Scherzo

THE NOCTURNE SYMPHONY

Scherzo

4 Horsemen
Publications, Inc.

LYRA R. SAENZ

Published By: 4 Horsemen Publications, Inc.

4 Horsemen Publications, Inc.
PO Box 417
Sylva, NC 28779
4horsemenpublications.com
info@4horsemenpublications.com

Cover by J. Kotick
Typesetting by Autumn Skye
Edited by Jen Paquette

Library of Congress Control Number: 2024937059

Paperback ISBN-13: 979-8-8232-0501-6
Hardcover ISBN-13: 979-8-8232-0502-3
Audiobook ISBN-13: 979-8-8232-0504-7
Ebook ISBN-13: 979-8-8232-0503-0

DEDICATION

To the unseen and unwanted.

TABLE OF CONTENTS

The Wastes
Aighneas
Seki
Ser
New
London
Orisumi
Ebele
Deri

him
Vatidomvs
City
Shinka
Temple
Lorelei
City
Tokiseishv
Avrevs
New
Chernobyl
Murasaki no umewarame
The Tar Tat
atierra

"Nothing is more painful to the human mind than, after the feelings have been worked up by a quick succession of events, the dead calmness of inaction and certainty which follows and deprives the soul both of hope and fear."

From Mary Shelley's *Frankenstein*

1
ACE OF CUPS

13th Day in the Month of Falling, 1877 A.P. - Calypso City Outskirts

ATZI IS LAUGHING AT SOME NEW PRANK Xipilli has pulled, not that Wren cares in the least what their brother has done now to inspire such a thing. All that matters is the sound: clear as bells and filled to the brim with mirth. Her sister's laughter is the best. Atzi is bashful though. Every time Wren says as much, her *hermana* blushes profusely and declares that, no, Wren's laughter is far better a sound than anything else. It's probably the only thing they'll never agree about. It's fine. However, this might very well be the last time she hears it in person.

"I do hope you have finished writing your maid of honor speech for tomorrow." Elisabeta's voice is severe, not an unusual thing when it comes to Wren. "You'll be speaking in front of a banquet hall full of some of the most important people in Deriva and Ebele."

High tide is coming in. Waves crash against beach sand blacker than obsidian...

"Oh, I thought I'd wing it."

The Vulcana sighs.

"Can you just once assure me that you won't muck something up without giving me grief?"

Her stepmother sounds defeated. That is unusual. Wren has never seen the woman like this, forlorn and nostalgic. Elisabeta is a force of nature. She has no reason to sound as such, especially not where Wren is concerned. Wren realizes her stepmother is sad. Wren supposes there are plenty of reasons for it. After all, in just a few short days, her daughter is to be married off to the prince of another country. Atzi will leave, disappearing across the sea with Chike to prepare to rule another nation. Wren understands. After all, she will be losing a sister. So, yes, she understands Elisabeta's heartache. Never mind that she and Papa were the ones who negotiated the match.

Wren sighs.

"I have something written out. I'll be tweaking it based on how the day goes, but the skeleton is there and ready to be delivered to both yours and Papa's satisfaction. I promise I will give due honor to our beautiful bride."

Her stepmother's face softens as she watches Atzi and Xipilli play in the sand, but then she turns back to Wren and her expression sours.

"Hmph! See that you do. Perhaps someone will find you charming enough to marry. Do make sure to catch the bouquet."

Ah, there's the Elisabeta she knows and loves, haughty with a healthy dose of disdain for her husband's "bastard." Wren isn't any more a bastard than Xipilli or Atzi. Her mother just wasn't the first wife.

"Sure, *mamá*."

The woman visibly bristles at Wren's sarcasm—it helps that she's always hated it when Wren calls her "*mamá*"—and storms away with all the pent-up bluster of a typhoon. It's all she can do now Wren's earned her place as a technomancer. Her poor stepmother's dreams of making marriage chattel out of her eternally dashed...

A notably larger wave barrels its way to shore, taking Xipilli's feet out from under him much to Atzi's delight. Wren smiles. Her sister's laughter really is the greatest thing left on this island. She'll have to cherish it for as long as she can. Another wave steals Atzi's balance, her laughter doused in the water.

High tide is coming in...

Waves crash and roll against the shore.

This is what Wren hears as she comes to. It's a familiar sound. Some people grow up to the sound of car horns and thundering trains. Wren grew up to the sound of Deriva's ever shifting tides, its calm washes and its raging storms. She knows this sound better than any other in the world, but these waves are markedly different. The water sounds sluggish and foamy, like the water is too heavy for the current forcing it to shore. The air smells different, too. Overly salty and acidic, it burns the lining of her nostrils. The acrid smell of rotting fish lingers as well, not the same as it would be in a fisherman's market early in the morning. Deriva always smelled like clean sea breeze and sand—healthy and alive. Protected by the laws of isles, the parts of the Cetoic Ocean that touch Deriva are blessed by the sea gods of Deus. They say Poseidon himself graces the waters along the Derivan coast. Not this; this is the scent of oceanic death left to ferment at the mercy of the elements. This is the smell of a dying ocean whose denizens have been left in the sand to rot.

And the birds! Hel above! The seagulls. There are way too many of them, squawking and carrying on like a bunch of foul-mouthed rioters.

Blinking her eyes open—they're crusty and sore as though she's been crying—she sees the sky's the wrong color. A mottled gray thick with ocean mist, she can hardly tell the difference between it and the dull brown of the sand she is lying in. It trails

down an embankment that would be pretty with the surplus of
sea glass scattered through the sand, but it's tainted by all the
weeds and man-made debris. The natural sand is barely even
visible by the time it is swallowed up by mottled, dark-green
water. Another glaring contrast to the waters around the island
on which she was raised: the isles of her homeland always have
crystal-clear, brilliant blue depths.

No, this is certainly not Deriva, which begs the question.
Where are we?

Movement draws her attention. Silje, housecat-sized and cute
as a button, lies coiled against her hip. The netherbeast would
look like an everyday housecat were it not for the dark, mist-
like energy swirling along the edges of her fur and the itty-bitty
horns peeking out along her brow. The feline opens one tired
eye to look at her. To think, just a few hours ago, the netherbeast
had been the size of a small horse, the displacer beast dripping
enough power to teleport them here with her very own brand of
displacement magic.

"I suppose you aren't going to tell me where 'here' is..."

Predictably, she gets nothing more than a twitch of a whisker
in response. Then, the animal "mffs" at her before curling into
an even tighter ball and returning to her sleep.

"I suppose you have a right to be tired. But did you have to
teleport us to such a disgusting beach? Whose idea was that,
because it couldn't have been mine?"

Can't she just go back to sleep and deal with everything she
doesn't remember happening later? Situation be damned, she
shifts to do just that, but the weight of something on her hip stalls
her. There's an arm thrown across her waist, the hand of which
loosely grips the folds of her clothing. Mindful of Silje, she rolls
over to look at the person next to her.

It's Kaito.

And at the sight of him, a flood of memories all come rushing
back. Encountering the Nightmare and Mishka dying in her
arms—an innocent witch/firefly who only wanted to help her
community. Everything that happened afterward: the Blixvi,

its pestilence on Chairomura, the kids, Silje... Then there's the Shard: a plot to kill Zenza, dancing with Hikaru, then her brother as pigheaded as always, the fight with Summer's pet basilisk, and lastly Summer—her ruse dissolved, slain by her lover's hand. *Curse you, Thames!* And *pinché pluma!* She outed herself when she outed Summer. They now know Atalia is dead and Wren Nocturne isn't. *Shit!* The League knows she's alive.

The Songstress of Lorelei came back from the dead just in time for them to declare hunting season on her ass, and on top of all that, she's now dragged Kaito into it, too. For a bleary second, she panics. He shouldn't be anywhere near her. It's too dangerous, too shameful, too damning to be a witch's companion. Let alone a witch as infamous as she is.

A flicker of silver shines from her finger, and the amethyst inlaid within the Miyazaki seal catches just enough light to give her pause.

"Oh... right..." she whispers.

I would rather stand in the dark with you than live in a synthetic light.

Kai's signet ring, given to her as he spoke the first lines of a vow held so sacred in their world that not even the feud between hexen and human+ could diminish its value. Noble, handsome, too-good-for-this-world, prince-of-righteousness Kaito Miyazaki has somehow decided that she (the flawed, pigheaded, and barely sane witch that she proves herself to be time and time again) is worth throwing everything away for: his title, his status, even his family. They'd been in the middle of the desert when League bullets caught up to them. The adepts didn't even give warning. They just opened fire, and Silje rallied up the little magic she had built back up to displace the three of them over Hecate knows how many miles.

"You reckless fool," she whispers, a fond look on her face. If she had had any modicum of sense, she would have held her tongue and kept from repeating the next part of the incantation, but recite the vows she had, and such magics are irrevocable, more so even than the most holy of marriage rites. As binding as the void that holds the stars in the sky and twice as ineffable.

"That means no take-backs, Miyazaki." She giggles quietly, wondering like a twitterpated schoolgirl if she is, in fact, speaking to herself or Kaito. (Technically, if they'd done the thing properly, she would have signed legal documentation to take his last name.) "I guess that makes two of us."

Kaito's hair has fallen from its usual topknot. Sand flecks through the locks, now tangled from the elements. She can't imagine her personage is any better for wear. They must have been sleeping for at least a few hours, considering they ran from the Shard in the middle of the night, and it is now just before dawn.

The Shard—talk about a living nightmare.

Summer's dead. Wren can barely fucking believe it, and Thames laughed about it right in her magic-damned face. That rat bastard! She swears, the next time she gets the chance, she is going to run him through with Lacuna.

Thunder rumbles on the horizon. Rain blowing in from the depths, she can already see the waves rising higher to welcome the torrent. They can't stay here. There's no telling how far up the beach the tide will come.

Pulling herself up, she winces at the sharp throb in her abdomen.

"Ngh!"

Fuck! The bullet wound.

Zenza got her good. The shot won't kill her; the girl missed her vitals, and the stim Kaito shot into her after saving her from becoming one with the pavement is doing its work to heal the damage, but it's going to make moving around difficult for at least a couple of days. It took her nearly a week to recover the last time she took a solid hit from Chike's techno-rifle. Looks like Agni was two for two on hitting her where it kind of counts. That cursed rifle. If she could, she would curse her dearly departed brother-in-law to the lowest levels of the underworld for making the damn thing. If she didn't already know how impossible it was (Yes, she did try. How do you think she got so well versed in resurrection lore?), she would yank his spirit out of Lacuna's hearth and give him a proper tongue-lashing over the weapon before sending him to a proper afterlife. After all, she put him there. Surely, she can summon him back out, and she promises she'll put him right back after she's given him a piece of her mind.

There's a loud squawk behind her. Probably a pair of birds fighting over a scrap of food. Yup, two seagulls flapping about in the air with something gross between them. It looks like entrails of some kind.

"Wren…"

Kaito's voice is grainy, no doubt from lack of sleep and the unclean air. Awoken by her sudden tensing, the prince opens his eyes to peer up at her.

"I'm fine," she hushes, trying for a light-hearted tone. It falls flat. "Just forgot I had a hole in my stomach."

He makes a disapproving sound and pushes himself out of the sand.

"Let me see."

"It's nothing."

"A wound from a technomancer weapon is never nothing."

He's right. Pretending the injury isn't there won't do her any favors, so she lifts her top, baring the wound to him. She makes a face as her lover's brow furrows.

"It isn't healing as I would like."

There is a definite hole in her side. Kaito gently palpates around the site, and Wren feels something very solid and very foreign shift in her insides. No exit wound which means the damned bullet is still in there.

"The nanos haven't yet degraded the bullet. You need another stim."

She shakes her head. *Absolutely not!*

"I can do it."

He looks at her in question. "I didn't realize you had surgical equipment."

"I don't."

"I don't understand."

Shaking her head with a crooked grin, she holds a hand a few inches above the wound, closes her eyes, and grits her teeth.

With a burst of magic, the bullet flies into her hand.

"Ah!"

"Wren!"

He clamps his hands down on her abdomen, applying pressure to staunch the fresh flow of blood. Perhaps, she should have done that with a bit more nuance.

"I'm good." She winces, swatting him away. "It's not the neatest way to remove a foreign body, but it is the quickest."

"Telekinesis is not an appropriate medical alternative."

Wren shrugs. "Neither are essential oils, but at least telekinesis works." Kaito's look is reproachful at best. Silje sits up, sniffs at the injury, makes a face, and yowls. Kaito raises an eyebrow at the cat.

"I think Silje and I are in agreement."

Wren looks at her familiar, a witch betrayed. "Yeah, yeah… Well, at least I don't lick my *culo*."

Silje sniffs, her whiskers bristling. Meanwhile, Kaito is already reaching for a stim.

"I don't want another stim. Do you realize how badly that stuff messes with my system?"

Kaito makes a noise of disapproval but tucks the syringe back into his belt. "Then, we will need to find you a doctor. A wound from Agni will not heal without medical intervention."

"Not sure there are many League doctors who'll work on a witch."

"So we will find a doctor outside the League. We are, I believe, no longer on League soil if my disconnection from the network is any indication."

"You're not connected to the network?!" He nods. "Then, where do you think we are 'cause I'm drawing a blank? This place is too damp to be Deriva."

Kai's sights turn on, spinning for a moment before deactivating with a shake of his head. He winces as though a headache is forming behind his eyes.

"I guess you're not exactly 100% either."

"The jump here seems to have damaged my system. We are in the Tai Tai, if my memory protocols are correct."

Oh, great! The land of pirates, criminals, and naysayers. Indiscriminate of Hexen, Human+, or Fae so long as people can prove their hands are dirty enough to continue churning out the dreck polluting the surrounding waters. She winces at her own thoughts. *Guess that means we'll fit right in.*

"Hmm, even more promising. Pretty sure the doctors here would view me as more of a science experiment than a patient." It's supposed to be a joke, but Kaito's face falls, and all she feels as a result is guilt. "Kaito, I'm okay."

"You quite nearly were not."

She knows. Oh, does she know... So, she leans forward and kisses him on the cheek, just below one of the nodes inset there. "You know, you really shouldn't worry so much. The stress will make your dangly bits shrink."

Wren is expecting him to at least scoff at her, but she's disappointed that he doesn't so much as blink at her dirty joke.

"The negative effects of stress are the least of my concern when it comes to you."

Her darling prince, as impermeable as ever... She sighs and lifts her fingertips to his face to nudge a few stray strands of hair out of his eyes. He breathes deeply into her touch before catching her fingers in hand and brushing his lips against her palm.

"Then I suppose I can mourn the loss of a few centimeters." She laughs at her own joke, which she immediately regrets when fire flares in her gut. Kaito gives her a reproachful look. "Sorry..."

He bandages her up as best he can with their limited supplies of gauze and medical tape, little more than a bandaid for a bullet hole. *Loki's Beard!* She'd forgotten how badly Agni could infringe on her natural healing factor. Not to mention, as drained as she is, it'll take a lot longer for her magical pools to recharge completely.

Thunder rumbles in the sky as Kaito applies the last piece of tape. The tide is rising, churning up loose seaweed from the depths. The birds are entirely unbothered, circling and jumping about their feast as though it were an all-you-can-eat buffet. (*What?! Did a shark beach itself or something?*) Wren and Kaito, on the other hand... they need to find cover if they don't want to get caught in the rain.

"So we are in the Tai Tai. Any idea which island?" asks Wren.

Kaito finishes putting up his materials as his sights alight once more. His eyes trained skyward, she watches as they spin clockwise then counterclockwise before blinking off. He shakes his head.

"There is a huge server just out of my range. I can't log into it without getting to an activation point. Until then, my servers are completely disconnected." He rubs a spot on his temple.

"Kai?"

"It's just the Disruption. I'm not getting much of any signal out here."

Disruption: not a pleasant feeling at all, Wren remembers. While she herself never had the same extensive neural implants as a Murasakan human+, she knows what a Disruption is. When tracking beyond the boundaries of the network, most augmentations have a tendency to lose connection—this can be as simple as not being able to get direct messages for a while to as life-threatening as an insulin pump not releasing a proper dosage because of interference. For Wren, a Disruption meant Mano and her other movement augmentations would go on the fritz, making it hard for her to retain her stability and balance. If it got bad enough, she lost feeling in her legs entirely thanks to her spinal adjustments.

For Kaito, it's even worse. A Disruption on a neural augmentation is absolute hell. It's like having three of the five major senses shut off. The ground doesn't feel right underfoot, and the world turns to black and white. A bit like vertigo, really. Only, it's not so much an inner ear problem as it is internal server instability. Someone can expect anything from shoddy signal, dropped navigations, and buffering comms to attachments going in and out and various glitches as the system tries to compensate for the lack of external network support.

"I'll be fine once we are back in range of a network. If needed, I can hack into the local web."

Wren snorts. "Yeah, because that sounds totally safe."

"There are unfortunately no better options at the moment."

"Wouldn't it be better to just go without? I thought you had a portable network linked in on your person?"

"I do."

"So, use that rather than connect to a local server set up by pirates?"

"It's not that simple."

She glares at him. "Why not?"

"I've essentially defected from the League. While we were on the run, one of their disruptor drones managed to damage my PN. I am running at 60% capacity right now."

"Oh, that sucks." Well, that's a fairly obvious reason, now that she has the information necessary to understand. "Can you repair it?"

"Possibly, but only if I can get back online." He blinks his sights back on, this time along with a handheld unit. Numbers flow across the screen too fast for Wren to garner any meaning from them before the unit glitches out, too. "Safety is not the question if the situation is dire enough."

"Kaito," she chides.

"My defenses are powerful enough to prevent any viable malware."

"Not if they were set up by a hacker."

"They would have to be a formidable one to infringe on my firewalls."

"We are in the Tai Tai. Where do you think the best hackers retire to when they're done causing mischief in the League?"

"I hear your concern, Wren."

But nothing is going to change his mind if he feels it necessary to log onto the network, no matter how dodgy the whole thing might be.

She sighs. "So be it..." A raindrop lands on her nose. "Well, as nice as it would be to have a romantic sit in the rain, it might be better to get to higher ground before the coast disappears into the ocean."

Kaito nods, rising to his feet. He offers her a hand and pulls her up. In turn, Wren scoops her sleeping familiar into her satchel. As they walk up the beach, the first drizzles of rain start to fall. As they crest the top of the hill, the skyline of an island metropolis comes into view, and on a broken sign post next to the canal, a metal marker reads, "Calypso City."

"The term schizoid refers to an individual, the totality of whose experience is split in two main ways: in the first place, there is a rent in his relation with his world and, in the second, there is a disruption of his relation with himself. Such a person is not able to experience himself 'together with' others or 'at home in' the world, but, on the contrary, he experiences himself in despairing aloneness and isolation; moreover, he does not experience himself as a complete person but rather as 'split' in various ways, perhaps as a mind more or less tenuously linked to a body, as two or more selves, and so on."

Excerpt from *The Divided Self: An Existential Study in Sanity and Madness*
By R.D. Laing, 1955 A.D.

2

THE PAGE OF SWORDS

13th Day in the Month of Falling - Snowfall Palace

RAGE HAS ALWAYS BEEN A STRANGER TO Renki, yet for the last three days, of all the other emotions he should and could be feeling, Rage sits at his bedside like a simmering vulture. The carrion bird paces as it waits for its next meal to roll over and die. Wings coated in sparks of fractious violence and beak stained with bitterness, Rage feasts on his other limp emotions while wrecking his reality. At its arrival, it tore around his quarters like a winter storm. It left behind a wreckage worthy of a toddler trapped in a high chair. It now hovers in his shadow, flapping its wings every few hours, a reminder of the last thing he said to Kaito.

Renki's hands wring into the tattered pink and blue fur of the little cat stuffy in his arms; he feels like a five-year-old again. Scylla—the little toy has been in his possession for as long as he can remember (Heck, before he can remember, really), and he is worrying at it now just like he used to as a half-orphaned child coming to Snowfall for the first time to meet Kaito, the man who would become his father.

It's so frustrating.

—— 15 ——

"*Stop treating me like a kid. I don't need to be coddled! Just tell me the truth!*"

To punctuate his words, he throws the toy. It collides with the far wall, sailing past Kaito's right shoulder.

The man glances at the abused toy before responding. "I have told you all the truth you need to know. There has been a misunderstanding regarding Lady Wren, and until I can rectify the situation, there is nothing more I can share with you."

"I don't understand. Why can't I just help you? If Lady Nocturne is in trouble, I want to help. She helped us when we got in trouble in Chairomura. Surely, it would be better for me to be with you doing something productive than here doing nothing. She said herself that you trained me well."

"Wren is..." Kaito falters. "The manner in which Lady Wren's return was accomplished has had complicated effects on her being. To exacerbate things, she has been gone from this world for twelve years. There are many things she is currently unaware of which I need to speak with her about in private, things which I fear she will not respond well to. I cannot risk you being in the crossfire."

"But you said she was someone I could trust."

"And she is, but it... I'm sorry, Renki but it is difficult to explain."

Always... Always, always, always, his father stops talking because he can't explain something properly, so it's easier just to not say anything. It's the same adage Renki has received every time he ever asks about his mother. Who was she? What was she like? What happened to her? All questions Kaito has historically only ever answered with "It is difficult to explain," and Renki is fed up with it.

"Maybe if you hadn't let my mother die, she would be able to explain it for you!"

Kaito doesn't respond. He doesn't even flinch. He, instead, picks up the thrown stuffed animal from the floor. Setting Sylla back on the dresser, his tousan suddenly looks far older than his 33 years.

"We will speak more when I return."

Now it's a question of whom he is angrier with: Kaito or himself.

The skin of his knuckles is bruised and broken. If Kaito were around, he'd be instructing Renki to apply healing salve to the injury, but Kaito is not around. He isn't even within communication range. He heard the news. He saw the upheaval that happened at the Spire. Kaito is gone. Gone through a magic portal, having declared his loyalty to the Songstress of Lorelei over his own family, and everybody is busting their circuits about it.

Not that Renki is innocent of his own busted circuitry.

While his room is no longer the wreckage it once was, Renki's comm unit is done for. Broken, no doubt, from angrily throwing it against the wall. It fizzles out and dies in his fist, and so what! What's the point of having a comm if the person he's trying to reach seems hellbent on ignoring him?

"Fine, be that way!" he yells into the dead unit. "See if I care! I don't need you anyway!"

And he tosses it into the waste bin. It rattles against the expired pods already within.

The anger boils under his skin, drives his pulse into dangerous heights, and despite his words, all he wants more than anything is for Kaito to answer his goddamned calls.

Beep... beep... beep...

A message comes through on his bedroom monitor, a beeping sound that immediately lifts his spirits. *Did he respond?*

The teen runs over to the monitor, opening the chat and pressing play on the message without even looking at the sender. To his disappointment, the voice that greets him sounds nothing like his father.

"Renki, it's been decided that you are to resume your training as normal. Report to the garage in an hour. Be ready for travel and a new assignment." It's Fumiko, calling him down for a missive. Not Kaito. Not Wren. Not anyone he wants to talk to right now, really. "I will be going with you so you can receive your mission brief..."

Renki listens dazedly to the recording. Apparently he is to meet Hikaru and Akari at the light rail station, and the grand master will be escorting him there herself despite her responsibilities to the rest of their trainees.

So he packs: a change of clothes, rations, his o-katana, extra medical supplies, a few rewire tools, and beacons. He changes into a set of battle leathers, plain blacks and the usual dark purple yukata underneath, and to finish off his uniform, the plain lavender sash he's worn since he was four years old—the symbol of his mourning for his mother and a perfect match to the lavender robes Kaito has worn throughout Renki's whole relationship with him. Until recently, of course. How queer that he would cast off his grieving garb in the wake of a witch's return from the dead...

Renki's brow furrows.

Yet another unanswered question. Maybe Kaito really is under a witch's spell. The thought leaves a bitter taste in his mouth.

"Young master," a computery voice chimes in from his room's monitoring sensors. "Fumiko-sensei is requesting confirmation you are on your way."

Renki's AYA program is an offshoot of Kaito's. Knowing the master program is who-knows-where in Kaito's portable personal networking (PPN) just adds more salt to the wound. He's never felt more like a kid being watched by his nanny than now. He never even had a nanny growing up. Kaito insisted on being his primary caregiver despite royal expectations. No nannies, no governesses, and definitely no wet nurses. Kaito raised him himself. Whenever the man took a mission that would send him off for an extended period of time, Renki stayed with Akari and her parents (them being second cousins of Kaito and Hikaru and technically making Akari Renki's 3rd cousin). He even shared a living space with the man, his bedroom being just on the far side of Kaito's receiving room until he was old enough to join the trainee corp. Then he was moved into the dormitories to live with the other adepts-in-training.

"Thank you, AYA."

He flings his pack over his shoulders, activates his room's security parameters, and heads for the door, pausing only to look at Scylla before, in a spur of impulsiveness, he picks the battered old stuffie up and tucks her in his satchel. Then, the door slides shut behind him, automatic locks activating with a hiss.

Fumiko is waiting for him in her convertible. He half expected her to be in battle garb, but instead, she stands in her usual plain training robes. He throws his pack into the back seat and slides into the passenger seat. Without a word, his great aunt slips the car into gear, and they are off, driving away from Snowfall and through Tokiseishu to the light rail station.

The journey is quiet, not an unexpected thing considering Fumiko's distaste for needless chatter, so he jumps when the woman addresses him.

"Renki, all your life you have been your father's first priority. I can understand how strange it must be to see him putting someone else before you, so know this. There are things a man needs to do not just for himself but for the people he cares most about, and that includes you. Kaito's focus on Lady Wren is not a lessening of his love for you. In fact..."

She trails off, and Renki's frustration flares.

"In fact what?!"

"I'm sorry, my boy, but that is something you need to hear from your father."

"And when will that be?" His frustration bleeds into his voice, and he winces.

"I wish I knew, child." Fumiko sighs heavily. "I wish I knew."

"Does this have anything to do with the fact that the rest of the world thinks I'm adopted?"

"I can't answer that, Renki."

"Yeah, yeah, of course, you can't."

It's unfair and immature. He's acting like a petulant child, yet he doesn't seem capable of breaking the pattern he's fallen into, so he turns his head and stares out the window as the city passes them by.

The conversation ends until they reach the station where his uncle meets them. Fumiko offers her nephew a quick greeting and disappears onto the train. It's like she can't get away fast enough, and when his uncle greets him, he thinks he might understand why.

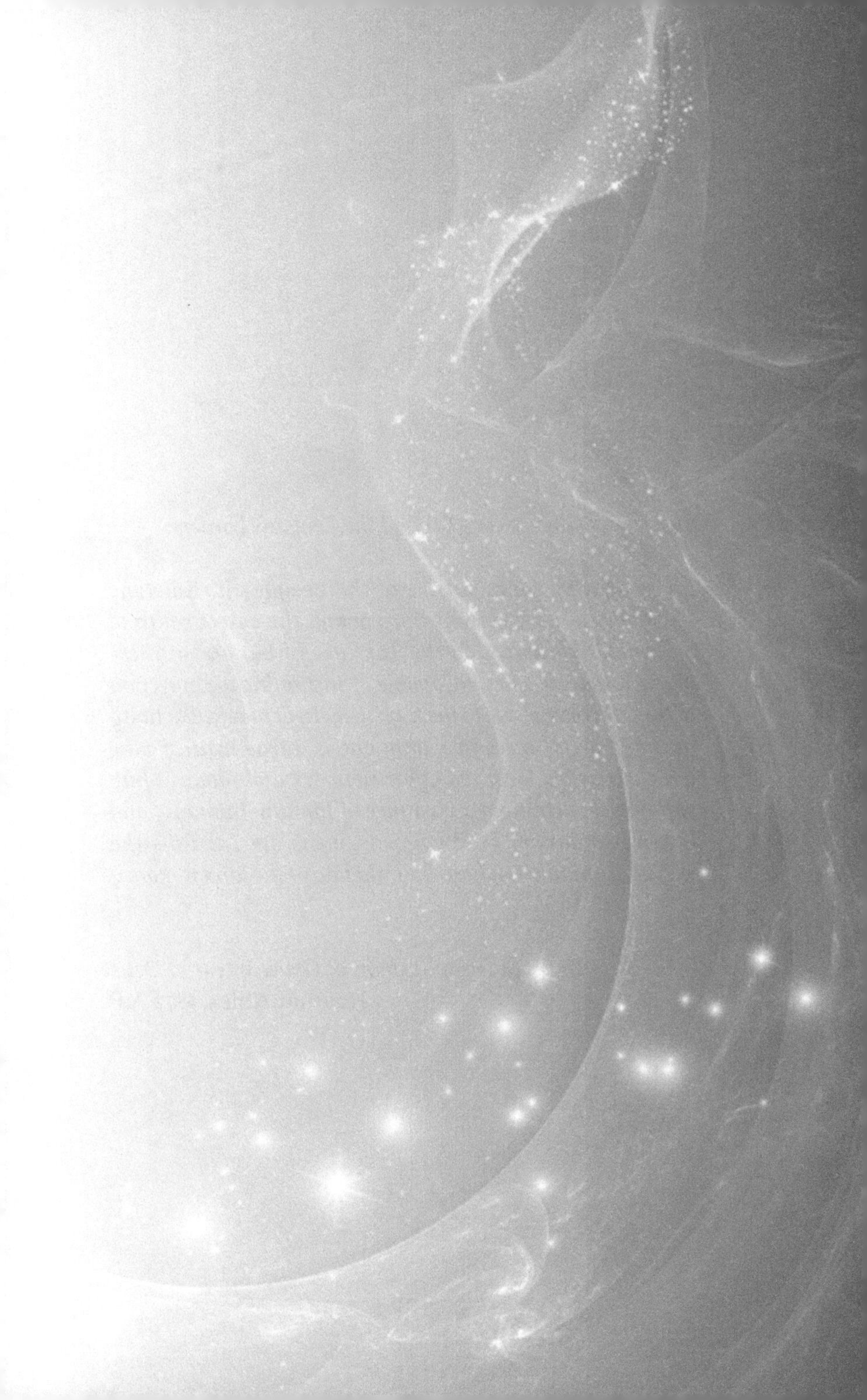

Systems of Governance Beyond the League's borders:

There are five zones outside of the League's jurisdiction: The Wastes, Lorelei, New Chernobyl, the desert south of Sekhmeti's borders, and the Tai Tai. All but one of these places are dead zones, incapable of sustaining a connection to the cyberscape due to the high density of magical activity in the area. Of these five, only one is a true neutral zone which boasts a localized cyber network and magical hub capable of sustaining a vast mix of human, human+, and hexen population. That neutral zone is the Tai Tai—the isles of criminals—where the only law of the land is money.

Excerpt from *Systems of Government in Deus*
Heather Ables, 1872 A.P.

3

THE PAGE OF WANDS

13th Day in the Month of Falling - Calypso City

THERE IS AN ARGUMENT OF SORTS AS THEY make their way through the outskirts of the city. Wren thinks it's more important to get Kaito access to the network while Kaito thinks tending to the barely-healing hole in Wren's side is a much higher priority.

"And how are you going to find a doctor without network connection?"

"I hear hospitals are fairly commonplace, even in crime-run cities."

"I'm not bleeding anymore."

"You require stitches."

"Yeah, hard pass. It'll heal on its own."

"Yes, it will," Kaito agrees. "Three or four days from now, after infection has set in and destroyed more tissue than a bullet ever could."

As if to emphasize the man's point, Silje—the little traitor—reaches up and paws her hurt side. Kaito takes Wren's resounding hiss of pain as his declaration of victory.

The sky opens as they enter the city's hub. Globular bullets of rain fall from the sky in torrents worthy of a cello's *furioso*. They *thawk* onto the pavement with audible percussive sounds until the ground is saturated enough to dampen the *vivaci* taking place.

It quickly becomes apparent that this certainly is not a League city. There is too much litter, too much waste, and too much pollution. Even Seraphim, a country desolated by nuclear radiation at least appears clean on the surface. Even so, Wren would be hard pressed to call this a human city. There are bright neon lights, huge moving holo-projection screens, and a hodgepodge of land-, water-, and aircraft all moving through the city at varying levels. And right beside, shifters for hire showing off their animal forms, blood clubs advertising a good time for all, vampyre or otherwise, and the occasional street performer weaving a bit of euphoria into their songs and shanties, magic as alive and present as technology.

Calypso City sits on a collection of man-made islands. The canals and rivers thread through the city as commonly as roads and railways while metal spires reach well into the cloud-line, though perhaps the better word for it is fog-line, discolored as it is. There are floating markets, sky plazas, and subterranean trading houses, all of which contribute to the layer of soot and grime coating the city.

The gondola they ride on is operated by an android but owned by a troll as tall as Wren's thigh. Metal from top to bottom with a tinny computerized voice, the android speaks for the hunched fae while the troll crunches his way through the crumbling brick and mortar of a nearby bridge. Occasionally, he spits a wad of cement at the android, making a metallic *thunk*.

"Fillius Stonebrook. Need a drift into the city, I own the best bridges, and the worst besides. 10 credits per passenger."

Gliding through the city's canals, Wren takes note of what she sees. There is a kelpie in the canal being fed by an old lady in a white veil. Farther along, more seagulls harass a scruffy-looking rat shifter seeking some shut eye on the side of a closed bar. The hexen waves a (mildly) feathered hat at the birds only to have one of the feathers plucked right from its brim. Eventually, the canal opens into the city's center where several canals converge in a central thoroughfare. The fishy smell is pungent here as well, just as it was at the beach. Here, however, the reason is far more apparent.

There are people everywhere, driving motorboats and motorbikes that burp thick, black smoke through their exhaust pipes. Cigarette butts litter the sidewalk. Animal feces—Wren assumes it's animal feces anyway—has been smeared along walls like some sort of graffiti made with nature's most organic of paints.

Looking down at the water, Wren can't help but grimace. Gray and cloudy, two things water should never be, with thick, sour foam collecting at the edges. In some places, the water even radiates a yellow-tinted steam. Isles of trash and excrement drift downstream like rat-infested boats, and she could swear at one point a two-headed fish swims under the boat. *Certainly wouldn't want to go for a dip in this water. You might not come back out with your skin still intact.*

"Now arriving at Sparrow's Square. Please, pay and disembark."

While Wren hops onto the cobblestone, Kaito swipes his credit chip—a microchip inlaid into the back of his left hand—across the robot's sternum to pay for the trip.

"Should you be using that? It can be traced back to you, can't it?"

"No. My private accounts are accessible to none but myself."

"But it's wired into your system."

"I've ensured that every aspect of my system is functionally separate from League networks, particularly my financial and identification units. Only those with access to my coding would be able to find it."

"Then, doesn't that mean your brother could track it back to you?"

"Hikaru is no longer privy to my system coding."

Emerald eyes go round and her eyebrows nearly disappear into her bangs.

"Wait! You recoded yourself! That's utterly insane! It's near suicide! You could have died!"

A technomancer, or even just a neurologically altered human+, can't just go about changing their coding. It's the equivalent of trying to change their fingerprints. No... worse... like restructuring a person's entire DNA. People do it, of course. It's highly illegal and incredibly dangerous. Most of the people who choose to do so are criminals and vagabonds.

"It needed to be done."

Wren doesn't know whether to smack him, hug him, or kill him herself for providing such a vague answer. Why would he do such a thing? For Kaito to have revoked Hikaru's access to his system would mean that the pair were on rocky footing even before this whole debacle of a reincarnation. To change his coding so substantially would require a full upheaval of his mainframe. We're talking about a complete override and system wipe! He told her a while back that his whole system was rebuilt after an attack fried his previous configuration. She'd been so horrified to discover it initially that her only concern then had been whether or not she was the person responsible for the shutdown. She didn't think to ask if he'd made any changes as notably altering as changing his coding.

What could have happened between Kaito and his brother? What could be so terrible that Kaito would decide to undergo such a dangerous procedure? What did Hikaru do?

Before she can ask, Kaito steps off the watercraft and begins climbing the stairs to the street level. Silje, riding in Wren's satchel, safe from both the rain and the prying eyes of strangers, wriggles in the bag, apparently uncomfortable now that Wren is upright again. Annoyance drips off the feline in waves.

"Oh, don't complain at me," she hisses at the bag, following Kaito up the stairs. "You're nice and warm in there while I'm out here in the wet."

"*Mrrp.*" More annoyance flicks across her psyche.

"Yes, yes, whine at me some more."

Despite the rain, the streets are flooded with people huddled under umbrellas making their way to their first appointments for the day. So many people, no one gives them a second glance. (Not that they would have any reason to. This is the Tai Tai. No one wants to be found here.) The flapping thuds made whenever a pair of umbrellas collide, normally so bothersome to Wren, fade under the hustle and bustle of city foot traffic. What's more irksome is the stifling onslaught of emotions barreling at her from every direction: annoyance, excitement, panic, happiness, sadness, desperation, impatience, pain, amusement, frustration, anger, even arousal out here in the middle of the street. Everything. It's all there, coming at her from every direction. So much so, her heart begins to pound, and sweat breaks out on the back of her neck.

So, she grips Kaito's hand, and thanks the goddess that his neural defenses are still online despite the Disruption. As much an anchor as a comfort, he exudes a smooth, unbroken nothingness, a perk of the protections his neural net provides him. Her empathy can't penetrate his consciousness without him overriding the settings on his system, and focusing on him as though she were trying to penetrate his defenses makes everything else fade away. She has never been more thankful for that.

She wonders if he can even feel her probing against his barriers. If he is bothered by her holding his hand, he doesn't show it. He actually squeezes her palm three times as if to say, "I'm here. I've got you," so she holds tight and allows her mind to float in his blank space. It's balm over the most strenuous of her discomforts. All the others, though, move to the forefront. Funny how once she gets relief in one area of disquiet, all of the others just ratchet up in level.

Wren, after nearly thirty minutes in the steady rainfall, is soaked to the bone. Her cloak isn't waterproof, and she doesn't have a jacket to wear underneath. The fabric isn't thick enough to keep her dry, and the water seeps into her clothing. As close as she's huddled into him, it doesn't take her technomancer long to notice when she starts shivering.

"You're freezing."

"It's just water."

"And how much blood have you lost in the last 24 hours?"

Kaito, who has the audacity to remain completely unfazed by the chill despite his hair hanging in limp, water-logged strands around his head, looks from her to the surrounding shops before tucking her into his side and steering her into a nearby coffee shop. She sighs on contact. His body feels like a furnace. (*Este vato*! His body temp regulators keep him warm and toasty while Wren is left to freeze to a second death.)

The bell above the door dings pleasantly enough as they enter, and a sweet-faced dame with short, curly brown hair greets them.

"Welcome to Cafe Diablo," she chirps with an uncharacteristic drawl to the word "diablo." A *gringa* for sure, saying it "die-aa-blow," but at least she tried. "Seat yourself wherever you'd like, and I'll be right with ya."

The woman's vibe is sweet enough, but with everyone else... A cacophony of noise intrudes on Wren's psyche: tired businessmen, excitable teenagers, a pair of love birds sharing a milkshake. Someone in the far corner is in a foul temper while the person across the aisle rides a synthetic high, pumped up by a cocktail of caffeine, hallucinogens, and stimulants. *How has he not had a heart attack, yet?*

"Not sure I want to be here right now," the witch grumbles.

There's a petite gal sitting at the counter eating a slice of cake and slurping a whipped cream-capped cup of hot cocoa with a jarringly carefree disposition. Why a character like that would wear a thick wrap over her head, Wren has no clue. She would much more expect the dark, antisocial ones to wear such adornments. Like, for instance the brooding broad in the corner. Wren really doesn't like the feel of her: too icy and chilly in texture despite the steaming bowl of porridge in front of her.

Wren shuffles her way into a booth as far away from everyone else as she can get, plopping down into the cushion and sinking far deeper into the seat than she expects. One of the springs protests her weight with a *twang*. Bully for it.

She lays her head on the table. *When did the world start spinning? Did I really get that wet? It isn't raining that hard, nor is it terribly cold. We're in the tropics for crying out loud!* Maybe it's the amount of emotion running rampant across the city.

Kaito peels the sopping-wet cloak from her shoulders and folds his leather coat around her like a blanket before stepping away. She notices that his clothes, having been covered by the coat, are bone dry. *That's Kaito for you, sensible to the end.* She hears his dusky baritone amidst the steady murmurs of the diner but can't make out what he's saying or to whom exactly. Silje pokes her head out of Wren's satchel, nudging Wren's side and licking the water from her skin.

Kaito returns, the waitress following behind him with a thick afghan in her arms.

"Oh, you poor dear. Caught in the rain like an alley cat, it seems."

Taking the blanket from the woman, he replaces his coat with the warm wool. Between that, Kai's body heat, and the heater overhead, she's already warming up despite her damp clothing.

"My name's Felice. What can I get for ya? Something to warm your bones? We've got a brilliant breakfast chili, hot and spicy. It'll warm ya right up. Chef's a bit of a kitchen witch as it were, puts all sorts of healing good stuff into his dishes though he ain't got a drop of real magic in him, but knowing your herbs and spices is its own type of magic, I suppose. Just the ticket with some eggs and hash, if you'd like?"

Wren decides she likes this woman. She's perky, boisterous, and unafraid to carry on talking.

"Just coffee, thanks."

"She'll have the breakfast chili," quips Kaito.

Wren gives him the side-eye. "I'm not hungry."

"When was the last time you ate?"

"When was the last time *you* ate? I don't see you ordering anything."

"Two orders of chili, then," he says, and Wren drops her head back to the table.

"Coming right up," says Felice. "Anything else I can get ya?"

"No, thank you."

Felice nods, walking off to put their orders in. Wren lifts her head again when an abrupt chill invades her right side. She growls as Kaito's body heat disappears.

"Where are you going?"

"There is a small clothing shop next door, and you need dry clothes and a better coat. I'll be back shortly. Then when the rain stalls, we can make our way to the hospital."

"Kaito..." She starts to say something, but the sentence dies on her tongue. He really ought to not be here. A prince of Murasaki no Yama, brushing elbows with local diners and shopping for a witch at a downtown thrift store... The thought churns her stomach.

"Wren," Kaito's gaze is firm, framed in conviction, "I am here, and I'm not going anywhere." He reaches over and takes her left hand in his. His thumb glides gently over the signet ring. "'Til the stars go dark..." With his other hand, he cradles the seashell necklace at his throat. "...and our bones are laid to rest."

He leans down to kiss the bridge of her knuckles, his breath warm and comforting, lips soft as silk.

"I'll be back soon. Save your strength."

She nods, wanting far more than a kiss on the hand, but doesn't resist as his fingers slip from hers to tighten his coat around his shoulders. She watches with bleary eyes as his back disappears through the door into what is now a full-on downpour. She hopes that coat is as waterproof as it feels on the outside.

"You've got a fine gent there, taking care of ya." It's Felice, back with her coffee.

Wren's lips quirk up into a small, sad smile. "He's a good man." A terribly misguided man, but a good one, nonetheless.

Felice sets her coffee on the table and leaves her to it. Wren blows on the plain black coffee absentmindedly. Unfortunately, it doesn't smell terribly heavenly, but at least it isn't the java mud some dives deem acceptable for human consumption. Her first sip wakes her up. The second makes her wince as she gets past the heat into the actual flavor. It's weak. Growing up in Deriva really spoiled her when it comes to coffee. Nothing beats a nice warm cup of island espresso brewed from the beans of trees grown in lava-enriched soil.

She takes a third sip, trying and failing not to make a face, as she takes in her surroundings. A swanky joint, the diner is a hodgepodge of aesthetics. From rainbow banners and unicorn coasters to ebony draping and a bat chandelier, the place seems to embody the full spectrum between bright/shiny and punk/gothic. The patrons match the decor. A pair of businessmen read the day's headlines, a pair of boys coo at each other in sporty polos and safety pinned jeans, and a permed/manicured beauty sits drinking her coffee with a small dog tucked into her pink purse. (*Is this what housewives look like around here?* The diamond ring she sports is larger than Wren's eyeball.) The hot-tempered man across the diner looks like a blue-collar worker while the manic pixie dream girl just can't seem to sit still as she savors her breakfast cake.

Wren pauses, however, when she notices the chilly brooder angled her direction. She's stopped eating and sits still as a statue staring directly at Wren. Icy blue eyes and pale blond hair, she's a pretty thing but young. Can't be more than sixteen. She cows as Wren's gaze meets hers, shifting her attention back to the bowl of porridge in front of her. Said bowl is no longer steaming as it was but a moment ago. Wren shivers and takes another sip of coffee.

Let her stare. What difference does it make to Wren?

The holoscreen at the far end of the diner projects the weather forecast. Rain with a chance of hail, apparently, and they are encouraging people to stay indoors as much as possible to avoid any inhalation of fog. Nothing like a day of acid rain to go with her breakfast. Another screen opposite plays a game of pro holoball. The players project their minds into the playing arena using their virtual bodies to score against the opposite team by knocking each other out of bounds with the ball. It's similar to rugby or dodgeball, only when the player is called out, their projection scatters into a billion cyber particles. The businessmen make bets with every new score.

Wren takes another sip of coffee and scratches Silje behind the ear, content to ignore the broadcasts when static fills the both screens.

"What the hell! Check the connection!" shouts one of the holoball fans.

"Breaking News! Witchcraft at League-sanctioned Conference!"

Wren looks back up at the new image on the holoscreen.

It's the Shard. Or rather, it's the pavement outside the Shard. Air security drones shine lights on a mess of broken glass, trashed vehicles, and a twenty-foot two-headed snake, coiled up dead in the rubble. Several patrons look at one another skeptically. One person even shouts to "get this League shit off the screen!"

"Early this morning, a hexen infiltration of the Shard led to dire consequences. The assassination of Ebele's Orisha, Chiamaka Nagi, leaves the technomancer council in shock as the Primarch grieves his murdered wife."

The footage cuts to a shot of Donarick Thames hunched over himself, covering his face from the camera view with the silk of a scarf 'Chiamaka' was seen wearing early that day. It's a charade, if she's ever seen one. Thames no more cared about Summer's death than he would have about a fly's.

"If this news does not in itself bring us into darkness, what is worse is the knowledge of the person responsible for this atrocity, and please be cautious because the horror of what you are about to see is not for the faint of heart."

A reel plays of the face-off in the lobby. Ghosts flit through the necrotic fog; flashes of green, purple, red, and yellow light flutter through the mist. There's screaming and explosions and the twisted coils of magic caught on film. At one point, a wraith screams directly into the camera before knocking an adept off his feet. Wren winces when his back breaks on impact with a nearby tabletop. Then the fog clears, and for just a moment, a clear shot of her appears on screen. The footage pauses, rewinds, and zooms in on the witch.

"You've got to be kidding me," she mumbles.

Wren sees her own face on the screen alight with battle fury: her hair whips around her face, eyes glowing green, the triskelion at her brow lit with power, and a song spilling from her parted lips.

Across the bottom of the screen the tagline flashes:

WREN NOCTURNE - THE SONGSTRESS OF LORELEI - BACK FROM THE DEAD

"It's a horror story many of our children have grown up with in the last twelve years. The Songstress of Lorelei. The mad witch who nearly tore our whole world apart..."

Wren averts her gaze, looking down into her mug of coffee as the anchor goes over her history.

Merde!

A League broadcast all the way out here! Looks like the aforementioned cat is officially out of the bag. Most of the diners aren't paying much mind to the broadcast, though many of them look up as footage of her summoning ghosts to fight off Seraphim forces trails along the screen. The businessmen have put down their newspapers.

"You think it's true."

"Eh, who knows? More League propaganda. Don't know why they bother paying the money to broadcast all the way out here."

"If it's true, though..."

Wren pulls the blanket higher over her head. She can feel eyes on her, and she isn't quite sure if it's her own paranoia talking or her sixth sense warning her that things are not alright.

"Wren Nocturne is armed and dangerous and not to be taken lightly. People are advised to note that there is a strong possibility she will not be traveling alone." A picture appears of Kaito. "The Crown Prince of Murasaki no Yama, Kaito Miyazaki, has been compromised and is now a prisoner to her thrall. The prince is a highly skilled technomancer and whatever spell has been cast upon him, it has clouded his mind and morality. Citizens are advised to avoid approach but are welcome to call local law enforcement. It is vital that he be apprehended for treatment."

Now everybody in and outside the League will have an eye out for a mad witch and her thrall.

"Additionally, direct from Primarch Thames, a handsome reward awaits any human, human+, or even hexen who can bring the witch to justice with a triple reward to any capable of bringing her into League custody alive."

Great... Where's Kaito? They need to get out of here, now.

Wren nudges Silje's head back into the satchel and scoots to the edge of the booth only to be cut off by Felice, arriving with their food.

"Alright, dearie. Two breakfast chili combos fresh from the kitchen. Can I get ya another cup of coffee? Oh! You off somewhere?"

Wren smiles sheepishly, pulling the blanket tighter around her shoulders.

"Uh, yeah. Where are your restrooms?"

"'Round the corner kitchen to the left."

"Thanks!"

Wren doesn't give Felice another glance backward before barreling up and out. She doesn't head to the bathroom, she heads for the door, past the pixie girl, past the two businessmen, and around the teenage couple. As she passes the icy gal, a wave of anger sends her tumbling sideways into the glamorous housewife. The woman's non-fat latte goes flying, spilling sweet and sticky all over the tabletop and dripping onto the woman's clothes.

"Oh! Watch it! Wait, aren't you—"

"*Perdoname*," she apologizes, angling around toward the door without really looking at the damage she caused.

She doesn't make it.

Her foot slips out from under her. Silje jumps from the satchel while Wren lands face-first on the tile—the suddenly very cold tile. When she lifts her head, she finds the floor is now covered with a thin sheet of ice.

"What the—"

The hair on the back of her neck prickles. A frosty flash of magic zips forward behind her. She rolls under a nearby table, startling the two dewy-eyed boys. The pair get up screaming from their seats, cutlery and plates going everywhere in their haste to get far away from the crazy woman currently under their table. When she turns back to look, a collection of deadly-sharp icicles have burst up from the floor. Had she been even a moment slower, they would have punctured her lungs.

And not far from the newly formed ice stands Miss Dark and Brooding. A snowflake indicia sparkles a cold blue on her left shoulder. Murder shines in her eyes.

Murder aimed directly at Wren.

Many that live deserve death. And some that die deserve life. Can you give it to them? Then do not be too eager to deal out death in judgment.

Quote from J.R.R. Tolkien's
The Fellowship of the Ring
Published posthumously in the year 3 A.P.

4
FIVE OF WANDS

THE SHOP KAITO VISITS IS OF DECENT ENOUGH quality. It doesn't take him long to find Wren a raincoat, proper boots, and a change of clothing. It is as he is checking out with the cashier that he spies a display of gloves behind the counter, and in their midst hangs a lovely, fur-lined leather set with lace insets—the kind of gloves Wren used to wear constantly whenever she needed to come into close contact with someone.

"A way to dampen the connection," she'd said once.

He wonders if maybe such an accessory might help her now. They are after all in the city, and Wren's empathy is nothing if not unrelenting.

"Shopping for a lady friend?" The clerk's tone is amicable and ever-so-slightly teasing. "A pair of fine gloves for a fine lady."

Wren would've cackled like a hyena had she been within earshot of anyone calling her a "fine lady."

"May I see the black pair?"

"Of course, sir."

The gloves are soft to the touch but durable enough to survive some roughhousing. They'll work perfectly.

Kaito pays for his goods, allows the gentleman to wrap and parcel his purchases, and then heads back to the diner. It is as he is crossing the intersection that he realizes all is not well within.

The youth, a waifish thing standing taller than Wren, glares daggers at the witch. Pale blonde hair, blue eyes, and a toffee-colored skin tone hinting of a mixed heritage, she can't be older than seventeen or eighteen. Just barely an adult with all of the teenage angst to be expected of a fifteen-year-old; a chilly angst, too, it drifts throughout the diner, inspiring the patrons to shiver in response. Amplified now that Wren has her complete attention on the girl, the youth's emotions are on rapid fire, flickering between anger, fear, grief, and pain, and every single one of those emotions seems to center around Wren.

Wren makes the mistake of poking her head out to look for the girl from under the table, and a flash of snow and ice nearly shaves the hair off her head before she can duck back under the wood. It hits the table leg instead. Hoarfrost spirals its way up the metal, and as Wren tucks herself away, her shoulder clips the now frozen metal. It's so cold, it burns a nice ring into her arm.

Instant frostbite. Wonderful!

The couple whose table Wren rolled under get up in a panicked shuffle and high-tail it to the edge of the room as Wren's attacker storms her way. The chairs get kicked away, so Wren telekinetically slides one into the witch's path. The back of it hits her in the stomach, and she angles around the other side, passing the housewife Wren already harassed. The lady chokes and sputters as the girl shoves past her, staining her dress with even more coffee as she knocks into the table.

"Excuse me! What do you think you're doing?"

The little dog barks loudly, yapping and snapping its tiny ineffectual jaws at the girl. Though, Wren supposes those teeth are at least decently sharp.

"Shut up!" snarls the frost witch, kicking the dog and its bag across the floor. The whimpers that follow are pathetic enough to make even Wren sympathize with the little ankle-biter.

The witch pushes a hand into the woman's face and screams; frost builds around the human's eyes and lips. Her screams are muted compared to the witch's banshee shriek, but the pain within is deafening to Wren.

"Hey! Cool it!"

Wren, now standing on the far side of the table, thrusts a hand forward. Her magic unfurls, flinging Ice Girl away from the human and into the counter. She tumbles heels over head to the far side, nearly taking Felice with her, but the waitress is quick enough to dive out of the way before a hundred-and-something pounds of angry witch can knock her out.

Wren shuffles to the housewife, screaming from frostbite, and lays her hand over the spell.

"Shh, shh, it's okay. You're going to be okay," Wren soothes, even though the skin of the woman's nose is already purpling and the ice has crusted over her eyes. She summons a dish towel from behind the counter and wraps the woman's head. "Get me some hot water!" she shouts to Felice, and the waitress runs to the kitchen shouting.

"You witch!" shouts the girl. Back on her feet, her jacket askew, Wren gets a good look at the girl's indicia: a simple six-pointed snowflake. There are some trail away, tiny flurries that would appear as freckles otherwise but now glow with power.

A frost witch in the Tai Tai of all places, thinks Wren. *Let's see if we can put her on ice.*

As the younger witch aims another spell Wren's way, Silje darts out from under a barstool and trips the girl. She stumbles into the businessmen's table, breaking a piping hot carafe of coffee all over her clothing.

"Stupid cat!" she yells after stripping her jacket off.

She aims a finger at Silje. Particles of ice spiral around the tip, gathering into a fine point. She screams again to release the gathered magic as Wren waves a hand up, deflecting the blast from Silje to the ceiling. Fiberglass rains down, scattering the diners unfortunate enough to have been underneath. Felice returns from the back with a pitcher of boiling water in hand.

"Get her out of here. Soak the cloth and melt the ice. Hurry before she needs more than a hot towel."

Another casting barrels Wren's way. She turns, batting the frosty magic heavenward as Felice scampers off with the housewife. It explodes against the ceiling. Snow cascades around them, but before it can fall to the floor, the girl commands it back into the air.

"Snöstorm!"

A blizzard bellows through the diner, knocking over tables, breaking light fixtures, and sending patrons darting for the door, their meals unfinished, their checks unpaid. Not that they make it very far. Half of them end up frozen mid-run while the other half realize seeking cover and warmth is a much more practical goal. Wren's own magic is the only thing that allows her to stand at the center of the witchfrost without becoming an icicle herself. But how long can she stave off the spell's effects?

"Silje," calls Wren, and the cat scampers her way over, dodging sleet and hail to tuck herself under Wren's blanket. The cat shivers violently. "Stop this now!" she yells at the other witch.

"You want me to stop. Fine! I'll stop when I've sent you back to Hel where you belong."

"Wanting to c-cash in on that n-nice bounty, I take it." She hates that she has to spit that out through chattering teeth. Already, she can't feel her toes in her boots, and her fingertips have gone numb.

Ice Girl shakes her head.

"I could care less about the money. I've wanted a piece of your stinking corpse for years."

Wren frowns.

This witchling, apparently, has a grudge against her. The resentment rolls off her psyche in nauseating waves, thick and cloying enough to make Wren almost want to repent for whatever wrongdoing she's being held accountable for. Not that Wren has ever given two shits about asking for forgiveness at every perceived slight. People develop inferiority complexes by doing far less, and it isn't like "sorry" has ever been a word people like to grace her with, so why should she bend over backward to make other people feel better?

"I don't kn-know when or how I wronged you, but you n-need to walk away if you know what's good for you. I have much bigger th-things to worry about than an angsty," she spits the word out, willing herself to not shiver through the next part of the sentence, "spoiled teenager with such miniscule control over her magic she thinks throwing icicles around is a valid show of strength."

"How dare you speak to me like that?!"

She throws a pair of icicles at Wren's face. A twist of the wrist and the frozen daggers change direction, hurtling back to their progenitor. Light brown eyes widen as Ice Girl makes to get out of the way, but she's not quite fast enough. One of the icicles tears through the back of her blanket.

"I'll speak to you how I like. You want to act like a fool, then I'll address you as one. Now unravel this blizzard before you kill everyone here."

"I will when you stop breathing."

The blizzard's fury intensifies. The few still warm-blooded patrons shudder and turn to flesh popsicles. Silje, curled up and freezing at her feet, has rime frost forming in her fur. Wren picks up the cat and holds her to her chest for shared body heat. Wren, already weak from magical exhaustion and injury, can feel her face going numb, warmth trickling across in place of the freezing cold. *Not good.* When the cold stops feeling cold, that's when things are going down the drain. Wren's bullet wound twinges, the literal pain in her side worsening from the exposure to the chill. She feels the first life vanish as it is snuffed out like a candle by the cold.

Alright, that's enough.

Mouth dry, lips turning blue, she croaks out her first note. The effect is instant. Two frigid patrons, now lifeless thanks to the extreme cold, begin to creak and croak against their frosty prisons. If ever there was a time to take advantage of a situation as a necromancer, it is in the event of a recent death. Bring the victim back to life and turn them against the person that killed them. A short and sweet revenge story fueled by necrotic magic, and Wren has played that game many, many times before. The undead shuffle their way to the frost witch.

Ice Girl stifles a gasp as the first walking dead ambles its way to her. Fear rolls off her in waves as she stares at the undead like a deer caught in headlights. The poppet raises its arm high into the air and brings it down over her head. The witch goes down, but the limb also hits the counter with a hefty *thunk*, and the frozen appendage shatters.

Right... Meat popsicles. Mierde...

The witch kicks the zombie away only to be caught from behind by the other. Wren's poppet wrangles the girl back to the ground. A flash of blue magic spears into the ceiling, taking the zombie's head clean off. The undead topples over lifeless. Behind Wren, the baby starts to cry, its little face turning blue in its mother's frozen arms. The woman's heart rate is dropping.

"Silje," she hushes, and the netherbeast jumps from her songstress's arms, rushing to the babe to keep it warm. "These people are innocent. Stop this before you kill everyone here."

"I won't stop until your corpse is frozen at my feet."

A scattering of frozen daggers *shing* her way. She flicks the projectiles away only for a sharp pain to stab into the meat of her back. A spike, drawn from the frozen ground and thrust into her core like a spear, anchors her to the floor right beside where Agni shot her just days ago.

Wren's body goes rigid, pain freezing through her core.

Remind you of anyone, Songstress?

Emerald eyes flare with wild magic. An echo drifts through her awareness, at once as close as her soul and distant as a star.

Who's there?

"How dare you! You of all the monsters in the bloody universe!"

Seems she's a little avenger as well.

Wren shakes the voice from her subconscious and breaks the spike in her back. Blood wells in her hand, hot and steaming compared to the ice surrounding her.

"I don't know how or when I wronged you or your kin, and for that I'm sorry, but these people are not a part of whatever feud you have with me. Call off this blizzard, and we'll settle this in private."

"You think I care about them?! I'll turn the whole world into a frozen tundra if it means sending you back to hell."

"It would be difficult to send someone back to a place they've never been."

"Shut up!" Ice Girl screams like a petulant toddler, and the storm grows in fury. The ghosts of the businessmen, newly expelled from their corpses, scratch and hammer against the floors, chains wound tight around their wrists and ankles. One of the lovestruck teens shrieks as his boyfriend is knocked over, a crack forming along the side of his frozen prison.

What a selfish child! Like a toddler throwing a tantrum—a tantrum capable of killing dozens of people, all for the sake of revenge. Wren's rage drowns out any and all latent emotions in the room. The diner falls away, so too does the cold and the wind. Her physical senses fall numb to the external world while her sixth sense, her magic sense, opens wide and swallows.

And when Wren next speaks, it is not with a voice she would call her own.

"No, witchling. You won't."

Completely devoid of emotion... Wren looks at the girl, dead lights in her eyes. The girl's light brown eyes glare furiously at her.

"I'm not scared of you."

The triskele glows a volatile viridian at her brow. Another witch dead at her hands. Fine! So mote it be.

"You should be."

Kaito couldn't have been gone for more than twenty minutes. *What's happened?*

The windows have frosted over and several patrons bang on the door, trying to get out, but the door is stuck fast, frozen in place by a sheet of ice. Magic, lots of it, untamed and unfocused runs amok in the diner, and it certainly is not his witch's.

He activates his sights. Lines of coding replace the vital world. He lifts his hand to manipulate the space, but the Disruption flares through his head like a spiced arrow. Pain floods his receptors, and before his sights can fully boot up, his cyber vision goes dark, leaving nothing but plain city buildings and suffering people... *Shit!*

"Back away," he shouts to the people inside before kicking in the door. The first hit doesn't break the glass, reinforced as it is with ice, so he directs power into his muscle enhancements. The nodes around his temple glow violet, and a pulse of electricity tinges through his torso into his legs. The next kick shatters the door and a whirlwind of ice and snow tumbles out onto the sidewalk. Passersby pause at the spectacle, but Kaito doesn't waste time dealing with them, rushing into the blizzard.

The inside of the diner is a frozen wasteland. Ice sculptures stand scattered throughout the diner. No, not sculptures—people. The diners who were caught in the crossfire of a clash between witches. Already some have lost all signs of life. Others are in dire straits. But that isn't the worst of it.

The worst is Wren. With frost forming in her hair and fingertips blackened from frostbite, she shivers at the center of the room, yet despite this, his witch stands tall, her magic floating about her in slow, angry circles. There is a dagger in her hand, a black blade soaked with necromantic magic. It's Lacuna. He'd recognize that blade anywhere. (*When did Wren recover her anthame?*) And before her floats a young woman. No, she's too young to be called a woman yet. She's a teenager, barely any older than Renki.

And the sound spilling from the girl's throat, blood-curdling and sharp, reminds him of a banshee he encountered several years back. But a banshee's cry, no matter how filled with sorrow, holds power and purpose. This scream does not. This is a death scream, filled with pain and suffering. She is dying and his witch is the reason why.

Wren's magical necrosis buries its way into the witch's meridians, destroying pathways as readily as a virus destroys data. If this keeps up, she'll not only be giving the witch a magical lobotomy but the trauma of it will, no doubt, kill the girl.

"Wren, stop!"

Bloodlust and magic: you'd be surprised how well the two go together. And Lacuna... Suffice to say, Wren's athame has always benefited from its mistress's knack for vengeance. She doesn't know if it was the first ping of another innocent death on her radar that did it or if it was the icicle being driven into her already wounded abdomen that nudged her just this side of sanity, but Wren's rage reaches a peak not long after the witchling decided to test her. Wren's magical fury has burned cold for many, many years. Not even a frost witch could compete. Ice may be cold to the touch, but Death freezes the soul.

How many witches are dead because of you?
Mishka... Summer... Yggfret
You abandoned us! I did what I needed to survive!
The Nameless ones...
You left us alone to die at the mercy of machines!
Jessabelle... Fae... What's another dead witch compared to all that?

Her body is moving. Her magic coils around her like a venomous snake, but she doesn't know what commands spill from her lips. There is only the bloodlust. *Berserkir.* The song she sings is horrid, like a nursery rhyme warped not for the temporary peace of sleep but for the permanent torment of Tartarus. Maybe the witchling will be able to freeze the underworld over. Not likely... Perhaps she'd be more comfortable in Helheim, where anguish awaits in the chill rather than the hellfire.

Someone is screaming. She's not sure who. It could be her. It could be the baby. It could be the souls of people desperate not to die. But she hears screaming, and it reminds her so much of another time, another day, another year, another life, when screams were music to her ears. Why did she ever give up that life? She can't remember why.

"Wren, stop!"

Kaito's voice penetrates the haze in Wren's head. Awareness slaps her across the face. Hovering before her, tangled in Wren's necrotic coils, is the ice witch, screaming her head off as Wren's decaying touch works its way into her system, shutting down magical pathways and decimating the child's magical network.

Odin's Eyepatch!

She drops the girl from her magical hold and her casting ceases just short of rending the flesh from the younger witch's bones. Kaito races to her, his hands warm on her chilled skin. *Skadi, it's cold!*

"What happened?" he asks as the frost witch sobs at Wren's feet, and for one horrific moment, Wren doesn't remember what she did in her fury. (Did she kill these people? When did she draw Lacuna from her belt?) But then, Silje lets out a fearsome growl followed by the timid wail of an ice-cold baby, and she remembers. The magic running wild in here is not her own, and the witch-made storm is about to kill off the handful of people still alive.

"Kai, can you dispel this?"

"I can."

"Do it! Quick! Before this whole place becomes a funeral home."

"No!" screams the frost witch. She yanks on Wren's ankle. Chilling cold winds up Wren's leg. Wren kicks the teen away, and Ice Girl goes rolling into the nearest set of barstools.

Kaito's sights spin, a dull glow compared to his normal bright lavender gaze. His barriers against her empathy drop, and his pain is hers. Agony courses through his head, alighting his nerve ending. It isn't fire, nor is it ice. There is no physical pain she can use to describe what is happening within his body as he fights to access his tech despite the Disruption. Her vision blurs and blackens, yet somehow, he remains tall, and *saibaki* floods the perimeter. The purple glare floods the diner, encasing tables and chairs, the bar and barstools, the little yappy dog, Wren and Silje, even the ice witch, and, of course, the people trapped within a grid of technomancy.

The gridlines fall into themselves, folding and unfolding until the code tightens on the wild magic, and Kaito bends it to warp the storm to his will. His fingers trace through the code nearest him, and already the unnatural chill wavers. The snow eases, and Wren's limbs regain a bit of feeling in her extremities, but then the girl rushes Kaito, an icicle in hand. Kaito blocks the teenager's assault with a simple lifting of his forearm. The teen's arms stall on his guards, and she bares her teeth at Kaito.

"Why would you help her?" the witch spits at Kaito. "You're a technomancer."

"Because I love her."

I love her... Wren just about wallops her head against the counter swinging around to stare at Kaito in disbelief. He says the words without even making a shift in expression, so matter-of-factly. Kaito's face is as passive as ever, like he's just declared the sky is blue or the grass is green. Like the words he's just spoken are just fact, inarguable and unchangeable. Surely, she's dreaming. Too much blood loss coupled with too much magical exertion can do that to any witch. Wren is no different.

"Then, you're in love with a murderer. She deserves to die."

"Yes, yes, yes," says Wren, shaking off her alleged hallucinations and turning back to Ice Girl. "And I suppose you think you're the one to do it? But I've got some business to take care of first, so if you'll excuse me, I don't have time to babysit wayward witches."

Wren's magic flares up, thrusting the girl off her feet and into the countertop mirror while Kaito sets back to work until the magic is caged within Kaito's cybernetic prison, and the blizzard ceases.

"Stop it!"

But it's already too late. The remaining patrons with a pulse thaw out in the wake of Kaito's dispel. They shiver and cry, and—oh good—the boy who got a good crack in his frozen state is just fine. The mother, seeing her baby deadly pale, draws the child close and coos at it while Felice nudges her toward the relit furnace. The teen screams, magic furling at her fingertips once more, but the girl's magic isn't the most deadly thing aimed Wren's way.

Bang!

Wren dives to the floor as a shotgun fires just to her right. It's Chef, apparently, chef's hat askew on his head with his weapon raised overhead and pointed to the ceiling. The goddamn barrel is still smoking.

"I don't give a lick of care who killed who, who died when, or who owes who what. The lot a ya are gonna pay off your tabs and get the hell outta my diner."

The ice witch screams one more wave of frost in their direction before making a break for the shattered window. Chef fires the shotgun two more times on her heels, but the girl disappears around the corner, a hexen promise on her tongue aimed at Wren.

"Silence the Songstress!"

Someone ought to put that on a banner. It has a nice ring to it. She can see it now, a whole host of protestors standing outside her door calling for her blood yelling, "Silence the Songstress! Silence the Songstress!" as though anybody actually listened to protestors anymore.

Wren wilts, the strength sapped from her limbs. Kaito's hands guide her to the floor. The damp of melted ice soaks into the seat of her pants, and it's still much colder than she would like, but at least it's a solid surface. It isn't even 9 o'clock in the morning, and already it's been a day.

Two smoking barrels aim her way.

"Whoa, whoa, whoa," she says, raising her hands.

"You keep yer magic-grimmed fingers on the goddamn floor, witch."

"Okay, okay. You got it," she says, spreading her palms flat on the tile. "Not here to stir up trouble."

"All you've done since you entered my diner is stir up trouble!"

Kaito steps between Wren and the irate chef. "We did not start this confrontation, and you'll do well to point your weapon elsewhere."

"Oh really? And I suppose you were here to witness how my diner ended up a fucking ice cave? Last I saw, you dumped her in a booth and took off. Pretty negligent of ya considering a woman like that stirs up trouble wherever she goes. Now get outta my sight before I—"

Having had enough of the man's postering, Wren flicks a finger toward the barrel of the shotgun, and the metal bends 180 degrees to point back at the man wielding it.

"What in the bloody world! This was my pop's vintage..."

The man's voice fades from her perception, rapidly gaining distance and washing out of reality. Wren, losing her last angle on the waking world, lets herself sink into the warm bergamot smell of Kaito's clothes. If anyone else needs to take a piece out of her, they can very well wait until she wakes back up.

The Technomancer Council and Primacy has never gone unquestioned. Just as any ruling body undergoes scrutiny from the media, the TCP has dealt with its fair share of bad press, yet somehow, all of those instances of potential scandal end up getting swept under the rug.

The largest, of course, being the execution/suicide of the Songstress of Lorelei.

Excerpt from *Systems of Government in Deus*
Heather Ables, 1872 A.P

5

THE EMPEROR.

HIKARU'S EYES, NORMALLY SO WARM compared to Kaito's cool silver, are cold. The emperor of Murasaki no Yama, who always seemed to save a smile for him ever since he was little, now regards Renki with a strange solemness the teen has never seen about him before, like some deep knowledge burdens him.

"Ah, Renki. Good to see you are rested." He isn't though, not even mildly. Can't his uncle see the bags under his eyes? "I have a mission for you."

Hikaru beckons him onto the train, a private affair used only by the royal family, complete with private compartments for each member of the household, Kaito included. Renki has only been aboard a handful of times and not since he was a small child. Everything was so much bigger back then.

At the front of the train is a compartment for adept escorts and royal guards. This is where Hikaru's formal guard will stay during the trip: a plain barracks with minimal comforts but plenty of tech and weapon maintenance equipment. No doubt this is where Akari has been staying to serve out her punishment for running off to Chairomura and nearly getting herself killed. No... That isn't fair. Renki is the one that nearly got her killed, chasing off into the unknown the way he did. Akari shouldn't have had to endure the penalty for following Renki into trouble, yet she did. He didn't even have the chance to apologize. That's how quickly Kaito whisked him back to Yuki ga Furo.

He'll need to rectify that.

The next few compartments are for any technomancers accompanying the royal family. The set up is much the same, except the sleeping arrangements are private and far more cushy, with places for Murasaki's greatest human+ warriors to lay their belongings and personalize the space should they choose. It looks like one of them has been recently in use.

They pass through the remaining compartments, each decorated to the taste of the family member or soldier class to which they belong. Fumiko's is minimally ornamented with various teaching tools and heirlooms of the Miyazaki family that are not precious enough to be kept in a vault but merit the respect of an honorable display. Things like letters written between lovers in the olden days of the war against magic, artwork finely painted but small enough to fit on a window pane, and journals written by their ancestors: scripts and scrolls of the war and of how the hexen first began to abuse their power.

Hikaru's compartment is elegant and comfortable, featuring a pull-out writing desk and a wall of computers for his use. Never is there a moment of rest for the ruler of a country. There are always reports to file, official documents to stamp, and correspondence to send. Rarely is there a time when Renki has ever seen his uncle without his comm unit or his sights inactive during the waking hours of the day. The only time he ever turns them off is when he is speaking to someone directly in front of him or referencing an external electronic device.

The last compartment is Kaito's. Neat, clean, and sparse, it would look no different from the adept compartments were it not for its size and the upgraded monitors on the walls. Kaito would never condone such fanfare for their missions, but with Hikaru, it was different. The emperor required maximum security for all his ventures, a limitation as far as stealth and efficiency went to be sure but necessary for his stature. Hikaru allows the scanner to process his retina and walks through once the doors open.

The back of the train is reserved for specialty needs (i.e. prisoner transport, evidence, corpse preservation, etc.). He wonders, with no small thrum of excitement, what could possibly be waiting for them there. Fumiko and Akari are already there along with a technomancer Renki has only seen a handful of times.

"Any word on Tanaka?" Fumiko asks the stranger.

"Dead, master. Culprit unknown, but it appears Kaito-sama was in the area at around the time of death."

The conversation ceases as they notice his presence. Akari waves to him immediately, but Fumiko is quick to hush the girl and usher her into the compartment before she can properly exclaim anything more than a small *meep*. Despite the grand master's scolding, Renki's mood lifts at the sight of his cousin and friend. Aside from the tiredness clinging to her brow from spending the last seventy-two hours as Hikaru's guard, she looks good as new. No sign of the sickness that nearly killed her in Chairomura. He's glad to see she's looking better. Lady Wren's treatments really did save her life.

"Renki, this is Orson." He beckons to the unknown technomancer once they've all assembled within the car. Wearing a viking-esque style of armor, not Murasakan standard but painted in Murasaki colors, the man is taller and bulkier than most any other Murasakan adept Renki knows, and with his shaved head, braided blond beard, and blue eyes, there is no doubt this man's heritage is of decidedly northern blood. The man nods in welcome. "You and Akari will be working under him for this case, after which he will be taking over as your mentor."

"Taking over?"

Hikaru doesn't answer him. He simply joins Fumiko and Orson where the pair have already gathered around the table.

"Renki, Akari, put these on." Orson gestures to a pair of liquidator-style masks on the side table.

"What for?" asks Akari.

"Some spells leave a residue behind which if inhaled can wreak havoc on the mind," he answers.

"But you're not wearing one."

"Orson specializes in dealing with psionics."

"Meaning?"

"Psychic attacks don't affect me."

"Quickly, you two, before you breathe in any of the trace." Fumiko-sensei's order is muffled behind her own mask.

A biohazard sheet covers something vaguely human shaped on the slate, and Renki nearly gags when Orson pulls back the sheet to unveil a rapidly decaying corpse. Discolored and oozing a gray tar-like substance, the body is nothing but skin and bone. What must amount to decades worth of mummification has left this man's body nothing but a leather-clad skeleton. A film of magical residue settles over the apparently male corpse like spider webbing. It traces the whole body and flakes off as the sheet is pulled down. The stray strands spin and drip around them like ectoplasm tainting the very molecules in the air.

Fumiko, Hikaru, and Orson snap on a pair of medical gloves before moving to stand on either side of the corpse.

"Cause of death?" asks Orson.

"Total body shut down from organ and brain failure due to dehydration and starvation. The body has also been completely drained of blood, the organs missing, almost as though taxidermied, yet there are no puncture or dissection lines to be found."

"Like the life was sapped from his very bones," inserts Fumiko.

"Remind you of anyone?" asks Hikaru, looking pointedly at Orson.

"All too much, Miyzaki-Tennō."

"It would appear her viciousness has worsened with the current circumstances."

"Being among the dead in Hel's desolate world for so long will do that."

"You make too many assumptions, Orson."

"Where else would a necromancer spend their afterlife?"

It takes a moment for Renki to shake off the stupor brought on by the vehemence in the emperor's voice before he figures out exactly who his uncle is speaking of. "You're wrong!"

"Renki," chides Fumiko, trying to intervene.

"No, I don't believe it!"

"This is not the time, boy," hisses Hikaru.

"Lady Nocturne didn't do this."

"Young man," Orson's voice is calm and leveled, the way one would speak to a toddler. Renki hates him all the more for it, "this body bears all the signs of having been felled by a necromancer. There is no denying that dark magic was in action here, and it is no coincidence that this poor soul's cadaver has turned up just as the Songstress returned to the world."

But Orson's words mean nothing to Renki.

"Why would she kill some no-account? I mean, this person isn't even augmented. The Songstress of Lorelei is—"

"A witch who has been brought back to life by unknown magics for an unknown purpose. She is bloodthirsty and unrepentant of her past actions," snaps Hikaru. "And you are too young to remember the atrocities she committed."

To emphasize his point, Hikaru thrusts his comm-bearing wrist forward. A holograph beam alights, and in the image stands Wren, covered in gore and surrounded by bodies. As the image unfolds, a technomancer rushes the witch, weapon drawn. Green energy catches him mid swing, and before Renki's eyes, the man's skin wrinkles and shrinks until the technomancer falls dead at the witch's feet. In all that time, the Songstress of Lorelei didn't even move. She simply continued a haunting song of destruction and torment.

"This is just a glimpse of what she is capable of, Renki."

"But that can't be..."

"You couldn't know this because there were efforts made to shelter you from such truths, but the Songstress of Lorelei is a killer, guilty of killing hundreds of Human+."

How can such statements be true of the person who saved Akari's life? How is he supposed to reconcile Miss Nocturne as a murderer when she looked him in the eye and told him he was worthy?

"It can be, and it is. Your father knows this better than anyone else, yet despite everything, your father has decided to align himself with a known murderer." Hikaru's rage is beyond anything that Renki has ever experienced from the man.

Without a response to give, Renki backs away from the emperor and runs to his father's compartment. As he runs, he can hear Fumiko scolding her nephew for his callousness.

"...you are hardly the one to judge your brother for acts of betrayal!"

There's a soft tap at the door.

It's Akari. He doesn't know how he knows it's Akari, but it is her.

"Ren Ren. Can I come in?" Sure enough, his best friend's head pops through the doorway.

"Hey, Akari."

The other teen lets herself in and settles herself at the foot of the bed where Renki has bundled himself in his father's sheets. The heavy knit of the topmost cover was originally his grandmother's and set with spiraling designs in purple, mauve, and burgundy.

"You know, it sucks that Kaito-sensei isn't going to be around for a while, but I think this Orson guy will be pretty cool to work with. He wants us on reconnaissance mostly..."

Akari's words float across his awareness. He's listening to her but not really listening. He lets her go on, though. On and on and on. She's trying to distract him from his thoughts. He gets it. He really does. A small part of him might even appreciate it, but the vast majority...

"Did she really kill that many people?"

"And then he said—What? Who?"

He gives her a look as if to say, "Who do you think?"

"I mean, all the stories say so."

"Stories?"

"Well, yeah. I guess you wouldn't know because Prince Kaito raised you in the palace, but when I was a kid, other children used to tell me that their mothers told them that if we didn't eat our vegetables, the Songstress of Lorelei would steal us from our bed and feed us to her garden gnomes."

"I don't believe that. She would never hurt a child."

"Maybe, maybe not. One of the reports I read said that she sacrificed her newborn nephew for some blood oath."

"Reports can be falsified."

"It was the same report that detailed Prince Chike's death. And everybody knows who was responsible for that."

Renki bites his tongue before he can blurt out that self-defense is a thing and says instead, "You really think Kaito-sama would work with a baby-killer?"

"Yeah, well, I mean, who knows? Miyzaki-Tennō says he might be enchanted."

"Did he look enchanted to you?"

"No... Yes... I don't know."

"You were there! How can you tell me you don't know?"

"I just don't know, okay!" she shouts back. "A lot was happening, and no one knew what to do. There were ghosts attacking people and the Songstress—"

"She has a name!"

Akari flinches, dumbfounded by the vehemence in his tone. Even Renki draws back in on himself at his own outburst, averting his gaze before Akari resumes her speech, slow and deliberate as though Renki were a wild boar.

"Lady Nocturne said she'd cast a spell on him, but he said she hadn't, and then next thing anybody knows, they've disappeared into some magical portal, leaving behind a mess of injured adepts and junked robo-guards."

"So, he's just gone. Fine. I'd rather be an actual orphan anyway."

"Renki, come on. You can't just—"

"I need to finish unpacking."

"Unpacking? It's only a few hours ride."

"Just go, Akari!"

The girl zips from the compartment as though fire were at her heels. Renki nearly slams the door shut, and for the first time since his *tousan* deposited him back in Snowfall like a troublesome child, the anger melts away to tears.

Renki cries, a raw nerve left exposed to the elements. The tears are hot on his face, and he can already feel the swelling starting in his cheeks and around his eyes. In a few minutes, he'll look like a puffy marshmallow man and his eyelashes will be all clumped together like a bad mascara job. At least, he doesn't cry ink like an overly made-up girl.

He takes out the new comm unit Hikaru gave him and dials. As predicted, his tousan's voicemail answers, but this time, he doesn't hang up on the answering service.

"They found a body at the Shard, and Uncle is convinced Lady Wren killed him. Fumiko-sensei isn't so sure. Either way, you've been implicated. They're assigning Akari and me to Orson for the mission. It's been less than a day since you vanished from the face of the planet." He hates how thick his voice sounds, and the tears stuck in his throat make the pitch rise uncomfortably high. "Did you really kill Tanaka? Where are you? Are you with her? You said you'd come back with Lady Wren, yet no one seems to expect you to return? Why? Are you in trouble? Why won't you answer me?"

Renki's head drops into his hands. A sob rattles out of his chest. Is this what it means to be abandoned? Why does it feel so familiar?

The Emperor.

"You said you'd come back, but how can you do that if even Uncle believes you are a traitor?"

Very few humans are able to tell you what sets Hexen apart from Faefolk.

It isn't hard to understand why. Both groups use magic, both are substantially different from humans, and both seem to walk the fine line between mortal and immortal. So few humans even get to see fairies these days, they are almost as much legend and mythology within League countries as they were in the old world before the witches vacated.

As such, I feel it is my duty to exposit the difference.

To put it bluntly, Fae are the naturally occurring magical beings in Deus. Hexen are, to put it bluntly, aliens from an unknown land. You see, back in the olden days before the hexen ever came here, Deus was home to the Gods and Goddess whom most witches worshiped. Their peoples are the fae. The fairies, the sirens, the satyrs, the dryads, the elves… All those creatures of "folklore" they told stories about in the old world are the indigenous residents of Deus.

It was only upon a great show of collective mercy that the gods brought their earthly worshipers to Deus, and once those witches set foot on the magic-rich soil—soil untainted by human hatred—the latent powers hidden in their blood sang to life, and the fae had no choice but to accept the newcomers into their lands.

It was the fae who named the witches and their ilk "hexen," for they were a hex cast upon them by the gods who had forsaken them.

Excerpt from *Of Fae and Fury:*
The untold histories of the unseen
Written by [Redacted/Unknown/Lost]

6

ACE OF CUPS

13th Day in the Month of Falling - Calypso City

KAITO LUNGES TO CATCH WREN BEFORE SHE hits the floor. The sudden action jolts through his wiring, battered from not only a magical jump but also the fatigue of battling the Disruption. Pain still splinters through his scalp, but he pushes it away. He'll take a dose of neuropozyne later. Now is not the time for a maintenance dose.

The chef rants on and on to no one and everyone in various languages, insulting Wren no doubt until a new voice enters the conversation.

"Oh, Vivo, don't get your wings in a twist. You were fixin' to do a total renovation anyway, and Big Daddy Boggs will fix you up nice and new in a jiffy. Where else is he gonna get his favorite cup of coffee?"

A petite, cloak-wearing woman, apparently unaffected by the recently dispelled blizzard, jumps down from the counter and dances around the chef. She twirls in front of him, her skirts sparkling as they fan out. Kaito spares her a glance before returning his attention to Wren. He doesn't like how shallow her breathing is.

"Stay outta this, Lyra," he hears Vivo say. "Drink your cocoa."

"Oh I finished it well before the snowstorm, thank you very much," the girl chirps back. "Lucky for you because I sure as heaven would not pay for something that was destroyed before I could enjoy it."

"You little..."

Kaito tunes them out. He hasn't the time for spats between normals. Wren's body is cold to the touch, and there's blood everywhere. She needs another stim. He reaches into his pack, pulling out the syringe, only for a pair of dusty hands to stop him before he can inject the medi-stim.

"Oh, you don't want to do that. At this point, it'll send her body into shock."

Kaito looks up to find a rather peculiar looking face less than two inches from his own. There is chocolate smeared across her lower lip and a bit of whipped cream lingering at the tip of her nose, but this is hardly worth noting compared to her other features. She looks at him with bright pink eyes framed in gauzy, silk-like eyelashes. Her skin, while a pale porcelain, seems to glitter around her cheekbones and chin. The shine gives her more of a rose hue which darkens to a true fuchsia speckled with white freckles around the hairline, and despite the scarf covering her head, he can see where the tone blends perfectly into her plum pink hair. And poking from the fabric is a set of pointed ears.

More jarring than her appearance, however, is how fast she appeared before him. *How did she get here so quickly?* He didn't even see her move.

This must be a fae creature of some sort. An elf, maybe? Or móg-fae? He's not sure. He's never encountered one up close.

"I'm Lyra, by the way, and your little witch has just about had it."

"Wait, stop—"

Before Kaito can react, the woman lifts a dainty hand over Wren's face, rubs her fingers together, and a cascade of pinkish dust shimmers over Wren's hair and face. It tangles in her blue-black locks like glitter, and the wild script of her face shivers at the contact, almost like her magic is giggling at the touch of the dust. As though by magic, Wren's body warms in his arms. The color returns to her cheeks, and her breathing evens.

What kind of magic is this? Kaito has never seen anything like it.

"Poor, chilly thing. That ought to do her some good 'til we get to my workshop. I can fix her up right and proper there."

She gets up and flutters her way over a nearby table; a pair of orange tipped pink wings peeking out from under her caplet to help her along the way.

"You're a fairy."

"In the flesh, love. And your witch needs some old-world medicine, if you catch my drift. That smattering of dust'll only hold so long."

She winks.

He remembers seeing the woman before leaving the diner earlier. In all this time, despite the magic being flung back and forth around the diner, the fae seems to have quietly and calmly finished her piece of cake and hot cocoa. Having been entirely unaffected by the witch-made blizzard, she now primly wipes her lips with a pair of napkins, one in each hand, before sidling up to Silje and unceremoniously patting the netherbeast on the head.

"You're awful cute in this form, but something tells me being so small irritates the living daylights out of you."

Silje's whiskers twitch, and she licks at the area the fae stroked before darting to Kaito.

"So, shall we head out? Her ladyship probably shouldn't be out in the open for much longer."

Silje's body language screams agitation, probably considering that her witch was just attacked by another witch, but the familiar doesn't seem averse to the fairy. Even with this, Kaito is distrustful. A total stranger, and a fairy no less, offers her service to them out of the blue. Surely, there is an expectation of payment or exchange here as is the norm with fae creatures.

"Thanks for the offer, but we'll continue on our own."

Kaito gathers Wren's things, double-checking the fast route to the hospital, but the fairy clicks her tongue and bats her eyelashes at him.

"Oh, I wouldn't advise that. You'll want to trust that there isn't anywhere else that can take care of your beauty's injuries. Metal people medicine doesn't sit too well with hexen like her. Besides, you'll be somewhat conspicuous trekking your way through the city."

"Is that supposed to be a threat?"

"Haha! Not at all. Didn't you see the news? Oh, wait, I guess you haven't connected to the local server. Here…"

Her eyes travel to the freshly reset holoscreen above the dessert bar. It's back on the game of holoball. Not for long, though. She snatches the remote from behind the register. With a click of her fingers the monitor flickers through several channels of static before a pair of news anchors appears.

"Ah, here we go. The Hexen headlines should prove interesting."

One of them is dressed in garb more akin to that of a Victorian lady or gentleman complete with florals in their cropped hair and a parasol overhead while the other wears a rather queer rain suit of sorts, entirely black with a bucket hat on his head and thick glasses over his eyes which seem perpetually fogged up. Nevermind that both are indoors. The screen gives their names and pronouns, though the pronouns for the one wearing Victorian garb have a tendency to flicker from he to she to they and back again.

Kaito frowns.

"We've just received reports of a clash between two witches at a local dive. Could it be related to the newly resurrected Songstress of Lorelei? I'm Cole Zalensky, and this is the midnight news report."

Lyra laughs.

"I've always found it funny that they call it the midnight news report no matter what time of day it is. Oh, look, look, look, this one is my favorite."

"Wren Nocturne in Calypso City? Could we be so lucky?" The second anchor, sporting a flowery headband and the name "Kay Downing" on their nameplate, looks starry-eyed and lovestruck by the idea. "Oh! To live in a day when the gods may once more walk among us."

Cole rolls his eyes at her antics, seemingly adjusting the cuffs of his sleeves before clearing his throat and pressing on with the newscast.

"Authorities are on their way to investigate. All civilians are advised to stay clear of the area. Any privateers looking for a quick score, stay on your toes. I'm sure you've already seen the bounty sent over by the League. Probably enough to cover your rent for the next five to ten years."

The second anchor huffs, hands on their hips and cheeks puffed up like a chipmunk. "Oh, have you no loyalty, Cole?!"

"I just say what the monitors tell me to say, Kay. You should try it sometime..."

A loud siren wails outside the diner, and bright lights flash through the windows. AYA is quick to pull up the aforementioned bounty. An impressive figure for both him and Wren, and an even higher number of credits on offer for anyone capable of capturing the Songstress of Lorelei alive.

"Whelp, that's the Hexen chat chit for you. I do so love that vampyre. Always good entertainment," giggles Lyra, spinning on a stool. "Can't wait to see what the metal mouths are saying? Clank clink. Vampyres, witches, and weres, oh my!" The woman jumps from her perch to spin past Kaito's left shoulder. The faintest of touches to his left hand and something folds into his palm. "Clank clink, clop clip, who's afraid of a witch's trick?"

The fairy winks at him as the chef scoffs.

"Thor, almighty. Cuckolded rumor-mongering fiends. Bootlegging hexen and +ies alike will be trekking mud through my kitchen looking for a goddamned ghost," Vivo mumbles, droning on and on in the background as Kaito glances at the small swatch of paper in his palm.

At first, he can't make heads or tails of the writing: strange swirling runes and shapes he hasn't a name for. He is about to look to the fae for clarity, but as if by magic, the symbols rearrange themselves into a name: *Lylilria Mchelogdea.*

"I'm sure I don't have to tell you what having ownership over a fairy's name means."

Wren's breathing stiffens and stutters before stalling entirely. The deathly stillness that falls over her nearly stops his own heart until a raspy inhale signals that she yet lives. He looks back to the fairy and makes his decision.

Meanwhile, the chef has continued his rant about the place.

"Felice, get the shotties. We got company coming, and like hell am I letting these gold-loving arseholes set foot in here."

"As if you don't serve gangsters' wives five times a week," calls Lyra.

"At least the wives tip well. So do the gangsters. The rest of the undergrounders though... Cheapest lot of penny-pinchers you'll ever meet." The man looks over to Kaito. "I don't know 'bout you or the little lady there, but you'd best make yourselves scarce before I decide to call in on those credits. Just look at this mess."

"No need," Kaito declares. He pulls out his portable unit. Connecting to the diner's systems, he hacks into the diner's financial accounts. Nothing grand, but not measly, the diner boasts a solid sum, but it's nothing that will cover the repairs necessary after the damages inflicted on the establishment today. A few quick maneuvers and a sum of credits large enough to more than cover the damages to the diner find their way from Kaito's private accounts to the diner's accounting system. Vivo, watching the transaction on the screen, nearly faints at the number of zeros.

"Who the heck does this guy think he is?"

"Someone who would appreciate your discretion." Kaito rises to his feet, Wren tucked safely in his arms, before addressing the fairy, "Lead the way, but be warned, fae. Turn on us, and it will be the last faulty decision you ever make."

Despite the threat to her person, Lyra smiles impishly.

"I would expect no less from the Songstress's yoke. Umm, Felice," she calls, waving a hand, "we'll be taking those meals to go, if it's all the same to you."

Felice's face falls.

14 Years Ago - 24th Day in the Month of Soil - Two Months After Seraphim's Fall

When the missive comes to Yuki ga Furu Palace, Hikaru is skeptical, reluctant even to allow Kaito accept the case based on the territory he would be heading into.

"The League has no jurisdiction over the Seraphim no-man's-lands. Nor does this case have anything to do with our country."

Hikaru's latest desire has been to return Murasaki no Yama to a place of neutrality and isolationism, accepting cases only involving their territory and immediate borders as it relates to their country, but Kaito stands firm. He is taking the case, and there is nothing his brother can do to stop him.

"Matters involving war criminals involve all of us, regardless of where our borders are drawn."

Hikaru sighs. The new emperor has been in his office for nearly three days without interruption trying to reorganize and balance their adept rosters, military budget, and incoming trainee applicants. Only Fumiko, Kaito, and a handful of service bots have seen him since he sequestered himself, and as Kaito peers at his brother from where he stands across the office, the difference is telling. Hikaru looks thin. Stress has aged him at least five years, pulling flyaways around his temple from his slicked-back hairstyle and darkening the pockets under his eyes.

"Don't you have responsibilities here that need attending?"

An untouched tray of food sits to Hikaru's left, his lunch. Kaito would not be surprised to learn it was probably delivered to him nearly an hour ago.

"I have overseen the redistribution of my immediate duties, and as Calyx of Murasaki, it is my obligation to represent you on the field in any missions involving international interference as this case does. Jamar Sahra of Sekhmeti is leading the mission as a retaliation for the initial attacks against Sekhmeti. Aighneas and Ebele are also sending their own operatives. As the only nation whose country did not suffer direct land fighting, our involvement is not only requested, it is expected."

And with only two spots remaining on the mission roster, he needs Hikaru to hurry up and submit his credentials to the system before he is locked out of the case.

"But why this case?"

Why indeed?

Taking a mission outside of the League's borders is never considered routine. Taking a mission to a former warzone is even more atypical, but in this case, the need is justified. Montwyatte, the last technomancer who fought for Seraphim during the war, has been spotted in Petalburg, a small outpost that sits in the no-mans-land between Seraphim and the Wastes. Somehow escaping the final siege which brought down his compatriots, Montwyatte's flight to a neutral zone should have been expected and, more importantly, of no concern to Murasaki, and yet...

A steel foot kicks the soft flesh of a ribcage... Blue-black hair yanked backward by a mechanical fist... "My man, Montwyatte, was a right beast."

"I have my reasons."

His brother sighs, the sound years older than it has any right to be for his age. He knows very well what Kaito's reasons are, and he won't dare push back against them. Kaito takes the bowl of rice on Hikaru's tray and sets it on top of the open tablet in front of his brother. The screen immediately darkens, saving any vital information, and Kaito proffers a pair of chopsticks. Hikaru begrudgingly accepts the utensils and takes a chastised bite of lukewarm rice. Small victories...

"I suppose I can't stop you, then."

Kaito shakes his head from left to right, a slow deliberate gesture confirming his brother's words.

"Fine then. You have my sanction." Hikaru stamps his electronic seal across the bottom of the case holograph, signing for Kaito's involvement. His name is immediately added to the roster of technomancers accepting the case. "You'll be seen as an immediate mark for anyone daring enough to make a bounty out of a League-sanctioned technomancer especially with the amount of reconstruction efforts currently taking up resources across the continent."

Wars involving technomancers are far-reaching and destructive. While none of their battles may have physically taken place in Petalburg, the war's effects, both vital and virtual, on the surrounding lands and the resulting influx of refugees would have undoubtedly affected their economy. Such shuffles of people, allegiances, and goods require organization. Organization which below-ground infrastructures and governments like that of the neutral zones tend to struggle to implement based on the chaotic nature of their political system.

"Perhaps, but Gewalt has specified this mission be taken by six certified technomancers for good reason. A force of that size would have been considered a full battalion during the war, and five spots have already been accounted for."

Who the last technomancer will be is anyone's guess, but it matters not to Kaito. He is going, and that's all that matters.

"Be safe, otouto."

Kaito bows his head and takes his leave. His equipment is already packed.

Two Days Later - St. Petalburg just Beyond the Edge of Seraphim's Borders.

St. Petalburg sits just below the permafrost at the northern edge of the mountain range that acts as a barrier to The Wastes. There are only two means of arrival: by water or by air. Kaito has chosen to travel by air, and he regrets that decision the moment they hit the storms.

The aircraft landing pads here are insidious at best, downright hazardous at worst. They are not maintained well, with broken boards and splintering support beams. He isn't sure what kind of wood they use to build their supports, but it does not seem to do well in the icy water, and he worries that the structures will simply crumble upon impact with the next violent wave to punch into its face.

And there are plenty of those considering the storm currently pummeling the mountains.

As he arrives at their mission rendezvous point, only three of his teammates have already assembled: Selene Fitzroy, Chike Nagi, and Jamar Sahra. They all look about as miserable as he feels. Chike has pulled his hood down as low as it can go and can't seem to decide whether standing in the rainwater is preferable to not standing in the rain. Jamar, equally discomfited, sports a respirator over his lower face, no doubt filtering the damp frost out of the air to aid his breathing. (Coming from a place as hot and arid as Sekhmeti, it's no surprise he's having difficulty breathing in the heavily saturated, freezing air.) Not that he is one to judge his colleagues. He too is quite out of his element.

This time of year, it's the height of the monsoon season in southern parts of the continent. That water deluge reaches all the way north with rains that are more sleet than water, especially compared to the temperate rains of his home which come with cool breezes and steady thunderstorms. Here, the rain dumps from the sky in buckets, and the winds cut through to the bone no matter how many layers of clothing worn. It makes him feel wet despite the waterproof cloak around his shoulders and the umbrella over his head. Though Selene, whose hair is a frizzy mess from the rain, claims he looks "as immaculate as ever." He chalks this up to the dark coloring of his clothing hiding the sweat stains. Jamar simply rolls his eyes while Chike just moves back into the rainfall; both of them are too hot and bothered to care what Selene thinks of their appearance.

"So, that makes four," says Chike. "Any idea who we're waiting on?"

"Art told me he was taking this mission," answers Selene. "I don't know the last person, though the last I checked I saw someone from Deriva was listed."

"Irene," provides Kaito easily, looking up as an Aighnean helicopter circles down to hover just above the ground. He saw her name appear on the roster during his trip here. Water splashes this way and that in response to the chopper's blades. Jamar gets blindsided by the splashing and chokes as water soaks beneath his mask. He wanders away to clear the system.

"Ah, that's why I missed it."

"What did you miss?"

From the aerial landing strip, Arturo Lionheart disembarks from the chopper. He's dressed appropriately for the weather with thigh-high rain boots over military fatigues and a waterproof poncho slung over his shoulders, so he sloshes through the water like a long-legged crane only lacking the grace of such a creature. Jamar greets the man with a fist bump.

"I didn't realize Irene was our fifth because I only look at last names on my mission tablet. Her last name was listed simply as Deriva."

"Of course it's listed as Deriva," inserts Jamar, strapping his mask back over his mouth. The accoutrement shifts his voice to a tinny echo. "She isn't exactly legitimate."

Selene rounds on Jamar. "And what exactly is that supposed to mean?"

Jamar gives the woman a bored look.

"I mean, she isn't descended from anyone notable. She's the first technomancer in her family."

"So what! I'm the first technomancer in my family. You calling me illegitimate?"

"You at least have adepts in your family. She's a slave's daughter, for crying out loud. Barely even transhuman."

"That doesn't make her any less legitimate than you."

"But it does make her new tech. Why do you think she pledged loyalty to Deriva? Her own country didn't want her after certification. The cost of keeping her outweighed the benefit. It's a miracle she even survived integration. Couple of years from now, I bet she makes a stupid decision that costs her her augmentations and her life. Most transhumans expire long before posthumans of more respectable pedigrees."

Selene opens her mouth to shout something else at Jamar, but Chike cuts in first.

"Which is probably why she beat your ass so thoroughly during the trials. Because she's had to work far harder to become a technomancer than you ever did."

Jamar's eyes narrow, dark and angry, but before he can snap anything back at the Ebelean prince, the horn of a docking submersible breaks the roar of the storm. A Derivan submarine breaks the surface at the end of the dock. It vibrates at such a low frequency it seems to calm the waters around it, floating there entirely unbothered by the turbulence. The hatch opens and out climbs Irene, her scythe strapped to her back. Strangely enough, she seems to be ranting to herself about something, harried and bothered as she scrambles up onto the dock and falls to her knees. More than a little green around the edges, she looks as though she is about to lose her lunch. He half expects her to begin kissing the ground.

Jamar turns away, looking back to the city skyline as Selene goes to greet her friend. If Kaito remembers correctly, the two used to team-up often during their trials. They ran with a group of girls from several different countries; however, only Irene and Selene graduated. Well, those two and...

"Wren Nocturne! I cannot believe you did that!" he hears Irene yell down into the hatch once her feet are firmly on the ground.

"We were perfectly fine. I had it all under control."

The second voice chimes through the hatch from the belly of the submarine to Kaito's surprise, and two seconds later, the witch herself hops her way out of the vessel, landing lightly on her feet on the dock, an umbrella pointed upward perfectly above her head and entirely unbothered by the subzero storm.

"Xipilli told me that we aren't supposed to spin the ship like that. You could have completely destroyed our surface tension and drowned us."

Wren waves her hand. "That's just something they tell you in piloting school. It's perfectly safe if you know what you're doing. Two hands on the wheel and all that."

"You only have one hand."

Wren shrugs.

"I have other skills to make up for it." As though to demonstrate, she floats a pack up the portal and closes the hatch with a small burst of magic, the locking mechanism clicking into place with the push of a button on her comm unit. With a gurgle of bubbles, the vessel sinks back below the surface, invisible to anyone who might come investigating the area. When she turns around, she waves pleasantly to Chike, Selene, and Arturo, and when she sees Kaito, her grin widens to a full smile that reaches into the greenest flecks of her eyes. She bounds his direction, looking all of sixteen again, and he meets her halfway up the dock.

"I didn't realize Kaito-kun would be accepting this mission," she teases. "The border zone is no place for a prince. Though I do like seeing you in the rain."

"And I suppose it is a better place for a lady?"

"Lady? Where?"

"Ahem, Irene and I are standing right here," says Selene.

"Hah! Speak for yourself, Fitzroy." Irene laughs. "Though I suppose you could include Arturo in your lady's club."

Arturo chuckles. "Yes and while I'll take that compliment any day, I don't think I'm even remotely worthy. You women are the reason our species is able to thrive. We would all be lost without the ladies of the world."

"Yes, yes, keep trying to sweet talk us."

The man gives an affronted scoff, hand on his chest in outrage.

"Sweet talk? Oh, the things you accuse this poor man of."

Selene and Art go back and forth in the most outright display of flirtation Kaito has ever seen despite this absolutely not being the time and place for it. Wren leans into Kaito, rising onto the balls of her feet to whisper a sweet melody of notes in his ear.

"And you used to call me shameless?"

Her breath dances over the shell of his ear, and he can just barely feel her lips brush over the skin of his neck. Gooseflesh breaks out along his shoulder and back, and his tech whirs to life to stabilize his temperature. He meets her eye to eye, spies the mischief in her sea-green ones, and leans down.

"And such a display is supposed to have me think otherwise, my lady?"

Wren chuckles, biting her lower lip to keep from outburst. She looks as though she is going to say something else, but an interruption stalls her.

"What do you think you're doing here?" Jamar's question, more than a little abrasive, pulls Wren's attention from Kaito, and her mood, light and breezy before, pivots to something more reflective of the ice spilling around her, a deathly chill shrouded within her gaze. Jamar's servers must sense it because his third-eye headset alights, and the activation lights around his oxygen mask pulse with an increase in speed.

The man himself, however, doesn't seem any the wiser to Wren's shift from at-ease to combat-ready.

"Well, I'm certainly not on vacation. It's monsoon season in Deriva and wet season everywhere else. If I was going anywhere, it would be somewhere much warmer and less wet."

"You know what I mean, Nocturne."

"No, I'm afraid I don't. You'll have to clarify."

"This is a mission for six technomancers. No more, no less. You were not on the roster; therefore, you are in violation of League protocols."

"On the contrary, *highness*," Wren sneers, "I'm not here as a member of your unit."

Wren throws a holopod at Jamar. It opens in his palm. On the projection is a different mission briefing from what was given to Kaito and the others. It is a Deriva-specific case, though it does involve their unit and case. It basically tasks the person on the case with aiding their company in any way possible but with an addendum regarding Montwyatte: Kill or capture with special assignment to Deriva's second-in-command Wren Nocturne and signed by council member Xipilli Moctezumo, Vulcan of Deriva.

Jamar's brow tightens. "My father was not informed of this. He would have vetoed such an assignment."

"The Primarch's signature is not required should a monarch and/or council member decide to mobilize an adept or technomancer of their own roster."

"This is an outrage. We don't need your help. You're barely even a technomancer!"

Kaito could cut the tension in the air with Amatsu and not even manage to leave a dent. Jamar, on the other hand, he could probably slice in two as easily as a stick of butter, and he isn't the only one with murder on his mind. Agni has fired up on Chike's back, and Selene looks about ready to fire an arrow into the Sekhmetian prince's backside. Irene shifts uncomfortably from one foot to the other, looking from her country's second-in-command to her mission captain. Wren, however, regards Jamar with an eerie calm.

"Welp, this 'barely even a technomancer' is here whether you like it or not, highness, and if you were half as intelligent as you claim to be, you'd happily accept my help, just, ya know... considering where we are." Wren gestures in a circle around her, and the umbrella above her head rotates in a steady ring, but it's not the umbrella she wants to draw attention to. It's to the surplus of magic lingering in the area. There are several fae creatures swimming below the ice behind them, the earth vibrates with chaos, and there is nothing normal about the thick essence in the air. "This is after all a wild zone, and those mountains are close enough to cause a Disruption should the refraction of the sun deem it so."

"Spoken like a true witch, Nocturne."

"Yeah, well, this witch is on your six whether you like it or not."

Judging by Jamar's dour look, having Wren at his back is not a tasteful thought. "Just stay out of my way, and I'll do you the honor of forgetting you were even here."

"How generous of you, Sahra."

"Hmph!"

And the man storms off, heading for the coach that will take them into the city. Chike approaches his sister-in-law with a half-hearted laugh.

"I suppose there are some perks to having a big brother who is both Vulcan and League Council Member."

Wren offers Chike a lopsided smile. "It helps that Xipilli also wants to see Montwyatte in the ground. How are Atzi and Zenza?"

"Zenza is fighting her first cold. Poor thing screams at all hours of the night unless either I or her mother are holding her."

"Poor tyke. I hope it isn't serious."

"Nothing a bit of acetaminophen and mother's milk can't fix."

"Good. I'm surprised Atzi let you out of her sight."

"She practically pushed me out the door. Says I fret too much, and I'm already sporting gray hairs."

"Ah, yes, I can see that. The salt and pepper in your goatee is rather dashing if you ask me."

"Humph!"

Chike shoulders Wren amicably before strolling off to catch up to Jamar. Irene follows after with a look toward Wren and Kaito. They do have a mission after all.

"Well, shall we dance?"

Wren's voice is a song on the air, her smile more than a little teasing coupled with her trademark two finger-framed wink, but the seriousness in her eyes is not lost to him.

"Wren, are you sure about this?"

"Deadly," she answers. "On your lead or mine, Prince?"

And without another word, Wren follows Selene and Arturo to the coach. And for this being their mission's beginning, Kaito has never felt so much dread.

An object in motion stays in motion.

Newton's Third Law of Motion

7

THE FIVE OF SWORDS

14 Years Ago - 26th Day in the Month of Soil - St. Petalburg, Seraphim

"KAI, ON YOUR SIX!"

Kaito swings blind, and Tsukuyomi impacts on the rogue adept with a squelch. Wren uses her magic to peel the man off his blade and send him flying into the nearby canal while Kaito directs Amatsu into the stomach of another foe. He joins his teammate over the edge of the bridge. Blood stains the water even through the murky gray coating at the surface. Wren has already stunned three others. Meanwhile, Irene, Chike, and Jamar have dealt with their opponents on the far side of the bridge. He's not sure whose bright idea it was to send Arturo and Selene in a separate direction for reconnaissance, but the lack of fire power is proving problematic now.

Jamar nurses a wound on his arm. When Irene moves to offer assistance, he coldly shoulders her aside.

"Well, I was expecting to find one Seraphim op, not half a dozen."

"Perhaps your daddy should have done better reconnaissance for you?"

"Shut it, Nocturne. That's what Fitzroy and Lionheart are for."

"Just saying."

Wren flits around to one of the dead adepts. This one doesn't look nearly as beaten up as the others thanks to the quick death the witch handed him by snapping his neck. She places her fingertips on the dead man's forehead and hums a short tune, like a wind chime tinkling in the night, though there is no breeze to speak of. It sounds vaguely familiar, like something he's heard on the radio but not. A moment later, the dead adept becomes an undead adept. His tech even lights back up. The coloration is different than before, now a rotten green where it was once red.

Jamar, seeing the undead rise to its feet, is quick to accost the witch. "There will be none of that, Nocturne."

"None of what, Sahra?"

"I'll not have none of your necromancy! This is my mission, and the last thing I want is your trickery compromising it. Desist at once."

Wren rolls her eyes and moves on to the next corpse.

"I said stop, Nocturne!"

Jamar reactivates his weapon, a triple-bladed katar which unfolds from his mechanical forearm. Christened Serket at their trials, the steel sparkles gold in the low light, the H-shaped handle folding easily over his clenched knuckles to create a perfect extension of his fist. The medallion at the base of the central blade glows a dull amber not unlike the sands of his home. Underneath that notch hides a machine-made toxin mixed with Jamar's own life blood and synthesized to deadly perfection. The poison is deadly enough to down a mammoth should he manage a direct injection.

"Lady Wren isn't on your roster, your highness," Irene inserts, blocking Jamar's view of the busy witch. "She has every right to use her own methods as she conducts her own mission."

"I don't recall asking your opinion, you—"

"Sahra," Kaito calls, "rather than squabble amongst ourselves, perhaps it would be best that we reevaluate our approach since we now know Montwyatte has several men at his disposal."

"*Had* several men at his disposal," the witch corrects as she dumps the corpse she was just working with into the canal. "These halfwits, apparently, thought he was too bossy to continue venturing with him any longer. That they came upon us was entirely happenstance and misfortune."

Two days of reconnaissance work to find Montwyatte's location yielded nothing to their group. This is the first lead they've found, and apparently it is moot.

"And you know this how?" asks Jamar.

Wren's eyes glitter in the darkness, and the corpse beside her speaks.

"Montwyatte is a cad and a coward who cares more about wine and whores than exacting revenge on the people who killed our Pontiflex. You want to find him? Go to the west end of town. There's a hexen bar there where only the most wily fancies may tread. Imagine, a technomancer as great as Montwyatte willingly consorting with hexen whores. It's despicable."

Wren snaps her fingers, and the magic giving it life cuts short. It falls limp to the ground, landing with a meaty squelch.

"The dead don't lie, my lord."

"Is that a fact?" quips the prince.

Wren turns to Kaito. "These guys were fed up with his preference for entertainment rather than action, so they thought they'd take matters into their own hands."

"And do what?"

"No idea. Maybe they just wanted a good old fashioned street brawl when they came across us, but they picked the wrong group. When have you ever met someone from Seraphim who was smart?"

"Good point."

"So where is Montwyatte?"

Wren's new poppet, freshly dead but already shambling like a centuries old mummy, is walking away toward the center of the city.

"Apparently, he is hiding out at a local dive. Come on. If what this guy's memories managed to serve up are correct, we can follow him there."

"This is the place."

Wren gestures to the small, dirty dive that seems to be the only local eatery around. The mural featuring the restaurant's name and a chipped away depiction of a family celebration is grimy and discolored with time and abuse. So much so, Kaito can't even make out the proper name of the establishment. On top of that, there doesn't even seem to be anyone inside.

"This hole in the wall? It looks like the kind of place that serves the local strays for dinner." Jamar's lip curls in disdain at the venue. Kaito himself has a hard time imagining a man like Montwyatte would want to hunker down in a place like this.

"Not the building, Sahra. The void waters."

"What the what, now?" asks Chike.

Wren clicks her tongue and chuckles, stepping forward with her hand raised to something unseen. The vacant space under her palm ripples, and as if from nothing, a doorway materializes. At the center of the door, a runic symbol (⋈) glistens, but just as quickly as she reveals it, it vanishes from their sight.

"Where'd it go?" asks Irene.

"It probably sensed too many technomancers in the area and hid itself again. No problem," answers Wren. "I can call it forth again. In the meantime, it's probably best that I let the rest of you in through the back. I doubt they'll let me in with a posse of +ies. You should circle around to the other side of the alley. Shouldn't take me but a moment to convince them that I belong."

"What's to stop you from just taking off on your own?"

Wren looks at the Sekhmetian prince. "At this point, Jamar, nothing. Perhaps you should remember that before you try to antagonize someone who shares the same immediate goals as you do."

Jamar, ruffled and put-off, turns to go, albeit reluctantly. As though in defiance, he starts clicking angrily at the communications unit embedded in the back of his forearm. Probably a mission update to Selene and Arturo on their present time and location in case Wren does indeed take matters into her own hands. Wren and Irene share a look.

"Make sure he doesn't muck all of this up, will you? I can't lose this lead."

"No to worry, my lady. I'll keep him in sight." Irene salutes before the woman follows the other technomancer away.

Chike laughs, shaking his head in amusement. "Man, I'd hate to be on the wrong end of your sarcasm, *Umakoti*."

Wren turns back to the blank space in the alley while Chike pats Kaito on the shoulder as he passes, disappearing out of the alley.

Kaito stays behind. No doubt in his mind that his witch can sense him.

"Hey, Kai."

It's the first moment they've had alone in months.

"Wren, may I?" His hands hover on either side of her hips, waiting for permission. She looks over her shoulder at him, a cat-like glint in her eye.

"Your highness, shouldn't you be more focused on the mission?"

"A small interlude is sometimes necessary for the full symphony to carry on."

She chuckles but nods her head, and Kaito winds his arms all the way around her small waist. Her body is warm in his arms. All the tension that has been radiating from her since their arrival melts into him, like a wilting tremolo on the edge of a musical theme.

"I didn't realize you would be accepting this mission."

She laughs.

"You still don't see Xipilli as a monarch. He has just as much authority to initiate a mission as Gewalt, Sahra, or your niisan. He just doesn't quite know how to do so as effectively as everyone else. He'd rather shout orders and have other people take care of it for him."

"Like you, you mean?"

"Of course, like me. Who do you think is the real brains of the operations in Deriva? Xipilli does the leading part. I do everything else. That's how we always said it would be ever since we were kids. We're just doing it all a bit sooner than planned."

There's a note of bitterness hidden near the end of her explanation. Some calm exasperation she may not wish to voice aloud but that Kaito catches all the same. The pair didn't realize how young they would be when it came to pass, nor the circumstances under which Xipilli would be forced to inherit the throne.

He understands. For all of Murasaki no Yama, he understands. He and Hikaru did not expect to fulfill their concurrent roles so soon either.

Wren's body trembles. For a moment, he worries she is crying, but then giggles well up like water out of a spring.

"My brother really needs to be more responsible with official council paperwork though. Hehe ha—"

"Wren..."

"Mande, mon prince?"

"Did you assign yourself this mission you're on?"

She bites her lip. "Maaaaybeeee..."

"Does your brother even know you left Deriva with Irene?"

"Possibly not."

"Do you realize how much trouble you could get yourself in if Jamar realizes you are here sans sovereign permission?"

Wren blows a raspberry. "Jamar is as stuffy as his father and twice as dense. You have to spell things out to that one if you want him to understand, and I personally don't plan on telling him. Do you?"

Kaito sighs, but once he shakes his head, no, she carries on.

"Besides, what is he going to do? Slap me on the wrist and tell me to go home? I'm the League's Hero, remember? There wouldn't even be a technomancer council if I hadn't given them the key to the Pontiflex's personal chamber pot."

She laughs even harder at her own joke.

"Wren," he attempts to chide her despite the half-smile threatening to split his face at the moment.

"Don't worry, Kai. Even if he does suspect something, my brother will smooth it all away. I know my brother can be a stubborn *burro* at times, but Xipilli will back me up. He always does."

Her fingertips continue to play with the space in front of her, unbothered and totally relaxed as she falls into a spellweave. The disjointed musicality of the humming is soothing just on its own. He is sure that if his neural blockers weren't on, they would be lulling him into a magical sleep even as she centers her power on a completely unrelated target. The new cat-like gleam to her eyes is intensely apparent, the byproduct of her witchsight.

"What do you see, now, that I can't?"

It's a question that has been lingering at the edge of his thoughts for a while now: her ability to recognize the forcefield in Vatidomus City, her strange manner of staring at the unseen, her new ability to see spirits and ghosts... What other unseen things in this world is she now able to recognize with her witchsight that are beyond even his human+ senses?

She chuckles at his question. "You can see it too, Kai. Just activate your sights."

He frowns, doubtful of that, but does as she says. The world, ever lined with unseen coding, turns from the subdued grays and blacks of a downtrodden civilization to the familiar number-lined lavenders and violets of his unnatural vision as his sights come online.

"I only see that which exists in the cyberscape, Wren. I can't visualize anything that exists outside the bounds of reality and its virtual counterparts."

"But don't you see?" she titters. "Magic is part of reality, the same way our breath is part of our bodies. You just need to look within to see without. Here," she lifts her hand to a space barely a few inches from his nose. "Focus on my hand."

He does. The coding around her nails is a darker shade of purple while the skin of her hand is a lovely lavender tinged with the emerald green of her energy signature. A part of him aches in remembrance of a time when her coding was lined in a brilliant golden hue, but this change is nothing new to him. He's examined her coding multiple times since her return.

"I feel as if I am going cross-eyed."

"Hehe. Good." She extends her hand out in front of them. He keeps a keen eye on the appendage, secretly thankful that his eyes aren't crossing anymore before she moves on with her instruction. "Now, look at the negative space between my fingers. Do you see the code sitting there?"

He grunts in affirmation.

"Excellent. Now, don't read the lines of code. Look behind them."

Look behind them? What does that mean: *look behind them*? "Wren—"

"Just try it, Kaito. This is as much an experiment for me as it is a lesson for you."

When he narrows the focus to the seemingly empty air before them, something quite frankly magical happens.

There *is* something there. Alive and pulsing, just like the energy signature surrounding her coding, a veil of some sort reveals itself on the far side of his code. With each twitch of her fingers, it reacts, ripples trailing away from her witch song, cascading over and under one another like still waters. Only these waters have no shoreline. The ripples cascade beyond the boundary of her hand into the coding outlining the buildings, pavements, and even the sky, reaching away to infinity just as if it were outer space.

"Void waters," she called them. It's a suitable descriptor.

"Safe spaces are not always safe, yet we seek refuge in them without any other option to take."

From the journal of a hexen refugee,
1437 A.P.

8
THE LOVERS

"**W**HAT EXACTLY IS THIS PLACE?**"

"This is Club Harborage."

About fifteen minutes ago, Kaito followed Wren into the magical doorway, and they found, on the other side, a strangely normal looking check-in station manned by the most uninteresting man Kaito has ever seen or met. Even now as he tries to remember the interaction between the witch and the doorman, he can't recall any details of the man's face. Several times now, he has gone into his retinal recordings to remember, but every time he turns off the reruns, it's as if he hadn't even bothered checking them at all.

The club itself is full of light, and none of it is of the electrical variety. Magical orbs hover in scattered coordinates throughout the room. They cycle through various hues in a steady rhythm, a rainbow of colors contained within a liminal space. He imagines for just a moment that he can hear the song in their dance, but the bass of the music is too loud.

"But we are nowhere near a harbor!" He has to shout to be heard.

A pair of beastly-looking fellows wearing very little fabric dance past them. So enraptured they are with one another, they hardly even notice how close they come to intruding on the space of a group of vampyres. But the vampyres are too blood-drunk to care, sipping healthy mouthfuls of the red fluid from their martini glasses.

These are not the only hexen about.

Lycans of multiple varieties, other types of shapeshifters, goblins, more vampyres, even a few golems dancing free of their witch masters, and he sees so many more hexen from other nations that he has little to no experience dealing with. He doesn't know if there are any witches about other than Wren, but he knows without a doubt that it was her status that allowed them such easy entry.

"It's not that definition." Wren winks at him. "Ah, absynthe," she declares, then promptly sashays over to the bar.

The last thing he wants to do is follow her through the crowd, but the only other option is to stay by the door alone while surrounded by hexen. Hexen who, by the way, seem to be doing things far beyond the scope of what he would call dancing, so he makes his way around the gyrating bodies to where Wren leans against the bar.

"Do you want anything?" she asks.

"We're working."

"You're working. I'm sleuthing. There's a difference."

The bartender hands her a drink that glows as virulent a green as her triskelion when it is alight.

He sighs, scanning the room for any tech signals. There are more than a few, surprisingly enough, none technomancer grade, but sure signs that human+ patron this place as regularly as the spell folk.

He wrinkles his nose at the prospect.

He can understand hexen wanting to indulge in pleasures of the flesh, but human+? They were supposed to be better than their organic bodies. If the legitimate brothels in the red-light districts of the League weren't distasteful enough, illicit nightclubs such as this, underground and secret to the average human, are even more out of touch with sanitation standards.

He won't even consider the amount of debauchery that probably takes place in the unseen shadows of such an establishment.

"I am not surprised Montwyatte would hide out in a Hexen brothel."

Wren shoots Kaito one of the meanest glares she has ever had directed at him. "This isn't a brothel, Kaito."

Wren takes her drink and walks straight into the undulating crowd of dancing bodies. The other hexen, as though responding to her witchiness, fold and unfold around her until she disappears directly into the heart of the pulse, leaving a confused Kaito behind.

What did he say? How could this not be a brothel? There are scantily clad men and women everywhere; several pairings dance and gyrate to the drum and bass as though to separate would be to commit a grievous sin against synchronicity.

"You have certainly fucked it, my dear," a slightly pitched voice says behind him.

Kaito turns to find the bartender peering directly at him. A dapper-looking gentleman, or perhaps a delicate lady fair, with rouge on their cheeks and a luscious wig full of purple, pink, and blue ringlets on their head. Their garb is strangely androgynous yet unspeakably fashionable—not that Kaito is a connoisseur of fashion; that's much more Hikaru's point of interest. For a top, they wear a pressed tuxedo in the unmistakable coloration of a flamingo; however, the bottom of the suit is probably the most extravagant of ballgowns Kaito has ever seen.

The person's appearance strikes him dumb.

"Harriety—psionic, my dear." A bejeweled hand is presented to him. "Your kind often confuse us for witches, but we don't really have magic in our blood the way they do. And you are apparently a master of stepping in it."

"I don't understand."

"Your lady friend is the first witch we've had here in months. Can't imagine she doesn't feel perfectly at ease at the harborage compared to all that mess of metal and steel you all call civilization, yet you look around and see a brothel. My, my, lad. You have no sense of hexen kin, do you?"

"I know hexen well enough to—" He cuts himself off by literally biting down on his lip, and the metallic taste of blood scrapes across his tongue. He nearly said he knew enough about hexen to hunt them down.

"That's what I thought." Harriety's words are sassy in more ways than one as though they knew what Kaito was thinking. That's not possible, of course. Kaito's neural blockers protect him from such invasions. "Don't worry. I can't read your mind. I just know peoples' expressions very, very well. Anyway, your lady friend is right. This is no brothel, though I can understand you making the mistake. Lots of people would see couples having sex in a public venue and assume the venue to be a palace of pleasure, but while there is plenty of bumping going on behind the curtains, this is certainly no whorehouse."

"So what is this place?"

"Club Harborage?" laughs Harriety. "It's a safe haven, of course. A sanctuary for the hunted, the outcast, the weary."

"A sanctuary?"

"Amazing what people do when they feel safe. You +ies! You've done some much to advance your societies, yet no one feels safe enough to be their true selves. This here—" Harriety juts their chin at a particularly enthusiastic couple tearing at what little clothing they wear as though it were a puritan sack. "This is how people are when they are free to be who they are. They dance, they sing, they fall in love only to fall out and do it all over again. This is how the world would be if we didn't put so many baseless rules on our own natures."

"Yet you house wanted criminals."

The bartender hardly seems fazed by Kaito's aggression.

"Everyone here is a criminal in the eyes of the League. We make no distinctions between those who earned the title and those who were born to it. And your lady fair, as much as ignorance kept her from persecution before, fits the latter description."

"Wren was not born a witch. She was a technomancer once."

"Oh? Who's to say there is really all that much of a difference?"

A tug on his sleeve pulls his focus away from Harriety's asinine theories.

"Kaito..."

A hushed whisper on the wind, an emerald tendril curls before him, twisting in the space in front of his face until it becomes less of a serpentine wisp and more of a vaguely human-shaped enchantment.

"Kaito," it whispers. The magic is whispering in Wren's smooth alto.

The tiny sparkle of magic spirals, dancing to the pulse of the music. It brushes playfully against his nose and eyelashes, sashaying sensually over his lips as though it had a mind of its own. Well, not so much a mind of its own as the voice of its master.

It tugs at his hair. Uncut ever since his mother's passing, it has now reached beyond his cheekbones, and the little sprite or spell, or whatever it is Wren has made, pulls him away from the bar and into the thick of the crowd. Amazingly enough, no one so much as brushes shoulders with him on his route to the witch.

When Wren dances, it's like being caught in a hurricane. The music surrounds her form, enfolding it in the same way a tornado spirals the falling water. She rolls her torso forward and back, side to side, sweat beading in the valley of her breasts. Her storm winds howl in all directions, clearing the people around her lest they be sucked into her typhoon. Her hips jerk and roll like thunder in the clouds. Her wild script sparkles in maddening pulses over her skin. Lightning strikes from within her very being. She is the power of the storm.

She is earth and life and pure electricity, and it is her power that bids his feet to walk ever in her direction.

"Wren..." he says, but his voice is so quiet, the music so loud, its recitation is more for him than her. A prayer to a mortal goddess.

When her eyes lift to find him, he is unsurprised to see the glow of her power shining in her triskele. However, Kaito is not prepared to see it reflected in her eyes, glowing a fearsome emerald green. He should be repulsed. A part of him screams at him to run. To turn away and never look back. The same part that would name her evil and seek to destroy her before she can destroy herself. The same part of him would see to it that every being in this club, Club Harborage, be annihilated.

But then Wren smiles. Not at him. Not for him. She smiles for herself. He is merely lucky enough, trusted enough, to witness it.

She holds out her hand. He takes it.

And another piece of that ignorant part of himself crackles into dust and is swept away by her storm as, for the first time in years, they fall into a dance. They move together face to face for a while. Well, Wren dances. Kaito mostly watches her, swaying back and forth from foot to foot enough to at least seem like he is dancing. He's never expected to nor felt the need to dance to music of this nature. Music with curse words and heavy basslines. Music about sex and getting high. Music designed so people could exercise such activities.

He feels out of place. Badly out of place.

"I'm sorry," he yells over the music.

"For what?"

"For my ignorance. I should not have spoken about this place the way that I did."

Wren sips the last of her absynthe with a nod of acknowledgment to his words before whooping as the DJ turns the tables onto a new song. The empty glass flies out of her hand in the general direction of the bar where Harriety catches it with an easy flourish.

"I love this song! Come here!" she shouts and abruptly turns herself away from Kaito. Taken aback at her sudden need to turn away from him, he moves to follow, only to find Wren's back pressed solidly into his front. "Relax, *mon rivage. No puedes perreando conmigo si no te relajas.*"

"What?!"

"Relax and move with me."

She pulls his arms around her waist and presses even closer, and to make the connection better, Kaito spreads his feet apart and bends his knees. It's a mistake though as the adjustment brings his crotch into intimate contact with her supple derriere.

"There you go. Just like that." She leans her head onto his shoulder. Long black curls spill over his arms and tickle his throat.

"Kaito," she purrs. She is so close her lips brush against his pulse. "Dance like you wanna fuck me."

He doesn't so much as hear her words as feel them, tiny zings of electricity through his entire body. Her hand snakes around to grope his ass. It jolts his body forward even harder into the witch, and once he's there, it seems ridiculous not to fall into her slow grind, so he does. He follows her lead, becoming a vessel for her watery movements to fall into. Heat generates between them, and Wren starts singing along.

We're gonna rock the bedposts 'til daybreak, whoa.
Don't cha wanna love me 'til I'm only yours.

Something happens as Wren sings. The whole room, already hyped up on ecstasy and bliss, reaches a fever pitch. The bodies surrounding them move infinitely more aggressively. Their amorous embraces become salacious. Kisses become lip locks, slip and drool and whatever else glides down faces and throats and chests.

Kaito himself, though unaffected by whatever influence Wren's voice seems to be having on everyone, trails his hands up her body to cup his partner's full breasts. Wren's moan echoes in his chest. "What's happening?"

"Nothing. They are just feeding off my energy."

"Like vampyres."

"No. Like hexen."

Wren's eyes sparkle with mischief. She turns in his grip, straddles his leg, and claims his lips for her own. To say Kaito loses clarity on everything that happens next would be a lie. He knows very well what he does. How Wren leads him to the far side of the dance floor. How he pulls her behind an unoccupied curtain. He doesn't stop her when she drops to her knees and pulls open his pants. He remembers very clearly begging under the wet heat of her mouth and being at her mercy until she decided to pull off. He is very intentional about the tempo and ferocity with which he makes love to her against the wall.

Volatile and maddening, and the entire while, she sings and hums her songs for the whole club to feed off, so the ruckus outside becomes more and more explosive. Lycans shift and howl, ravenously fucking and brawling. The vampyres watch and enjoy, drinking down all of the emotions ricocheting throughout the room.

There's more. So much more that he is aware of only through his connection to Wren. Later, looking back in hindsight, it was the fastest coupling they have ever indulged in, yet to Kaito, as everything unfolds, it goes on and...

on and on...

and on...

and...

"What took you so long?! We've been waiting out here for over an hour."

"Oh, I'm sorry. I must have lost track of time trying to get past the security guard."

Jamar is clearly miffed by the prospect of being left outside while Kaito was allowed in.

"Any sign of Montwyatte?"

"Not yet," Wren answers. "The bartender told me he typically arrives around this time."

"Well, what are we waiting for? Everybody is in position. The moment he walks through that door, I want him warded, destabilized, and handcuffed."

Jamar shoves past Wren to enter a club where he is most certainly not welcome. Kaito grabs him by the upper arm. "This mission is Montwyatte. You will do no harm to any hexen within. Am I understood?"

Jamar shoves Kaito's hand off. "The day I take an order from you will be the day I roll over and die."

"I can't be certain about the rolling over part, but your death will come today should you jeopardize this mission with any out-of-bounds maneuvers."

"Sir, yes, sir."

It isn't even worth asking why Kaito feels like he's just being placated.

Capturing Montwyatte, all things considered, is anticlimactic. He shows up. Chike confronts him, and to all of their surprise, he acquiesces to being taken prisoner. Jamar, controlling ponce that he is, takes control of the situation and practically yanks the fugitive away from Chike and Irene to process him himself.

Wren is displeased. Kaito is one hundred percent certain that she was ready to tear him limb from limb. The man even took one look at her, saw her indicia alight, and winked at the witch as though knowing the exchange between her and the Sekhmetian prince just before he arrived at the club.

"I tell you what, Jamar. If he goes peacefully, he's all yours, but if he puts up even a little bit of a fight, all bets are off. I'll kill him, rip out his heart, and you can have the spare parts."

Alas, he decides to go peacefully. He even surrenders his weapon to Irene and allows Kaito to put tech suppressors on him. He's now being escorted to the train by Irene. The remaining three of them stand outside Club Harborage for a debrief. Kaito waits for Jamar to leave so he can have a personal conversation with Wren. There is something that has been weighing on his mind as of late, but it's hardly a conversation he wants to have in front of company, especially this brand of company.

"Well, Nocturne, better luck next time, I guess. You'll have to inform Xipilli that his sister came in second best on this one."

Wren doesn't even grace the man with a look. "Oh, I'm certain it isn't over yet. Montwyatte may be going into custody willingly, but a jail cell won't protect him from me."

"You can't break into a prison to kill him, Nocturne. That would be illegal."

"My very existence is illegal, Sahra. Perhaps you'd better think with your actual brain instead of just spouting off loose threats like your father."

"My father is the most brilliant man in the entire League. His very title demands it, but if you need a demonstration, I'm happy to oblige."

Kaito's eyes narrow as the other prince reaches for a device hidden in his back pocket. It's a detonator, something Kaito would usually expect to find on the other side of a bomb. Before he or Wren can do anything, Jamar's thumb compresses the central button and the device lights up a blinding red.

"What is that?" asks Kaito.

"Oh, just a new invention my father has been working on with some of the resources left behind by Seraphim. We always knew they were the forerunners in nuclear technology, but did you know they're working on smaller but no less deadly weapons? Apparently, the Pontiflex was concerned with having a supply of weapons solely capable of causing planetary destruction. Funny how all these egotistical types start to think outside themselves when other people's troubles come knocking at their door."

Jamar keeps his eyes focused into the distance. Wren and Kaito glance all around, expecting an explosion of some sort to occur, but nothing happens.

"Nothing is happening," says Wren.

"Patience, Nocturne. It'll happen."

A shudder ripples through the forcefield hiding the establishment and the building comes into view. Already, cries of fear penetrate the magical walls of Club Harborage. The windows break and pounding begins at the door, but it doesn't yield. Someone has locked everyone in.

Wren's eyes widen in horror. "What did you do?"

Jamar chuckles. "A new prototype that we are quite proud of. It's called an assassin drone. Tiny flying nanobots no bigger than your thumbnail. They wriggle their way into the ear cavity and burst, destroying the brain stem. Chances of survival: 0%."

Kaito rushes forward, his right hand flashing out to catch Jamar around the collar. "Call them off right now, Sahra."

"And defy a direct order from the Primarch?"

"I never read anything about an order for genocide."

"Probably because while you and our little witch were inside fooling around with all of those hexen, I sent an update to my father. He's been looking for an opportunity to test out these little buggers and was so thankful to Lady Nocturne for giving us a prime circumstance to do so."

He starts laughing.

"You monster!" shouts Wren. "Those are innocent people in there."

"Those are monsters in there, and they all deserve what's coming to them."

Kaito punches the man in the face. The other technomancer lands flat on his back on the pavement, out cold. The riff raff dealt with, he turns around, sights active and saibaki swirling into his receptors.

"Can you stop them?" asks Wren.

"I don't know."

With his infrared vision, he can see inside the building. Lycans swat and bat at the robots, trying and failing to eliminate as many as possible. The vampyres, their abilities useless against cold steel and metal, cover their ears and cower behind their larger counterparts. The few casters attempt to magic themselves away to no avail.

There are countless electrical receptors flitting throughout the club, thousands of tiny software systems, each operating off of one executive order. It should be easy enough to nullify the kill command, but the signal is so scrambled he can't trace it back to a single source. In fact, there seem to be multiple sources sending in the signal, as though they were drone bees responding to various queens residing in their hives. "I can't. There's too many. By the time I could work my way through the hives' commands, they'll have done their jobs."

"No…" Wren's mouth forms the word, but he can barely hear the sound come out. "I won't let them kill all of those people."

She starts to run forward, but Kaito grabs her arm. "Wren, you can't go in there!"

"They're dying, Kaito. I can feel them!"

"If you go in there, those bugs will just turn around and attack you, too, and what good will that do?"

She flings her hand forward, and the doors to the club swing open. A few hexen, once outside, attempt to flee, but run headlong into an electrical force field. There are wards keeping them from leaving the vicinity. Jamar, that cursed bigoted bastard, must have placed anti-magic wards around the building knowing they would try to escape.

"No!" shouts Wren.

Kaito reroutes his targeting system to the wards. "I'm going to deactivate those wards."

"There's no time."

She's right, and he doesn't require his technolyzed sight to confirm it. His vital eyesight can see plainly as day the people collapsing within.

She widens her stance and extends her hand. Her voice echoes through the alley as darksome magic circles and collects around her.

"Wren, what are you doing?"

She doesn't answer him. The triskele shines bright on her forehead as emerald energy swirls around her. He can't understand what she is singing; it sounds like Hexen speech, dark and ethereal. It sounds awful to his ears, not the usual beautiful tones and cadences he is accustomed to hearing her sing. This is eerily violent, reminiscent of that day in Deriva when Wren rose from the figurative "dead" and reappeared after a year-and-a-half MIA. That day, Kaito witnessed witchcraft being performed firsthand by a person he never, in a million years, thought he would see perform such an abominable act. His perception of Wren that day nearly changed forever for the worst.

Seeing this side of her magic once more makes shivers race up and down his spine. The chill in the air pales in comparison to how cold his body becomes in response. This time, however, her powers are being used to save people who are more similar to her than they are to him.

Wren's breathing quickens. The very air around them thickens. Each breath he takes seems heavier and heavier, less and less effective. His skin aches from the build-up of power. He drowns above water, and his support systems activate. His AI warms him that he is in a dangerous proximity to a magical deluge. But as damning and draining as the effects of her magic are on him, they seem to be affecting her much worse.

Jaw lined with tension and her throat straining to summon the forces of necrosis to her whim, the strain of the casting is apparent in her face. Her eyes glow a bright virulent green, her breath comes in bursts and spurts, but most troubling is the blood slowly trickling from her nose and ears.

"Wren, you can't do this."

Yet, despite his calls for her stop, she presses on. If anything, the music becomes even louder, more prominent, more distressing. He activates his auditory blockers it becomes so intense.

"Stop this before you kill yourself!"

"I can do this!"

And for the first time since she began her song weave, he looks up at Club Harborage. Her magic encircles the building. Green light shines within and without, reflecting in the glass of the windows and the ice on the street. In his sights, he sees the robots beginning to succumb to her energy. She is holding them locked in place with her telekinetic abilities.

The fingers of her hand slowly start to close into a fist. The first curve eliminates roughly a hundred bots. The second another two hundred. By the time she reaches the third curve of her fingertips, something fights back. A pulse of anti-magic force penetrates through her spell.

The question now becomes, who will win: Wren or the robots whose entire existence is based entirely upon the accomplishment of their mission to kill as many hexen as possible within the building where they have been planted. That's the horrific truth behind the efficiency of technology. It knows only its programming. There are no "buts," no "ifs," not even "ands" beyond what their systems tell them to do. The mission is the holy grail, and once accomplished, they have no further function.

And the scary thing is, Kaito thinks, *we build them that way. We build them to be emotionless and effective. They feel no pain. They feel no remorse ... all for the sake of the objective.*

Technomancers are different. There is, allegedly, a human aspect to every human+. Humans are inventors and tool-users by nature. Technomancy is merely an extension of that natural propensity. The hexen would say otherwise. The hexen believe that the integration of the unnatural into a body is a surefire way to strangle the soul within. The exact opposite viewpoint is held by the technomancers who see the integration of magic into a soul as an invitation for the destruction of a person's humanity. It's as surefire as ending a life with a bullet.

Humanity's natural propensity for innovation brought forth these tiny monstrosities of metal, dynamite, and intelligence. As though learning from the magic being directed against their efforts, the nanobots rally forth as a unit, moving against the magic holding them back.

Blood flows from Wren's eyes. He's seen her move singular objects at a time. Right now, she is trying to wrestle with thousands. He cannot imagine the strain on her synapses.

"Wren, you're killing yourself."

"Leave me alone, Kai."

"I won't let you kill yourself here. There are too many of them."

"I can do this!" she screams.

But she can't. The bots rally, their programming far stronger than the magic of a single witch, and Kaito watches as the last bit of life is snuffed out inside the club, and with it, Wren's magic puffs out like a candle flame.

Spent, Wren collapses to the ground. Kaito catches her around the shoulders before she can hit the pavement. Goddess above, he can see the bodies piled in the entrance where escape proved futile. You would never be able to guess how they died. Their bodies look completely unscathed. He guesses that's the beauty of technology. It makes death less messy and therefore more appealing to look at.

"Wren, there was nothing you could do."

"Why am I not strong enough?"

"You are only one person."

She cries. The tears mingle with the blood still dripping down her face.

As he leads her away from the area, he tries not to look back, but the ache in his chest pulls his eyes back for a single glance. It's a sight he will never forget as long as he lives. To think, just moments ago this was a place full of more life than he had ever witnessed.

Club Harborage: a safe space turned into a graveyard.

No bigger than a grain of rice but loaded with enough juice to power a satellite, S33Ds are installed into the base of the human skull, flush with the brainstem, where they sprout specially designed axons. These axons twist and embed themselves into the patient's central nervous system in a process that is both painful and dangerous. The goal of the integration is for the S33D to exist in perfect homogeneity with its now posthuman user, providing them with in-brain computers. Capable of storing memories, synchronizing with computational systems, or simply acting as an ingrained comm unit, these neural augmentations are the core of the Miyazaki family's posthuman tech systems, and by extension, all of Murasaki has access to the civilian grade version of the implant.

To barter in S33D integration outside of Murasaki's borders— or rather to barter in knock-off versions of the technology— is to purchase a one-way ticket into the dankest, darkest holding cell kept special for any surgeon willing to make a profit off people's lives. The counterfeit versions of the S33D are too unpredictable and too dangerous to sanction.

Technolyze Me: Making the Superhuman Brain
C. R. Ashworth, 1847 A.P

9

QUEEN OF PENTACLES.

WITH AS MUCH POLITICAL FREEDOM AS IS afforded to the Tai Tai, much of Calypso City has been overrun by grimy mold and mildew, bleeding rust, and unchecked decay. Canal-traced cities do not fare well within laissez faire governments. Pollution levels go unchecked, businesses are allowed jurisdiction over themselves, and people... Well, people do what they like just short of mass murder. Emergency vehicles fly past, their sirens wailing for the attention of uncaring traffic. Shady characters wander in the shadows of their wake, their attention drawn to the worst possible thing they could possibly latch onto. Excerpts of the broadcast he missed while he was in the clothier's shop play on repeat every direction he looks, and he is not comforted by it.

"Hack or payoff? How did the League broadcast into our networks? Is this a declaration of war?"

"The Songstress of Lorelei returns, and she's taken a technomancer for a hostage. Farting fairy films! I'll drink to that!"

"Prince Kaito Miyazaki: enchanted hostage or rebel defector?"

The local news sources are discussing the League's broadcast across every screen, billboard, and projection panel they pass as Kaito follows the fairy through the city.

No one gives them a second glance, most of them too busy fretting over the League pushing their way into their broadcasting systems, but he can't help but feel exposed. *Is Thames so desperate for Wren that he would pay off Tai Tai officials to get a hand in the outlying country?* Even more concerning is that the bounty for catching Wren alive is so much higher than capturing her dead.

Why does he want her alive? The League worked so hard to kill her twelve years ago.

It is almost a relief when Lyra pulls aside a manhole cover and directs Kaito into the belly of the city. Down here, the smell of saltwater is almost overpowered by the rot of waste. The salt kills most of the foulness of humanity, but it leaves instead a chronic stench of rotting seaweed and fish. In fact, there are more than a few dying mackerel flapping about on the platform. Their coloration is concerning to say the least. Silje, reluctant to tread through water like a typical feline, settles herself on Kaito's shoulders. In her miniaturized form, the netherbeast weighs hardly anything, but now he is balancing both a cat and his lover on his shoulders while descending into the underground.

"Here through, go we."

With a rip of velcro, Lyra leads him through a sanitation curtain into a circular connection chamber. Six other tunnels converge on the chamber, making a hexagon of stormwater lines. With the rain still pouring down topside, the water rushes in rapids to the central drain. Lyra tugs on a pair of levers, one hand on each, near the drain, and the water swirls violently into a whirlpool just wide enough to fit a person. At the center of the pool, a pole extends up from the tunnel.

"Make sure you swallow. Your ears might pop." Without further fanfare, the fae jumps down the tunnel.

Kaito helps Silje into Wren's satchel and adjusts Wren onto his back, strapping her in with the coils of his blades and sheaths.

He steps up to the pole and carefully guides himself and his cargo down the shaft.

The fairy wasn't kidding about his ears popping. The distance down is substantial, but with mist spraying into his face the whole way, it's hard to tell how many meters he descends before his feet reach another platform. All he knows is he has to pause several times to equalize the pressure on his inner ear, and sweat has beaded on his brow from the added weight of his lover and her familiar. By the time he reaches the final foothold, the stench of the sewers has dispersed, so all he smells now is volcanic rock. When he looks down between the grating, sure enough, lava flows several miles below their feet.

"You've set up your workshop within the caverns of a volcano?"

The fairy titters in amusement. "Along you come. Along you come. To close the path, we need."

Two thousand years ago, humans would have described Lyra's voice as otherworldly, but here in Deus, it's just par for the course. Kaito steps toward the voice as the overhead grate closes, cutting off the flow of water. Several gaslights flare to life to reveal a garage of sorts. Lyra hovers near the roof, another pair of levers in hand until the grate closes completely. She then flutters down, kicks a brick in the wall, and a door slides open on the far wall, unveiling a rather cozy living space.

There's wood furniture and wall paintings, plants blooming under solar lamps, and controlled waterfalls weaving their way down the walls and doors. Everywhere he looks, he sees sections of soil inset into the floors, glowing mushrooms popping up out of the beds. All of the light fixtures are either bioluminescent plant and bug-life or fairy fire housed in a gaslight. As he enters, a cluster of sprites skip up from under the floor to greet him like bright little sparks of color.

It's a homey space, despite its strangeness. *Were it not for the lack of sunlight*, he thinks, *this would be fitting for a fairy.* But there is no such sunlight. Which begs the question: Why would a fairy choose to live underground? Don't these creatures need the constant freshness of the air and water? Though, he supposes, in a place like Calypso City, "fresh" is not exactly how he would describe the outside.

He shifts Wren from his back into his arms once more as the fairy addresses him.

"This way. I can patch her up in my workshop."

Wren is still very much out of it by the time he sets foot in the fairy's so-called workshop. While the bleeding has slowed, her head lolls from side to side as Kaito moves. The entire way here, she's barely even twitched; only the warm pulse of her wild script assures Kaito that she's stable. What gives Kaito pause, however, is the appearance of the workshop. Where he was expecting a medical clinic of some sort, he finds instead wrenches and power drills, spare cogs and wheels, screwdrivers and hammers. None of which are meant to be used on organic flesh.

"You aren't a doctor."

"No, I'm a mechanic. Same thing."

"It is not the same thing, You told me you could heal her."

"I can," snips the fairy, hands on her hips. "You saw what my dust did for her earlier."

"Mechanics do not repair people."

"Eh, fixin' an android ain't much different from fixin' a person, and I've done plenty of both, thank ye very much. The vascular system of a bot's just oil instead of blood."

"Not sure I agree with that statement..."

"Yeah, and how much of your insides is made of metal?"

Biomechanically speaking, none of his insides are made of metal. They are simply lined with mechanical accoutrements and wiring designed to enhance his biological abilities (i.e. increase/decreased oxygenation levels, slowing/speeding his metabolism, stimulating hormone production such as adrenaline and/or oxytocin to intensify muscular acuity and performance, so on and so forth). They don't give him anything he couldn't already do naturally, just amped up to superhuman levels for better advantage against hexen kin.

Were it not for his neural net and the S33D embedded in his cerebral cortex, Kaito would be able to undergo de-integration with close to zero repercussions. If he didn't have a S33D linking through his entire system, Kaito's body would continue to function as a normal human being without his augmentations—a privilege many human+ cannot claim. This is opposed to augmentations like Wren once had, like Mano, her mechanical hand, and the muscular rehabilitators that made up for the damaged tissue in her legs. Without those augmentations, Wren would have been unable to walk correctly, and after discovering her witchcraft, she used her telekinesis to make up for her missing augmentations. It's the difference between having a mechanical heart and a pacemaker. One replaces the faulty organ, the other helps the organic material meet optimal standards of operation.

"Wren is not augmented."

"Which just makes it easier." She gives him a wink and a smile before taking on a more serious expression. "Look, I know I'm not exactly the kind of person you're used to dealing with, but I promise you, the fact that I can fix machines is way more impressive than my ability to heal plants and animals. Fairies are kind of designed that way. Now, set her down here while I get my medical kit."

Lyra gestures to a small cot before fluttering into the rafters, leaving a sprinkling of dust behind. Temporarily placated, Kaito lays her on the plain mattress, leather padded and more like a daybed. Her breathing is heavier than he'd like, but at least it is steady.

"So you're the ones everybody's been flapping on about?"

"Everybody?"

"Oh, you know. The forest spirits and the ground gnomes. Everyone's been buzzing about some resurrected witch wreaking havoc along the countryside. Here I thought they were talking tales, but to see her in action. Whoa! Never thought I'd be thankful for a sugar craving so early in the morning."

Lyra sets a hard case on the table nearest Wren's feet. The contents of the case are so archaic, Kaito has only ever seen them in old world textbooks on medicine—books, which by the way, are no longer used in the medical field. They've long ago advanced beyond scalpels and bone saws, yet here he sees a case full of various such accoutrements.

"You're going to stitch her wounds closed," he points out as she pulls out a pair of needles and a long spool of medical thread.

"Yup. I'm gonna stitch up these nasty bits peasy easy. She's leaking magic like a drippy faucet, and it ain't gonna help her heal up none spiraling down the drain."

"Yes, but by using such instruments, you increase her chance of infection. There's a reason we don't use hand tools in surgery anymore."

"Maybe not on you +ies, but I guarantee if you keep using all those fancy lasers and injections on a witch, you'll eventually poison their system to the point where they can't flush it out. And me you mind, that is not a pretty sight to see on any hexen."

With a needle in each hand, the fae sets about sewing the bullet hole shut. She mumbles as she goes, an unending conversation between herself and her tools the technomancer isn't privy to. He can't even tell what language she is speaking. Perhaps something unique to the fae? At the very least, there doesn't appear to be any magical happenings taking place in reaction. Even so, Kaito keeps a close eye on her ministrations, monitoring so nothing untoward occurs, while taking in their surroundings.

Lyra's workshop is a mechanic's dream. Walls of tools, maintenance bays, a software library, and enough parts to build a handful of human-sized robots from scratch. But the more Kaito looks around, the more he wants to pick Wren back up and walk out the door. The only thing that keeps him is the knowledge that he has no skill in manual medical procedures. A severe oversight now that he thinks on it, one he should bring up to Fumiko when he's home—

He cuts off the thought before its completion. Renki... *Kami, the boy must be so confused.*

"Since when do the fae run chop shops?"

"Your highness, fairies have been trading body parts on people since long before they started doing it to themselves. My great grandmama traded a baby for a changeling, and my mum once stole the peg off a pirate in exchange for a newborn pup. But, I ain't no chop shop. These folks don't have the means to see a real doctor about their augmentations, so they come to me."

He almost asks if she has a permit to work on or install human augmentations but reminds himself this is The Tai Tai. He shouldn't expect anyone to have any kind of official paperwork for conducting their business, certainly not for League standards.

Lyra makes quick work of Wren's wounds, even tops off the finish with an antibiotic ointment of some kind and another dusting to prevent infection. Silje jumps up onto Wren's hip as soon as the fairy steps away, and Kaito steps over to assess the work. It's solid as far as he can tell.

"Ya know, I can tell you're anxious about your lady, but there's not much sitting there staring at me is gonna do to help her. Why don't you hook into my network hub? You can look up all my history and records if you so choose, and the best part is you can check your own servers in the process. Take your pick on software if you see an upgrade you want, though I'm sure an upright gentleman like you would have no interest in the types of upgrades I have on hand."

Kaito frowns, doubting there are any illicit upgrades that could do anything for him, but it's worth checking. Besides, he'll be severely impaired without access to a server. There is only so far his personal network can get him before it proves wanting in a conflict.

Logging into his personal network is like finding solid ground. He didn't realize it before, more focused on Wren's injuries, but the lack of connection was wearing on his nerves. Now that he's reconnected to a server, the tension headache behind his eyes is lifting, but it rapidly returns as an influx of messages ping through his neural net.

Missed Calls:

Renki
Renki

SCHERZO

Fumiko
Hikaru
Renki
Tomi

His voicemail is full, and there are text messages popping up through his sights in rapid fire.

[Hikaru: What the hell are you thinking? Do you realize what you've done? The Primarch is calling for your head, and I don't have the means to change his mind.]

[Renki: Are you alright?]
[Where are you?]
[Uncle is losing his mind. He's reassigning me to Orson's unit!]
[Why aren't you answering?!!!]

[Tomi: Call me back when you get a chance. You won't believe what I've found.]

[Fumiko: Kaito, I don't need to know where you are or what you are doing, but please just let me know you're alright.]

[Renki: Are you really cursed?]
[Who is Lady Wren? Why is she so important?]
[Why aren't you answering?]

The surplus of the messages flash through so quickly, he barely has time to process them before he indignantly deactivates the notification setting on his net.

He'd forgotten what a pain it could be to reconnect after a disconnection, and not for any other reason than when people cannot get ahold of someone they would otherwise have access to, they have a tendency to demand more than they would otherwise. Even when said individual is far beyond their reach.

Tomi's face in his message is two parts amused to one part disbelieving.

"Well, I suppose I can't blame you for not telling me your lady fair was actually the Songstress of Lorelei back from the dead to assassinate the Orisha of Ebele, but you could have at least told me your girlfriend was a witch. It would have clarified things. Not to mention, I wouldn't have been so goddamned confused by her movement patterns. Anyway, I'm calling…"

Kaito hits fast-forward on the voice message and moves onto the next one. Renki's voice drifts through the comm.

"Hikaru is assigning me a new mentor. It's been less than a day since you vanished from the face of the planet. Why would he do that? You said you'd come back with Lady Wren, yet he doesn't seem to expect you to return? Why? Are you in trouble? Why won't you answer me?"

Kaito digs the meat of his thumbs into his sinuses, rubbing a rough circle around his temple before dragging the tension to the back of his scalp. Renki… Poor child is probably confused and angry. The last he saw Renki, he was untying the teen from a trap affixed by Wren. The witch tied up Renki, Akari, and Zenza as a means of keeping the three from wandering off while their respective guardians came to fetch them—respective guardians being Xipilli for Zenza and Kaito for Akari and Renki. While he'd left Akari with his brother for her punishment, Kaito escorted Renki back to Snowfall Palace himself, an endeavor that nearly cost him the time necessary to catch Wren. He should have rightly grounded the child for running into danger the way he had, something he had never felt the need to do before.

And oh, the tantrum Renki threw when Kaito refused to answer his questions…

I don't need you anyway!

Now, Renki has watched his father toss off all of the teachings they have both so steadfastly learned for a witch who is a complete stranger to him. Not that Renki seems to find Wren strange at all. The teen had been hellbent on chasing after Wren himself.

"Why do you get to run after her? You've taken me on countless hunts. Why not this one? I have as much right to hunt a witch as you."

"I am not hunting Lady Wren."

"Then, what are you doing?!"

What is he doing? Outside of League servers, the name of a fairy in his pocket, sitting in said fairy's apartments while his newly resurrected soulmate is basically being stitched back together once again by said fae. Now, his witch's familiar is digging around in a flowerpot on the far side of the room. He's never been further out of his depth.

By the time Kaito finished filtering through all of his messages, the netherbeast had wandered her way out of the workshop, looking far more relaxed, not only with her surroundings but with their current predicament. He takes it as a sign that Wren truly is in good hands. If a creature as distrusting as a feline netherbeast can get comfortable in a strange place, then surely he can as well. Unlikely, but the sentiment is there.

At present, Silje is sniffing about in one of the planters, occasionally digging a paw into the dirt. *Is there a bug or something?* Wouldn't surprise him if there was; they are underground. The cat moves to a different patch of soil, circles herself, and digs even more fervently at the base of the new plant—some breed of hibiscus it looks like. Her tail flicks upward as though preparing to sit, and Kaito quirks an eyebrow.

Perhaps a little too comfortable, actually. The last thing he needs is for Silje to make a litter box out of one of the fairy's planters.

"Silje," he calls, and the cat pauses her digging. The feline's tail twitches in annoyance, but she allows him to pick her up and set her down on a pile of newspaper instead, not that she apparently has any intention of going to the bathroom there. She simply scratches at the edges of the paper and sniffs. Then, with a twitch of her whiskers, she displaces.

Probably onto another plane to take care of her business elsewhere. He hasn't any idea, and the creature returns so quickly, Kaito almost wonders whether or not he imagined the cat's disappearance.

Ah, the displacer beast's power of disillusion. Enough to make even a technomancer question what he is seeing. But Kaito knows better, has been around the feline enough to dispel the magical doubt without much cause for concern.

It helps that he is now able to map the animal into his cyberscape—something he was unable to do 12 years ago. And doing so now is probably the most unsettling sight he's ever recorded.

To the trained eye, Silje's coat has regained its misty halo, but you'd have to be following the cat's movements closely to notice the incorporeality of her edges. To the average person, she simply appears as a regular black-furred member of felis domesticus. In Kaito's sights, however, the netherbeast's signature is more akin to a ghost's than a living creature. Perhaps this is what makes Silje such an appropriate familiar for Wren's necromantic persuasion, or is it Wren's ghostly inclination that makes her an appropriate witch for the netherbeast?

Either way, he's always been intrigued by the magical bond between them. Was it forged the day Wren released the feline from Summer's chimera experiments? Or did it happen later? What kept Silje in this realm? Free will? Or was it some unspoken call to a witch?

Technomancers know so little about familiars and their relationships to their witches. There is no such parallel in the field of science. Two hundred years ago, they speculated the relationship was a parasitic one. The witch would mooch off the netherbeast's power, using it for themselves all while ordering the creature to perform their bidding. But then, they realized that wasn't right either because the netherbeast could draw on its witch's power, redirecting it to make itself stronger, faster, even more potent in its magical ability. So maybe it was a more mutual symbiotic relationship, a give and take between two complete organisms? A mimicry of the relationship between wolves and ravens. The ravens lead the wolves to their prey, and when the wolf makes the kill, the ravens get a fat helping of leftovers.

The familiar flits back and forth around the apartment, flickering in and out of reality. She hops up onto the sofa only to displace herself, reappearing on top of the cabinets from which she disappears again before rematerializing seven feet away atop a basket of lavender potpourri. "Conservation of Mass" would dictate that Silje's extra mass would need to be stored somewhere while the netherbeast recovers from her injuries. He would imagine, what with Silje's disposition for dimensional travel, that she probably tucks it away elsewhere when she assumes her smaller form.

"She's a feisty little thing, isn't she?"

"She's no housecat, if that's what you're wondering."

"No, I suppose not. Netherbeasts never make the best pets. Though fae creatures don't much either. Monsters however... Monsters never bite the hand that feeds them. I once kept a small collection of hippocampus in the canals. People'd pay to ride them up and down the city's waterways never once realizing they were riding the children of Poseidon. Eventually though, the city passed a mandate against owning marine equines, so I had to give them up. Still miss them to this day, especially Bubbles. She was a fun one to ride."

Unsure how to respond to that, Kaito turns his attention to the door of the workshop. "How is Wren?"

The fae blinks. "Oh, your lady friend should be good as new come the morning. Stitch, stitch makes the skin reknit."

The door left ajar, he can only just see the tool rack on the far wall, fully stocked with various power tools, hand saws, a staple gun, and... a microfridge? What could she possibly have in there that she can't keep in her kitchen—her kitchen less than ten feet from the workshop door?

"Why would you help us?" asks Kaito. "It's been awhile since I dealt with a fairy, but it's my understanding that trades should market an equivalent exchange of goods and/or services."

"Mmmm... I like your aura?"

Kaito doesn't buy it. His expression is pinched, the underside of his nose tensed like he just smelled something sour.

The fae must sense it because she backtracks. Her cheeks turn an even darker magenta, almost as though she's blushing. "Okay, okay, I'll admit it. I'm a huge fan of her music. I have all of her albums from before she... well, you know."

Yeah... he knows.

10
SIX OF CUPS

Present Day - 14th Day in the Month of Falling - 12:30AM - Calypso City

"DO YOU EVER WONDER WHAT THINGS would be like if your mother hadn't died?"

Summer stands behind Wren at the banister as the songstress looks out on the city. It's peaceful. The city lights flicker as cars pass below them, though she can't exactly tell where they are. One of the buildings reminds her of Sekhmeti's trade center, but just to the left of it is Aighneas's Babylon Tower—a giant exoskeleton of a structure which zigzags into the sky like an iron lightning bolt. Just beyond the city limit lies a mountain that reminds Wren of Deriva's main volcano, Pele, but then the plants and decor look too much like Tokiseshu to be anything else. To top it all off, everything feels like it's underwater, even though she can feel the coolness of the air and smell the dust in the curtains. The world, a cacophony of sensation, narrows down to one finite point.

Summer... so close, her breath fans over Wren's neck.

"My mother was human," whispers the witch. When the wind blows, the redhead's silky nightgown glances along Wren's bare back. Her fingertips card through Wren's hair, weaving gold thread into the dark locks as she twines each lock this way and that into an extravagant array of braids. Every so often a sharp nail scratches along her scalp, causing gooseflesh to prickle up her arms. "I know because she left an electronic letter on my belly when she rolled me into a towel and left me at the edge of the woods to die or be collected by someone else. I was still covered in afterbirth. My mother was human+, but my father must have been a witch. I don't know how I was conceived. Probably the product of an accident or assault 'cause there's no way in Helheim I was the product of love and a plan. Why she didn't just abort me I'll never know. Maybe she didn't get the choice."

Summer's hands leave Wren's hair.

"Hmm... Which do you think is better, Songstress? Hung from the hanger or hung from the noose?"

The summoner snorts at her own twisted joke. Not the kind of black comedy Wren appreciates. The brunette turns from the cityscape to regard the other witch. The redhead looks younger and older at once. Her hair is a darker red but white decorates her temple. One moment, she has wrinkles around her eyes; the next, she is a fresh-faced little girl, no horns, no scars, just wide brown eyes. Her eyes are the only things that don't change; gone are the void-lights of the Summer Wren met in the catacombs of Lorelei. Only wide open browns, like warm coffee with just a splash of milk, remain.

"I guess after I was born, she saw my indicia and decided she didn't want to raise a witch, so she abandoned me to the wilds. Do you think she thought it would be better that way? That's why they gave me the name Helsdottir, another unwanted daughter to be parented by Pain and Death."

Wren watches herself lean into the wind away from Summer's dark touch, warm on her skin but cold in her bones. "Perhaps you should find her and ask."

"Oh, I did," Summer chuckles. "She didn't have an answer for me. I guess I should have waited a little longer before I had one of my netherbeasts rip her voice box from her throat, but they'd gotten tired of playing with her husband's corpse."

"You killed your own mother."

"Oh, goddess, no! Just left her muted and defenseless as a babe on the edge of town for her much loved children to find. I do love poetic justice."

"I've never been much for poetry."

"Yes, you much prefer songs. Don't you, Songstress?"

Summer sweeps a stray strand of Wren's hair behind her ear. "No, I just find poets to be unbearably narcissistic."

Summer giggles, a pitched girlish sound that coming from anyone else would have sounded sweet as honey. From Summer, it just sounds sickly.

"Do you think there was ever a chance your mother would have abandoned you? No, why would she? Your mother worked hard to find your father. Hel, if the rumors are true, she outright bewitched him into her bed, didn't she?"

"That's not true."

Summer's eyes roll skyward.

"If you say so. But really, Songstress, do you think you inherited her natural talent for bewitchment?" Summer leans into Wren's face, her eyes sliding down to the other witch's lips.

"I prefer 'charisma.'"

The redhead smirks. "Of course, *min dronning*. As you say."

The nerve endings in Wren's lips scream as Summer presses forward—

"Stop!"

Wren wakes with a shout and immediately regrets the outburst for the pain in her abdomen. "Argh! *Mierde...*"

Lifting her top, she finds gauze taped to her belly. Ripping the fabric off, she finds Agni's piercing stitched together with three fine pieces of clear thread. It's neat work, clean and tidy with the remains of some sort of ointment rubbed around the edges. *Who did this? Where's Kaito?*

She twists around and winces-the itchy pain of another healing wound.. Reaching around, she touches another piece of gauze. Oh right, that's where the frost witch's ice spike impaled her. She can probably assume the same treatment has been bestowed to that injury as well, but who stitched her back together?

Not Kaito surely. The prince barely knows how to sew clothing, let alone flesh. And why should he? Technomancer healing agents are far superior and user-friendly. Heck, most League doctors would be hard pressed to make a stitch by heart for how uncommon the procedure is these days. And if they do decide to sew someone back together, they typically use a handheld device called a skin-knitter. Surgeons will apply it to virtually any kind of wound or incision, and the device metabolizes lab-grown skin cells into a patchwork stitch to repair the injury. It promotes better healing, results in less scar tissue, and better yet, it's cheaper for both the patient and the surgeon.

Do you ever wonder...

A shudder trails up her spine, goosebumps prickle up her arms and legs, and the sensation brings her thoughts back to her dream. Dreaming of a dead witch, what a wonderful way to spend her recovery! Wren closes her eyes, willing away the tension growing behind them.

Pixie Stix! Summer was murdered by her own husband. If anything were to make the foundation for a vengeful spirit, that is sure to be one of them. Now the question becomes: is it her own overactive imagination bringing her visions of a murdered witch, or is there an Echo in the room?

Speaking of rooms...

Wren has woken up in a workshop of some kind, equipment for tinkering everywhere she looks. Even though the lights are off, her witchy vision allows her just enough visibilities to make out the various screwdrivers and wrenches that decorate the walls. There are hammers large enough for nailing wood pieces together sitting right next to small more delicate mallets designed for small clocks and wristwatches. Gears of varying size and arrangement lie scattered in an organized mess on the workbench, and springs hang from the ceiling reminiscent of how Jessabelle used to hang plants to dry in the kitchen.

The tension drips from Wren's shoulders.

The technomancer part of her feels strangely at home here. This is the kind of place she would have considered a perfect haven once upon a time. When she was a girl, Wren would have walked into a place like this, picked up the first screwdriver within reach, and started taking apart the nearest piece of machinery just to see how it worked. Now though, with not just living years under her belt, she's a little more cautious. Workshops are only as safe as the people who go to work in them. She doesn't sense anything outright malevolent in the area, but she isn't foolish enough to assume the lack thereof.

"Kai," she calls.

No response. However, now that she's focusing on the world around her, she hears a humming sound coming from the doorway.

Legs stiff with fatigue, Wren rolls from the cot, feeling more like a turtle than a witch for the amount of times she has to sway back and forth just to get her feet over the edge without aggravating her stomach wound, but she does eventually manage it. Her bare feet slap onto the floor, a smooth concrete coated in alloy designed to cushion the joints of anyone planning to spend an excessive amount of time standing here.

Wren makes her way across the room and into the doorway. The light shouldn't be blinding, yet still she squints into the new space.

Kaito is there, and before even a thought can cross her mind, she runs/falls to him. Ever her shore, he catches her tidal wave in his arms, the best home she has ever known. And the kiss that comes next...

Peace. Pure peace.

The moment, long and soft like a sugared sigh, passes far too quickly. They part when Wren's lungs ache for air, but they do not separate. Wren settles into Kaito's warmth as easily as a cat settles on a windowsill. She closes her eyes and presses her ear to his chest.

Seated on the sofa with his sights active, he seems to be working heavily in his cyberscape. She hopes he's running some system maintenance. Their last jump could've screwed up his coding in some miniscule way, but she realizes fairly quickly that this is not what he is doing. On the table in front of him is a router and not a fancy Murasakan one either. This one looks ancient, bulky and boxy, and she can feel the heat radiating off it from here despite the internal fans working to keep the device cool. This is the source of the humming, and Kaito is hooked in via one of his forearm cables.

Wren frowns. She thought they'd agreed that was a bad idea until they knew exactly how hostile the local servers were.

The only thing which keeps her from an outburst is Silje sitting curled up on the back of the sofa. The familiar is taking turns grooming herself and Kaito in even, unhurried licks as though she had all the time in the world to lounge away in the bath. *And doesn't a long, undisturbed bath sound like nirvana right now...*

Wren lays her head in his lap.

"I am glad to see you awake."

Wren smiles at the sound of the technomancer's voice. "You haven't exactly seen me yet."

"I'm reading your coding right now."

"Not the same thing."

"You're right," he says, his sights clearing to reveal molten silver. "But in regard to your state of being, I garner more information from your coding than from you, Miss Fine–until–another–witch–knocks-me-on-my–ass Nocturne."

"I was just—" She cuts herself off before she can say "fine." Clearly, she was not fine to have ended up in whatever makeshift hospital this place has become. "You aren't normally so entrenched in your scape," she says.

"The servers here are proving difficult to enter."

"Odd. I thought Kaito Miyazaki was the best hacker in all of Murasaki no Yama."

"I am not the best hacker in Murasaki."

"What!? Who knocked Prince Kaito from his throne?"

Kaito's lips quirk up at one corner. "Their name is Tomi. I was their senpai while they trained as an adept. They never made it to the trials, but they make a better career out of hacking than some of the locals in the Tai Tai do."

"Fair enough."

The router on the table goes quiet as Kaito disconnects from the hardware. "How do you feel?"

"Surprisingly *not* like an icicle was just shoved through my back," she says, turning so Kaito can see the patch of gauze still intact on her lower back. His fingers are cool as they prod gently at the area around the wound. "Not sure who you found to patch me up, but they did a hell of a job."

"That would be me."

From the other side of the room, a petite child-like woman glides through the entryway portal. With bright pink hair and skin, it's no difficult task to guess she must be a fae. Her aura, as well, is familiar. Reminiscent of—

"You were at the diner."

The fae giggles. "Indeed. I must ask: whatever did you do to that teenage witch to make her hate you so?"

Beats Wren. As far as she can tell, she's never met the girl in either of her lives. But that's beside the question.

"I'm more interested in learning what benefit you reap from helping me."

"Oh, I'm just being a good citizen of the people. Altruism, I think you people call it."

"Fairies don't understand the meaning of altruism."

The fairy feints hurt. "You can't possibly mean that."

"I always mean what I say."

Wren's magic curls around her fingertips. Her hair rustles from the self-made force of it. Even this much of a flex is draining, but the last time she trusted a fae, she lost the most precious of treasures for her foolishness.

"Wren," calls Kaito, setting a hand on her shoulder, "it's alright. She gave me her name. Here, look."

A diner receipt has a name spelt out in Fae speech. At least she assumes its Fae speech. To her, it just looks like a mess of scribbles masquerading as runes and symbols.

"You honestly accepted that mess of writing as her name... Kai, really?"

"The written names of the fae only make sense to those upon whom the writing has been bestowed," the aforementioned fae inserts. Her wings fluff out on either side of her with a rustle. She titters under Wren's gaze, then bows her head. "I mean no offense, Lady Songstress, but you wouldn't be able to read it no matter how long you stared at it. It simply isn't meant for your eyes."

"Is that so?"

A spark of irritation zips at her heels at the way the fae smiles in Kaito's direction, but when she turns to look at her technomancer, his eyes are focused wholly on her. She simmers down.

"It says her name is Lylilria. I'm afraid I can't pronounce the last name."

"Mchelogdea. As in Mick-Cloud-egg-a."

Right... She has a feeling the humanesque spelling on the receipt only somewhat hinted to that particular pronunciation, but she'll digress.

"Last I checked, Puck isn't the only trickster in the fairy court."

"Perhaps, but I guarantee you, my reason for saving your life has far less to do with any kind of trick and more to do with..." she waffles, shuffling from foot to foot. "Okay, I guess I haven't been completely honest."

"What do you mean?"

"I knew who you were the moment you entered the diner and not just because you are the Songstress of Lorelei resurrected and all that." Wren's eyebrow twitches. "Don't get me right, that's cool and all, but it's more to do with... well... okay, here."

From the nearby shelf, the fairy pulls a vinyl. The medallion-shaped titanium reflects the light back in iridescent rainbows of disk-stored data, and printed across the front of the disk is a triskele framing the name Nocturne.

Wren recognizes it instantly and rushes forward. The vinyl is light in her hands. The graphics sparkle and shimmer as she twists it this way and that, a cheap replication of her actual magic. Physically, it weighs less than a pack of gum, but the contents recorded within represent a goodly portion of her creative life.

"How do you have this?! I thought they were all destroyed after I—"

"Defected," Kaito finishes.

"I was going to say 'died' but that's also accurate."

Kaito's face falls, and Wren immediately regrets her callousness. *Dang it, why am I always putting my foot in it with this man?*

"Suffice to say, I am a huge fan, and I was kind of hoping you would give me an autograph."

"An autograph..."

"Yes, an autograph."

Wren looks at the fae through her bangs. "You saved my life because you want an autograph?"

"Is that so hard to believe?! You were a total legend. Your single 'My Heart to the Sea' was at the toppity-tip of the charts for months. The only reason they banned it was because... well, I'm sure you know why they banned it, and then you bucketed the kick."

Wren frowns. "Don't you mean 'kicked the bucket'?"

"You understand my meaning. Kicked it was, and people went crazy, not just in the 'magic is dead' way, either. People would have killed to find anything with your name signed on it. Something to do with priceless nomenclatures and celebrity infamy post-mortem." The pitch of Lyra's voice is steadily rising higher and higher the more agitated she gets at the prospect of Wren signing her album. "I witnessed some of the insanity myself. Two lycans got into a tiff over a signed copy of 'Algorithm,' and only one of them had a full coat of fur left at the end of it. Anyway, getting your autograph on this baby now would be like getting Mozart to rise from the dead and sign an original rendition of his Requiem while it was being played on a 1756 edition violin by his star performer. Legendary and authentically post-mortem!"

The fairy looks, for all the world, like she could bounce up and down and up and down about this for the next several hours, but rather than encourage any additional trauma to either hers or Kaito's hearing, she simply nabs the record from rapidly twitching fingers.

"OH! You're really going to sign it!"

"Considering you saved my backside..." (*Quite literally*) "...and my ever-astute companion deems you harmless. I see no problem with it, even if your simile is grossly overexaggerated."

Wren grabs a pen from the coffee table.

"No wait. Use this one. It's my special autograph pen."

Lyra produces from her coat pocket a fuchsia monstrosity of a *pluma*. And she isn't using that as slang, either. The feather is easily the length of her arm, longer even. She would assume it was a peacock feather, but the patterning on it is wrong: striped like a zebra but spotted like a cheetah and in an entirely inappropriate color scheme of virulent pink, bubbly purple, and worst of all an obnoxious shade of orange.

"Okay, I'll use your pen. Don't give yourself an aneurysm."

"Yay!" The fairy pirouettes on her toes, dipping the feather's gold-plated tip in a well of strangely colorless ink. She then thrusts the instrument under Wren's nose. The witch's aforementioned body part twitches from the proximity, her hand snatching the potential weapon away before it can rid her of the tip of it.

It's warm from the fairy's body heat. Almost hot to the touch. *Jeez! Do fae run at furnace-level temperatures or something?*

She turns the album over, finds the signature sleeve within, and without much preamble, scribbles her signature across the corner.

To my winged friend, Wren Nocturne

She finalizes the text with a curly music note drawn in place of a period and smiles. It's kind of nice signing one of her albums again. Nice to know there are still people out there who appreciate her music, not for its magical prowess, but simply because they enjoy listening to it. It almost makes her feel normal, whatever that dumb word means.

"Thank you! I will cherish it forever!" Lyra takes the record in hand and hugs it to her chest in a painfully adorable way.

"No problem. It's the least I can do, really. Thanks for your help."

Silje mews from the couch.

"Right," Wre- says to the cat. "Well, we really should be going. Can't be spending too much time here, right Kaito?"

Kaito nods, bowing his head to Lyra.

"Hai. *Arigato gozaimasu.* We will take our leave now that we are both able to travel again."

"Oh, must you really go so soon?"

"I'm afraid so."

The fairy sighs. "I suppose you're right. It is my understanding that wanted fugitives make for bad house guests."

Kaito rises from his seat, collecting their things. He wraps Wr—'s cloak around her shoulders and slings her satchel over his own. W—'s familiar jumps from the couch arm into her witch's arms.

Lyra takes a step forward. "But wait—"

Silje hisses at the fairy.

"I'm sorry, but there's something I forgot to mention."

The fairy sets the signed record down on the coffee table. A noise at the entryway draws the witch's attention. "Lyra, did you do it?"

"Who is that?" demands Kaito.

"Just a friend."

"You told me no one would follow us." Anger tinges Kaito's voice.

"He didn't follow us. I called him here."

"You did what?" the songstress asks. Dizziness impinges on her senses. Has she been drugged? No, that's not possible. She hasn't eaten anything, nor does she smell anything on the air.

"Lyra! Did you get the witch?!"

Her eyes dart to the newcomer. The man at the entryway is older, weathered like an old seafaring ship that was once the talk of the ocean. His appearance boasts of a rugged handsomeness that has grown mature with time.

"Who are you?"

He ignores her. "This the witch?"

"Yes, Leon. I told you I found the perfect witch."

"What's going on here?!" Her own anger rises, her magic tingling at her fingertips. "Explain it to me now."

"Miss Nocturne, please. No need to posture. I promise I will explain everything—"

"Cut the magic now, witch, before I put a bullet through you!"

The pistol's barrel is dusty with disuse, but she can see straight down its shaft to the angry brown eyes trained on her. *Fine. You want to be a fool, stranger? Be a dead fool.*

The songstress's lips part. Which note? A siren song or should she cut straight to a deafening tremolo? Either one would suffice to teach a needling, gun-toting fool a lesson. No wait! Better choice. A Fool's Song.

She sings.

But no notes ring out. In fact, with a sharp inhale, coughing doubles her over, like her lungs are trying to escape through her throat.

"What's wrong?! What happened!" asks Kaito.

With a mighty heave, she clears the blockage. "I'm fine."

She must have swallowed wrong. She purses her lips and hums the starting note.

Nothing. Another coughing fit fills the room where a cadenza should be. This one brings her to her knees. The blood rushes loud in her ears. Just underneath the tumultuous noise of her own life blood, she hears Kaito yelling and Silje meowing. *What is going on?*

The fit passes. Kaito's face, so terribly handsome in his worry, swims before her blurred vision. She takes a deep breath. Exhales, then draws another, shaping her lips into a perfect "O."

The whistle should be a sharpened F.

Instead, air passes over her teeth, empty and quiet, and she swallows her own tongue. Mucus floods the back of her throat, enough to block her airways, and the coughing resumes with a vengeance.

She doesn't understand.

What is going on? Why can't she sing? Why can't she cast? A songstress without song is just...

"I'm sorry, mistress." Lyra's voice is soft in her head. "You'll understand once you wake back up."

And the world fades away as Kaito draws his blades. The last thing she feels as her head hits the floor is the crash of the newcomer's desperation washing her out to sea.

"Even a man who is pure in heart,

And says his prayers by night,

May become a wolf when the wolfbane blooms,

And the moon is full and bright."

-Curt Siodmak

11
EIGHT OF CUPS

15th Day in the Month of Falling - 6:20AM - Wakeville

RENKI FEELS OUT OF PLACE. OR MAYBE OUT of time is the better way to describe it. Everyone here is dressed like they are living in the dark ages.

The cities of the outer rim are less human+ more human-. This is where the technologically infirm go to avoid as much scientific innovation as they possibly can. However, these cities are far too close to League central areas, so hexen avoid them like the plague. It results in an area saturated with untapped magic which in turn results in a population of people prone to Wúxíng Syndrome. Not the kind of place a league adept-in-training would have any business visiting.

Yet, here he is, wrestling with this weird ickiness in his gut.

This town is called Wakeville. He's never been here before. He's absolutely sure he's never been here before, and yet why does he have this boundless sense of déjà vu knocking around his head? Kaito always made a point to keep him safe within the borders of Murasaki no Yama. The few times he was allowed to venture outside of those borders, it was under strict supervision and an unshakable escort.

"What do you think, sir? Should we conduct interviews with people in the area?"

"We'll get around to that in a moment, Akari. First, I want to get the lay of the land."

Akari and their new mentor are just ahead of him discussing the particulars of their new case. He can hear them well enough from where he is standing but doesn't care to insert himself into the conversation. Is that petty of him? He isn't sure. He isn't trying to be petty, but he has nothing to say. Nothing constructive anyway.

"Hey, Renki. Do you see that?"

He sees it alright. A "fire breather" entertains a group of people in the middle of the plaza. He can smell the kerosene from here. It's play magic without any such dabbling in actual magic. The performer lines their mouth with vaseline or some other sundry flame-repellent balm, drinks down a mouthful of highly flammable liquid, and then blows a steady stream through a blazing torch.

"I see it, Akari."

The kid/fire-breather is pretty young. The boy couldn't be any older than Renki, if even that. He is shorter than Akari with tawny brown skin and a head decorated with beaded dreadlocks. If Renki didn't know any better, he would think the child a hexen, but no hexen would be stupid enough to come within sixty kilometers of this place.

"But he's so young! I didn't think people did that kind of stuff anymore."

"An entertaining form of begging, Akari. They can't earn in the usual way, so street urchins will do anything so long as it can earn them some credits."

He doesn't appreciate Orson's two cents. It's unnecessarily dismissive. *Is it their fault they are unable to make money in the "usual" fashion?*

"He's a kid. He should have someone looking after him, yet he doesn't. Do you really think that's his fault?"

"My young highness, I mean no disrespect in my assessment. Merely that street performers are little more than beggars, and to their disadvantage as well. They give of themselves in hopes someone will offer them money for their time, but there is no guarantee anything will come of their craft."

He opens his mouth, a rebuttal on his lips. He isn't quite sure why he disagrees so vehemently, but the comment has struck a chord in him that he doesn't think anyone has strummed in a long time. A memory cord of an angelic voice and dancing barefoot along the cobblestone paths traipses across his servers, a memory from a time before he even donned his augmentations. That is to say, no such memory should even exist on his servers by the sheer mechanics of how the S33D works.

Renki huffs, biting back the retort that is sure to get him sent back to base camp.

"I'm going to start with the street peddlers. Maybe they saw something that can help us."

"But Renki, Orson wants us to stick together."

"It's alright, Akari. Renki will be fine."

"But, sensei..."

"Daijōbuda."

Before Orson can insert his thoughts, Renki turns and disappears into the oncoming gaggle of pedestrians. His comm unit beeps with a missive from Orson.

STAY WITHIN 100 METERS OF MY RADIUS

Sure, he can do that. Not like he has much choice in the matter. Never mind. It's fine. He'll deal.

He shakes his head, cards his fingers through his hair, and steps to it.

Renki has always had problems navigating public markets. He isn't sure why. It's just one of his special quirks, he supposes. Too many sights to see, too many interesting smells, too much muchness, really; it makes for a very discombobulating experience.

A passerby rams in his shoulder. They don't even say sorry to him. They just carry on, head down, at a near half-run.

"Hey," he shouts but then recoils as Kaito's voice in his head reminds him, *We act in anger because we know not empathy.* The first time his oto-san told him this saying was when he was seven years old. He'd gotten into a fight with some of the other boys in school. They were bullying him for how small he was, and Renki, with all the wisdom of a hurt seven-year-old, had punched one of them across the face. The others retaliated, of course, the way they would against any other boy on the playground, but Renki, being augmented as he was, suffered little more than a few minor cuts and bruises. The boy he punched, however, ended up in the hospital with a cracked skull.

We have power others do not, and we must always be aware of how we use it.

Kaito's words, though they were said with the gentlest sternness he ever heard in his life, chide him. It seems more than a bit hypocritical that Kaito's voice would lecture him when the man in question is probably miles away on what is apparently considered a severe enough venture to alienate even the emperor of Murasaki from being on his own brother's side.

"Oi, thief!"

Renki turns to find the young performer from earlier running straight for the person who just ran into him.

"No, they just ran into me. There's no reason to—"

Just as he is about to defend the person, they take off running in the opposite direction, and Renki sees for the first time that they have a pistol in their hands that looks curiously like an adept issue model. His hand goes to his belt. They have his pistol!

"Stop!" shouts the younger boy again, giving chase.

Renki follows. The thief makes a turn down a side alley, knocking a woman off her feet and nearly upending a stroller. Renki launches himself over a cabbage seller's wagon, despite the irate seller's waving fist, and races down the alley after the performer. The dark-skinned boy does a forward layout into a handspring. He lands feet first on the thief, knocking both of them into the dirt.

"You sorry sack of shit! Stealing from one of the League's finest. And a weapon, no less!"

"I'll show you sorry!"

The thief, a middle-age looking gentleman of maybe Sekhmetian descent, attempts to fire the pistol on the performer. The trigger, however, doesn't release the hammer.

In Renki's sights flows the words: "Attempt to discharge ammo from weapon # 727 recorded despite safety commands. Did you authorize this usage?"

He sends a quick thank you to every time one of his instructors gave him steps down and up Shinka temple for forgetting to set his weapons on safety mode before putting them up. It only took two failures on his part, but there are exactly 1,122 steps from the base of the mountain to that confounded temple. He should know. He counted them anytime he and Kaito made the trek up to the royal family quarters of the temple, and that was more than just twice.

"Howls of a halfmoon!" growls the man before he begins hurriedly trying to manually unravel the safety codes.

Renki gives pause at the thief's curse.

Halfmoon? There isn't a halfmoon tonight. The last full moon was barely a fortnight ago. It'll be another five weeks before Dei even reaches its waning gibbous.

"Get that pistol out of his hands before he gets the safety off!" shouts Renki.

The command is moot though because no sooner does he shout the command that the man tosses the weapon away in favor of gritting his teeth in anger. A menacing aura fills the alley. Renki's eyes bulge in horror as the muscles of the man's face ripple, pulling away from his skull.

"Shoot him! Get the gun and shoot him!" shouts the boy gesturing wildly to Renki. The youth in question stands frozen in horror as the thief's bones shift and break. His nose elongates, his teeth sharpen, and fur ripples across his chin and cheeks.

A Koi lycan. There is a Koi lycan shifting in broad daylight even though his corresponding moon is no longer full.

"What are you doing? Hurry before he finishes shifting—oof!"

The wind goes from the boy's body as a huge muscled leg, easily twice its normal size, kicks him square in the chest. There is a gross crunching sound, and the boy goes spinning into the far wall of the alley, hitting the bricks and then bouncing onto the side of the nearby dumpster with a hollow thump.

Renki snaps to life as two human, lupin eyes turn on him. He grips for his comm. "Orson, lycan! There's a lycan in the marketplace!"

Static greets him.

"Orson, Akari? Does anyone read me?"

"Foolish borg scum… I'll make a meal… on a skewer."

The voice is gruff and mangled, filled with an emotion that makes his stomach turn. He turns to see the lycan a mere foot in front of him. He didn't know lycans were even capable of speech once their jaws separated.

With a roar, the hexen lunges for him. The adept swerves to avoid the attack. He escapes with his body intact, but a piece of his sleeve gets left behind, caught between sharpened claws. He rolls across the dirty pavement, aggravating the pre-existing bruises from his cycle crash just two days ago.

I'm only glad you wore your damned helmets.

The lady Nocturne's words echo in his ear, and all of the negative emotions of yesterday come racing back. The anger, the confusion, the needless irritation that made him throw one of his most prized possessions across the room.

He winces as his hurt arm reminds him of his stupidity, but it's worth the pain. There's not enough armor in the world to cushion a blow from a raging beast man.

"Argh!"

Claws bared and teeth gnashing, the lycan howls in anger, making a wolf's line for him. Renki backpedals, hands and boots scratching into the ground as he scrambles backward until his back meets the wall.

Shimata!

A meaty paw rises overhead and comes down.

Bang! Bang!

The strike never falls, and the lycan's body seizes and then falls over sideways. Behind him, the performer boy stands breathing heavily with Renki's pistol in his hand.

"How did you—"

"I don't know what happened. I picked it up and it went off."

Renki picks himself up off the ground, sights activating in his eyes with a pale gold glow. A quick glance of the lycan's vitals confirms he's dead. No chance of recovery from the shot that killed him. One of the blasts went straight through his spinal cord. Even if he did manage to pull through, he'd be paralyzed for life, not that it's anything for him to worry about now. He is most assuredly no longer for this world.

"That shouldn't have been possible."

There is no way the blaster could have gone off. He saw it for himself. The lycan tried to fire the weapon and nothing happened. He had the safety on. Only he would have been able to turn it off. So how could it have fired just by some kid who just happened to pick it up?

"Do I look like someone who knows how to even work one of these things?"

Renki looks at him for the first real time. Despite the bright coloration of his costume, the boy beneath is as ordinary as they come. Brown hair, brown eyes, brown skin, and the kind of features one would forget were it not for the makeup working hard to make his face more interesting.

So does this kid look like a master hacker?

No, he really doesn't. Between the boy's bare feet, the matted locks of his hair, and the dirt caked to his chin and neck, there is no way he could have the exposure to, let alone the knowledge of such technology to do anything with it. But Renki has more to worry about than if this kid could hack into his safety protocol.

"What's your name?"

"I didn't mean to kill him. I swear it."

The boy is hysterical, tears in his eyes, sweat at his brow, fingers twitching around the pistol's handle. The barrel of which is aiming directly in Renki's direction.

"I know. You didn't mean it. Why don't you tell me your name?"

"Gideon."

"Gideon," Renki says the name as slowly and as calmly as he can. "Gideon, my name is Renki."

"Renki?"

"Yes. Renki. I'm Renki and you're Gideon."

A new trail of tears forms along his cheek. "I've never shot anyone before."

"I know, Gideon. It's okay."

"Is he dead?!"

"Gideon, you're in shock. Just hand me the pistol, and everything is going to be just fine."

The boy looks at Renki, eyebrows scrunched up. Then he looks down and sees the gun rattling in his grip. His reaction is akin to finding a venomous snake winding around his fingers. He drops the blaster before it can bite him.

"No—wait!"

The blaster falls to the pavement.

"Duck!"

A laser beam pings against the brick wall behind him as Renki falls forward onto his face.

"I'm sorry. I'm sorry."

"It's alright." Renki pulls himself back to his feet and retrieves the fallen weapon.

"Are you hurt?"

"I'm fine, thanks. Are you alright?"

Gideon doesn't answer his question in favor of pointing in the general vicinity of Renki's waist where his belt sits.

"Oh no, your sash."

"My sash?"

His lavender sash, the same sash he has worn every day since he was five years old, is torn. For ten years, he's kept this one piece of fabric in pristine condition. He scrubbed it by hand every week since Kaito taught him how, folded it carefully away every night for safekeeping on the flat top of his dresser, donned with all the careful pride and elegance owed to such a trinket, and even fought with primary school bullies over it when one of the older boys thought it would be a good laugh taking from him. A large tear has shredded the fabric straight down the middle, and nearly every other bit of fabric is mottled with back-alley grime.

Now that hurts. Somewhere deep in the aching place where his last conversation with Kaito plays over and over again, something more breaks where an already fragmented piece of his heart lies.

"Was that for your mother?"

Renki stares at Gideon, about to answer when...

"Renki! Praise the gods you're alright!"

Orson and Akari, racing down the alley, seem as harried as he feels. The pair completely bypass Gideon in favor of inspecting Renki as thoroughly as possible in such a confined space. Orson checks him over with his scanner. The blue of his sights projects a thin beam of light over him from head to toe. Akari is more hands on. The girl often forgets the capabilities of her own tech, choosing instead to grope him up and down his arms and shoulders. (Were he a more appalling kind of boy and were she not like a sister to him, he might have made some appropriately teenage jibe at the manhandling. But, alas, Renki is not like other boys his age, and he's quite certain his oto-san would be highly unimpressed were he to employ such behavior. He knows he has always been unimpressed by other boys being unnecessarily rude to their female counterparts.)

Orson frowns. "You've dinged yourself up pretty good. We'll stop by the nearest clinic to make sure there isn't anything more extensive than a few cuts and bruises."

"I'm fine, Thorgard-san. Many of those are old."

"Regardless, I want you to get checked up. The last thing I need is for a prince under my charge to end up infected with lycanthropy."

"He didn't actually hit me. He went down before he had the chance."

Orson steps toward the hexen and squats down. "A Koi lycan transforming in the middle of the day; it's unthinkable."

"Renki!" Akari shouts. "Your sash. it's completely ruined. The lycan did this." Akari touches the fileted pieces of his mourning sash in horror. She'll have to come up with her own explanation, for Renki can't bring himself to answer her.

"You're lucky the only thing torn up was your clothes. What were you thinking, engaging a lycan by yourself?"

Renki angles around his so-called mentor. "I wasn't by myself. I was with—" He cuts himself off. When he looks around Orson to gesture to the boy who effectively saved his life, all he sees is an empty alley. "He was right there."

"Renki Miyazaki!"

Renki takes off down the mouth of the alley to find the boy, but when he reaches the market street, there is no sign of him. With too many people, too many trading carts, too much noise, he can't see beyond the street line. Even the performing troop he was with has vacated the premises.

"Renki, why did you take off like that?" Akari's question comes with a hand on his shoulder.

"He was right here. Gideon. The performer boy."

"What performer boy? Explain yourself, lad. You're not making sense."

He thinks the technomancer's words are meant to be gentle, but all he hears is words tinged with a gruff northern accent uncommon to Murasaki no Yama. Orson may speak Hanasu perfectly, but he will always have the edgier texture of his root language in his voice.

"The lycan stole my pistol off my belt. I wouldn't even have noticed if it hadn't been for Gideon."

"Gideon? Who is this Gideon?"

"That's the name of the performer who was breathing fire at the entrance of the grounds not thirty minutes ago."

"What fire breather?" asks Orson.

"The kid! The one who was performing at the entrance!"

"It's alright, your highness. You're not in trouble. There's no need to make up a lie."

"I'm not lying. The kid is real. His name is Gideon." Renki's protests are met by deaf ears. Orson is already walking away. "You saw him, didn't you, Akari?"

"I'm sorry, Ren, but I didn't see him."

"But he was in the middle of the plaza!"

"There was no kid, Ren." Akari is looking at him like he has a few screws loose. He's had a lot of people look at him that way in his life. Unaugmented strangers in the street when a much younger Renki would say something aloud in response to a message his oto-san had sent him over their shared server. He hadn't quite yet gotten the hang of responding via their nodes, so he would just answer verbally. Prepubescent classmates in school whenever something regarding magic or hexen was brought up, and Renki would have the gall to contradict something the teacher was saying. *Is it really wrong to correct an adult when they say witches maintain their power by organizing human sacrifices and stealing babies from their beds?* Apparently so when everyone else in the room has been going to sleep with the threat of the Songstress of Lorelei coming to steal them out of their beds for misbehavior.

None of them, despite their best efforts, ever made him feel inferior, but from Akari, it's like a slap in the face.

"...'Tis folly to be wise."

From the poem,
"Ode on a Distant Prospect of Eton College"
Thomas Grey 1742 A.P

12
THREE OF CUPS

14th Day in the Month of Falling - 11AM - Somewhere Underneath Calypso City

THE BACK OF HER HEAD IS THROBBING. WASN'T she just awake?

"Oh, quickly, quickly, she's waking up."

The witch groans. "Mmm…" she murmurs into a clothed thigh. Oh, her head is in Kaito's lap. "Kai?"

"I'm here." There's tension in his muscles. *From battle maybe?* He feels as wound up as a jack-in-the-box. *Was there a fight?* Her head is throbbing. Didn't she hit the floor? He must have moved her at some point, but wait… what did happen? The last thing she remembers is a gunslinging git and losing her voice.

"What happened?!" She jolts upright and instantly regrets the rapidity of the movement. Her head splits into quarters at the action. "Ah!"

She buries her head back in Kaito's leg.

"Here, put this on her head. It will ease the pain."

A warm, minty-smelling compress is placed at her temple. She blinks, peering through her aching eyelashes to see white freckles, pink hair, and glittering wings. *Lyra! That two-faced trickster of a fae!*

She kicks out again, nearly head-butting Kaito. Magic spins at her fingertips. "What did you do to me?!"

The fairy doesn't even flinch backward despite the triskele glowing at the woman's forehead. Her indicia flickers, uncharacteristically weak despite the amount of rage fueling her casting.

"Calm down, W—" Kaito's voice cracks. Coughs shake his frame, and every time he tries to finish his statement, specifically her name, it's like something punches him in the throat each time.

"What did you do to him?!" She tries to sing, but all that comes out is moth dust.

"Now, now, Songstress. You'll give yourself another psychic wallop if you try any of that mischief on me."

"What have you done to me?"

The fairy holds up the record and the Songstress of Lorelei's autographed name. The ink, translucent before, now gleams magenta. Before her eyes, the letters become scrambled and warped. She cannot read her own name, and even as she tries to grasp for it, the knowledge drips through her fingertips, a memory evaporated into nothing. As one last test, she reaches into her pack for Lacuna. She prays, willing the blade to recognize her, to tell her who she rightfully is, but when she unsheathes her athame, there is nothing. The blade lies black and dormant in her hands. It does not recognize its master.

Understanding dawns as ugly as an ice bath. "You stole my name."

"To put it simply, yes."

"You lying, manipulative wretch. You stole my name which therefore means you've stolen my magic!"

"Not stolen, borrowed."

"It all amounts to the same thing! Give me back my name this instant!"

"Sorry, Songstress, but I had no choice, you see, and I can't by rights return it free of charge. There's, first, something I need from you."

"Well, I've nothing for you to take. You've already taken it all."

"Not so, your grace."

"And stop calling me that!"

"I don't understand." Kaito, his voice raw from the coughing fit, comes up behind her. His hand closes on her shoulder before she can right and truly pummel the fairy to dust. The witch calms but only enough to power down Mångata who had somehow, miraculously come to life in retrospect. Kaito's silver gaze falls on the fairy. "You gave your word. Your word which is beholden to me as the owner of your name. You can't take the name of any living being. Your promise was tied to this inscription."

"Apologies for the subterfuge, but I didn't actually say that, did I?"

"But you did."

"No, I didn't. I said I could not steal the name of anyone in full possession of their own facilities. You, my dear witch, are not exactly in full possession of yourself, now are you?"

"What? But that's—"

Wait! She sets her hand on Kaito's arm and the technomancer goes quiet. *Is that true?* It is true. She isn't in possession of her whole self.

"She's right."

Kaito stalls, looking down at the witch in askance. "What does she mean? How is she right?"

"The curse."

"What curse?"

Damnit! She doesn't have the time to deal with this. Okay, well maybe she does, but she *so* did not want to deal with this yet. She didn't want to deal with this at all. Is it so hard to meet the prerequisites of a curse without having to involve every person within a quarter of a mile of her? Apparently not, as here she is, once again, dragging Kaito into the crosshairs aimed at her stupid head.

"It's the blood curse that brought me back from the dead. It's still in play."

"In play for what?"

She smiles sheepishly up at him before covering her face with the still damp towel. It stinks of medicine, but at least it gives her a veritable reason to avoid eye contact. "Oh, you know. Blood for blood and all that overexaggerated mess."

Kaito looks about ready to murder her himself for how vague she's being, but surprisingly enough, Lyra comes to her rescue.

"Exactly. 'Blood for blood.' Miss Singsong, here, is still indebted to her resurrectionists, as such her being is not actually hers to possess."

"So who does it belong to?"

Kaito looks at her with large pale eyes, well, large for Kaito. Anyone who didn't know him would just assume his facial expression was the same as normal.

"It belongs to the dead."

Kaito deflates. She's always found that to be a strange word to use in reference to a person. It isn't like her prince is a balloon which can lose its air, but that's exactly what he does. He doesn't get any smaller. He doesn't lose any mass. He doesn't even so much as move. It's so much worse than that. It's like something nameless goes out in him. Hope maybe? She isn't sure. Where ignorance is bliss and all that. Her stepmother always did say that people only stay optimistic so long as they don't know the truth of their circumstances.

(She used to hate every time Elisabeta threw that line out. She never said it to her husband's second daughter. No, she always said it to her own children whenever their younger sister had finally just convinced them to ease up on their duties and have some fun. It was like she wanted Atzi and Xipilli to become allergic to fun. Atzi never took it to heart, but Xipilli... well, it was just a few days ago that he wanted to run her through for making a harmless joke.)

"Look! I don't have time for this! Give me back my name! And I promise I won't hold it against you."

"Sorrrrrry," the fairy whines in a tinny voice. The apology couldn't be any less grating. "But I cannot do that. I can, however, arrange a deal."

Right, because that's not suspicious at all. A fairy wants to make a deal with a witch? No telling what kind of good will come of that.

"A deal?"

"Yes, a deal. You see, my friends have been going missing."

"Missing? What do you mean 'missing'?"

"She means that the fae folk in this area have been turning up as rotten corpses on the beach for the last seven years."

Ah, it's the old sea-raggled gentleman from before, the one who thought it best to aim a bullet-sneezer at her. Only now, instead of toting one of those archaic boom sticks, he has in one hand a silver stirring spoon and a cup of what she assumes to be tea in the other.

"Who are you?"

The man gives a low hum of dismissal as the hand bearing the stirring spoon takes up action. The cling, clang, clinking of the silver against the teacup sounds almost melodic. (She wonders if she's lost all aspects of her musical might, or if the spell just affects her voice.)

"Ah, yes. This is Leon, one of my regulars. I'm glad he could make it, actually. You see, he's the first one who noticed the same problem I have been observing."

"And I take it you want us to figure out why your so-called friends have been turning up dead?" asks the witch.

Leon's face hardens. If he were a woman, she would wonder if he had any gorgon blood in him, but everyone knows Medusa and the rest of her ilk are female as a matter of course. No anomalies. No exceptions. "My husband has gone missing."

Leon is tall and tanned with sun-kissed fringe and a handsome salt-n-pepper goatee.

"Your husband?"

He hits the edge of the carpet, and the empathic witch's world goes upside-down. "Yes, my husband."

Cursed were-monkeys! It's amazing how some people can feel so deeply but show nothing on the surface. She calls them heart grenades, ever so lovingly. Unobtrusive on the outside but downright explosive once the trigger is pulled on their carefully bottled emotions. Unfortunately, her empathic abilities give her a front row seat to every explosion. Her lover is one of those such people. He's shielded from her at the moment; thank every goddess in existence for working neural blockers. He is terribly overwhelming when he isn't guarding.

At least, heart grenades aren't very common. In fact, she's only met a handful in her lifetimes, but every time she's had to deal with one, they give her a headache.

This one, despite his steely disposition and cold stare, is a migraine bubble primed and ready to burst behind her eyes. There's anger and frustration, deep-set sorrow and longing, a touch of jealousy toward Kaito (that's interesting), and just a hair of admiration for Lyra. These are all surface level, though. Something any low-life vampyre could identify with a taste of blood. The witch's empathy, though, really likes to poke and prod at things without her say-so. Her passive abilities go for the deep lunge, as such, she finds the root cause of all of his core emotions: He's in love.

There it is, clear as daylight at the mouth of a cave and louder than a crash of thunder overhead. But it's no honeymoon phase. It lacks the fiery, passionate love she often feels inside adorations of this volume and magnitude. Newly-in-love people are noisy. They shout their feelings to the high heavens for all to hear; dammit all to any empaths who cross the path of that kind of amore. No, his is the enduring kind of love. The kind of love so deep she could drown in its depths if she made the mistake of going for a swim.

"Right, well. Since, I've put you on loan, I'm afraid your voice, and therefore your magics, are at my call and beck until such a time as I deem to return them to you once more, and that won't be until after we've gotten to the bottom of all these disappearances."

Kaito's ear twitches. "Disappearances?"

"Yes, fae of all natures have been disappearing across the city. Lyra seems to think you and that no-account witch are the half-wits capable of figuring out this mystery."

"Who are you calling a 'half-wit,' half-wit?"

"Songbird, please. You're in no position to be insulting our hosts."

Our hosts!

She is about to turn to give the vagabond prince a piece of her mind, but he is already shifting her out of his lap as he rises from his seat, gently settling her lengthwise across the cushion.

"It is no use haggling with the fae. State your desire, Lyra, and I will see it is done in exchange for my witch's magic and name being returned to her."

"She's not making a deal with you, metal man. She needs the witch for this, not you. You're just a convenient plus-one."

"My name," declares her technomancer, severity pressing in at the edges of his voice, "is Kaito Miyazaki, not metal man, and this witch is—"

"I know who she is, *Miyazaki-san*," Leon sneers out Kaito's surname like it is a curse word. "The Songstress of Lorelei, second daughter to the former Vulcan of Deriva, and only child of the firefly, Freya." Leon's eyes turn impossibly darker as they settle on her. "You're the one whose mother's death led to the culling of merfolk all along the coast of Deriva. If it weren't for your father's war on the ocean fae, Thale and I never would have needed to relocate to the Tai Tai for safety, and we'd still be living happily and peacefully on the Derivan coast together with our children."

The witch withdraws as though slapped. What is she supposed to say to that? *Sorry my mum was killed by a sea monster when I was ten years old, and my father was so devastated he declared war on every sentient being in the surround waters?* Maybe she should have done more to prevent that while she lay, a child amputee, in a hospital bed waiting to undergo the incredibly painful procedure of having a mechanical limb grafted to her mutilated stump of a wrist.

"I take it Thale is a merman."

Kaito's redirection couldn't come at a better time as the songbird teeters between launching into a full-on lesson in manners or curling into a ball as she regresses back to that day of pain, confusion, and grief.

"That's right."

"And you are—"

"His husband, obviously. I said so already, didn't I!"

"Yes, you did indeed say your spouse had disappeared. I was going to say 'human+.' Beyond the metal prosthetics around your hands, I am picking up augmentations on your person; however, none of them are listed with an active registration. Are you in disuse? If so, I can assist you in making repairs."

"Well, don't you worry your pretty head, highness. I got plenty of 'em. And they're all working just fine. Registration or no registration."

"Are they up-to-date or stale?"

Leon draws back, his demeanor suddenly much less offensive than a moment ago. "Not sure that's something I want someone like you to know."

"Someone like me?"

"A League machine." Interesting choice of words.

"Very well. Then I'm sure I don't need to mention that your social cue metronome is entirely offline. Either you've been neglectful of your maintenance protocols, or your mechanic is a hack."

"Watch your mouth, big timer. My mechanic is the best in the city."

"Clearly not."

"Kai," warns the songstress. Her expression says it all. Now, it's her turn to err on the side of caution. *We are not in the position to antagonize these people.*

"Miyazaki-san," inserts the fairy, "while I understand your concern for Leon's tech, I can certify it is in prime working order. His mechanic is thorough if not accurate."

"And I take it that would be you," the witch says, looking over at the fairy hovering two feet off the ground.

"Yeah, well, I run maintenance on Leon's augmentations. He has an amazing endoskeleton lining his spine. You should've seen what it looked like when I first started working on him. It hadn't been adjusted in years and was about to destroy his cervical vertebrae. Just the bad luck of dealing with counterfeit augmentations, I know, but hell holy bats, you would think these bastards would take an ounce of pride in their work."

No, she really wouldn't. Why do something the right way when it can be done the cheap way? So is written the secret to capitalism on every desk, in every office, across every billboard in the world. People only care about other people when greed is not in their best interest.

"Well then, Lyra, my so-called name-holder, care to explain to me why you went through such trouble just to steal my voice and make my day even worse?"

"Leon's husband is just the most recent of dozens of fae folk who have gone missing in the last several years, and quite frankly, I'm tired of watching my friends go missing."

"They just disappear? No one ever sees them again."

"No one but the birds eating their carcasses." She frowns. *The seagulls by the beach.* She had thought it strange that they would congregate despite the refuse. "The locals know about the bodies that turn up randomly, be they in the canals, the backwater resacas, or on the shoreline, but they can't be bothered to do anything about them."

"Hard to care about a few dead fairies when everyone around you has a target on their back."

"Exactly."

So fairies have been going missing. What does that have to do with her? Nothing. Nothing unless someone decides to make it her problem. *Which apparently...*

"So you've stolen my name because you want me to find and rescue these missing fae."

"Precisely."

Lyra's smile is far too chipper for someone who essentially just put a leash on one of the most feared witches this side of the veil.

"There's one problem with your plan, fairy mine. How am I supposed to recover your lost friends without my powers? You've practically rendered me a normal."

"Not quite. Your powers are tied to my will. You can use them but only as I see fit. Here, why don't you carry a tune for my plants? They could use some perking up."

On command, a bright andante trickles from her throat. It isn't one of her scores. It isn't even a song she likes. Something poppy and outdated, probably from the fairy side of the river, but it's her voice singing it.

The itsy bitsy spider,
Went up the water spout
Down came the rain
And washed the spider out.

Her magic weaves through the room. Still a vibrant emerald, still sparkling and healthy as usual, but it's tracing a pattern that makes utterly no sense. Its usual spirals become backward-facing ovals. It crosses its own trails, gets tangled in itself, and seems to bounce like a ping pong ball through the room as tickles the sleeping leaves, touches the vines hanging from the ceiling, and dips into the soil of each pot like a happy little gnome.

Out came the sun
And Dried up all the Rain
So the itsy bitsy spider
Went up the spout again

Annoyance bubbles up, hot and ugly under her skin. What is she? Some service bitch dog for hire? *Sit, girl. Roll over. Good dog! Here's a biscuit. Now, sing! Good job! Make a zombie for mama!*
Not likely!

This black widow spider
Still has a lot of bite.
Make me fall down and
I'll send you underground.

She exerts her will, the little of it she has left, at least, and as the lyrics change, so too does the texture of her magic. The plants, once green and lively, turn brown and dry as her magic makes them wilt and die. When one of the roses starts to lose its petals, she stops, turning to Lyra with a smug grin on her face, arms crossed over her chest.

"Sorry, I never did have a knack for gardening. Thanks for the permission, though. Nice to know I still have some power."

Lyra looks at her the way one would look at a puppy who's just peed in the wrong place. She imagines if she had a tail, it would be wagging in pleasure despite her "owner's" displeasure.

"I suppose I asked for that, telling a necromancer to tend to my plants." The fairy flutters her wings, causing a sprinkling of dust to fall over her now sad excuse for a garden. Glittery fairy dust blankets the dying plants, and with a little magic of her own, the color returns to their stems, their spines return upright, and a few new buds burst open on the flowers in a vibrant array of color. It doesn't save everything, however. Witch magic, as volatile as it is, is stronger than fairy magic. "No matter. Plants are easily resurrected. Glad to see you found a means to use your particular flavor of magic. I only ask you to not abuse the length on your leash."

"Stop referring to it as a leash and I'll think about it," grumbles the witch.

The fae ignores her. "Well, as you can see, you have permission to use your magic within whatever parameters I set. As such, I give this stipulation: you have my full support to use your magic so long as it works toward meeting my requirement of finding Thale and the other missing fae of Calypso City. No more. No less. Any spell work beyond those parameters and I'm afraid you'll find yourself more than a little hoarse."

"And once I solve your case, my name will be returned to me?"

"Naturally."

"I need you to say it," growls the witch. "No tricks, no fancy wording."

The fairy sighs but holds her right hand up as though pledging her allegiance. "I promise, on my name which your lover holds, that once you find the culprit behind all of these disappearances and set up a means by which to save my lost friends, I, Lyra Mchelogdea, will return your name and full autonomy over your magics. In doing so, I give up all licenses to your person and waive any ability to steal your name from you again, even though I get to keep the autograph."

Yeah, we'll see about that one, she thinks, though she is presently satisfied with that oath. She turns to Leon. "How often does Thale go swimming?"

5AM - Calypso City Flooded District

It is decided in no uncertain terms that morning would be a better time to embark on this madman's mission. After all, it would give them time to prepare, collect supplies, do some data-driven reconnaissance, so on and so forth, et cetera, et cetera, so at the break of dawn—*Odin's Beard! What is it with humans and rising early!*—she ambles her way behind Kaito and Leon to the last place Thale was seen on land. She sips on a heavily sweetened, heavily milked fairy coffee just willing her eyes to stay open while the two men discuss various mission-related topics that she probably should pay half of her attention to but doesn't have the right, oh, she doesn't know, *enthusiasm* for at the moment.

The underground of Calypso City is less subterranean and more subaquatic. What else would you expect from a city that sits more on the in-between of several isles than on actual land mass?

Winding tunnels, some flooded and some bone dry, make up the subway and sewage system. Lyra's home, tucked neatly away in one of the drier parts is soundly disconnected from the main lines, a feature which took no small feat of magic and technological intervention to keep the whole place from molding every five hours according to the fae's complaints of excess moisture.

The tunnels that make up the subways and sewers are as treacherous as any underwater cave, requiring spelunking equipment and diving equipment for any average person to even stand a chance of ever seeing the surface again.

The sun hasn't even risen above the horizon, yet already she and Kaito are about to bid it goodbye. When up is no longer an option, there is no place to go but down.

"Thale's been missing for how long exactly?"

"Almost 24 hours."

"And I take it that's abnormal."

"Without my know ahead, yes."

The man wrings his hands. A titanium ring embedded with a single black and red pearl catches her eye. Nested on his heart finger, the ring is simple but elegant. The stone itself pulses with magic. Not witch magic, not even Hexen magic: Fairy Magic. It zings across the witch's sixth sense, sounding like an early spring sea breeze, smelling like sand in the summer, and tasting like the salt of a clean, fresh ocean.

A mermaid tear. Or, more correctly, a merman's tear.

"When did you last see Thale on two feet?"

"Two days ago."

Two days... What happened two days ago? Let's see. She was on a mission to murder another witch as a requirement of a blood pact placed on her in exchange for this new life she is presently living. Said witch's husband, however, beat her to the gun, and as a result, her masquerade came to an end putting herself once again on Deus' Most Wanted. Not that that's anything new. She had to be resurrected for a reason, after all.

Kaito looks her way. There's a question in his eyes, but she can't for the life of her figure out what it might be.

Oh... Right.

She's not the only one making the front pages. A certain prince decided she was worth throwing everything he ever worked for away. He hasn't lowered his mental guards since they left the Shard. Understandably so. It's been far too dangerous for him to unarm himself, yet she aches for the feel of his psyche, both familiar and alien in the best possible way.

Instead here is this human+ standing before her, unaware of her power. Unaware that his whole soul is bared to her. That his disdain for her was like salt on a blister but beneath that was a heartbreaking emptiness. That emptiness makes her want to cry as much as scream because it is an emptiness which aches for his own lost love.

"This is where Thale last submerged," declares Leon as they approach a narrow dip in the nearby resaca. Resacas are a fairly unique thing to this part of the world. You won't find them anywhere else in Deus. The island chain that makes up the Tai Tai is essentially a man-made linkage of floating isles. As much as they are the result of volcanic activity, they are also disconnected from the ocean floor. The reason for this is because as the people of the isles settled, they broke the natural rivers apart with the purpose of creating more landmass for people to live on. The resacas are the leftover evidence of those rivers.

This one is a sordid affair. Discolored from city pollution and sewage run off, the water is a gray tinged green that smells about as appetizing as it looks. On the far end of the bank is an open flood gate carved from cement. Right now the reservoir is shallow enough that about half a meter is showing above the waterline. That won't be the case once the next batch of rains come about.

She looks up at the sky. Not a cloud in sight, quite the contrary to yesterday when the downpour sent them scurrying for that diner. Not that a clear sky means anything at this latitude/longitude.

"Kai, do you know what the forecast is going to be for the next twelve hours?"

Kaito's sights spin sluggishly in his eyes. It's concerning how slow his servers are operating here. He didn't try to connect to the network, did he? They were interrupted before she could get a clear answer from him about it back in Lyra's workshop.

"According to the weather reports, it's supposed to be light showers later this afternoon. Nothing to be concerned about in regard to flooding."

"I wouldn't be so sure about that. Thale says the weather system here is less accurate than a drunk monkey playing darts."

"Well, that's all we have to go on. Lest we want to wait until the dry season comes, which would be, oh, in about three months."

Leon sneers at her. "I doubt either you or Thale have that kind of time, princess."

She ignores the jibe. She may have been the child of a king, but she's never been a princess.

"Does Thale go diving here often?"

"No. He can't stand the clean-up, but he went looking for a friend of ours who disappeared a few weeks ago."

Kaito's brow lifts. "A friend?"

"Loupe, an old seafaring friend of mine."

There's a note of hesitation in the man's description of this Loupe, and the witch is quick to pick up on it. "By seafaring, you mean pirate, don't you?"

"Perhaps. Perhaps not. Not like I'd tell the likes of either of you. You're League-born and he's League aristocracy."

"I haven't been considered of-the-League since long before my first death, and Kai's relationship to the League right now isn't any more companionable than yours might be." In fact, she would venture to call it more hostile. The songstress turns her attention back to the water. Frothy with seafoam and run-off, the canal is less a body of moving water and more a trudge along of ichor. She can't imagine the merman would have been happy submerging in it. "Anyway, tell me about Loupe. What happened to him?"

"Loupe disappeared not long after his wife was taken. She's a half-elf, abducted just like all the others a little more than a month ago. He thought since he wasn't a fae or a hexen, he could go looking for her without much danger, but we haven't seen him since he went searching. I've been looking everywhere for both of them, but there's only so many places an old +y like me can go, so Thale decided to go looking for him, against my wishes."

"And you let him go?" asks Kai.

"Thale is his own person. I may be his husband, and to that end I have some say over his actions, but I have no right to forbid him from doing anything once he's set his mind to it. I can only support him."

"Hmm, sounds utterly frustrating," says the witch, smiling crookedly at Kaito.

"You have no idea," huffs the former pirate.

Kaito gives his lover a sidelong glance. "Somehow, I completely understand the sentiment."

"You know you love me."

Leon makes a disgusted noise and mumbles something, probably derogatory, about straight people. She imagines he is thinking something along the lines of "disgusting heteronormatives." Gotta love the elder gays. Good thing she's bisexual.

"Well, while you two flirt your way into some roundabout plan, I'm going to run interference up here. The news programs have had a field day with your presence here."

She can imagine. It's been a day since the broadcast she saw in the diner. What else might be waiting to be screened across the entire island?

"Your assistance in that is appreciated. Give Lyra our love."

"Yeah, whatever." Leon turns on his heel and walks away.

"Kai, are we sure we want to do this? The last time you and I went traipsing about below sea level wasn't exactly a walk in the park, and as much as I would love a repeat of the more pleasurable parts of that case, aren't we past the point of needing a cave-in as an excuse for bedroom games?"

The look she gets in response could freeze a small lake, but the songstress's resultant laughter would melt it right back down. Eventually, the technomancer softens, leaning down to her ear and lifting her chin with one long digit before setting a still kiss on that dancing mouth. Her laughter fades away into a long quiet, interrupted by an annoyed *tsk* when her lover pulls away.

"I would hardly consider this a pleasurable walk, *Ore no Kaiyo*. Your present predicament somewhat demands our acquiescence."

"Right, I was trying to forget." And failing miserably at it.

"Besides, my dismal performance that day is not worth repeating."

"Oh, I wouldn't say that. You were seventeen. What do you expect?"

Piano player's fingers thread through her hair, effortlessly winding through the curly locks without hitting a single snag. "You deserve better than the inexperienced hands of an angsty teenager. Perhaps, later, when you are no longer at the behest of a manic fae. Then I will be able to properly speak your name and declare to you everything I wish to do to you once more. Then, we can rewrite that data memory."

Her face burns. "Kaito Miyazaki! Is that any way for a prince to speak?!"

"Perhaps not a prince, per se," he says, leaning in close, "but, surely, a vagabond would speak as such."

He leaves the sentence hanging in her ear and promptly turns on his heel and strides into the tunnel.

The Songstress of Lorelei, for her part, stands stunned and more than a little shocked by that shameless display of flirting. Before she gathers her bearings, she reminds herself that she is the proper tease and jogs after him with a shouted:

"You think you're so cool now after one act of defiance. Listen here, highness: I made a living dancing in the shadows. I'm the original boogeyman, a bona fide criminal. You can't just..."

She keeps going, but the nonsense she spews isn't important. What is important is the deep rumble of Kai's amusement.

Ever heard of a pithing needle? It's a specialty tool used by doctors in the Victorian Era.

They used to believe that the only way to settle a mad person's ailment was to prescribe unending rest and relaxation. Sounds great in theory, but in practice, this results in sensory deprivation for 99% of patients undergoing such treatment.

"The Yellow Wallpaper" is a wonderful testament to this phenomena. A woman, postpartum, is deprived of her time with her infant in favor of having to sit all day in a room bedecked with the most hideous wallpaper. Some say it is a vampire story, others a ghostly tale; I say it is just what it claims to be: a woman's descent into madness.

How does this fit in with a pithing needle?

Well, when patients were particularly antsy, they would insert a needle into the spinal column of said patient so as to render them immobile from the waist down, thus preventing the infirm from moving or running away. It worked, of course, even laid the foundation for what would one day be called an epidural; however, they didn't count on how well it would work. You see, the first patients to undergo the procedure never regained the use of their legs.

Excerpt from *Magical Maladies*
By Dr. Lovecraft

13

ACE OF WANDS (PART 1)

15th Day in the Month of Falling - 5:30AM - Calypso City

SHE ISN'T QUITE SURE WHAT SHE WAS expecting to find once they entered the mouth of the abandoned subway. Filth, sure. A bit of putridity, yes. Vermin, absolutely. But artwork... No, she most certainly was not expecting to find whole murals splashed across the grime-flecked walls of the underground.

Graffiti is a lot of things to a lot of people. A nuisance, a crime, vandalism, etc. Lots of the negatives go with the term, but she can only see the beauty of it. It is an avenue of expression and a harmless means by which to "stick it to the man" as it were. Hip Hop is a lifestyle, not just a trend, and in the inner city, you can expect plenty of people to adhere to the culture.

There are more people down here than she was expecting. A few lycans cultivate together around a stereo lifted above the water on a stack of cardboard boxes. The music echoes off the walls, a hypnotizing drum and bass. It ricochets through the witch's rib cage in the most delicious way. The gathering of lycans jams to the beats echoing around the chamber, low, visceral movements that embody the earthiness of the body. Groundedness, as much as every creature is born hearkened to the earth, is a learned quality for most people. We waste so much time idolizing the heavens, we forget the sanctity of the ground.

The lycans pay them no mind as they pass. They're too busy howling up a storm as one of them splashes about in an impressive windmill. His feet flair seemingly in all directions at once, spinning like a top in space. It's like gravity and friction have no effect on him.

She remembers when she used to study ballet. In that artform, the emphasis is on balance and defying the body's natural desire to fall—the goal to reach for the clouds and appear weightless to an audience.

There is no such illusion here. Simply a mastery of momentum.

Art in its finest incarnation: living, breathing, moving at 200 km/s.

"You always did have a love for dancing." Kaito's voice is smooth in her ear.

"And you will forever deny your own love for it."

"I have no love for such gyrations."

"I bet you would if I were the one dancing with you."

"I seem to recall a certain time when I did indeed dance with you to this kind of music."

"Ah, yes. Harborage." She remembers, now. The hexen club where they went in search of Montwyatte. "I'd forgotten."

The sound of the stereo diminishes as they move deeper into the caverns.

As they continue, the people they pass dwindle in number. There is a human wrapped up in newspaper/magazine leaflets, apparently sleeping in a relatively dry hollow in the wall. A pair of women kneel in front of a small statuette. It seems to be a rendition of Poseidon. He sits astride a kelpie, trident held aloft. She is reminded for a brief moment of her brother and his weapon, Opochtli. Sea serpents, she doesn't even want to think about how he must feel about her right now. Probably somewhere between scalping her and flaying her alive, neither of which seem like fun experiences.

Naturally, the thought of her brother dearest makes her mind wander over to Kaito's brother. His esteemed imperial highness is probably dreaming about cutting her head off himself. *Do they still have beheadings in Murasaki no Yama?* Eh, she's sure he'll make the exception for her. He warned her to stay away from his baby brother. Is it really her fault if said baby brother felt absolutely no need to steer clear of her?

Deeper inside, a few children play in the runoff water. They look to be building a dam of some sort, either uncaring or unknowing of the kind of filth they are playing in. They're just old enough to wander about without a chaperone, though their choice of play yard is probably not what their parents had in mind. That is, of course, if they even have parents.

There were a lot of orphans left behind when the Reckoning happened. Childless parents and parentless children were forced to find one another in the wreckage that remained of the various hexen and fae communities. The demolition is probably the reason hexen are so readily accepted in the Tai Tai. The humans vastly outnumber any vamps, lycans, or witches—definitely witches—that may be lurking about. No reason to be scared of something when there are plenty of pitchforks available to exorcise any bad behavior.

What are the chances that she would run into a witch in the first bo-hunk diner she set foot in? That girl was probably one of a handful of witches living in the city. Naturally, she would have a vendetta against the Songstress of Lorelei because that's just the kind of luck she has.

"Do you remember what you said to me that day?"

The water moves slower down here even though the slope of their descent steepens. Probably a sign that the water is dirtier and therefore unable to run as nature would otherwise dictate.

She chuckles at Kai's question. "I say a lot of things all the time. You'll have to be specific."

"It was regarding my comment of the place being a brothel."

"I told you it wasn't a brothel."

"Mmm," the man hums in amusement, "I meant after that."

"To stop being elitist?" she asks, not entirely sure where this conversation is going. He shakes his head. "Sorry, I honestly don't remember."

He sighs. "You told me I was looking at the place like an infantile bigot."

"I did not! I just told you to grow up and get out of your aunt's classroom."

When she looks back at Kaito, there's a small half-smile lingering at the edge of his mouth. *Well played, Kaito. Way to jog my memory.*

"Does that not basically amount to the same thing?"

Well, I guess when you put it that way...

There was a particular course on hexen that she distinctly remembers being less than secular. She believes the description that was used to describe witches was, oh yes, "cannibalistic heathens who would just as soon rip your face off as look at you."

"Well... Okay, yes it kind of does. What I really wanted to say was to get your head out of your perfectly clenched butt cheeks and stop turning your nose up at something just because you don't understand it."

"I gathered that. You were simply too kind to say so."

"More like preoccupied."

"Yes. You realize I had no idea what you meant back then."

"Well, why would you? We were stupid teenagers." *War-forged teenagers but, hey, details, details...*

Kaito snorts. "I never got to tell you when I finally understood what you were saying."

"What do you mean?"

"After..." he trails off, silver eyes looking anywhere but her. "After Lorelei was destroyed, I started to understand what you meant. Having a place where one can be their true self is a precious treasure—the loss of that can leave an irreparable scar on a person."

The witch frowns. "I don't understand. What does this have to do with what we are doing right now?"

"I noticed you were looking at those children."

"So..."

"I didn't get the chance to tell you before my brother sent you away. It's about Fae."

Her boots splash into shallow water. Her ears start to ring. "I don't want to talk about Fae."

"No, Songbird, listen. You don't understand. When you—"

"It's over, Kaito!" she interrupts him. "She's not coming back. I know it was my fault. I don't need you to bring it back up."

"No, that's not what I—"

"Must we dredge up the past? I mean, don't we have more important things to worry about?"

The woman angles away from Kaito and hurries down the tunnel. The sound of the children splashing around in the water is starting to die out. Now all she can hear is her own feet slapping in the shallow puddles. She chalks up the wet at the corner of her eyes to the mildew irritating her sinuses.

"Yes, but—"

"Yow!!" Her heel hits something jelly-like below the surface of the water, and without a chance at catching her balance, she wheels backward straight into Kaito. The impact takes both of them down into the slick.

If you've ever been to a water park, you know that there are certain attractions specifically made for the daredevils who want to have their swim trunks blown away. There was one in Deriva. She remembers going there every summer with her family up until her mother's death. There were certain water slides that you had to cross your hands over your chest and pinch your nose closed for risk of losing your swim top and getting a good gallon of water into your brain if you didn't do it right.

Those slides were bad enough on their own. Despite her fear of heights, she was willing to brave those with her sister close behind her. It was the other kind that scared the bejesus out of her. The monster slides that started with a 90 degree drop.

She hated those.

The lifeguard would usher their next victim into a standing capsule and shut the door. When she did it, he instructed her to stand all the way against the wall and assume the position. Then, before she could say she was ready, the machine began a countdown from 10.

Once the timer reached 0, the trapdoor under her feet opened and swallowed her screams as she hit the water slide below.

Xipilli loved going on those slides. His younger sister, however—8-years-old and terribly scared of heights—did not. She did it once on a dare and never again.

That, of course, was a simulation of danger. Something designed for fun and entertainment that was, in fact, perfectly safe.

This, the sewage slide she and Kaito are currently riding, is not. And when the ground drops out from under them, just like those trap doors at the water park, the witch really starts to shriek.

"Can you slow us down?!" Kaito's shout, though not nearly as loud as hers, echoes in her ear.

"I don't know!"

Her feet hit an alcove with a jolt. Water rushes up her nose into her mouth, effectively silencing her. Her shoulder grazes a nearby arch. She can't see, she can't hear, and worst of all, she can't sing!

Nothing escapes her throat. Her magic, under the beck and call of another, does not come to her. "I can't stop us!"

"Hold onto me!" shouts Kai.

Her fingers knot into his jacket. There's a *shing*—the telltale sound that Kaito has drawn at least one of his swords.

The steel of the blade makes the most horrible screeching sound as Kaito drags it against the side wall until finally it embeds into the stone. Their descent slows until finally, with one last jerk, the swords catch and the coils linking them to Kaito's arms reach an end. Water rushes past them as the pair come to a halt, Kaito's arms held akimbo as they dangle against the steep incline of the ledge.

She spits foul-tasting water out of her mouth. "I swear to everything holy and unholy, when I get my hands on that fairy, I will personally make sure her sparkle needs some serious polish!"

No sooner are the words out of her mouth than a massive spark zings through her spine, like a taser being pressed to the base of her tailbone. The shock loosens her hands, and she slips down Kaito's body.

"You okay?!"

"It's fine!" she shouts, catching herself around his shins. "Damned fairy spell. Can't even speak ill of her without suffering some sort of recompense."

"That is the way of most curses."

"Talk about a serious oversight. I can use my powers to accomplish her means but not to keep us from plummeting to our deaths."

"Unless we weren't actually in any danger?"

"Yeah, tell that to my adrenals. *Puta Madre!* Now what?"

"Can you see what's below us?" Kaito's voice sounds more than a little strained. She can't imagine why...

She peers into the blackness below. With all the water pouring around them, it's hard to make out anything other than foam, but she thinks she can make out a small pool below them.

"Do you have a light?"

"On my hip."

She reaches up, but just before she can reach his belt, gravity tugs them down. "Shit! What's happening?"

"My swords. The wall is crumbling."

Loki's daggers, of course. With this amount of moisture around them, the metal is too sharp against water-logged cement. A few more seconds and they'll resume their descent without any chance of stopping.

"*Pinché pedo*, alright. I think there's a pool of some kind below us, but I can't tell how deep it is."

"Do you see a ledge nearby?"

Rubble falls past her head. They fall another few inches. She grabs the flashlight off his belt, flicks it on, and looks for something to catch onto. This is a sewer, after all. There has to be something people can use to get down safely.

Blank wall, broken stone, a strangely shaped rock... *Aha!* A ladder. Unfortunately, it's an enclosed ladder, the kind with metal grating circling the apparatus, meaning that she cannot actually grab onto it from where she's positioned. If they want to get ahold of the rungs, they'll have to bust their way through the metal.

"Kai, do you—"

A strangled cry from Kaito above her is the only warning she gets before they descend another foot.

"My heart! Not much time here."

"There's a ladder to our left but it's caged."

"Can you bend the steel apart?"

"I can try."

Extending a hand toward the ladder, the witch tries to whistle. A few notes come out, *Thank the goddess,* but over the roar of the waterfall, she can't hear herself. The cage shivers at her magic, but it isn't strong enough to merit anything substantial.

"I can't get it. Maybe if we get closer."

"Okay," he says. "We'll swing our way over. Move your legs left first. We'll start on 3."

Kaito counts up, and together, they coordinate their momentum. It's slow going. The waterfall, despite its meagerness, acts as an impingement on their natural force. But eventually, they manage to pick up enough momentum that she is just able to scrape her fingertips against the cage of the ladder.

"Almost. One more swing."

"Alright." The strain in Kaito's voice is thicker now. Hanging onto him as she is, her arms are starting to burn from exertion. She can't imagine how Kai's must be feeling, held straight over his head as they are. Her hands would have gone numb by now. His arms must be killing him, augmentations or no. With a mighty kick of his legs, they swing over. She keeps one hand anchored to his belt, next to where Mångata is strapped, and extends herself as far out as she possibly can.

"Got it! Okay. I think you can retract your swords—Ahh!"

As though by will, something above them gives. Kaito's cables retract, and the prince plummets, her hand still wound in his belt. Her shoulder shudders with a sickening pop. It takes all her will not to drop Kaito outright, but the prince has enough sense to get a handhold on the ladder's cage, lest her arm end up yanked clean out of the socket. Well, it wouldn't be clean. It would be quite messy, really. Especially down here... no one to clean up the mess.

She adjusts her grip on Kaito. Mångata's hilt falls into the space between her teeth.

"You okay?" asks Kaito. "Your shoulder has come out of place."

The witch juggles the hilt of her former technomancer weapon between her jaw and her good shoulder so she can talk.

"It'll keep," she grits through clenched teeth.

"If we end up taking another fall, I won't be able to catch you without possibly destroying your entire arm."

"It's fine. If I can get us inside this cursed ladder..."

She trails off. She shifts the weapon back between her teeth and jerks her head to the side, banging the hilt against the cage. Trying to trip the activation mechanism, she repeats the motion again. There's a light clicking sound, so she knows she's just about there. She just hopes against all hope that her ability to form the blade isn't compromised by the loss of her name.

Her hilt clicks against the edge of the grate, and the witch pulls all of her focus to the weapon between her teeth. It sputters under the water, but sure enough, emerald light as vibrant as her magical essence bursts to life. It turns on, and with a small whizzing sound, the blade cuts through the grating. The friction makes her teeth rattle. If anyone has ever complained about grinding their teeth, they have nothing on this. It feels like a thousand tiny drills are trying to dig their way between each individual molar and canine. It hurts so badly she lets the hilt drop from her mouth.

"W—!"

Kaito's attempt to shout the witch's name results in him nearly choking on his own throat. Thankfully, the witch catches the blade with her foot. The weapon would've sliced him to ribbons otherwise. He yanks it away before she loses her hold on it again.

"Sorry. Can you help me up?" The emerald glow disappears as Kaito powers down the aetherkalis.

"Yeah, give me a second."

Kaito's body is warm despite the waterlogged clothing. She relishes the feel of him as he climbs up past her. He grunts with exertion as he rips the wound in the metal open far enough to accommodate their passage and climbs inside. His hands are the last thing she sees before her vision blurs, and he yanks her into the tiny almost-prison cell. Chalk it up to technomancer-level agility, but Kaito is able to get her back upright and slung over his shoulders all while balancing on a few crooked ladder rungs.

Once they are both safely on the inside of the ladder's cage, the shaky songstress takes stock of her arm. It dangles there like a limp noodle.

"Whelp, this is a great start to an adventure in spelunking."

Kaito breathes, elbows wrapped around the rungs. His own exhaustion is apparent on his face.

"We are in a man-made underground, not a cave. This is hardly what I would call spelunking."

"At least we haven't mucked up our escape plan yet."

"So long as this ladder holds out, yes."

The witch squints up into the droplets of water falling lazily from above. "Any idea how far we fell?"

"My cables extend up to thirty meters. We've fallen farther than that." Kaito's sights are dimmer than normal.

"Your arms alright?"

"I'll survive."

"Yes, and I suppose you are about to climb us both down, all on the merit of your nearly pulled sockets."

"It would be better than you gimping your way down with a dislocated shoulder. Come on. I'll carry you until we are back on flat ground."

Well, she can't really argue with that.

Bracing one foot against the cage grating and the other on the ladder rail, Kaito helps her maneuver around to his back. He then hoists her good arm around his neck while she straddles his lower back. Her thighs clench around him. In any other situation, were there fewer layers of clothing between them, this would be a much more pleasurable activity. At least, she can pretend to feel the rippling of his muscles as he begins the however long descent down the ladder.

Funnily enough, it isn't a very long descent. Barely a few heartbeats pass before Kaito's boots hit solid, stable, and thankfully dry ground. Kaito bends at the knees to let her down.

Clenching her loose shoulder in her good hand, the witch goes to the nearest wall and rams her injured side into it. The head of her humerus pops back into the bundle of muscle and sinew that comprises her rotator cuff. The process, as satisfying as it may have been, hurts like a *puta madre*.

"Ten-minute break?"

About fifteen years ago, a younger, more pigheaded version of the witch would have taken offense to the question. *How dare he offer her any such handicap! She isn't some damsel in distress.* Yeah, her teenage self was a piece of work.

Now, however: "Ten-minute break."

There are benefits to spelunking about in an abandoned subway station. For example, not only are there items like ladders and footholds regularly scattered about the place for their climbing convenience, but there is also this little thing called electricity.

During their little water break, Kaito did some looking around and found an old fuse box. Tech-savvy cyborg that he is, it was no problem to get the circuits reconnected. Yes, a good chunk of the light fixtures are broken, and several of the lights right above their heads burst at the unexpected power surge, but the resulting light definitely makes it easier to form a contingency plan should their direction of choice go belly-up. Which, the witch quickly finds, is exactly what happens.

Nothing goes wrong. At least not in any way they can't handle. She and Kaito are perfectly capable people after all. No, it's the next obstacle they come to that has her reluctant to proceed any farther.

The tunnel, carved out to accommodate the passage of a submarine rail car, is naturally flooded. With the drainage systems redirected to keep buildings from sinking below the surface, it makes sense that an unused tunnel system would be allowed to go to seed. The water systems here have basically become an underground river.

Murky water. All Derivans hate murky water. Anyone who grew up by any body of water knows the rule: don't go wading through murky water. And this water is murky. She can't see her own hand after submerging it just an inch or two underwater.

"I'm not going in that water."

"There is no other path forward."

"Doubtful, but I'm not going in that water even if you do have an extra rebreather."

"Songbird?"

"Tell me. Does this remind you of any particular circumstance once upon a time?"

"I seem to recall a similar situation while we were stranded in the catacombs below Lorelei."

"Yeah... good times. That water wasn't nearly as murky."

"It was an underwater foray into the largest tomb in Deus. I couldn't tell you how many dead bodies, skeletons, and globs of viscera we swam past in that water. Yet you mean to tell me you refuse to dive in this water just because it's a little muddy."

"Not 'muddy,' murky, Kai. There's a big difference."

The ex-prince gives her a long-suffering look. A younger version of herself would have cackled with glee at the sight, but now, well, okay she still titters a little, but she'll probably feel a touch guilty about it later.

"Okay, in my defense, did I or did I not gain the moniker Queen of the Dead upon my return to the public eye? Dead bodies are predictable, skeletons are misunderstood, and viscera is just a byproduct of what happens when a body reaches its expiration date. It happens! Like gloopy milk! It's just a thing!"

"You just likened human sinew to fermented milk fat."

The first rebuttal she wants to give to that is "Well, humans produce milk, too, so it's really not that far off," but she restrains herself. No need to get confrontational over spilled milk.

"Yes, I know."

"So we're diving," he declares and proceeds to step into the water.

"Kai!" she shouts as his head disappears into the water. Unbelievable man! So much for approaching this mission with even an iota of caution. A part of her hopes something swims up and bites him in the ass, even if it means that ass wouldn't be as pretty to look at. She digs her heels into the ground wanting to be stubborn. It's irrational, she knows. She's faced zombies and netherbeasts, kraken and sharks, heck she's even faced the odd vampyre and lycan in life-or-death odds, yet here she is afraid of a little water.

"Oh, I know I'm going to regret this."

She fixes the rebreather to her face, tucks the loose ends of her hair into a messy bun, and steps into the water after her lover. Prince Charming had better not have already found himself face-to-face with anything that has even a single tentacle or so help her goddess!

Magdalena and Olga brought the kids to play today. I think it was good for Fae to spend some time with other children. The little one, Lisa, isn't much older than Fae, but she's already coming into her magic. It's no wonder Summer had the child kidnapped however many years ago. She's going to grow up to be a powerful witch. I just wish she would stop throwing snowballs at Fae. I don't want her to get sick again.

From the diary of W--n N--t---
1864 A.P.

14
THE CAT (PART 1)

Cats are magnificent creatures.
Just ask them.

No one who ever spent time with a cat would tell you it was time wasted. In fact, there is a particular situation I can think of in which a famous writer owned not one, not two but twenty cats, and he went down in history as one of the greatest writers of the 19th century.

This, of course, was before the great pilgrimage.

All that to say at her core, of course, Silje is no cat. She is a displacer beast. Yes, she has a feline visage, and whenever she's not in her true bestial form, she looks like a regular house cat. Sort of... Meaning, of course, that if the untrained eye were to squint a little bit—make the spikes and subtly glowing fur patches blur away—someone could see the resemblance. But Silje is no housecat, so to be sitting on the back of a couch with a so-called fairy stroking her as though she were some sort of pet! Let's just say, Silje is annoyed.

It's annoying enough that her witch has gone off gallivanting again. Without her, nonetheless. She could swear to the whiskers above, if that witch gets herself killed again, Silje is going to personally go find her in the afterlife dimension and kill her again. Really, what does a familiar have to do around here to get some respect?

"You know, I have never met a witch's familiar, and I must say you are just the neatest little thing I've ever met."

The fairy is positively insufferable. If she touches her paws again, there is going to be hell to pay. Silje is a netherbeast. If anyone knows how to pay hell to mortals, she does.

"Lyra, do you really think this is a good idea?"

And then, there's the other one. The man who tried to shoot her witch. It's taking all of her self-respect not to scratch his eyes out.

"I know, Leon. I know you don't trust witches. I know you don't think that this is a bright idea, but we had no more options. Okay? What else do you want me to do?"

"All I'm saying, Lyra, is we don't know anything about these people. I mean, a technomancer and a witch. What kind of weird combination is that?"

There are plenty of creatures in this world who'd think a pirate and a merman to be an equally perplexing combination, thinks Silje in response. But who is she to judge? She's just a "cat."

"This isn't just any witch, Leon. This is the Songstress of Lorelei. That's a big deal."

"I'm supposed to be impressed just because she came back from the dead to be with her boyfriend?"

"Oh I wouldn't that say," the fairy titters. "Something tells me our dear lady witch came back from the dead for far more reasons than just to kiss that pretty face. Though you must admit, it is a very kissable face."

"That's beside the point."

The man kicks the TV in anger. The fairy seems unfazed. She just tilts her head slightly to the side as the image on the monitor skews in a slight rotation.

"You're right. She probably won't manage it. It's not like that woman brought the League to its knees twelve years ago. She had no allies, no resources, and no means to do it, yet still whole nations were put into upheaval because of her. Just imagine what she could accomplish with a few notable people on her side."

"We interrupt this program to bring you an urgent news bulletin."

Silje's ears twitch as the television's screen blinks to static one moment then to a bright blue news station floor then next. The letters "VBS" spin across the top while a scroller with various headlines floats across the bottom.

[MIA: Jamar Sahra | Devastating Storm to hit New Chernobyl: How will the Lycan Packs Manage? | Total Upheaval in Ebele: Is Zenza Nagi the Rightful Orisha? | Primarch Thames to release prototype of new anti-magic collar]

"An update on the status of the latest menace to the League."

The familiar jumps from the back of the couch and onto the top of the TV. It's one of those old fashioned... ones she used to find in the old world, boxy and impractical for the way the human+ manage their tech these days but perfect as a nesting post.

An image of her witch's face pops up on the screen. It isn't the most flattering photo. Silje's songstress is mid-spell call while a blast of light zings past her head, meaning her hair is floating around her head somewhat akin to a gorgon's snakes. The picture is inside of a box on the screen, and it looks like a nametag is supposed to be shown on the bottom, but the letters and numbers are all mixed up, upside-down, and backward.

The news anchor looks to where the image appears as a hologram on his desk.

"Lydia, can we fix the monitors, please?! The name is all scrambled."

Silje would love to know what is happening on the other side of the camera right now. The text is rearranged several times, to no avail. The letters just won't straighten out. When a name is stolen by a fairy, it stays stolen in all incarnations of the name including the written word. Eventually, the label settles on Songstress of Lorelei.

The anchor gives a terse "thank you" to whichever aide managed to fix the issue and turns back to address the camera.

"We have reason to believe that the resurrected Songstress of Lorelei is presently hiding in the Tai Tai with traitor Kaito Miyazaki. Primarch Thames is presently in negotiations to allow the safe passage of several technomancers for the purpose of locating W—"

The anchorman stops short to choke and cough.

"Water-Water!"

A harried-looking aide comes forward with a glass of water. The anchor drinks and clears his throat.

"Sorry about that interruption. Yes, Donarick Thames is working diligently to locate W—"

Another bout of coughs, and this one is especially violent. The same aide comes forward to pat the man on his back.

"I said, he is working to locate W—!!"

This time the convulsions lay him out on the anchor desk. He makes a slashing motion across his neck and then rolls his wrist with his finger pointing somewhere off screen. The screen flashes, much to Silje's chagrin, over to a clip of her witch from twelve years ago.

The Songstress of Lorelei stands bloodied and angry in an arena, Mångata at her feet. Her mechanical opponent lies dead on the ground. There is a riot of terror as Lacuna returns to her injured hand, its latest victim slumping over dead in the viewing pavilion.

Silje growls as the scene unfolds. They are leaving out the fact that the person the witch killed had just finished calling for her head in an unfair ruling despite her win in the arena. It was the moment when the witch realized she would have to fight her way out if she wanted to survive. But they allow the carnage to play out until the broadcast is once again replaced with a VBS station newsroom. A new anchor has replaced the previous.

"As you can see, it is imperative that all information regarding this person is given to the proper authorities. The Songstress of Lorelei is dangerous and not to be trusted. Even saying her name is dangerous."

What is this propaganda?! They can't defame her witch like this.

Silje shakes her tail out, jumps off the TV, and wanders over to the door.

"What is that animal doing?" asks the pirate.

"No idea."

A ripple of energy later, and the displacer beast disappears into the ether.

There is a legend in the Tai Tai concerning the underground. They say if one were to venture deep enough, they would walk straight into the circles of hell. It is a place of change, more mercurial than even the most hostile tides of Deus. It is a place of loss. Anyone who dares to venture below the surface does so at their own risk because they will lose something. Whether that be something as simple as their own shadow or as devastating as their soul.

Cassandra was one such venturer, and despite her powers of foresight, not even she could predict what she would lose beneath the too-still surface of the Tai Tai's waters.

The start of an old Hexen folktale,
Passed down through the generations by
storytellers unknown.

15

EIGHT OF SWORDS

15th Day in the Month of Falling - Somewhere beneath Calypso City

S HE'S DONE HER FAIR SHARE OF DIVING. IT was kind of a natural part of her life, considering she grew up in Deriva. Shoreline skiing, reef diving, pond diving, even deep-sea diving have been just a few of the standard dives she's undertaken in her life. She's sure she is forgetting a few other instances, but one thing is for certain. She ain't never been on a sewer dive. Okay, she has never been on a sewer dive.

"Did I ever mention how romantic I find underground dives through sewage?"

Kaito gives her a long look from across the channel.

"It's not a sewer, my love. It's an abandoned subway station, not a sewage line."

The witch rolls her eyes. So far, they've swum about 200 meters without event. The flooded tunnels are so winding it's hard to judge just how much progress they've made. Even more so, ascending and descending with the caverns as they go, she's lost all perception of what level of the underground they are on.

The glow of Kaito's holo-projection is the only light in the cavern they are presently sitting in. The witch is only glad the damned fairy had the good sense to loan them a set of wetsuits before sending them down here. Oh, Silje would be having a full-on fit were she to have followed the witch down through these tunnels.

"Standing water is still standing water regardless of whether it's in a sewage line or in the middle of the street. You and I both know we'll be in dire need of a sanitation dip after this."

"I'm sure we can make arrangements with a regenerator."

There's nothing suggestive in Kaito's words, not even a hint of salaciousness, yet her mind falls deeper into the gutter than her physical body is.

"Only if you can promise we have one together. You know I hate sitting in those oversized coffins."

Ah, Kaito, her oh so handsome technomancer Kaito, looks quite the picture with his hair in a tighter than normal topknot and stubble decorating his face. Guess that must be the consequence to becoming a vagabond overnight. The skin-tight suit doesn't hurt either. Normally, Kaito's garments hide his physique, well-maintained by rigorous training and hours in the field fighting and hunting down various menaces to society, but in their swim gear, she can make out every perfect ridge of every perfect muscle.

"Regenerators are not typically designed for two people."

"Oh, I'm sure we can make it work."

Kaito's eyes hold a smile within them, even if the man himself is too stoic to humor such flirting. Must have something to do with the fact that she has no actual way to insure they get an actual regeneration machine for their use any time soon. Confounded, sensible man.

"I'm sure between your stubborn nature and your natural talents, we can surely do so, but right now, we've an underground river to navigate."

"Not sure I'd call this a river." It's more like a cesspool, not that she says that aloud. The whole situation is already aggravating enough. "I find it hard to believe any mer-person would lower themselves so far as to go swimming in this. I don't care how golden-hearted they may be. Why would they degrade themselves like this?"

"This is where Leon said his husband disappeared."

"Perhaps our ex-pirate friend was terribly mistaken when he said Thale went diving in this place. What made him think this was where he should be looking for the missing fae?"

"I don't know," answers Kaito. "Lyra and Leon seemed fairly tightlipped about that."

"You'd think their mutual desire for our success would encourage them to give us as many details as they could manage."

"I can't explain it either. Come on, there should be another cavern where we can surface just beyond this rail tunnel. We seem to be running adjacent to the active tunnels."

"Hm, maybe we'll be lucky enough to find a working terminal and hitch a ride down deeper."

Kai raises his eyebrow at her. She just grins, gesturing to the pool and then delivering her trademark wink and finger twirl. "After you, my prince."

Kaito fixes his rebreather and dives, the songbird following close behind. Kaito may be a more than decent swimmer, but the witch is Derivan. While Kai keeps relatively close to the ceiling, the Derivan-born witch is more comfortable diving deep. It's less claustrophobic knowing she isn't going to bonk her head should she surface too early. It also serves the purpose of making her work harder which keeps her warmer in the long run—wetsuits only do so much against the chill.

The floor of the flood water is also quite the interesting little environment. (Yes, yes it doesn't make any sense for her to go spelunking about considering how abysmal she feels for the situation, but I mean, if you're going to go diving in the dunk—even if it is a putrid dunk—you might as well look around.) So far she's found abandoned shoes, some clothes hangers, and a lost suitcase. In this tunnel, even more interestingly, there's a whole subway car.

Kaito surfaces ahead of her, and she follows. The new cavern is a boarding platform. The waterline has risen about halfway up the platform. The old rail is obviously lifeless in the wake of disuse and flooding, but the witch isn't about to risk a run in with the ever-*peligroso* third rail even if it was designed to see underwater traffic.

There's a reason Deriva doesn't have a subterranean public transit system. Whatever nonsensical madness runs the Tai Tai can just stay right wherever the fuck it is, thank you very much. She might be crazy, but she's not crazy enough to run an electric system under a city built on a canal system.

As she wades out of the water, she notes that Kaito's earlier tampering with the fuse boxes farther back are starting to lose their juice. The bulbs here, while lit, are dull at best, and most of them flicker at inconsistent rates. They're obviously not long for this world.

Her prince is over on a center panel which appears to display an old map of the tunnels. A lavender grid of light, originating from Kaito's ocular augmentations, swishes this way and that over the images.

"Scanning waterlogged maps for historical accuracy?" she chirps, making her way over to him.

He chuckles as her hands come around his shoulders. "No, I am comparing these to the scans I got from Lyra. Something isn't lining up. According to the information I already have, we should have surfaced at docking platform 8C. This is platform 5A."

"Perhaps we took a wrong turn."

"That's what I would assume as well if we had actually made any turns anywhere."

Well, isn't this a conundrum? "Cave-in maybe?"

"Possibly, or someone altered the tunnels somehow. That's what I'm trying to figure out now. Do you know what I did with my comm unit?"

She looks at him, puzzled. "Don't you have one in your head?"

"Normally, yes, but ever since we woke up on the beach, I've restricted myself to my aux unit. I swear I just had it a moment ago."

"Are you telling me the great Kaito Miyazaki misplaces anything that doesn't readily attach to his own body?"

"No." He scowls at her. "I set it down to take my rebreather off, and now I can't find it."

She gives him a lopsided smile. Her great technomancer, known for his speed, cunning and skill, really is a darling, pathetic man sometimes. He starts looking around the immediate area. His sights spin slowly. She would imagine that he has some way to locate his own tech, but if he's trying to conserve energy, maybe manual searching really does work best, at least when magic is not your go-to skill set.

She whistles a series of four notes. It's probably a moot point. If her magic won't work in an effort to save her own skin from plummeting down an underground waterfall, what good will it do in finding a comm unit?

Surprisingly enough, the device levitates quite docilely out from behind an overturned trash bin and plants itself in Kaito's hand.

"Seriously..." She sighs, glaring up at the ceiling. "My magic works on that but not in a life-or-death situation. How stupid can your fairy magic be?!"

"Songbird," Kaito cautions.

"No, it makes no sense! Don't I need to be alive to fulfill my end of the bargain?"

"The fae work in mysterious ways." He sounds bemused if not equally annoyed with the whole situation. "You know that better than anyone."

She pouts, crossing her arms over her chest like a bratty teenager. "Remind me never to so much as look at a fairy again. I may just throw a pot of honey at them."

He shakes his head, turning back to the subway map. "In this instance, apparently my needing to finish analyzing the differences between my digital map and this decrepit one is more pertinent to our success."

She affixes her goggles back over her eyes. "Yeah, well, while you figure that out, I'm going back down to investigate something."

"Did you find something?" he asks, powering down the grid scanner. Now, his sights spin sluggishly over just his irises. She really doesn't like how slow his processors are running.

She shrugs. "There's a subway car down there. Its lights are still on, and I want to check it out. Perhaps Thale made a pit stop there."

Kaito looks at her with a hint of worry at his brow. "You found an abandoned subway car that's still working?"

"Not working per se, just lit up."

She's not sure what the difference might be there, but she won't know if it actually works until she gets her hands on the controls.

"Are you sure you're up for it? I've been trying to keep our excursions underwater to a minimum."

"Hey! I resent that. Am I Derivan or was I just born on an island?"

The man gives her a skeptical look. She isn't exactly at one hundred percent should anything happen while she is on her own. But this is just a quick dive. She'll be down and out before he can finish scanning his configurations again, and considering how fast that is in practice, that's pretty fast.

"Oh, come on. I'll be fine. Two minutes, then you can come drag me out yourself."

She only feels like a resurrected zombie now rather than death warmed over.

He gestures to Mångata, now tied to her belt. "I know you aren't exactly keen on using your old weapon..."

"Kai—"

"...but don't hesitate to use it."

She sighs. "Of course, your highness."

"*Ore no Kaiyo*, your teasing use of my title is more than a little taxing at the moment."

The witch winces. Right, considering he's probably on the League's shit list right now. Closing the distance between them, she winds her arms around his neck. Despite the damp, his body radiates with warmth.

"*Lo siento, mon rivage.* I was being insensitive."

The tension wilts from his shoulders, and he ducks his head down to press their foreheads together.

"No, it's alright. You weren't trying to be malicious."

"And don't you know it." She coos at him. His lips quirk up in a smile for just a second.

"I do," he says simply and captures her lips in his.

Yeah, this witch knows her own nature better than anyone, and the only person who might best Kaito on that list is Xipilli, but she doubts that to be the case after all the time that's passed. There has always been a darkness in her—a tendency for lying when it suits her, a tendency to cause trouble, an aversion to following rules. It's the kind of darkness that helps her tongue cut through a person. Cut to the quick, her stepmother once said. She's never been belligerent about it. Some people take it the wrong way; others deserve the tongue-lashing she gives them.

Kaito has seen her do this on multiple occasions: to Chike, to Jamar, to Xipilli. It was never without good cause. If you asked her, she'd tell you they very much deserved the ire they received.

Kaito pulls away too soon, thus ending the kiss.

"Don't take long."

"Sure thing."

She's not sure if she's imagining it or not, but it looks as though the man's face darkens in the glow of his holo. Her empathy tingles as a flash of worry, not her own, cascades over her psyche. His neural guards must be flickering on and off as well.

She has half a mind to address it with him, but in the face of being underground, it probably isn't the most pertinent thing ever. After all, who's going to take advantage of him? *The Songstress of Lorelei! Ha! That bitch ain't got nothing on me.*

She pecks him once more on the lip, relishes in the surprise that passes through him, and then turns back to the water.

It seems murkier under the surface than before, which is utterly ridiculous because she was literally just down here. Perhaps the pair of them stirred up some debris when they surfaced. The subway car is about a league from the terminal;

with the fins attached to her feet, it doesn't take too long to get down there. Mångata in hand, she activates the weapon. The double-bladed weapon activates, shedding a bluish-green aura in approximately a five-meter radius around her.

It's perfect for cutting through the murk, at least visually if not actually.

In Mångata's glow, she can better see how much the metal has corroded due to the salt water. This thing must have been sitting down here for at least twenty-five or thirty years. She'll need to ask Kaito when the station was abandoned. But something about that doesn't sit right with her. The glass of the front car's windshield is still intact, surprisingly enough. She would have expected it to have been destroyed or weathered away by the currents down here. Maybe some of the fish might have rammed into it enough to put a few cracks in it, but no. It's still perfectly pristine.

The door onto the train is locked shut. If Kaito were with her, she would have him shove it open with his human+ strength, but she can make do without.

She snaps her fingers and a spark of light flickers in front of her hands. The spell reaches for the door's central latch point but fizzles out just before it can do anything substantial.

Blasted fairy magic...

She moves Mångata in front of her, powering down one end. Taking it in both hands, she drives the aura-made blade into the seam at the top of the door. Mångata shears through the metal like a saw blade, heating and melting as it goes. She works the blade through the door bit by bit until she can pry the doors a part. It takes time. Time that she doesn't really have. Magic would have been faster. Magic is always faster.

The inside of the train is overgrown with various seaweeds and brine. There are left behind pieces of baggage that have fallen from the overhead compartments along with other human debris: a cane fallen lengthwise in the aisle, a few hats—one a top hat and another a baseball cap—a cosmetic mirror sits on one of the eaten-up seats, and an old handbag sits next to one of the handrails. When she picks it up, a weird-colored fish swims out of it. It lets out a slew of bubbles and swims away. Everything is covered in a fine layer of undersea sediment: dirt, sand, and the gunk leftover from when this place was a working station.

She stalls for just a moment when she sees the first skeleton. Whatever destroyed these tunnels did so while there were people still inside.

It's almost comical the way it's seated, upright and leaning slightly into the arm rest as though posed there by a prop shop tech. Even as she watches, a family of fish appear from inside the eye socket only to re-enter through the open jaw and then disappear into the ribcage.

"Dost thou sunken to the briny depth, care to shamble at my behest?" she sings. Her voice resonates inside her mask. The echo of her own voice makes her face gear vibrate. It kind of tickles. She's always loved singing underwater. Xipilli used to tease her for it. "It's not like anyone can hear you," he'd say, trying to make her stop. "Besides, you sound like a jellyfish farting."

Don't ask her to make sense of what a farting jellyfish sounds like. Prepubescent boys are the absolute worst, and Xipilli made a point to pull her pigtails as often as he very well could. Not that it ever worked. She would find delight wherever she found delight and bully for him if he thought her joy so annoying as to begrudge it. Such instances ended after her mother died. Looking back on it, she can imagine why he stopped teasing her. She only started singing more, both below the surface and above.

It's no wonder she became the Songstress of Lorelei. Even in the face of having everything taken from her, she never lost her voice.

But even now, the singing makes her feel like a mermaid. Mermaids don't actually sing underwater. Any sailor will tell you, beware the siren's call, for she has surfaced not for pleasure but for slaughter. "Silent stranger, hear my song, rise up once more. Let us surface again."

A simple touch to the skeleton's brow, and the former fish apartment complex jumps up, ready to shake, rattle, and roll on her command.

Nice to know her necromantic touch is working, at least in this instance. Who's to say it'll work later? For all she knows, the reanimated skeleton will simply drop dead in thirty minutes or so.

There are four more skeletons scattered across the floor. They are positioned in a way she would more readily expect, considering the situation. Clearly, the animals have been messing with these, and whatever killed them to begin with probably knocked them all flat.

The lights that attracted her attention to begin with are nowhere to be found. Were it not for the pulsing green glow of Mångata, this first car would be as dark as can be, so she moves on. The next three cars look much the same as the first: a few more skeletons, abandoned belongings, and some fish to keep her company. Her new skeletal companion marches silently behind her as she swims through the gaps. The fifth car, however, looks like a massacre took place within. Bones carpet the floor, picked clean, whether by the watery decay or by the local fauna.

Wait a minute. Something strikes her as more than a little peculiar.

"Hey, Kai?"

"Songbird," he responds over the radio static on their swim gear.

"Don't bones dissolve in saltwater?"

"Yes," he answers, sounding unsure. "Shouldn't you know better than I?"

"Yes, but I'm just remembering. Could you look up how long it takes for that to happen?"

"Up to a year, depending on the temperature and acidity of the water."

"How long ago did these tunnels get shut down?" Her frown rings through her question.

"According to Lyra and Leon, this particular line of track went out of commission roughly fifty years ago."

So, there shouldn't be any bodies down here, in other words. *Interesting...*

As she swims through the space between cars, her goggles fog up, and a wave of warmth passes over her legs.

What was that?

She swings around to peer into the darkness behind her. When nothing reveals itself, she continues along into the final car where the dull glowing light seems to originate.

The door to the car is hanging caddy-wonk in its frame. The witch isn't entirely sure how it managed to be struck diagonally within its sliding frame, but a slice through it with Mångata and it falls away from its home. It's not the greatest passageway, but she swims her way through the opening, her skeleton following a ways behind.

The last car is unlike anything she has seen thus far. It's like she's stepped into an underwater fairyland. The floor is littered with glowing pearls. The railing and seats have all been overcome by corals and seaweeds, none of the kind anyone would find in a city's flooded district. These are ocean corals beautiful enough to rival the reefs surrounding Cresta de Corail, luscious and vibrant with life. And if that wasn't already strange, there are pieces of still active tech floating just right in the middle of the space.

What is going on here? she thinks, thoroughly fascinated by the floating tech.

To see all of this tech not only free-floating in the water but active, to boot, is strange.

Mechanical devices, by nature of material density, have a tendency to sink. Even the smallest of artifacts will descend into the briny depths should they go overboard a ship, and only specialized technologies, like adept and technomancer augmentations, maintain all of their function upon contact with water.

Yes, people still have to pay extra if they want a comm unit that is waterproof, and if they wanted augmentations that will still work while damp, they'll be looking to pay at least 20% more for specialized coating. There are exceptions to this, of course. Military personnel and high-ranking officials have a tendency to get waterproof augmentations by default, but she has known several lower-class cyborgs who have to remove bits and pieces of themselves just to take a shower.

The witch never could quite understand why people felt the need to choke as much money out of others as possible. Water and bathing are a basic human necessity, yet the butchers charge extra just to make it so someone can go swimming without having to remove a limb or two. But, then again, money has never really cared much for human comfort. Why sell a thing for a reasonable price when you can sell it for twice that? It's the most basic law of finances.

She takes the nearest piece of tech in hand and checks it over.

It's not every day you see someone chucking a computer into a canal, and if the sight before her is to be believed, she can infer that several someones, whether they are with or without tech, seem to have gone ahead and thrown a number of mechanical devices into this very sewer track.

It's a diver's pro cam—the kind of camera you affix to your head or suit to record your adventures with. It works perfectly underwater. And this one, despite being down here for however long, is in perfect working condition, like time and salt water have barely even touched the thing. She clicks through the buttons until the screen lights up with a vaguely familiar tunnel frozen on its screen.

"Let's see what you've got on you?"

Static crackles over the comm.

"Songbird, have you resurfaced yet?"

The witch reaches for the comm unit at her side to respond but stalls as the video starts to play.

Never give your name to a fairy, for once something is lost, it may never be found.

Never give your name to a fairy, for while the fae will always remember, we mortals are prone to forgetfulness.

Taken from *Book of Wings and Dust*
By Mothram Gryme, 24 A.P.

16
THE TWO OF SWORDS

As Kaito is about to finish off his analysis of the tram station map, a buzzing sound comes from his comm unit. After checking the ID, he answers, "Miyazaki."

"Kaito, what the hell are you doing?"

It's Tomi.

"Tomi, I really don't have time for this right now."

Tomi blows a raspberry on the opposite side of the call.

"Are you nuts? The entire league is looking for you. And not in a good way. I'm over here surfing through propaganda about how W—, I mean Walpurgis—, I mean Wom—! Oh! Forget it! Propaganda about how a certain somebody has returned from the dead and is now seeking to overthrow the Primarch, and apparently, you're her pet technomancer enslaved to do her bidding because of some kind of enchantment she's placed on you, but I know it's not an enchantment because, first of all, the Songstress of Lorelei doesn't typically perform that kind of magic, and secondly, you were looking for some chick named Atalia last we spoke, so please, if you don't mind explaining it all to me: What the hell is going on?!"

"Yes, Tomi. She is back. I couldn't tell you this earlier for her protection. I have known since before I came to see you."

"And you didn't tell me that your ex-girlfriend was back from the dead! (Or maybe I should say current girlfriend?) Gods man, you mean you had me looking up a dead person? How is that even possible? Wait... She's not a zombie, is she 'cause, I mean, ick?"

"No, Tomi. The songstress is not a zombie. She's as whole a person as you or I. As to how it's possible... all that matters to me is she's back."

There's a sound like Tomi falling against his chair.

"I knew something was different about you when you came to see me. So that's it then. Your one true love is back from the grave, and now you've gone AWOL."

"I have not gone AWOL."

"From where the rest of the League is standing, it sure looks like it."

"I am working to clear her name. There are many charges against her which I believe to be the fault of someone else."

"And to do that you needed to make yourself a criminal as well? Yeah, I suppose that makes sense." The sarcasm in the other adept's voice is not lost on Kaito, so he remains quiet, working steadily on his previous task until the other shoe drops, which it does in just a few short moments. "Kaito! You know if I wasn't into all of this illegal stuff, I would not be talking to you right now."

"I guess it's lucky for me that you have a tendency to specialize in the less than legal."

"Okay, fair. So your message said you were in the Tai Tai, but that doesn't explain why your signal is so messed up. Where are you exactly?"

Kaito looks around at the ceiling, at the decay clinging to its edges, at the water clogging what was once a brilliant subway system.

"I am presently underground. It would appear that many fae creatures have been going missing in this area. As to the reason no one is capable of using the songbird's name, one of the high fae in Calypso City was clever enough to get a hold of the witch's name. As such, we are trying to get to the bottom of the situation so that she might have her name back."

Tommy laughs. "Well that explains how the news programs all of the sudden seemed to forget the name of the world's most wanted hexen. Why am I not surprised that your girlfriend would be so special? Only that the most beloved of your royal highnesses could possibly manage such a feat. Where did you even encounter a fairy? I mean, I guess it could happen to any of us. They aren't exactly uncommon. They just prefer green places to skyscrapers."

"Well this one lives quite contentedly among all manner of augmented quite easily."

A clip-clopping sound to the side draws Kaito's attention.

"Hold on, Tomi. *Ore no Kaiyo*, is that you?"

Over the comm, Tomi says, "Everything okay?"

"I'll have to call you back. It's not exactly safe where I am right now."

"Got it. Alright, boss. You let me know when you're ready to chat. I want to know the whole story. Genesis begone, if that isn't the love story of the century. Fair maiden, dead in a moment, her prince spends twelve years mourning her loss. Won't even consider a simple, noncommittal date. Next thing you know, she's back, good as new and witchy as ever. Now my boy's getting some action—"

"Tomi," growls Kaito.

"I'm sorry. You're right. You're right. I'm sorry. You probably haven't gotten any action yet because I know who you are."

"Tomi," the second warning call sparks over the connection.

"Ah! Yes, anyway, TTYL. Tomi, out."

Kaito rolls his eyes to the ceiling as the call disconnects. He doesn't even bother to set his comm unit back in his pocket, simply setting it down atop the nearest broken-down bench edge.

A chattering sound comes from somewhere near where the ticket or reception used to be. He can't see anything from where he's standing, but the lights dim and die not far from that part of the room, obscuring his human vision.

Unfortunately, when he turns his sights on, they flicker, not even close to maximum capacity. His night vision is blotchy and unclear, as though trying to see through water. Maybe it's because he's in the Tai Tai and not actually connected to the network, but this is getting kind of ridiculous. What use is a technomancer who can only perform at 50% capacity? Is he even at 50%? With AYA offline, he can't even run a proper diagnostics, not without stopping everything he is doing and falling into a dedicated unconscious state specifically for repairing and renovating his internal systems.

He speaks into his diving headset to his lover. Maybe she came up a while ago and is messing around over where he is hearing these noises.

"Songbird, have you resurfaced yet?"

No answer. Just static. Odd...

The area near the reception booths is flooded with water. It's far enough down toward the railing that the water has seeped up into the reception. Another splash echoes through the vast open chamber.

He draws his katana. No Technomancer would be foolish enough to ask, "Is anyone there?" when clearly there's something trying to hide itself from the human+. So, Kaito merely sidesteps away from the map and makes his way around the reception desk. There's a panel of glass that probably used to be much nicer that is now covered in plant life of some sort.

He reaches up to pull the plants out of the way, suddenly reminded of Mishka, a witch who would still be alive were it not for the machinations of a certain Primarch and his sociopathic witch wife. As he moves the plant away, a rat scurries past his feet.

Well, that would explain the noise. With a deep sigh, Kaito resheathes his sword.

It's tricky being on a case like this because he knows he is in an area where there is danger lurking about somewhere, but he hasn't any clue what sort of danger their foe actually is. All he knows of is disappearing fae folk.

It's not his favorite kind of case. He would much rather know exactly what he's about to play against. Could be magic, could be a monster, could be a hair dryer someone left plugged into the bathroom wall. It could be that all of the missing fairies simply came down here, slipped and hurt themselves, and never made it back out.

Hard to say.

He holds his comm to his mouth and presses the call button, but immediately forgets who he is trying to speak to. His partner, surely, but what was his partner doing that he needed to check on? He can't remember. Like the thought came and went as quickly as a bolt of lightning. Meanwhile, here he is needlessly paranoid that rats are going to race out at him and gnaw on his boots. With the mysterious noise dealt with, he should finish doublechecking that map again. As he's about to turn around, a pair of slim appendages clench tight around his waist, clawed fingertips digging into his abdomen.

His heart stops... until he notices the sharp nails do not penetrate his skin. It takes him all of a half second to realize exactly what is happening. It's a half second too long, but his heart resumes its beats. He keeps himself from having any sort of reaction whatsoever because he knows that presently the "monster" that has him right now is little more than his favorite witch playing a prank on him.

"*Ore no Kaiyo*, is now really the time for pranks?"

He can feel the witch smile into his back.

"Anytime is a good time for pranks, especially when a certain somebody is being way too serious about the situation at hand."

"You didn't respond to my call."

"I heard it. I just wasn't in a place to respond."

Kaito's brow furrows as he turns in his captor's arms to face her.

"How were you not in a place to respond?"

"I—"

SPLASH!

Behind the witch, a skeleton ambles crookedly out of the water. Kaito's saibaki crackles as he steps forward to destroy the fiend, but...

"Wait. The skeleton is mine."

Whose?

He turns around to see his lover smiling at him with glittering, playful eyes. Of course. How did he forget she was there after just a second of looking away from her?

"There were human remains down there?"

"Yup. I don't understand it either. When did you say this place was abandoned?"

"Leon said at least forty years ago."

Her brow furrows. "Then how is there any remote possibility of there still being bones down there? They should have been completely corroded away."

CRASH!

The witch turns with an exasperated eye roll to her skeleton, who has just scattered itself all over the floor after running into the subway schedule display.

"Enchanted skeletons. They have eye sockets but no eyeballs, so they run into everything. Great for when you give them direction, but when they don't know what to do with themselves, they can be literally all over the place. Anyway, I found this while I was down there."

The songstress produces what looks like a GoPro.

"This looks relatively new."

"So did everything else down there. A whole slew of tech just floating inside of the submarine car. I happened to pick up this one and amazingly enough, the video on it is still intact."

Kai presses play on the camera. The screen turns on to someone swimming through the canals much the same way Kaito and his companion did not too long ago, except this person seems to be moving much faster. Much faster even than most human+.

"This person isn't human."

"No tech. I noticed that too."

"You don't think it's Thale?"

"Who knows? It could be a mermaid; it could be a tide walker. Those are humanoid hands holding the cam. But look, it gets better."

The cam zooms in and out along the passage walls, pointing out details that neither of them took note of during their own foray along the tunnels. There are paintings lining the walls. Strange sigils that even Kaito, in all of his research of hexen sigils and wiccan hexcraft, doesn't recognize.

"Are those witch wards?"

"Not that I have ever seen. Though they look more like alchemical symbols to me. Only someone has morphed them with medical jargon."

"What do you mean?"

"They are made from numbers. Look."

The witch pauses the video and blows up the frame onto a skull-like symbol. It looks to be composed of the alchemical symbols for earth and fire, only they are encircled by a sun symbol. Dancing amid all those known symbols are numbers. Interestingly enough, even as the footage is paused, the symbol glows, the numbers shimmering beneath the footage.

"Do you see that? It's like it's super-imprinted onto the digital with a life of its own."

Saibaki surges through his body as his sights activate. Sure enough, the numbers are changing. He sets his scanners to analyze for any kind of pattern and turns to W— after.

"Keep going. I want to see something."

"There's plenty more."

The video resumes, revealing more of the same until the person reaches the train the witch went to investigate only moments ago. A shadow passes over the screen. The video stalls out, goes to black, then returns to the perspective of the interior of the train cars. There are skeletons there scattered across the floor. He recognizes his necromancer's new crew member sitting on the edge of the seat. The video carries through several of the cars.

"This here," points out the witch. "This is completely different from what I found when I went to investigate. The last car was completely obstructed by a downed door. I had to cut my way through. This person just passes straight through without issue."

"Do you think something caused the rupture?"

"Watch."

He does.

A flood of bubbles rises up before the camera lens. The flash of a red-tipped fin graces the frame as the person reels back in surprise. The train's casing rattles, as though something large just impacted with the transport.

A high-pitched singing resonates from the footage.

A large black tentacle-looking thing swings out of the darkness, knocking the camera from the recorder's hands. The device spins through the water, bubbles and hair and scales clouding the image. The singing reaches a fervor as gemstones trail to the ground, glowing a rainbow of colors. Their glow grows and grows until the dark creature swims off, taking the person with him. Then, after moments of nothing, the screen goes black.

"It was a mermaid."

"Merman. I think it was Thale."

"Leon said nothing about him having a camera."

"No, but he must have brought it down just in case he ran into something unsavory. Turns out, he did."

But where is the merman now? That's the question.

"It's been two days since his disappearance," says Kaito. "If he was attacked by something down here, surely it would have moved on by now."

"Not necessarily. It could be bound to this place."

"Then why haven't we seen it yet?"

"It's amazing how easily underwater creatures find hiding spots. For all we know, it's simply lying in wait for the opportune time to attack us," the songstress says. She has a valid point, but he still doubts that a beast that size would be able to keep a low profile all this time. Unless maybe it was functioning under duress. "What do you think the chances are he's still alive?"

"Not sure. There's no way to know whether he survived the encounter, but if he did make it out of the creature's grasp alive, what is preventing him from returning home?"

"I can think of a few things."

He looks at her curiously. The witch has that devious look in her eye like she is putting herself in the enemies' shoes for a chance to see through their eyes. The witch's name forms in his mouth, turns to ash, and tangles his tongue.

"Songbird?"

"I was just thinking about something that used to happen in Deriva before the fae were chased out of the surrounding oceans. It wasn't uncommon for mermaids to be captured in Deriva by tear harvesters. The tearers would torture the poor creatures for their pearl-like tears and sell them on the black market. It was a horrible practice. Papa always hated it."

"You think someone is harvesting tears."

"No... Maybe... I don't know. More than a few fae have gone missing in the last few months, right?"

"That is what we were told, yes."

"Well what if they were using them for their magic? Can you think of any other purposes one might have for fairy magic?"

Kaito frowns. "You don't mean..."

She nods, and Kaito curses.

As with any civilization, there are times in history that are less than shining examples of what the civilization is capable of, and the human+ of Deus are no exception. Before technomancers discovered methods for unlocking their abilities from within, before the trials determined which human+ were even capable of being technomancers and adepts, the warriors of the past used to hunt fae. Not for sport or games or even to establish the safety of their realms... No, they hunted them for their magic.

It's a complex process, harvesting magic from the fairy folk, but when dealing with witches, and with no other alternative, non-magical humans would steal magic—fairy dust for powering weapons, mermaid scales and tears for armor. They found that if they cut the tail off a huldra and stripped its back of bark, they could hold dominion over the nearby plants of the forest. If they took the fangs off a red cap, they could use them to counter vampyre syndrome.

Whoever has Thale, whoever has been kidnapping fae folk, if they're a medical practitioner, there is a good chance they have decided to revitalize these barbaric practices.

Kaito routes a pathway forward after sending a message to the surface for Leon and Lyra. He also has the foresight to send them a link to his comm unit in the event the pair decide to intervene. He doubts they will. Why would a high fae dirty their wings when they have their own personal witch to do their bidding?

The next dive takes them a few hundred meters further into the caverns. Unfortunately, however, there is no surface-able area where Kaito was expecting another alcove. Yay for cavern collapses. No wonder the city decided to abandon this part of the subaquatic transport system.

So they press on, his lover just ahead of him as they navigate the tunnels.

It's amazing really. Twelve years of more life experience in his favor, and still she out paces him as a swimmer. It's not so much a testament to any lack of ability on his part. Contrarily, it's an indicator of how vital swimming is to the lifestyle of the islanders of Deriva. She is simply that much stronger of a swimmer, and incredibly, without the hindrance of tech, she is even more suited for traversing currents below the surface.

The songstress twists and weaves through the water as well as any fish he might have seen in the ocean, so when they come to another collapse which forces them to go steadily one at a time into a tight squeeze, Kaito has no concern anything could possibly hurt her.

He however...

"Are you going to be able to fit?"

They are treading water at the top of the tunnel, a narrow space for them to discuss their plan by which to progress farther. Kaito, whose shoulders are much broader than his companion's, will barely be able to fit through the mouth of the caverns, and who's to know what will happen if it continues to narrow as they go. There is a very real likelihood that he will become unable to go back, and should a cave-in occur, he'll be up a creek without a paddle.

"I'm not sure. Not with my swords for sure, and if it narrows at all, it's a moot point to even try."

"And leaving behind Tsukuyomi and Amatsu is really not an option." How strange it is to hear the names of his weapons fall from the lips of a nameless woman. "Any idea how far this goes before it opens up again?"

He is already comparing their vision field to the tunnel maps he found earlier.

"I'd say we're looking at a minimum of thirty meters," he says. "But there's no telling if what I am looking at is up-to-date. With cave-ins and new flood zones, it could be much farther."

Lyra didn't have any Derivan-grade rebreathers. Why should she? They were special-issue to the islands with a near infinite ability to cycle the carbon dioxide out of a puff of air and convert it back into oxygen. Such equipment is incredibly specialized, not to mention very illegal to smuggle out should someone decide to export one without the proper credentials, and what need does a winged fairy have to go underwater? None. It would in fact be a great detriment to any ability she has to fly. As such, all she had in her possession were counterfeit mouthpieces that could be used to recycle a person's air for a limited amount of time before the filter needed a fresh sweep of atmosphere.

By Kaito's estimate, that time limit is about thirty minutes. Not nearly long enough for him to reasonably risk becoming trapped in a narrow crevice.

"So we turn back and find another route. Wasn't there another fork a few leagues back?"

The witch has a valid point, but the prospect of putting them even further behind schedule doesn't sit well with him, especially considering the video she found.

"No. I'll circle back myself and meet you on the other side. You should go through. We don't have time to waste."

"But what if—"

"It's fine, W—." His tongue tangles in his mouth. The frustration surges through him. He can't say his own lover's name as though it were some sort of sour note played at the end of a symphony, an unspeakable flaw in the score, an accidental written in by a cruel-intentioned composer. Worse, the music has been so tarnished by foreign hands, he can't even remember or give a guess to what the correct note might be. It's just an unintelligible mass of sound expelled by a crooked brass instrument when it should be a lilting cadenza played by a violin or higher pitched woodwind.

The notes, the letters, are right there at the edge of his understanding, but the more he grasps for them, they more they fall out of his reach, like sand falling through his fingers, and as a result, another piece of his lover seems to get lost in the abyss of a magic-made oblivion.

"It's fine, dear. I'll meet you on the other side. It shouldn't take me more than twenty minutes to backtrack around."

"I don't like the idea of splitting up."

"This coming from the woman who used to insist on doing things solo."

She flinches. A feeling of wrongness settles in his gut. *Is that right? Has she really always been so fiercely independent?*

"And I've seen just how badly things can turn out because of it, haven't I?"

What is she talking about? The fog encroaches further on his psyche. He can't think of a time when her independence ever hurt a mission.

"You've got Mångata, and while your magic is on the fritz, you should still be able to defend yourself. Your skeleton friend is seemingly prepared to protect you."

"But who's going to protect you should something go wrong?"

He can't help but chuckle. "My dear witch, I'm a technomancer. I don't need protecting."

"Sure," she drawls.

"Go on. I'll see you on the other side."

The witch gives him a long, worried look but ducks into the water to disappear through the maw of the cavern. She'll probably surface on the other side in some ten to fifteen minutes. He turns in the water and dives in the opposite direction.

As he swims his way down the tunnels, the mist gets thicker and thicker until he doesn't quite know why he is swimming through these hell-begotten tunnels to begin with. There are strange shadows shifting about the caverns. Odd bubbles crop up here and there, but he ignores them. Should anything wish to attack him, they are welcome to do so. He has his blades and his mind. He will defeat it.

But does he have his heart? Why is he even here in the first place?

Eventually, the face of the woman he has loved for most of his lifetime blurs and fades into the haze as though she never even existed. As though no one ever knocked him into the pond at Shinka, no one ever taught him how to see the veils between worlds, and no one left him a reason to live that was far more important than his own life.

Renki...

The name crosses through his head unbidden, but he can't fathom why. He doesn't know anyone by that name.

Wren...

Why is he thinking of birds? There aren't any wrens in Tokiseishu. There aren't even any around Shinka Temple, so why is he imagining the little brown things? He hasn't seen a songbird in so long.

Then, even the little bird just disappears from his thoughts into the haze. All he is left with is the gloomy expanse of water and rock and cement. He has no recollection of why he is here, traversing the underground. He doesn't even realize, in his confusion, that the shadows moving along the channel are not nearly so stationary as he first believed.

When the shadows attack, he never sees them coming.

There isn't a whole lot to say about what happens when a fairy steals a person's name. We can speculate all we want, but there's no way to know. Once a name is taken, it is lost to all, not only in speech and memory, but also on paper, and maybe even in recorded footage.

How many people, do you think, have been forgotten from history because a fairy stole their memory from us?

There is much debate though on how these people are forgotten. Some say that bonds of blood and love are stronger than the fae's curse; others, however, will tell you it is your closest friends and family who will forget about you first.

Excerpt from *Of Fae and Fury:*
The untold histories of the unseen
Written by [Redacted/Unknown/Lost]

17

THE THREE OF WANDS

15th Day in the Month of Falling - 3:52PM - Wakeville

THE MORE TIME RENKI SPENDS WITH ORSON on this mission, the more annoyed he becomes, and it's terribly out of character. Even Akari is starting to notice how unnecessarily foul his mood is rapidly becoming.

"*Pst!*" Akari elbows him in the hip. "What is with you? I feel like I'm about to be attacked, and it's because you are giving off the worst vibes I've ever felt in my life."

The boy wilts. "Sorry. I don't mean to be uptight but..."

Through the wall comes the hum of the current talk show discussion.

"Kennedy," says some uptight sounding show host, "I don't mean to interrupt you, but you have got to take into consideration that all of this was happening right under the Primarch's nose. How can we trust that he'll do what needs to be done when there was a witch literally in his own bed?"

"Well, that's the thing, Barb," an answering voice starts. "These witches can be anybody. They could be your neighbor, your grocer, your dog walker. Hell, even your own wife might be a witch, and you would never know it. Even the Primarch, the technomancer leader of this continent, was fooled by a witch. That isn't a reflection on him. It's a testament to how dangerous those witches are. Listen, you're young; you don't remember the days before the Songstress of Lorelei. Witches used to run this world, and the things they would do to people... Gods above. We can't go back to that. And this is only the latest in a long history of terror the hexen community has committed against humanity."

Orson's communications unit drones on and on and on. It's unceasing the way he seems to keep a constant stream of information coming his direction. News reports, weather updates, and even the occasional political celebrity speaker going off about how the League is washed up. Every talk show is talking about how Summer Helsdottir somehow snuck her way into the seat of Orisha. People are theorizing that the Songstress of Lorelei put her in position to do so herself, but then that makes no sense because it would have been the songstress's own niece and sister who most suffered from that upheaval.

"I just don't understand how these programs keep talking about Wren like she is some boogeyman."

Akari's eyebrows screw tight together. "You're getting annoyed by his constant radio, aren't you?"

"Aren't you? He hasn't turned it off once since we got to the hotel. I wouldn't be so bad if I couldn't hear it from the other room."

"Hey, count your blessings that he didn't insist we share a room with him. You know Miyazaki-sensei always speaks about frugality and all that." Her smile, pretty as it is normally, is forced. She's trying hard to cheer him up. He wants to cheer up. Really he does, but it's like a dark cloud is sapping away all of the positive emotions in him, so he looks away, downcast, hoping that his mood won't spread to her like the virus such things can be. The girl sighs. "Well, he's a technomancer, Renki. He has to know what's going on with the world around him, you know."

"Yeah, I know, but why doesn't he just read everything in his sights like—" He cuts himself off. He doesn't want to think about

Kaito right now. His oto-san has all but abandoned him. "I'm tired of hearing everyone bashing Ms. Nocturne."

"Bashing who?"

Renki looks at her with a puzzled look. Akari merely looks back, confusion spread across her face.

"You know! Lady Nocturne. The person who saved your life in Chairomura. She kept us from getting in trouble and nearly bit all of our heads off for running away from home without telling anybody."

Her confusion deepens. "Lady N—" Akari starts to cough as she tries to say the witch's name.

"It's Wren, Akari. Wren Nocturne. The Songstress of Lorelei. The witch our mentor is, apparently, willing to give up everything for, but I haven't the slightest idea why he would do such a thing, and he won't tell."

"Who's W—?!" She coughs again. "Why can't I repeat the name? I keep hearing you say it. Why can't I repeat it?"

"What do you mean you can't say it? Wren Nocturne. It's her name. It's always been her name. You've said it before."

"What are you two talking about?"

The pair look up to see Orson has returned from investigating the lycan's body. There was a whole ordeal to call the local mortician to have the body autopsied, but there's no way around it. For whatever reason, Orson had felt the need to put a bullet in the creature's head before calling the coroner. Seems unnecessary to Renki. There was no way he would have gotten back up anytime soon. The beast was already as dead as can be thanks to the missing boy.

"Nothing."

"No idea. Sorry, sensei. Renki was just talking about some witch."

"Some witch? Will you stop acting like you don't remember her name? She saved your life, remember?"

Akari looks at him like he's grown a second head. "What are you talking about, Renki? Kaito-sama saved my life."

"No, he didn't. He only showed up after and released us from the binding Wren tied us up in. He then threw you on the train to Sekhmeti so you could learn a thing or two about leaving home without permission."

Akari's mouth opens to argue back, but Orson interrupts. "That's enough, you two."

"But sensei—"

"The search continues for the rogue witch who has taken our Prince Kaito Miyazaki hostage," Orson's broadcast continues as though to emphasize the current fight taking place between the two underage adepts. "Miraculously, though, no one seems to remember seeing her in recent memory. Are we even certain this person is real? Did the Miyazaki prince simply defect after suffering years of incompetence from our Primarch?"

"What! How can they say they haven't seen her in recent memory? Akari, you saw her yourself in Sekhmeti."

"Saw who, Renki?"

He is about to rip his own hair out with how clueless Akari is acting, but Orson intercedes again. "What Renki is referencing has more to do with witchcraft than either one of you might understand. It is not unheard of for a witch to cast a memory charm in order to avoid detection. The witch the headlines continue to reference must have done such a spell."

"Lady Nocturne doesn't do that kind of magic."

"Who?" asks the technomancer.

"Oh! Forget it!"

Renki pivots on his heel and storms off, ignoring Akari's cries of shock and Orson's orders to stop. Let them come after him. If Orson wants to report his bad behavior, let him. He's not about to sit still while the rest of the world goes insane.

"How can they not know? She's only the most famous witch to have lived this century. They've got to be pulling my leg."

Renki marches through the crowds with his shoulders squared in anger, his booted feet stomping gracelessly across the pavement. An aura of rage and hurt surrounds him, and the townsfolk have enough sense to give the young adept a wide berth. More than a few children have felt the need to follow along beside him, mimicking his angry steps like a miniature posse.

"I don't get it. First, oto-san won't tell me anything. Then, Akari refuses to tell me anything she saw at the Shard. Now, the whole world miraculously forgets that Wren Nocturne is even a person."

He wonders if somehow he stepped into a fairy ring at some point, coming out on the opposite side to a mirror world where up is down, down is sideways, pigs fly and fish speak. *That must be it, right? It's in a parallel universe.* That must be the only explanation for the fact that his father, his steadfast, dedicated, ever-there oto-san has all but abandoned him for a total stranger, and he refuses to say anything whatsoever to Renki about why he is doing the things he is doing.

Renki angles himself off the main thoroughfare and pulls out his comm as he leans against a sizable statue of a Chinese dragon. He types out:

[To Tousan: Have you even looked at my messages? Are you ever going to answer me? Who is Wr—?!!]

As he types out the message, his comm unit keeps erasing and rewriting the name for some reason. He wrestles with it, typing—it replaces the words with a "world"—and erasing, typing—this time it replaces the text with the worry emoji—and erasing, typing—"wire," "whole," "wrong," "wring," "write!"—and erasing, cursing the autocorrect with each and every mishap. No matter how many times he tries to write the name, the comm refuses to let it go through.

"What is wrong with this piece of sh—"

"Look out!"

Renki looks up to see a mechanical robot, scorpion-like but with a strange human-ness about it, come flying directly for his face. The device splays its "fingers," and before he can react, it latches onto his face; the robotic facehugger hits him so hard he tumbles backward and lands flat on his back.

The sky comes into view, spinning and twisting, as the little prosthetic jumps off his face to sit on his chest. *Great...* That's exactly what he needed: a concussion.

"Bad, Raffi!" an approaching voice shouts. "Bad! You weren't supposed to attack the first adept you found. I told you we were looking for Wren Nocturne."

At the sound of her name, Renki perks up. He blinks and rolls onto his side. As his vision clears, he can now see that the thing he thought to be a scorpion is actually a mechanical hand that's been augmented to look like a scorpion. It rolls off to stand on its fingertips on the ground, its added "stinger" held aloft. He groans. Renki's nose feels like it is about three sizes too big, and his sinus cavities feel like they've been mashed into discs.

A pair of human hands pick up the mechanical one, chiding the automaton in a language that Renki vaguely recognizes as Derivan.

"Sorry about that. I'm still trying to get a handle on how this stupid machine works. I knew I should have convinced uncle to let me augment an actual animal companion rather than deal with someone else's—You!"

Renki peers up to see a girl, no more than a year younger than him, standing over him. She has on Derivan working leathers and her hair is pulled into a turban. "Ugh! Why is it always you?"

"Me?" asks Zenza, affronted. "Why is it always you!?"

The boy pulls himself up, dusting the grass and dirt off his robes. "You know," he says remembering that the last time she ran into him, it was with her steam cycle into his light cycle, "it wouldn't be so bad if you would at least do me the favor of announcing yourself before something under your operation crashed into me."

"I don't know why it zeroed in on you. It was supposed to be looking for the Songstress of Lorelei. I'll have you know I'm here in an official capacity. My uncle has me heading up a murder investigation."

Renki looks at the girl like she's grown a second head.

"Your uncle, the Vulcan of Deriva, has sent you, a fourteen-year-old adept, on a murder investigation."

"Yes."

"You expect me to believe that."

Zenza shuffles from one foot to the other.

"Well, yeah."

"I don't believe that."

"But it's true!"

Renki stares at her.

"Okay, it's not true. Damn it. I stole the mission brief because they mentioned my aunt Wren."

"You can say her name?"

"Don't look at me like that. Of course, I can say her name. She's my aunt. Stop looking at me like that."

Zenza hits him.

"Now what are you doing here? I, at least, have a mission dossier. What's your excu—?"

"Oh, you again."

Before Renki can answer Zenza's question, they are interrupted by the fire breathing boy from before. He has just walked up to them.

"Who are you?" asks Zenza.

The boy smiles. He has three dimples, two on one side of his mouth and a third on the top side of the other.

"My name is Gideon, and sorry for eavesdropping, but I think I can help you both with this murder investigation you're on."

Renka and Zenza trade glances.

"What do you know about it?"

Gideon's smile stretches across his face. "Know anything about the fae in this area?"

18
THE CAT (PART 2)

Downtown Calypso City - Silje

A CAR BUZZES OVERHEAD, NEARLY SHAVING off the tips of her ears. Almost immediately, a carriage driven by a robotic horse clip clops past her tail. And if that isn't bad enough a semi truck's horn blasts her in the face as she jumps up, fur sticking out in all directions like a porcupine rather than a cat, and does a back flip to avoid being flattened underneath at least 40 tons of steel and oil.

Silje hates cities. There will never be a more appropriate word for how she feels about metropolitan areas than "hate." She hates the smells. She hates the people. She hates the machinery. Most of all, she hates the lack of personal space.

She's been on the surface for a mere five minutes, and already she has brushed shoulders with at least six alley cats, woven herself between countless human/non-human feet, and been swept up by no less than three street-cleaning bots. The organics at least know enough not to try and hurt her on purpose. It's the inorganics that run the risk of grinding her in particles.

Why doesn't she just travel through the ozone?

Displacement, despite popular belief, requires a certain amount of area for success. It doesn't work if someone interrupts her, unless she wants to take a bystander along with her through the veil. Not sure that's a very wise decision, so naturally, she avoids such occurrences. It also doesn't work if the place she is trying to get to just so happens to be warded against netherbeasts, as most inner-city headquarters are.

The news station is a multi-story building. Not quite a skyscraper, but definitely bigger than your average apartment complex.

Presently, she sits across the street from it, having avoided becoming roadkill, and watches as the humanoids come and go at an increasing rate the later into the day it becomes. Her witch has been underground for nearing five hours. By now, her witch should have discovered at least some inkling of what has occurred with the merman, but who's to say what her witch has been up to? Honestly, she wouldn't be surprised to find out her witch and her witch's chosen mate decided to waste time by "blowing bubbles" at one another. Truly, she wishes her witch nothing but happiness, and if a stuffy half-metal man makes her happy, then by all means, she should have at him all she wants.

It's just the other thing that grates on her nerves. The other aura hovering at the edge of her awareness. It fades in and out like a flickering lightbulb.

But she can't deal with that right now. She has bigger mice to catch, if she can just sneak her way into that newsroom.

Opportunity presents itself as a lycan pushes a cart full of boxes toward the front entrance. Perfect.

The netherbeast dashes forward, risking tail and hide to get to the far side of the road despite the traffic zooming back and forth. The delivery lycan is checking in with the security guard as Silje pops open one of the boxes and dives inside, making herself impossibly smaller in the process. If anyone were to open her hiding spot, they would find a black, thumb-sized nugget of a kitten rather than a tiger-sized displacer beast.

Purr-fect for subterfuge.

Her box comes to a stop after several right turns and an elevator ride that managed to make her ears pop. Someone picks up her box and slides her onto what she assumes would be a desk or a shelf at around human eye-level.

"Is this everything?"

"Yeah, transcripts from the League's most recent broadcasts. Vaishi wants us to mimic them as closely as we can."

"Since when does the Tai Tai deliver League news?"

"Since the Primarch himself is presenting us with the choice that only a fool would fuck up: getting paid hundreds of credits or prepare for every technomancer on his roster to invade just to find one witch that nobody here really gives a fuck about."

"The hexen won't like it though. They are already up in arms over the legislation the +ies keep passing against them around here. The 'don't say magic' bill died on the house floor after a vamp took out the governor, but that isn't stopping them from proposing an ID band for all the hexen in the city. Allegedly, if one of them's caught without it, they'll be thrown in prison and made to clean the sewers for the rest of their days."

So even here in the Tai Tai, where money is the accepted governing body, hexen are being outlawed. Humans really are such cowardly creatures.

Silje wonders, idly, if there might be any information regarding the missing fae creatures.

"Have you heard anything about that news story Brigit has been trying to push? The old witch doesn't seem to understand that fairies are the last people anyone around here cares about. You remember the time she tried to do a whole undercover scope on how netherbeasts were being kept in cages in the old subway tunnels? No one cared. Netherbeast are the kind of monsters ain't nobody cares about. They ain't exactly natural in these parts, are they?"

Silje suppresses a growl.

Netherbeasts are to monsters what hexen are to fae folk. Monsters (i.e. sea serpents, nokken, thunderbirds, etc.) are the naturally occurring creatures of this world. Less than sentient and more bite and brimstone than their fairy counterparts, these are the creatures the fair folk call upon when they are in need of some assistance. Netherbeasts and hexen are unnatural to Deus. Ever since the witches disembarked on this particular planet, they've been seen as an invasive species, pushing the fae out of their territory for a place to call their own.

It's why most hexen settlements are in undesirable places on Deus. They are strangers who came to a strange land, and if it weren't for their gods and goddesses, the witches would have been thrown out with the rest of the human garbage they brought with them, but the gods have always given favor to their human followers, fae and fae folk be damned. With the witches, of course, came the thinning of the veil. They brought their magics and introduced all sorts of creatures to this world that were not naturally occurring.

Silje is one of those creatures.

Summoned to Deus years ago by one Summer Helsdottir, Silje was less than enthusiastic to suddenly be trapped in a cage with an overbearing witch attempting to enslave her. Her witch saved her, the only person she has ever seen outright help a netherbeast. She vaguely remembers Kaito being there as well. If he'd had his way, he'd have killed her on the spot, but the then slumbering witch didn't let him. Back then her witch was a technomancer, her magic dormant in her blood, slumbering until such a time as it could be called upon to save her life.

When Silje found the female technomancer again after her rescue, she'd been afraid that she'd arrived too late and her witch, a pulsing font of potential energy, was already dead.

Silje had put everything of her power into keeping the damned necromancer alive, and her hard labor was paid for in the woman's first resurrection. Everything that happened after, though, had been less than ideal.

She should have expected the witch would react negatively to her sudden and jarring change in circumstances, but she came through in the end with a little help from a fellow witch and Silje's unending dedication to her witchling's welfare.

"Don't you think there are enough ghost stories flitting around the webs? We have the League butting their heads into our business all because they believe some witch is back from the dead. The last thing we need to do is put the whole city in an uproar because fairies are going missing. I mean, honestly, fae go missing all the time. They come and go as they please."

"Mermaids don't do that."

"Yeah, well, who's to say they didn't just go back out to sea?"

"There was an autopsy."

"Yeah, and people die, don't they? Ain't no evidence of foul play."

"Well, don't the people have a right to know there is a chance their neighbors are disappearing?"

"This is a city of pirates, Morgan. There's always a chance their neighbors are going to disappear, whether that be because they owed the wrong person money, the League got to 'em, or if, y'know, they just up and left. There's no mystery in that."

"I don't know. The seagulls weird me out."

"That's just 'cause you're from the mainland. There are no seagulls in Aighneas. It's too far inland."

The door clicks shut as the pair leave the premises.

Silje nudges open the box she's hidden away in. It takes some time being as small she is, but eventually, she gets it open. Now, she begs the question, does she dig around in here for more information, or should she locate this Brigid witch and see if she can find more from her records? Witches and netherbeasts go hand in hand. Perhaps this Brigid person might prove helpful.

Decision made, she jumps from the desk she was placed atop and worms her way into the air ducts. It takes some work to get the grate unscrewed, but nothing she can't manage with her tail and determination.

Disappearing is not an option though. Not in a building with this much anti-magic security. Just being in here is making her whiskers curl. How could any witch manage to work here day in and day out? They must suffer some serious headaches as a result. No wonder witches are prone to substance abuse. Her own witch could barely sit in Cresta de Corail without a shot of absynthe in hand. Her sister used to get onto her all the time about alcoholism in the months leading up to her banishment from the League.

But Silje knows. It was never about the alcohol. Empathy sucks when you are hanging around a bunch of unfiltered ethos, and her witch's brother carried enough ethos with him to power a small lighthouse.

It isn't difficult for a netherbeast to feel out the aura of a witch. They are, after all, the closest thing to home this side of the veil. The energy signature she finds is on the far side of the building. Now imagine a black cat trying to slink its way around busy bodies, past bustling carts of paperwork, and under various checkpoints throughout the building.

There are reporters, journalists, interns, even the occasional black market information dealer to contend with. Everyone is racing about like the apocalypse was scheduled for twenty minutes from now, and they're still not sure what to do about it.

However, despite the obstacles, she makes it to a small cubicle at the edge of the floor where a plump man in a rainbow striped sweater and a frothy coffee in hand types away at the keyboard while a video of the League's recent airwaves plays in the background. He is playing more images of her witch, only this one is from twelve years ago. The trial by combat was held between her and Montwyatte. Her witch had every right to end that fight the way she did, even with the faulty weapon in hand.

Those arseholes had handed a single-handed person a two-handed weapon and expected her to use it! Had Silje not been tied up in a magically sealed sack at the time, she would have torn apart the committee who made that decision.

Silje's fur rustles in agitation as she hops up onto the edge of the cubicle. She is about to jump down onto the man's desk when another rather distasteful looking reporter rounds the corner, so instead, she ducks down behind the leaves of an artificial tree.

"Hey, Brig, you got the final draft of that report done yet?"

The intruder stands taller than the man in the cubicle, towering over him like some faux giant. It's abrasive, and his aura is that of a pompous blowhard. It makes her claws itch.

"I was under the impression it wasn't due until the morning."

"Vaishi changed his mind. He wants it today. You'd best hurry up on it because I don't know how many heads he plans to make roll around here, but I'm sure you don't want yours to be one of them."

The sneer on the man's face makes Silje want to puke up a hairball.

"Okay, but I have my missing fae report to finish. You'll have to finish it up yourself."

The tall man laughs.

"Good joke, Brig, but you know you're the one who's going to have to finish it."

"But you were assigned the report originally."

"Yeah, well, I told them I handed it off to you. You're so much more knowledgeable on this kind of stuff anyway. Too doo loo! And good luck!"

"But the fae!"

The round man's pleas fall on deaf ears.

Well if that doesn't make for a right bastard. Silje has always despised bullies.

The feline hops over the computer monitor to land with nimble paws on the keyboard. As you can imagine, the round-faced man jumps a solid three feet into the air. "What the devil?!"

That's beast to you, sir, thinks Silje.

"You're a-a-a..." *Cat got your tongue, dear sir?* "You're a cat! Wait... No, you're not a cat. You're a—"

Silje sets a paw on the man's mouth and is immediately disappointed by what she senses within the man's fiber. The two delivery guys in the storage closet called him a witch, but this person has the magical pool of a dodo bird. (Never mind that the creatures are actually quite magical. Why do you think the humans hunted them to extinction? All for nothing, though. They simply haven't the capacity for any serious spellcraft. They're dodos, for goddess' sake.) Witches and wiccans are not the same thing, though +ies have a tendency to make all manner of hasty generalizations about any act of magic, and the normals overexaggerate anything and everything that they fail to understand.

No, the magical presence Silje followed to the man's desk is, in actuality, a silver statuette sitting just left of the keyboard. It radiates with magic, not that that will do Silje any good. She needs information on the fairies, and she needs it now.

"You're not a cat."

The displacer beast nods.

"What are you?"

Her tail flicks the statuette.

"You're a familiar. Wait." The man glances to the right to where a few more images of Silje and her witch are depicted together prior to the Songstress's capture. The cat and the witch walking through the cobblestone paths of Lorelei, Silje keeping a keen eye out for danger. "You're her familiar."

The cat winks, but just as the man is about to rise from his seat—

"Oh, and Brig—What the hell?!" The tall man is back, and his eyes meet Silje instantly. "Somebody call security. The songstress's familiar is here!"

Flouncing furballs, and she's still too weak to take on her true form.

The tall man lunges for Silje. The cat jumps out of the way and darts for the door. Behind her, Brig stands up and catches the other man around the shoulders. "Stop, no!"

"Get off me, you sorry excuse for a witch. I'm getting that payload."

"No, you're not!"

THE CAT (PART 2)

Silje hears the punch but doesn't see it as she rounds the corner. She makes the mistake of looking back. When she turns her attention back forward, she runs straight into an anti-magic bag.

Koi is a magnificent sight when full. If you look at it just right, you can see the swirling movement of the blizzards constantly blowing across its surface. Oh what it would be like to stand in the midst of one of those icy storms. It isn't to be though. Our space flight programs have deemed Koi unsafe for human visitation. We did manage to send a robot rover there for the first time just last year.

Dedication has managed to stay in communication with our base past its mission timeline of just three months. I can't wait to discover how that icy terrain so vastly affects magic users here on the ground. Scientists speculate that there is some sort of radioactive element interfering with our atmosphere.

I think it's simpler than that. We should never underestimate the power of gravity.

An excerpt from *Moondance*
By E.X. Icarus, 1762. A.P.

19

THE QUEEN OF WANDS (REVERSED)

15th Day in the Month of Falling - 1:15 PM - Somewhere beneath Calypso City

S HE'S NEVER BEEN MORE THANKFUL FOR HER complete lack of claustrophobia. Navigating through tight underwater tunnels is a basic part of Derivan adept training, but it's been years since she had to call on those skills. After everything went pear-shaped in her past life, she had very little need to venture into the ocean. Living in a landlocked part of the world would do that, and Lorelei forest, while surrounded by rivers, was as far from any ocean as any territory could be, and despite her forays into the lake with Jessabelle and Fae, there was never much need for swimming, and if you asked this witch, she would tell you that river monsters were twice as awful as sea monsters.

Something about the lack of space gave them a serious complex. Not to mention they were incredibly territorial. She made the mistake of upsetting a nokken not long after Jessabelle finally coaxed her out of her near-death bed. That ended about as well any anyone could imagine. Only Kara's intervention had kept her from being drowned to within an inch of her life. The huldra had been salty about it. Said she'd only done it because she didn't want to see Jessabelle's hard work healing her gone to nothing. Not that it was any of the Songstress's concern at the time. She'd had other things that were far more pressing to worry about.

All that to say, while she is out of practice in regard to deep water cave dives, the witch manages to come out on the other side just fine.

"Kai, I'm through the passages alright. What's your ETA?"

Only static greets her on the other side of the comm unit. Great, he's misplaced his unit again. If you'd asked her when she was sixteen if she ever thought the Miyazaki prince was forgetful, she would have looked at that person like they had a second head growing out of their ass. But after being in the Tai Tai for the last few days, she's starting to think that the man would forget his own head if it wasn't wired to his shoulders.

Yes, "wired." She is beginning to doubt even muscle and sinew would make the man remember himself better. Clearly, tech is a necessity.

A twang of pain pierces through her arm. "Ow, shit! What the—"

She rolls up the sleeve of her diving suit to see blood soaking the inside. One of the curse marks is bleeding.

"Pinche pedo..."

She knows what this means, and it's not a comforting idea. The curse is hungry for its next kill. Summer's death healed the fourth wound on her arm. Another two fiends are called for by the last two, and apparently, two days is too long without a sacrifice.

"I do not have time for this."

How is she supposed to run a rescue mission and an assassination mission at once? She doesn't even know who she needs to be hunting, and why would she find them down here in these tunnels, anyway? This place is a pigsty.

She appears to have surfaced in a maintenance shaft of some sort. A dry platform rises out of the water, and there is a wall of tools and cleaning supplies hung up on the far wall. Beyond that a maintenance ladder sits across the way. A ladder to where? She has no idea. According to the maps they got from Lyra, and the platform map, she should be at least two or three levels down from the surface. So the ladder can go anywhere really. Which begs the question: does she sit here and wait for her beau? Or does she move on and investigate on her own?

She sits with the questions for two, three heartbeats before deciding. Of course she's going to investigate on her own. That's what she does. Kaito would be disappointed otherwise.

She surfaces in a strange room. Still below ground, yet this space is distinctly different from the rest of the tunnels. It's clean, for one. Second, there are active monitors lining the walls. Camera feeds flicker on them with various timestamps.

"Someone's been monitoring the tunnels?"

Several monitors are unfamiliar, most likely other parts of the underground that she and Kaito haven't explored, but there are two that she very readily recognizes: a camera feed for the submerged subway car and a second for the platform they found nearby. But who would be monitoring a bunch of abandoned tunnels? More importantly, why would someone care to monitor a bunch of abandoned tunnels? Seems like a waste of resources.

One of the unfamiliar feeds flickers, drawing the witch's attention, and as she looks over Kaito's form materializes out of the gloom around the feed. He swims by unabashed and unaware that he is being watched.

Interesting. She reaches for her comm. "Hey, Kai. I found something you should take a look at whenever you get here."

The only response she gets is static.

She huffs. Two thousand years of developing communications technology, you would think a society filled with mechanically augmented people who literally have computers in their fucking skulls would have figured out reliable forms of communication, and yet, here she is incommunicado with her lover because the tunnels below Calypso City have horrible signal.

There's a keyboard and input system on the floor—not even a desk—just sitting on the floor to collect dust and grime. She hunches down and starts fiddling with the board. Maybe she can pull up some old recordings. The screen nearest to her eye level switches at her command to a different camera feed. This one she recognizes. It's the mouth of the cavern where she and Kaito decided to split up. Well, more like he decided to split up. The idea of separating at this point in the game still seems like a bad idea to her, but he didn't seem to think so. She is not sure what timetable he's on, but it's not the same one as hers.

That's neither here nor there, now, though. Separate they did. Now if the man can just swim his way to her, that would do wonders for her stress levels.

This feed is different though, and almost immediately after she flips over to it, the water where they had just been treading ripples as though something were passing underneath the surface. Could have been a fish or a stray current, but there's no way to tell as the creature doesn't actually break the surface of the water.

She toggles over the screen with the subway car on it and hits the rewind button. The timestamp ticks backward faster than her eyes can keep up with. *Ha!* At least this tech is of reasonable age. Any older models would have ticked backward at a snail's pace, and she would have been here for hours.

Fish flit back and forth, there is a constant coming and going of a particular barracuda, and she thinks she even recognizes a few rare breeds of stingray swimming about. When she hits about two days into the past, she sees the merman being attacked and pauses the rewind.

"Holy shit!"

The beast that attacked Thale is unlike anything the witch has ever seen. Where she was expecting scales and or fins, there is instead fur and the slick mammalian physique of a whale or a dolphin. Featuring an elongated snout and what appears to be prehensile jaws, the creature's face is a monstrous patchwork of feline, canine, and reptilian anatomy. Its body is lopsided as though a reptilian was split down the center and forced to conform to a human body type. Its tail is that of a crocodile while its legs and/or hindquarters seem like a set of shark fins.

Whatever it is, there is no doubt in her mind that someone made this poor creature. Frankenstein's swamp, sea, or river monster all mashed together by a mad person's idea of scary. Even Summer's chimera weren't nearly so terrifying. At least, their shared anatomy made some semblance of sense to an onlooker—the pieces were picked for their efficiency and moldability to one another. This, though... This creature was made to do damage and destroy things without having a care for everyday functionality.

"Who would make something like this?"

She rewinds the feed a little further to see how Thale's capture actually unfolded. The footage confirms her suspicions about a prehensile jaw when a second set of teeth extends from the creature's mouth to catch the merman around the middle. From its back tentacle, something black and apparently viscous spews and winds around the merman, tangling him up as though in a spider's web. From there, the beast drags the helpless fae into the darkness of a nearby tunnel, and after that, the footage returns to total redundancy.

Nothing happening here. Don't mind us. We'll just keep on with the status quo. Never mind that someone was just kidnapped on camera.

"Was anyone even here to see what happened?"

She looks back at the control screen, typing like mad at the keys to find some idea of who is in charge of this stuff. There are records to be found for sure. Purchase receipts, addendums, maintenance logs, and finally, at the seeming bottom of the computer's storage systems, she finds something that at least hints at who is responsible for all of this equipment.

A logo with a large V, E, and W interwoven with one another. In the background, a vintage style camera painted in a minty green pops out against the letters. There is no other text. *What does "VEW" stand for?*

"When was the last shift scheduled for, anyway?" A door to her left clicks as someone unlocks the bolt.

Shit!

She quickly returns the screen to where she found it, closing out windows and making it appear as though nothing and no one has been messing around with the system at all, before ducking back down into the maintenance hatch.

The door opens, and a man walks through. He is carrying a cup of coffee and a large—she assumes—jelly-filled donut. He doesn't appear to be augmented, but unlike Kaito, she can't very well scan him for tech, and with her magic on the fritz, she can't exactly do any warding against any tech he may or may not have either, so she huddles on the ladder, one ear pressed to the trapdoor above her for any sounds she may or may not hear.

There is shuffling and something heavy being set on the ground. A backpack, she assumes, has been set right on top of her head.

A heavy sigh permeates the barrier as the man settles, seemingly not too far from where she is sitting.

"Now to stare at nothing for another six hours. Why does the doc even bother monitoring these tunnels? Aside from the occasional fish, nothing comes through here, and Levi will take care of anything stupid enough to come exploring."

The sound of a walkie talkie scratches through the air. The witch puts her shoulder into the door and pushes. *Damn!* The backpack is way too heavy. *What is with this guy? Doesn't he know that carrying a ton of weight on his back will lead to poor posture? Obviously not.* Augmentations or no augmentations, he has to be toting around at least four dictionaries' worth of weight in his bag.

"Ian, I'm at my designation. Anything interesting on your end?"

There's a scratch of connection, and a voice chimes over the walkie. "Levi was being a bit aggressive, so I let him out for a swim. Make sure your hatch is locked. You know how he gets when he's hungry."

"You let that thing out for my shift! Ian, what the hell, man?"

"Faust wants Levi to get regular exercise. He even said," the other man's voice shifts to mimic someone else's over the walkie talkie, "'If he gets antsy at all, make sure to let him stretch his fins. We don't want an angry monster on sight. Too many breakables around.' And ya know, I don't think he was talking so much about the equipment as the fairies that seem to keep showing up around here. Do you think he plans to stop collecting anytime soon?"

Collecting? Faust? Did that coward really escape from the asylum just to continue operations in the Tai Tai? But Lyra said that fae have been disappearing for years.

"I don't really care what he wants. I just wish he hadn't fired ole' Hannigan. At least she gave a shit about her employees. That arsehole only cares about his experiments and collecting more samples. What is he trying to do anyway? You can't steal fairy magic for free."

"No, but..." the person on the other side of the walkie pauses as though considering whether or not he should reveal some big secret or not. "Did you see that last broadcast from the League about the Songstress coming back?"

"Everyone saw that. So what?"

"I heard Faust claim that he was the one who turned her into a witch."

Excuse me! Dr. Dumpkin is claiming what?! You can't turn someone into a witch. That is not the way it works. You can't science experiment someone into something they weren't already.

Some people are born with a natural genius of intellect or with innate physical prowess or an affinity for the arts. Magic is the same. Everyone is born with the potential for magic craft, and witches are a natural extension of that insofar as they possess a naturally deep well of blood bound magical might, but of course, like any muscle, when left to disuse, it will degrade away to nearly nothing. In some, the talent will remain dormant their whole lives for lack of depth, lack of interest, or lack of attunement.

The Songstress of Lorelei could easily have been one of those who never awoke their abilities. She has no doubt that it was through the efforts of her mother that her powers had been repressed by the tech that had been installed in her body at a young age. Freya was no fool, and these days, the daughter she left behind suspects the rumors about the firefly being a sorceress of some sort might have had more than a little truth behind them. Of course she would want her daughter to avoid persecution by having her embrace the technomancer heritage given to her by her father more so than any witchy ancestry that was liable to be snuffed out the moment it was discovered.

No, Faust was not the reason this witch came into her power.

The man continues to gab with the other person on the walkie as the witch climbs her way back out of the hatch. He is so oblivious she manages to make her way past him to the door he left ajar on his way in.

The hallway she steps out into is nowhere near what she was expecting. She assumed she would find more dark passages, maybe some water dripping from the ceiling, some more graffiti, you get the idea. Instead, she steps out into a brightly lit, perfectly maintained hospital corridor, and she, wearing a water-logged diving suit with grime and salt water in her hair, sticks out like a sore thumb amidst the bright white of clean and sanitized.

The sound of wheels rolling along the linoleum greets her ear.

Shit!

She dives under a clothed gurney, careful not to mark up the perfectly pressed fabric with all of the mud still clinging to her body. The trolley rattles past, but there are no feet pushing the mechanism, so she dares to peek out. A hover droid pushes a cart full of pill cups.

What is this place?

The asylum where she was resurrected was not nearly this well maintained. The walls had been practically falling apart as she'd crazy-ed her way out of there wearing Atalia's face. Faust's name echoes in her head. *Is he behind the operations here as well, or is he working for someone else, merely going wherever he is told to go to wreak havoc where plenty already exists?*

Either way, the unsavory man being anywhere nearby makes her feel itchy. That must be why her curse scar has reopened. Faust was the doctor responsible for the torture and death of countless patients in his little house of horrors. His mistreatment of his inmates is the whole reason she is even here to begin with. Eight patients, all of different backgrounds, genders, and hardships decided it would be worth it to sacrifice their own bodies and souls to return hers from the dead.

The whole thing makes her want to curl up and die all over again.

No one deserves to have that much life shed for them, yet they did anyway, for her, for themselves, for revenge. That was how bad their situation was. Death was better, death was desired, and if vengeance could be integral to that death, it would be even more worthwhile.

Katrina, LuQin, Atalia, Sarah, Emilio, Hoshi, Amani, and Nadia... For as long as she has this second life, she'll never forget their names (regardless of whether that is twenty minutes from now, twenty days from now, or twenty years from now). It was Atalia's body that made the framework for her new and improved physicality: all her old scars gone as though they never existed, her missing hand returned to her, and even her magic seems more powerful than she remembers, unhindered by the stressors of surviving in a body once integrated with tech.

The gurney disappears around the corner, and the witch peeks her head out to make sure the coast is clear. All clear. Time to go. And the first order of business is to change into something more appropriate for navigating dry land.

Déjà vu is the worst. At least in this witch's opinion. As she walks through the corridors, she can't help but feel something niggling in the back of her head, like a worm trying to gnaw its way into her cerebrum. It's rather disconcerting and makes her feel like she is being eaten alive even though there's technically nothing wrong.

It gets especially disconcerting in front of a tapestry hanging at the end of the second corridor she ventures down. It strikes her as an odd place for there to be a dead end, but she isn't exactly well-versed in architecture. That doesn't stop the pull of negative emotions seemingly calling to her from the tapestry's fibers, and no wonder.

The tapestry itself is nothing impressive. Made from what she assumes to be a mix of silk and cotton fibers, the tapestry is a copy of the classical unicorn tapestry. She thinks the name was something along the lines of "A Unicorn Rests in a Garden." It's quite popular as a home staple. She's seen it in hotels and palaces. There was a version of it in Cresta de Corail. People sell photos of it on postcards. Why would someone put it in a hospital though? It seems a bit of a tasteless choice considering unicorns are a symbol of life and vitality. The people here are trapped in their beds much like the unicorn sits within a fence. However, the unicorn can jump out of its enclosure. The sick and infirm are reliant on someone else opening the gate for them to escape.

The nice thing about being in a hospital is the surplus supply of bandages for her use. She wraps her bleeding arm and carries on with her investigation, though she has no idea where to go. Does she try to find an office? Are there files anywhere that she can peek into? There might be, but everything, surprisingly enough, looks to be aboveground. Every robot is in perfect order: they carry clipboards that are perfectly organized, and they execute their duties with the utmost organization.

They don't even seem to mind her at all.

One spotted her at one point, and instead of sounding all of the alarms, the bot merely directed her to the front desk where an android modeled after a librarian, she guesses, stood typing away at a computer. Why a robot needs to type away at a computer, she isn't entirely sure. Perhaps it's just to keep the uncanny valley from triggering as intensely.

"Welcome to Calypso City Hospice Care Facility. How may I help you?"

"This is a hospice center."

"Yes, ma'am. We serve our patients until their last breath so that you don't have to."

A hospice facility? Underground? Last she checked, most cultures bury their dead, not their dying.

"And you keep all kinds of people? Human+, fairies, hexen?"

"At this time, we only service unaugmented individuals. We don't have the capability to tend to human+ needs at the moment."

She considers this information for a moment and decides to try her hand at a different line of questioning. "Is Dr. Faust around? I was hoping to see him on a very important matter."

"Dr. Faust is our executive director and is presently very busy with his work both local and overseas." The lights that sit where the bot's "mouth" would be otherwise flicker, two quick pulses followed by a long glow. "Your name, ma'am?"

Haha! Good question! What is my name again? "Is that necessary? I forgot my ID."

"Yes, ma'am. I will need to enter you into the visitor's log."

"Miyazaki, Larkin," she blurts out. It's the first collection of names she can think of.

"Thank you, Miss Miyazaki—"

"That's Missus."

"Very well, Mrs. Miyazaki. Were you visiting or dropping off?"

"Visiting. I'm a social worker, and I'm working on reaching out to the downtrodden in our community." The lie spills from her lips as easily as melted butter slides over toast. "Singing can be very uplifting for the sick even if they can't necessarily interact, and I really think I could do some good here for your patients. Are there any patients that have been here for an extended amount of time? More than six months? Preferably someone who might be lonely."

"Let me check our rosters."

The bot stops typing at the computer, and the lenses of her glasses flicker with light, not terribly unlike how Kaito's irises glow when his sights are active. However, this bot isn't so much reading the changes in its lens as living them. The visualization of the bot's search in the lenses is purely for the witch's benefit.

Eventually, the flickering settles on a room number.

"Patient #2047 is currently located in room 108. She is a coma patient, I'm afraid, without any family to speak of. Here is your visitor's pass. If you have need of further assistance, feel free to press the buzzer."

The witch nods her head and makes her way to the assigned room. Coma patient rooms are perfect for her needs. No one will be coming in or out, and the likelihood of getting caught will be slim.

Room 109 is as isolated from the rest of the facility as she can expect. As she enters the room, a quaint little thing painted in muted greens and beiges, a strange sensation tings her senses. An unseen energy pulses just beyond her comprehension like an insect fluttering in her peripheral vision, but the sensation comes and goes as quickly as a whisper.

Curiouser and curiouser.

Patient #2047 lies still in the bed. The songstress isn't quite sure what she was expecting, maybe an elderly person or a disfigured mummy wrapped up in gauze from some tragic accident. Instead, the woman lying still under a carefully tended quilt—it's made by hand as far as she can tell, every stitch lovingly pressed and folded and threaded through the fabric—is terribly young and heartbreakingly beautiful. The songstress doesn't even think it possible for her to be much older than she or Kaito, certainly no older than 35.

More disturbing, though, is Summer's ghost hovering in the corner, a young girl standing in front of her incorporeal form. The little girl is a carbon copy of the woman on the bed, just younger. If spirits could look exhausted, this one would be. The little girl's eyes are hollow and miserable.

She looks at the witch with pleading eyes and mouths a single word.

Please...

This is no ghost. This is the astral form of the comatose woman, locked eternally into the age she was when she first fell into a coma—a spirit of the living dead.

"Patient #2047 has been resting here for 21 years, 5 months, and 8 days."

The intercom on the bedside table answers the witch's unasked question.

"21 years?"

"Yes. Her condition is the result of an encounter with a magical being, the likes of whom was never found or even identified."

"What sort of encounter? Who was the witch? Did they ever catch them?"

"Unfortunately, my records are unable to relay any relevant data to Patient #2047's condition. It is as though the records containing the encounter have been wiped clean."

"Is there anything you can share with me?"

"Only a recording."

The speaker shifts from the tinny voice of the reception bot to a staticky replay of an old comm recording. The first thing she hears is the sound of singing. There is a bubbly laughing sound. A feminine voice chimes in.

"I can't believe how lucky we are right now.
Look, Anna, the deer are grazing in the meadow."
"Look at the baby, mama," a tiny toddler voice exclaims.
"The baby deer is called a fawn, sweetie.
That one is only just learning how to walk."
The child giggles. Neither mother nor daughter
seem to hear the way the singing increases in volume.
"Mama, what is that?"
"What is what, sweetheart—Anna!"

The recording cuts off from there. The scream, the music, the wail of magic hurtling toward the comm, it sounds like mother and daughter were on a nice calm walk in the forest when they came across a malevolent witch, one who felt the need to either defend her territory against intruders or simply wanted to see a happy moment turn sour.

"This is all that exists in my accessible records. This unit believes there used to be more, but for some unknown reason, the remainder is inaccessible."

The witch approaches the bed, one hand extended to touch the slumbering woman's skin. There, thrumming just beneath the surface, writhes a mass of uncontrolled power, but this isn't the witchy system of wild magic that forms naturally in a witch's blood. No, this is something cancerous like a tumor inserted beneath the derma and left to grow unchecked. Well, it would be unchecked were it not for the various wires and tubes designed to pry the energy from her network when it builds too high.

She's seen this before. Wuxing Syndrome is one of the worst magical maladies that can ail a non-magical human or human+. People once believed radiation poisoning to be the worst condition to recover from. Those people would have a hard time believing there was anything worse. Cancerous and irreversible, normally, the protocol would be to install filters that would collect the energy and release it from the body in a way that was safe for both the patient and those around them.

Patient #2047, though, was probably too young to undergo such augmentations when she was exposed to the magic that sickened her so. The witch wonders idly if maybe she killed the cold-hearted wretch responsible when she destroyed Seraphim's Koven all those years ago, not that it matters. Vengeance won't give the woman back her life.

"Why do you keep her here? Wouldn't it be more merciful to let her go?"

"Patient #2047 is a vested interest to our executive director. Dr. Faust has been working for years to unearth a cure for her condition."

Why? What does Faust care about one girl being in a magical coma?

"Does Patient #2047 have a name?"

"Anna Elizabeth Faust."

Well, isn't that just a coincidence?

"And how has Dr. Faust been hoping to achieve this cure?"

"I should think you could infer a proper answer to that question yourself, Mrs. Miyazaki."

A new voice enters the conversation. The witch's hair swings across her face as she whips around to find Dr. Faust himself standing in the doorway.

"Dr. Faust."

"You know me?"

Right, the last time he saw her, she was wearing Atalia's face. "I know of you. Your reputation precedes you. Here I thought you only dabbled in managing insane asylums for the poor and accused, but now I find you work in the hospice sector as well."

"What are you, a reporter? What does a reporter learn from sneaking their way into my daughter's care room?"

"I'm not a reporter."

"Good. Then, nobody will miss you. Guards!"

A pair of mechanized muscles rush into the room. The witch throws her powers at them with a burst of song. The first pulse of magic hits, sending the first guard down on the far side of the room, but the second fizzles to nothing before anything can be done. Before she can recover from the surprise of her magic once again failing her in a moment of self-defense, she finds herself face to chest with a burly cyborg, sporting four robotic arms and a face half encased in titanium. Those arms, thick as I-beams, wrap around her body and lift her off her feet.

He squeezes her so hard, the air is forced from her lungs.

Mira cabron, she thinks as she twists around in his hold, getting an arm free. She drives her nails, sharp as daggers, across the fleshy half of his face. He screams as the skin shreds to bits. He curses at her in a language she doesn't care to know and tightens his hold. In response, she swings out a leg, hooking her foot around the back of his knee and flexes outward, pulling the joint into an angle it is really not supposed to go in. The man crumples, his leg unable to support his weight.

The witch lands in a heap on the ground, fighting to regain the breath that was forced out of her. Before she can recover, the second guard is up and on her, and this one doesn't make the mistake of engaging her in such tight quarters. He stomps on the small of her back, then kicks her in the stomach. She pushes him away with a flash of bright emerald magic (*Yeah... So that one worked! Curse you, Lyra.*), but before she can get up and make her return attack, a glass something-or-other is broken over her head.

The Atomic Bomb was considered the most devastating attack to have ever been made against another nation in a time of war. This is true of the old world where magic was snuffed out to near extinction but not in Deus.

The Vanquishing was the most destructive tactic ever used in the war between science and magic.

In the last days of the Songstress of Lorelei's reign of terror, the League's council of technomancers gathered together to make a decision that would forever change the course of Deus's future.

Excerpt from <u>A World on Fire:</u>
<u>The Last Days of Magic</u>
Monsieur Lafayette de Leonard, 1876 A.P.

20

THE PAGE OF SWORDS

Memory Bank Retrieval - 14 Years Ago - 12th Day in the Month of Hearths, 1863 A.P.

KAITO'S MISSION WAS A FAIRLY straightforward one. A beast had been terrorizing one of the border towns between Murasaki no Yama and the boundaries of Lorelei forest. The reports were vague. No one who had encountered the beast had gotten a clear look at it, but it was, by all accounts, massive, dark, and extremely aggressive.

At this time of year, snow cakes the ground in this part of the world. The trees of the forest just beyond the safety barriers are tipped in white and icily silent. Most of the birds have migrated south, some of the animals have gone into hibernation for the winter, and any creatures that remain wandering the brush move slowly and silently to conserve energy. Food is scarce. Fruitless hunting is a surefire way to starve to death, and the freezing temperatures will eat up an animal's heat stores if they do not shelter correctly, so the chances of it being an everyday beast is slim.

Kaito hunts and finds himself blade to teeth with a jabberwocky. The dragon-like creature, mad with hunger, attacks Kaito without any regard for its own preservation.

He kills it as easily as he would a training dummy back home. The corpse is a gruesome thing. He does a scan to see what made the creature so volatile. Despite common belief, monsters of this sort rarely attack people. They much prefer to isolate themselves in their forests and mountains. He suspects this one came down from its ridge due to an infection of rabies, but how could such a creature get rabies?

"'Twas brillig, and the slithy toves
Did gyre and gimble in the wabe:
All mimsy were the borogoves,
And the mome raths outgrabe."

Kaito turns prepared to attack when singing enters the clearing from behind him but stalls the moment he sees exactly who it is.

"Beware the Jabberwock, my son.
The jaws that bite, the claws that catch!
Beware the Jubjub bird, and shun
The frumious Bandersnatch!"

"W—?" His lips form the name, but he cannot hear the sound they make.

The woman looks just as she did the last time he saw her, albeit less bloody and far calmer. She wears a simple black camisole dress, knee-length with a purple long-sleeve top underneath. The sleeves are pulled halfway over her hands and hooked on her thumbs. Her black boots disappear underneath the hemline of the dress. For armor, she wears a long black corset.

As a witch, she probably doesn't want to be encumbered by heavy or even medium-weight armor. Channeling the energies of the world requires attunement, and too many obstacles between skin and air can hinder such a thing.

"I always loved that silly old ditty. Can't say my stepmother ever enjoyed my taste for the weird and whimsical, but we live in the world where Carroll stumbled over himself and found inspiration for a nightmarish children's book."

"W—"

"You took my kill, you know. I've been tracking that thing for days. I needed its claws to claim a bounty. There are plenty of potions masters would love jabberwocky dust for their shops."

"W—"

"'And hast thou slain the Jabberwock?
Come to my arms, my beamish boy!
O frabjous day! Callooh! Callay!'
He chortled in his joy."

She continues singing as though she hasn't been missing for months.

"W—"

"That was never my favorite part of the song, but it fits this scenario nicely. Are you my beamish boy? No, you've seen too much and survived too much."

"W—!"

"I know what you're thinking," she cuts him off, hands in front of her chest in defense. "You're thinking, 'What the hell is she doing here? She's been gone for months. She's a wanted criminal... blah, blah, blah.' I told you." She's rambling. She always does this when she's nervous. Kaito strides toward her, sheathing his weapons as he moves. "I told you. I was hunting the Jabberwock for parts, but you got to it first, so if you'll excuse me." She shuffles on her feet—bird-like fluttering. "I'll just be going before you come to your senses..." She isn't backing up, at least not fast enough to evade the technomancer heading her way. He meets her. "...and start trying to kill me..." he winds his arm around her back. "...like you right properly should be doing if you had any sense whatso—"

He cuts her off with a kiss.

It's the only way to shut her up after all. She wilts into his hold. The witch, previously rising steadily in agitation, calms and sinks into the intimacy. My goddess, he's missed her. It's been two months. Countless people are searching for her. Some for good—her brother with Deriva's banner at his beck and call and her sister, whose husband fully supports the idea of finding his sister-in-law before anyone else can. Some bad—Sekhmeti wants revenge for the death of their pharaoh. Half the League is on the hunt for the witch who killed the Primarch in cold blood. Not to mention the countless hexen who are probably out for her blood as well for her role during the war—she killed at least a hundred witches who were working for Seraphim.

That kind of culling has upset the balance within hexen circles. He's been tracking the change. The vampyre clans and the lycan packs have risen against one another, vying for the dominant role in hexen politics. You see, witches are at the top of the hypothetical food chain. They run the show because so much of hexen culture originates and is sustained by their magic.

There are theories written everywhere in League libraries that hypothesize that if the League could simply destroy the witch population, cull it down enough to initiate weakness in all of the other hexen races, then winning the war would be a matter of shooting fish in a barrel so to speak.

There's been no observation of this yet. Koven, for all their hundred strength, did not comprise more than 35% of the estimated witch population in Hexen-led territories like Lorelei, the Wastes, and New Chernobyl. They don't have a count of how many witches live in the Tai Tai, and he isn't stupid enough to believe that there isn't a substantial number of witches currently in hiding throughout League nations, dulling their magics, practicing in secret, and keeping their heads down to avoid persecution.

Koven had been composed of the most dangerous and powerful witches of the time. Naturally, when a hole is left in a place of power, the next contenders line up for a chance to fill that void. It's disconcerting to know that the balance of hexen power may now lie in the ranks of either the vampyres or lycans, but he's been hearing whispers among the common folk.

The name of a new witch rising to power: The Songstress of Lorelei.

On his last mission, he'd had to deal with a street howler spreading anti-technomancer propaganda. He went on and on about how the peoples' rights would be taken from them; the League, if left unchecked, would see to it that the common people became little more than slaves under their regime, but never fear…

"The Songstress of Lorelei will tear the League from power. The hexen will once again rule. The old monarchies will be restored!"

The man was no hexen, merely a paranoid schizophrenic disturbing the peace. He hadn't paid much attention to it at the time, but then he came upon a conversation at a local dive bar in Oahu.

"There is a new witch in Lorelei. I hear she is building an army."

"I hear she's an old hag who wants to avenge Koven."

"No, no, no, no. She's not an old hag. She's half-orc and an accident in her youth scarred her for life."

"Scarred? I heard she's an unparalleled beauty, taught to sing by Hathor, bathed by Aphrodite, and bestowed her magic by Freya herself."

He didn't know of whom they spoke. The whispers had only begun three weeks ago.

But all of that is in the background. What does any of it matter when his heart is here, warm in his arms?

When they break their kiss, his long-lost lover looks up at him with half-lidded eyes.

"I'm happy to see you are doing alright."

"Alright is relative, but I'm alive; I make do, take care of my business, and I manage to keep a roof over my head. A wanted criminal can't ask for much more than that."

"Where are you staying?"

She leers at him, a joke on the edge of her quirked lips. "Hoping for an invite back?"

He sputters, "No. That's not—"

"Relax. I'm kidding. Besides, as charming as you are, it doesn't change the fact that I'm mad at you."

"You're displeased with me?"

"You took my kill. I needed those parts to sell. I'll need to find something else now."

He looks from her face, the dejection hiding in the twist of her smile, to the carcass.

"There may yet be something salvageable. The battle was not long. I doubt too much damage was done."

"It's illegal to poach parts off of the native beasts, especially dragons and unicorns. A Jabberwock is somewhere in-between. You would be within your rights to arrest me if I so much as touch the creature for its parts."

"From my perspective, the beast is already dead, nor was it killed by your hand. It would be wasteful not to use what you can of it."

"Alright. If you say so."

She takes a few minutes to collect various parts of the beast: the talons, both eyes, a piece of the tongue. She even cuts open its belly to extract its gallbladder and kidneys. He's surprised she doesn't take the heart as well, something about it being extremely poisonous and no good ever coming from anybody who decides to use said part.

With all the parts she wants collected and sealed into various jars and bags, she rises with her backpack slung over her shoulder.

"I guess this is goodbye. It was nice seeing you."

She walks past his shoulder, and before she can disappear, he reaches out and grabs her hand. "Wait. Let me come with you."

She laughs. "And put yourself on the chopping block should anyone find out? Sounds like a bad idea to me."

"I mean it, bad idea or not. You're in League territory. If someone sees you, they won't arrest you; they will kill you on sight."

She shuffles side to side on her feet.

"At least let me take you out to dinner, for old times' sake. Afterward, you can go on your way." *And I'll never see you again,* he finishes to himself, pushing aside the preemptive loneliness. *She's still here, baka.* It is best to be in the here and now.

It occurs to him that he has never seen her waffle about a decision. It's always either a "yes" or a "no" with her, never a "maybe" or an "I don't know." Yet here she is waffling very uncharacteristically about just allowing him to accompany her while she is in town.

She does one more circling of her feet without moving from her place, glances backward toward the woods before looking at him once more. When she speaks, he half expects her to say "no," but...

"Alright." A single word has never sounded like such a life-altering declaration. "We can go to dinner, but there's something I need to do first."

The witch leads him to a secluded meadow much deeper in the woods. There are a few deer nosing for frozen roots under the snow. None of them so much as react to the singer when she arrives in the clearing, but upon seeing Kaito, despite his calm demeanor and careful approach, their ears twitch and the does lead their fawns back into the tree line.

She stands in the center of the clearing and whistles a series of notes. Two low, a slide into the midrange, back to the lower pitch, and then three more in a high pitch.

For a moment, nothing happens. Kaito looks around, waiting for something to happen. Perhaps a portal will appear. Maybe she is summoning her familiar. Maybe she is meeting someone to make the trade of goods.

But none of those things come to be. Instead, the sound of small feet crunching through the snow greets his ear.

A child, no, a toddler, a little girl by all appearances, races through the meadow toward the witch. Bundled up in layers of cotton and wool, the child wears a tiny warm cloak, a wooly pair of leggings, and a long-sleeve dress. There is a knit hat on her hair, black wavy strands sticking out of the edges.

Kaito has no idea where the little one came from. She seemed to simply materialize at the behest of the singer's whistle.

Rosy-cheeked and happy, the toddler catches the brunette around the legs before the woman leans down to pick the child up in one arm. Her handless arm holds the toddler under their bum onto her hip while she points at Kaito. The child points at him as well, and the song witch gestures for him to approach.

"Hi!" says the little one in a high-pitched voice that rings through the whole clearing.

The little girl has almond-shaped eyes in the most enchanting shade of blue-green.

"This is my friend, Kai. Kai, this is Fae. She's an orphan from the war. I've taken her in."

Too stunned to think of anything else to say, Kaito extends his hand to the tiny person before him and says, "It's a pleasure to meet you, Fae."

The child doesn't shake his hand, but a smile splits that small face to show off eight tiny front teeth.

The most merciful thing in the world, I think, is the inability of the human mind to correlate all its contents. We live on a placid island of ignorance in the midst of black seas of infinity, and it was not meant that we should voyage far. The sciences, each straining in its own direction, have hitherto harmed us little, but some day the piecing together of dissociated knowledge will open up such terrifying vistas of reality, and of our frightful position therein, that we shall either go mad from the revelation or flee from the deadly light into the peace and safety of a new dark age.

Excerpt from "The Call of Cthulhu"
By H.P. Lovecraft, 1928 A.D.

21
THE EIGHT OF SWORDS

15th Day in the Month of Falling, 1877 A.P. - Somewhere in the Facility

SUMMER STANDS AT THE EDGE OF THE enclosed terrace in a simple nightgown, a shawl drawn tight around her head and shoulders as she looks out at the skyline. The witch with the triskele indicia stops a few feet from the woman, watching her watching the city, and knows. This isn't really Summer.

"You know, most of us can't stand the city. It's too noisy, too full, too interrupted, but I think I'll miss it."

There is no wind in the greenhouse, enclosed as it is, and the humidity sinks under her collar. She wonders how high up they are. 50, maybe 60 stories up. If she pays close attention, she can feel the subtle shifting of the building under her feet. It makes her stomach curl. Her fear of heights acts up even though there is solid ground beneath her feet.

"You can come closer, you know. I promise I won't bite."

She is just fine right where she is standing, plenty far from the window and any temptation of looking down. "You can't bite. You're not really here."

Summer turns slowly from the glass, face twisting into a mockery of a smile as she leans back on the railing, her silk nightgown falling in glossy lines over her curves, the plunging neckline barely leaving anything to the imagination.

"No, I suppose I'm not, but neither are you."

"What?"

"They have you under a Neural-Dephaser. They are trying to get you to stay quiet and stay out of it."

"But why?"

"'Why?' You silly, girl. Don't you remember who you are?"

The songstress gapes at the question. Of course she knows who she is, but... who is she? What was her name? Wyona, no. Wendy, no. Wanda? No, that isn't right either. Why can't she remember her own name?

"It's the fae magic, you foolish witch. Luckily for you, the dead have no such restrictions on our memory. Come here."

Summer takes her by the elbow and leads her over to a television. No, it isn't a monitor like she is used to seeing in this day and age. It is a vintage, two-antennae-jutting-out-the-top television. Summer's ghost pushes her down into a recliner she is certain wasn't there a moment ago before drifting over to the old TV. The ghost makes a fist and pounds on the top of the device which miraculously turns on. There's no power cable anywhere to be seen, so it's anyone's guess as to why it works.

There is a moment of darkness before the camera focuses. A man in a dirty lab coat stands in the center of the screen. His face is obscured with a leather mask shaped reminiscently of a crane's beak.

"I don't want to see this," says the witch who knows not her own name.

"You have to see this, my dear. You have to remember who you are and how you came to be."

"I don't want to remember."

"Forgetting is easy. Being forgotten is even easier, but there are some of us to whom neither is an option."

The mask-wearing man in the footage clears his throat as he is adjusting the camera. When satisfied, he takes a step back, adjusts his lab coat, and speaks.

"We have been trying to merge biology, alchemy, and arcane techniques. With genetic splicing and netherbeast summonings, we have been attempting to knit magic into the developing systems of unborn babies by altering the mother's genetic structure during gestation. Every subject thus far has perished at one stage of the experiment or another. We haven't yet had a viable live birth or surviving mother subject. Oftentimes, during labor, the accumulation of energy in the fetus ends up ripping the mother apart or vice versa. The few times we have managed a live birth, the child was too horribly disfigured from the introduction of nether-beast DNA to serve our purposes, thus the poor creatures had to be disposed of. The Pontiflex will not stand for this failure for much longer, but we have been given one last batch of test subjects."

The camera, at that point, splits to showcase several patient cells, each one holding a woman in various stages of pregnancy. Many of them are dirty and underweight for pregnant women, but they seem hopeful. Happy to eat the food being provided to them and thankful to the nurses taking their vital signs. It's sickening: the poor and destitute cast from their homes for their unborn babies, now here thinking they are with someone who is going to help them.

"These are the last subjects that we will be given. Most are the usual prostitutes and street whores that are found and brought to us, but I fear that all hope is lost."

There is some footage of the women undergoing treatment over the course of the next minute. For a while, the women seem to improve. Their color gets better, they gain the necessary weight, and the rosy glow of pregnancy permeates their forms as they come into good health once more, but as more time goes on and the treatments given to the women take on an otherworldly nature, their progress takes a different turn. Invariably, each woman ends up in a body bag.

A tear falls down the cheek of the witch watching.

"What does this have to do with me?" she asks Summer.

"Just keep watching."

"All of the subjects in Lot 27 have expired," the crane-masked man is speaking again. *"We have no further means of experimentation. We are out of time. I can only pray that my death will be swift at the hands of His Grace."*

The screen goes black for just a moment before the camera lights back up.

"There is hope after all. A prisoner of war has been brought to us by the Goblin King himself. She was given to us for disposal. Archibald is a cruel man, indeed, delivering a woman all but dead and torn to pieces to our door. 'Use her for parts' he said. Ugh, what a foul man! As usual, we begin with fresh blood and DNA samples, and lo and behold what a wonder that has been bestowed upon me. This technomancer has come to us approximately six weeks pregnant.

"I am prepared to keep these records sealed from access to anyone outside of my most trusted doctors. If His Excellency discovers I kept a technomancer meant for deletion, I will be hanged on the spot. But how could I possibly pass up this opportunity to experiment on a technomancer, someone whose body is accustomed to harnessing techno-magic! It is the perfect opportunity. Emergency surgery has successfully stabilized her for the time being. More procedures will need to be followed. She has a broken pelvis and several other serious injuries that will compromise her condition if left for too long. It will take all my medical knowledge and skill to salvage her, and she will need around the clock monitoring. If she can survive the week, we may have the answer to all of my prayers."

The camera angle changes once more to a hospital bed. The patient appears to be sedated or sleeping, strapped into place by a series of tubes and an oxygen mask seemingly locked in place over her head. Additionally, bandages cover her eyes, making it impossible to identify the technomancer who was taken hostage. The mechanical accessories inlaid into her right arm and both legs are dulled and covered in a contrasting wiring—power suppressors no doubt. The foreign tech glows red against the muted aquamarine sigils of her integrated accoutrement. Bruises decorate her flesh everywhere that skin is visible, bruises from bindings around her wrists, a handprint encircling her throat, scratches and fingerprints along her calves and thighs.

In the back of her mind, she thinks the tech might originate from Deriva.

The date marker in the corner of the screen advances by two weeks. The inmate's condition, which was dismal in the initial frame, has only improved in so much as the bruises are no longer visible on her skin. However, new injuries have replaced them. The mechanical modifications that were present along her right arm and both legs have been removed and each limb is poorly bandaged in bloody cloths. A collar has been braced about her neck and various wires and tubes have been inset into her arms, legs, and torso. An additional tube feeds into the facemask.

"Subject 127452 has undergone preliminary injections and genetic simulations, and it is promising that she has not fallen ill as many of our prior subjects have in the past. A feeding tube has been inserted to ensure maximum nutrition is absorbed into her body for the fetus growing inside her. She must have been a strong technomancer, indeed. Merely a week since her last surgery, and she has almost fully recovered. Despite her weakened state, the subject is violent and prone to outburst. In her short time here, she has injured several members of the staff and even killed one of my best doctors. As additional precaution, her mechanical augmentations, which were already supposedly deactivated upon arrival, have been surgically removed. We don't know if she was somehow able to reactivate her tools or if the job was not done properly to begin with, but it is an oversight that will not happen again."

The date advances forward again.

The doctors are shown administering injections three times daily. Sometimes the woman goes into convulsions but is easily stabilized, much to the delight of the head doctor. The camera still captures moments of fight from her. In one frame, she kicks an orderly across the room. In another, she struggles hard enough against her restraints that they cut into her wrists. During a transfer, she manages to break the knee of one of her escorts and takes off running down the hall. They have to shoot her with a tranquilizer to stop her.

After this incident, she is further restrained in an exoskeleton. As the date reaches several months past the initial date shown, it is obvious that the woman's pregnancy has progressed. She does not glow with a happily pregnant aura. There is a more sinister discoloration to her skin. The meager hospital gown she wears does nothing to hide the veins that pulse just under her skin, and a sickening pattern of wires have been inserted into her belly.

"This is incredible. Subject 127452 has progressed through her first trimester. The rate of miscarriage and death by this point sits somewhere at 90% for all our other patients, but Subject 127452 shows stable enough vitals that we are going to begin phase two of the experiment. The suspension tank and the brazen head. Now it is time to test whether the treatments have begun to alter her cellular make-up as well as the developing fetus within her."

The next few minutes of the recording feature the woman submerged in a large water tank while he continues to expound.

"Blood samples are promising. She is presenting an increase in blood density and cellular reproduction. White blood cell count is normal, but a new cell-type has joined the red and white blood cells. They don't appear to be hostile in nature and if anything, seem to carry a surplus of information in the mitochondria. How the body integrates this information remains to be seen. We have seen these appear in a few other patients but not in this volume. The patient's body seems to be healing faster as well, which is good. We monitor this by tracking a daily incision series upon her body, and incisions made as recently as three days ago have already healed with very little scarring. This will make phase 2 easier as we begin to introduce radiation and electroconvulsive therapy."

The screen flips through the implementation of the various phase 2 "therapies." She witnesses the woman's skin burn from radiation only to resurface just days later, no longer a warm tan but a paler gray. For a few sickening moments, active electrical nodes are applied to the girl's temple. You can never know abject horror until you watch a person's muscles go stiff as a board under the onslaught of high electrical current. At one point, Summer herself enters the facility to set an array which they set the inmate inside of while several hooded figures chant around her.

"As we enter the next phase of therapy, the fetus's cerebral tissue will begin to develop at an exponential rate. We seek to increase the percentage of brain function by simulating the development of more neural pathways than an average human would possess. This opens us up to a whole new realm of possibility for psychic ability in the babe, but I have miscalculated. As a teenager, the girl's own brain is still adolescent and therefore not yet fully developed. I never anticipated treatments would increase the mother's neural activity as well. Several accidents have occurred."

The footage flashes through several of these accidents. The glass of the suspension tank shatters while she is inside. Her attempt to run out of the room is thwarted by a large orderly who ensnares her in magnetic netting before she can get too far. She screams as she is strapped down to a table for electric shock. It is during this session that one of the doctors is thrown backward into a wall with no apparent cause. His neck breaks on impact, and the girl is immediately sedated.

"We are now keeping the patient on a regiment of tranquilizers. Hopefully, the fetus has developed enough at this point to not be too negatively impacted by the drugs. Subject 127452 is progressing at a marvelous rate, and we can only pray that the super soldier growing in her womb will remain viable just a bit longer. Once we reach the eighth month of gestation, a Cesarean can be performed in the event the mother's body expires before delivery. I can only hope it inherits its mother's ferocity. Goodness! Just imagine if the father was also a technomancer. The possibilities are endless."

The man devolves into a fit of maniacal laughter before the screen switches once again.

The experiments continue with more injections, more serums, more rituals. Drugs and nutrients are forced into her system through the tubes. The woman wastes away before their eyes as the days continue to progress. At about the start of what would be the woman's third trimester, a dramatic change takes place.

"Last night, Subject 127452 went into cardiac arrest. The subject's heart stopped for approximately 53 seconds. With adrenaline and defibrillators, we managed to stabilize her. I am beginning to lose hope. We are a month from minimal viable delivery. If she doesn't make it, that will be the end for us. We hope to keep her calm and comfortable using neural stimuli. Maybe by transitioning her consciousness into a virtual dreamscape, we can lower her stress."

When the screen next puts her on display, her condition has improved, but the woman is locked inside of a VR system and suspended by an intense tangle of cabling. Only the most minute movements and twitches reveal that she is still living. More time passes with her in this state, marked only by the constant flow of orderlies and doctors and the ticking date at the corner of the screen.

"We have done it. Subject 127452 has reached the 8th month of her pregnancy. Of course, we won't opt for an early delivery, but we now have the option of forsaking the mother in the event of catastrophe. I've ordered 24/7 monitoring of her. It is time to move on to the last series of injections. If the child can withstand this, we will have succeeded in our mission, and all of the death that has resulted from these procedures will prove worth it."

A camera remains constant over a hospital bed containing Subject 127452 as several more days pass. She is strapped down and hooked up to several machines. An arcane array encircles her. One appears to be monitoring her vitals and while another monitors her unborn's vitals. A bag of fluids and blood sit next to the bed as well, being steadily pumped into her system. Another bag of luminescent liquid hooks directly into her skull through the VR helmet.

An orderly enters the room and injects a syringe-full of something into the IV on her arm before stepping back out. The video monitors her chest rising and falling before stillness sweeps over the prone body. The machine begins to wail as her whole body falls into a seizure. Lines of black decorate her skin, and blood begins to pool beneath the VR helmet.

The head doctor is there within moments, demanding a C-section be performed immediately. The next few minutes are difficult to watch, and several of the aristocrats in the room turn away, sick at the very sound of the woman's screams as they rip her apart. Several minutes pass before her screams shudder and die only to be replaced by the cries of a newborn. Several on-lookers sigil themselves, praying for the dying girl, though what they are watching is all pre-recorded. The doctor stares at the child with wonder, greed and sick pride shining in his features.

"She's perfect! Our super soldier! Finally, we have accomplished our mission."

The doctor continues to preen as he hands the screaming infant off to a waiting orderly who sets the baby in a sterile NICU container before wheeling her out of the room.

"Sir?" One of the doctor's underlings pipes up.

"Yes, Dawson?"

"The mother... She is still alive."

A gasp resounds through the court as indeed the woman is still moving, the faintest of breaths raising her chest, her abdomen a landscape of gore and viscera. "Butchers," one of the appalled sect leaders gasps.

"Hmm. She'll be dead soon enough. Take the appropriate samples and then dispose of the trash. Remove the repressors first so we can recharge them. We may need them for the baby."

Dawson nods before turning back to the patient. His eyes look almost sad as he surveys the woman. Her breath rattles, and with each draw of air into her lungs, more and more blood spurts from the open incision site. He wrinkles his nose at the mess when blood flows fresh and pulls a sheet up to cover the gore to start working.

"Commencing removal of repressors," announces the man.

He carefully removes each and every blood-soaked apparatus, the sigils now gone dark. Without a host to feed energy from, the devices have deactivated. He turns his back to her as he moves to clean the repressors in a nearby basin. Slowly, the woman's breathing stills, and her body goes lax.

After just a few heartbeats, the black veins that have laced her skin begin to glow with a lime-green luminescence. A seizure overtakes the corpse, blood continues to flow, only now it is tinted with an ethereal glow, menacing to look at and filled to the brim with magical power. If the orderly hears her, he ignores her in favor of finishing his task.

A shadow falls over the camera and just as quickly disappears, and the girl takes a breath. Her hand clenches, and the bleeding stops.

By the time the orderly has turned back around, she appears just as she had been a moment before, apparently dead and gone. He needles a syringe, but just as he is about to draw from her arm, a flash of light whites out the screen and the man screams as glass flies into his eyes. Green light pulses around her and the restraints let loose. She rises from the table, shaky and in pain. She tears at the tubes embedded into her skin before attacking the VR device still strapped to her head.

She gags as she peels it off, and blood rushes from her mouth as she pulls the tubes out of her mouth and nose. She throws everything across the room. Her hand goes straight to the open incision in her lower abdomen, and she breathes, teeth clenched, trying not to scream.

Her dark hair obstructs her face as she throws her legs over the edge of the bed and tries to stand. Weak from inactivity and blood loss, she crumples to the floor and crawls her way to the table holding various medical supplies all while holding her insides from spilling onto the floor. A bandaged hand grasps for a cauterizing gun before dragging it off the table and onto the floor. The tool sparks in her hand as she tests it before she lowers it to the gaping hole in her stomach. This time she does scream as the device burns and sears the flesh closed until the open incision is a line of burnt muscle and skin.

She rises to her feet shakily, holding onto the table for balance. Her face lifts to the camera.

The woman's eyes sparkle green like a cat's in the footage, a ghost risen from the dead, her witch's indicia burning green at her forehead. Shadows shift around her frame, and then the picture shudders as an explosion of bright green light short circuits the camera.

The observer recognizes those eyes. She recognizes that indicia.

Static fills the screen.

Abruptly, a new image floods the screen, and the cries of a newborn overwhelm the speakers. The infant lies on a steel medical table as two doctors examine her. The crane mask wearing doctor is present in the room as well. He hovers over the child like a proud father. They haven't even bothered to clean her of her mother's blood and the birth fluids before they started the exams. The umbilical cord is overly long as well.

"The infant weighs 2.75 kilograms, and measures 45cm. Excellent statistics for a moderately premature delivery. The child, which will henceforth be known as Subject X1001, is a promising start to the X-series. After administering an ultrasound, all internal organs appear to be fully formed. No heart defects. The lungs are a tad underdeveloped, but judging from her cries, that doesn't seem to be an inhibition."

The baby is small, to be expected from a premature birth, but her lungs are full and there is power in those tiny thrashing limbs, so much so that the men have trouble keeping her still long enough to get her vitals. The doctors move about the room prepping additional equipment. As they prepare for blood extraction, a noise sounds from the hallway followed by a deep thud as something collides with the wall.

"Rowan, will you go check that please?"

"Yes, professor."

The younger doctor makes his way to the door. As he reaches for the handle, the heavy metal is thrown open, sending him backward to be crushed on the other side of it. The other doctor panics at the death of his colleague and makes to set off an alarm. Black tendrils of energy reach in and wind around his head and torso. He jerks as the energy snaps his neck. The lead doctor calls for back-up, picking up the child and retreating farther into the laboratory as the mad witch pulls her way into the room, one arm outstretched and glowing with dark magic.

"I need armed reinforcements in Lab 15 now. We have a subject on the loose."

"Give me my baby!"

A shrieking sound surrounds the woman's form as the dark energies around her thicken and multiply.

"Stay back. I'm warning you. I will kill her if you don't stay back."

"Give them to me." She takes another shaky step into the room.

"I said, stay back!"

The doctor brandishes a scalpel about the baby's face. The child's screeches reach a fever pitch.

"Don't touch my light," shouts the woman, and the scalpel flies from the man's hand and embeds itself into his throat. His arm flings backward from the force of the blow, and he topples over. The mother throws herself onto the ground in a lunge to catch the babe before she can hit the floor, but she is too far away.

"No!"

The dark energy swirls around the child and catches her in midair. Tears fall from the young mother's face to the floor as the babe is floated into her arms. She presses the infant into her body heat. The newborn's cries quiet as she enfolds herself around the tiny body. The child must have been freezing from the lack of body heat.

"That child doesn't belong to you!"

The sound of a weapon charging pierces the silence. A yellow streak of light burns into her back. She cries out before crouching down, animal-like with the babe in hand. Her fingertips light up green as a second shot is aimed at her. The dart freezes in midair, and a pulse of power flings the shot back to its originator.

The doctor shouts as the dark tendrils knock the mask off his face. On the screen is Professor Faust.

Another wave of energy lashes out at him, and he is flung back hard enough into the wall that it crumbles around him. The woman's mouth opens and a sound that makes even the observing spectator cover her ears spills forth. A green appendage reaches from her hand to rip the ceiling down on top of him. As the structure collapses, the guards arrive. They bare their weapons at the young mother as she tucks her infant closer to her body.

"That's me," says the observer, W—.

"Yes. It is."

On the TV, Wr—'s eyes close, her lips moving in fast whispers, and a vaguely cat-shaped green energy swirls around her, furling in and molding to her shape. It condenses down to a small glowing ball, the pair absent from the space, and then bursts, green flames scattering throughout the room and quickly igniting the woodwork. The camera view melts from the heat of the fire.

The screen goes black as the footage comes to an end.

"Do you remember, yet? Do you remember who you are?"

Wre- shakes her head.

"That can't be me."

"But it is you, Wren. That is *Wren Nocturne*."

22

FOUR OF PENTACLES

Memory Bank Retrieval - 14 Years Ago - 12th Day in the Month of Hearths, 1863 A.P.

"HOW OLD IS SHE?"

~~Wren~~ looks up from her steaming cup of egg drop soup to glance at the toddler currently pressing her face against the sizable aquarium beside their table.

"A little less than two. Their birthday is in about three months."

Barely more than a babe. "Where did you find her?"

Her eyes shift from left to right, her spoon held aloft before her mouth as though his words shocked her from her next bite of food. Surely, it's an easy enough question. She's chewing on her lip, not answering. She takes in another spoonful of soup despite the fact that she has yet to answer the question.

"Oh, you know," she begins, dabbing her mouth with a napkin, "plenty of orphans all across the continent. Pretty easy to just pick one up at an orphanage or on the side of the road."

"You picked a baby up on the side of the road?"

"No, we were in the woods."

"Someone left a baby in the woods."

Wren shrugs. "People have done weirder things to protect their infants. Moses was put in a basket and floated down a crocodile-infested river by his mother."

"So you're raising a toddler by yourself."

"Should I have just left her there?" she asks pointedly. "Or should I have drowned her first as a means of mercy?"

"Of course not. It's just—" Kaito looks at the child again, a niggling feeling in his gut. There is a lie of omission somewhere in those words, an important bit of information that she is very intentionally leaving out. Whether he is untrustworthy of such information or she is simply being protective of her ward, he cannot tell.

"I know I don't seem like the mothering type," she goes on while picking at her vegetables. "But I'm trying to do as best I can for them. This world is already dark enough. I want to introduce as much light into their life as I can. That's why I was hunting the Jabberwocky. These parts are going to give me some of the extra pocket cash I'll need for their Solstice present."

"I could get them something," he blurts without thinking. He certainly has the means to buy both of them just about anything they may want or need at any time, not just Solstice.

"That's kind of you, Kaito, but Fae is my responsibility. I'm the one who should be making sure their holidays are worthwhile."

"Whoooaah," the toddler oohs and awes as a particularly colorful fish swims right by her nose.

"Fae, come eat your rice."

"Oh-Kay," she says, sitting at her guardian's direction and grabbing a fistful of the food on her plate. The witch then looks to him.

"So, tell me what is going on in the world as I hermit in the forest."

Kaito's lips quirk up.

They stay at the restaurant far later than either one of them intended. So late, in fact, that Fae has curled up in her adoptive mother's arms and gone straight to sleep on her chest. The songstress wonders aloud how she is going to make the trek back in the dark without waking the babe, so Kaito offers her the pull-out couch in his hotel room. She smiles as she accepts.

His witch is outside, rocking herself and her ward side to side in the night breeze as he pays the bill. Their waiter smiles at him.

"You have a beautiful family, sir. Your little girl looks just like her mama. Thank you for your patronage."

He is so stunned by the compliment he doesn't find the words to refute the man's assumption.

Once they reach the hotel room, Kai leaves the two to themselves, moving into the adjacent room. He can hear her as she sings the child into a deeper sleep. Her song floods the space he inhabits even though she is a room apart from him. The songbird's voice cascades over him as he lays down. His eyes grow heavy, and sleep comes easy to him for the first time in a long while.

The sound of clothes rustling rouses him, and when a hand brushes against his collarbone, he snaps fully awake. In a quick movement, he pulls the person touching him off of their feet and onto their back on the bed. He uses his full body weight to hold them down, though it doesn't seem terribly necessary. The body beneath him is soft and pliant, having relaxed into the maneuver rather than fought against it.

"Sorry, I didn't mean to wake you."

His eyes come into focus in the dark as he blinks the leftover sleep from them. There she is, solid and seemingly close to laughing at his reaction to being woken.

"What are you doing in here?"

She bites her lip.

"I was coming to bed. I can sleep elsewhere if you prefer."

"I thought you would wish to sleep with Fae."

She hums in understanding. "I thought so too, but I couldn't fall asleep, so I thought I would come in here. Forgive me if I was presumptuous."

She wears her smile like armor as she moves to rise from under him. He places his other hand down in the sheets, far enough from her form that she does not feel caged by him but effectively stopping her progress lest she change direction. She seems to understand his intention and stops moving, choosing instead to cast her gaze back on his face. She breathes slowly, calmly.

"You need not apologize."

The steel in her smile melts, and she relaxes back into the pillows behind her. He thinks he imagines her sigh in relief, but the tension drains from her body. He should move off her now that he understands her intentions.

"I've missed you..." she breathes, so softly he can barely hear her.

Her hand lifts to the exposed skin of his shoulder where his sleep shirt has moved askew in their small tussle. Her fingers are cool on his skin, almost cold. They trail from the peak of his shoulder, along his collarbone, up the line of his throat to his jaw where she slides them across his cheek to the corner of his mouth where she stalls.

He grasps her fingers in his hand. She stiffens, no doubt thinking she has overstepped again. He turns his head, his lips finding her palm. His silver gaze finds hers. In the moonlight streaming in through the window, her eyes glow with a feline luminescence. Another change from her two-year absence that should unsettle him but doesn't. Not anymore.

"Your Highness."

"My Lady."

He allows her to guide him down, and she rises to meet him. It's been nearly six months since their last conversation that nearly ended in a kiss. It is different but the same. They are different but the same. Into the touch, he pours his longing, his grief, his anger, his need, and she returns in kind. He nearly succumbs to the intensity of her. He is not an empath like her, but even the depth of her suffering, her hatred, her rage is not lost to him. But those dark emotions are tempered by want, by her abounding joy in this moment, by the secret affection they share, and dare he dream it... Could he even hope that someone so untamed possibly would ever allow themselves to feel the damning ties of love toward him?

Long moments pass before they pull apart, breathless and panting. They shift as one, her legs parting on either side of his hips as he settles himself between them and their mouths find each other again. She coaxes his hands to her body, and he reaches under the hem of her chemise, touching bare skin. He releases her mouth to find his way to her throat where his teeth find purchase. He sucks hard, and the moan that escapes her is loud enough to give him pause.

He pulls back. "The child?"

She beams. "Fae is a very sound sleeper for a child her age. Once she is down, she does not wake, not even during a thunderstorm or the passing of a train. So long as we are quiet, we won't disturb her."

He nods at this, a hum on his lips before he finds hers again.

She lifts her upper body. His hands go to the hem of her shirt. She has not allowed herself to be bare before him since before the war, and a part of him does not expect her to remove her top tonight either, but then her hands come down on top of his, and she lifts the hem, and when the garment is pulled up and off of her body, his breath is stolen from his lungs. Her breasts are fuller now than when she was sixteen. Pert nipples stand taut against the darker pink of her areola before cascading into soft pale mounds. She sighs as his hands reach up to tease at their peaks, mouthing at the space between and around before his lips close around one, his tongue swirling, drawing delightful gasps from her. His arms link around to embrace her more fully, supporting her as she tries to remove his own clothing with her one hand. She makes decent progress before his patience gives way.

He lowers her back to the sheets and pulls away to rid himself of his garments while she pulls her legs through the holes of her panties, leaving her bare before him and him bare before her.

This is the first time she has allowed him to see her body since their time in the catacombs.

Their bodies bear the effects of war time. New scars yet to be explored, they are the blood sewn writing of their stories during their time apart. He knows there is an ugly scar on his left shoulder from a stab wound he'd taken early on. Faint burn scars line his right side from explosions. There is also, of course, the evidence of his newer tech. The trace lines of wires glow a steady violet under the skin of his arms and legs, powerful artifacts that gave him the ability to surpass the gear-grinding, bone-shattering power of augmented soldiers with their mechanical limbs.

The witch's body is decorated with the tattoo-like sigils she returned with. Their outlines are a faint gray-green at present since they are inactive. He'd only ever seen the ones on her arms and face, but they trace through her entire being along the sides of her torso, her spine, her legs. Artifacts brimming with power when he touches them, her whole body hums with potential energy just begging to be unleashed. There are scars too, faint punctures in her arms, the signs of shredding around her left wrist where her augmented arm was removed and never reinstalled. Most noticeable is the long horizontal scar that sits just above the line of her pubis, jagged and raised like a wound that never healed correctly. He has never seen such a scar from battle, or at the very least, he'd never met anyone who had survived the kind of wound such a scar would indicate.

She hisses when he touches it.

"What is this from?"

A strange look passes across her face then. A forlorn look of shame and sadness, of heartache and long dead anger.

"A nightmare and a gift all at once."

"Does it hurt?"

"No," she whispers, pulling his hand away and winding her fingers into his hair, pulling him back down. She is nothing but efficient as she effectively pulls his attention back to the present.

He is hard, and she grinds up into his pelvis, wrapping her arms and legs around him, pulling him forward. She has him held completely captive in her embrace. But he does not press into her. Not yet. He knows more now, and with that knowledge comes the abject question of how she had not completely shirked away from his touch their first time together, fumbling, clueless teenager that he was. He wonders how he did not cause her lasting damage those times during the war when their passions were little more than angry fights and desperate attempts to connect.

While his left hand tangles in her hair, his right snakes down between them. His index finger draws light teasing circles around the blooming bud of her clit before descending farther to press into her, his thumb staying in place to give more attention to that sensitive button.

"Kai."

His name falls from her lips like a wish. She arches into him as he nuzzles the skin of her bosom, his other hand snaking its way to her lower back, and she arches farther into his touch as he breeches her with a second digit. He angles his wrist and quirks his fingers in a "come hither" motion to brush against that soft bundle of nerves within her. She turns her head into the pillow and bites down to muffle her exclamation at his ministrations.

He works her with his hand, a slow torment of heat and pleasure, until she is a mess of soft sobs and pretty pleads. He does not stop, even as her first orgasm wrecks her form.

"Kai, please!"

He arches, sealing their lips together once more. He moves his hand from her core and repositions himself, smearing her damp pleasure against the head of his cock. He presses forward, listening and watching her carefully as he proceeds, thrusting shallowly at first and then deeper and deeper until the whole of his cock is sheathed in her tight heat.

By the time he is fully seated within her, her thighs are quivering around him, and she is drawn taut as a bow prepped to release. He dips his head down and swallows her moans as he begins to thrust. His hips work to elicit more of those sweet sounds from her. His own pleasure coils in the pit of his stomach, but he forces it down, determined for this coupling to last.

Her hand comes to his shoulder and pushes. He rolls them over and angles himself to lean against the headboard. He gives her full control, and her arms wind once more around his neck. She sits astride him, forehead braced against his, and with his hands on her hips, she begins to pulse fervently in his lap. She grinds into him and he angles his hips to hit that spot within her with each hard descent of her body onto his length. She cries out through gritted teeth.

Sweat gathers on their bodies. His fingers glide up to her shoulders, and he helps her move. Minutes pass between the shared heat of their bodies. The power in his arms pulls her down while his legs push his pelvis up to meet hers with every motion. Her cunt clenches around him, and she throws her head back, dark curls cascading like a waterfall down her back, mouth parted in silent ecstasy as she comes for the second time.

He surges forward then, flipping their positions, hips driving forward and back with raw fury. Her legs wrap high around his back, and he crooks one of her knees in his elbow, giving him more depth. Her moans reach a fever pitch, and she closes her teeth around her forearm to dampen the sound. She bites down so hard that the smell of blood reaches his nose. He grabs the limb and moves it. Her cries don't stop. His hand wraps around her throat and she mewls in pleasure, straining to capture his lips all while he continues to piston into her, and she meets him thrust for thrust until his own orgasm rocks through him.

His teeth close down on her shoulder as a deep groan shudders through his chest, her walls clamping down around him as a third peak rips through her. His sight goes dark for a full second.

They fall together. He collapses over her, spent, head resting against the line of her shoulder. She is sweaty and panting and beautiful in the moonlight, hair a messy spill around her head and a high flush across her skin. An exhale shakes from his lungs as he pulls from her, rolling them and rearranging them until she is cradled against him. Her lashes tickle the skin of his collarbone as her eyes flutter open.

"Wow," she breathes, and if his lips quirk as he moves to press them to her temple, he feels not an ounce of shame for it. They are dirty and sticky, and he doesn't have it in him to care. Her eyes fall shut again, and her breathing deepens as slumber takes her over. He follows her easily after tugging the sheets over them.

The next morning, he wakes at his usual time. The sunlight pours in through the window, filtered through the parted blinds. He is reticent to rise. His witch is warm in his arms.

It is dangerous being here. After yesterday's events, having dinner together, talking to her without any pressures of time or duty, carrying on the same easy banter of their summit days, just being with her. Were it not for the scars on their bodies and the state of the world on their shoulders, he would have thought them teenagers again. Even meeting her young ward only serves to make the moment sweeter.

His heart aches.

"You didn't come here on a simple assignment, did you?" she asks him as they prepare to part ways a few hours later. After a quick breakfast, the witch led him on a short trek to the forest that marks Murasaki's border. The witch keeps keen eyes on Fae, the small child now playing ahead of them in the brush. "Any adept could have handled that Jabberwock. Such a case is far beneath your skillset."

Rather than answer her outright, he looks away to where Fae has begun to pile balls of snow on top of her hooded head. She laughs, a sad look in her eye. "You've never been good at lying, Kaito-kun."

She turns her attention to the girl. "Fae, it's time to go!"

"No, mama!!"

"No 'no's,' Little One. It's time to go."

Fae pouts but begins to make her way down the tree she was just climbing up. Kaito speaks up as her little feet touch the ground.

"She is the right age."

She stills next to him, and when he turns to look at her, she doesn't dare to meet his gaze.

"The last case we went on together before the war... you got sick unexpectedly. The facility we raided. The scar on your abdomen."

He doesn't dare say more. Fae makes it to them and the woman bends to pick her up. When she is upright again, Fae's face curls into her bosom. As the girl looks at him, he notices for the first time the same glimmer reminiscent of a cat's eye in her gaze, only hers is a more orange luminescent than his mother's. The next words she speaks are spoken in Kaito's own language, broken and choppy but clear enough in their meaning.

"No one can know she lives. No one."

"Wren..." He wants to tell her that she doesn't have to face this alone, but his words catch in his throat, and she cuts him off before he can spit them out.

"Thank you for your kindness, Prince Kaito. I'm happy you got to meet my ward, but you shouldn't come back here. It's too dangerous."

She closes off to him once again. He breathes deeply even as his chest constricts. From the tree line, a low rumbling growl pierces the silence.

"Easy, Silje. Kaito is a friend."

The netherbeast who came to her call the day she became a fugitive steps out of the shadow of the forest, its giant paw crunching into the snow.

"Si Si!"

Fae wiggles in excitement at the sight of the great cat, so she lets the toddler down and the child runs to the netherbeast. Kai almost flinches as the creature nudges its great maw against the little one, but then the girl squeals in delight, and not for the first time, Kai guesses.

The girl's mother watches him watch his daughter play with a creature he has been taught his whole life should be killed on sight. She watches as he struggles to reconcile the gentle handling it, no... *she* treats the child with.

"We live in two different worlds now, Kai. You should return to yours."

"There was a time when you would have returned with me."

She looks at him sadly. "Some dreams are never meant to see the light of day." She laughs and reaches as though to touch him, but she catches herself as though an innocent touch in the daylight was more forbidden than the touches they shared in the dark of the night. "I'm sorry, Kai. I shouldn't have stayed with you last night."

She steps away from him, moving toward the forest. She turns back to him at the edge of the ward.

"Don't come back here, Kai. I wouldn't be able to take it if something happened to you, too."

She picks up Fae, and she crosses the ward, disappearing from his sight though he can still hear their voices.

"Mama, will the cyber man come back?"

"Probably not, Little One."

"Why not?"

"He has his own life to live, and it's very important that he live it."

"But why?"

"Sometimes, there isn't always an answer to that question. Sometimes things just are what they are."

"Can't you change them?"

"No, my love. Some things can't be changed."

"Mama..." The next time the child speaks, they sound farther away. "You're crying."

"Hush."

Kaito does return though. Time and time and time again. How could he stay away, knowing this is where his family is?

When the Songstress of Lorelei's name first appeared in League records, no one had any clue who the name might be in reference to. There were rumors everywhere of a witch who was going to take the place of Koven and become the ruling power of the hexen.

The Primarch of the time, a newly elected Morrigan Gewalt, felt only that any witch who tried to defy the League would be swiftly dealt with and made an example of. She put a bounty on her head.

100,000 credits to anyone who can bring forward the head of the witch responsible for killing however many technomancers were being attributed to her name. No one realized that the Songstress was far more than a powerful witch. She was, in fact, a witch with a knowledge of technomancy, and such a thing had never been seen before.

Excerpt from <u>A World on Fire: The Last Days of Magic</u>
Monsieur Lafayette de Leonard, 1876 A.P.

23
THE EMPRESS

"DID YOU KNOW THAT BABIES CAN HEAR the world around them before they're even born?"

Summer's voice is matter-of-fact, a barely interested observer commenting merely for the sake of filling in the silence.

"I wonder what part of my life my son heard before he died coming into this world."

"You had a son."

The other witch, draped in shadows and not much else, nods. "He would have been perfect, but he wasn't strong enough to draw his first breath."

She can't imagine what that must be like.

"My fault of course. I was too much. Did too much. Used too much. He would have had a better chance if someone else had been his mother. Maybe someone like you."

What is this witch on about? She was not the kind of person anyone associated with motherhood. At least not in any positive way. Her own brother once said she was better suited for the combat grounds than nurseries, and she hadn't a mind to disagree with him.

"Did your baby cry when they were born?"

Summer's question catches her off guard.

"What baby?"

"'What baby' she says. What baby do you think I'm talking about?! Your baby, you fool. I'm asking about the baby that was ripped from your cursed body! Did they cry?!"

The words sting. How could she know?

"I-I don't know."

She had been too close to death to remember if Fae cried when she was born or not. All she remembers is the pain, the rage, and then the ugly truth that settled in her corpse as the world shifted irrevocably from sense and sensibility to complete and utter nonsense.

"Yes, you do," snips Summer. "You've just forgotten and henceforth made no attempts to remember, so fix it! Stop running from your past and remember! Did your baby cry?!"

Yes, because it's just that easy. *Simply close your eyes and remember. It can't be that hard.*

Except, it really is that easy in this strange place. No sooner does Summer give the command than her reality tilts off-axis. It occurs without her bidding, this shift, as easy as changing a shirt.

"It was cold in the room..."

It's the first thing she recalls. It's the first thing because there is a very unique feeling when your insides meet the open air. Worse even than being stabbed in the gut. At least when someone runs you through with a sword, they don't make a point to pin the flaps apart.

"Why was it cold?"

If she'd been in less pain, she would probably have likened the sensation to that of one of the fortune-telling finger boxes, the ones that open and close in different directions. The player gives an arbitrary number and the caster counts up to so many folds before lifting the corresponding flap and reading some other arbitrarily decided number aloud. When she was a teenager, she remembers most of the girls counting silly things like how many babies someone would pump out or how many weddings they would have, what the first letter of their soul mate's name was, et cetera, et cetera. She never really participated. At least not after one of the flaps revealed she would one day be a proud mother of four bouncing babies.

Back then, one would have been too many. Probably even now, one would be too many. Woe to the child that calls her mother.

The doctors play with her insides. Their hands tickle and grope at her innards as they rummage around as though looking for a lost battery in a cluttered drawer.

"They were taking something out of me."

"Go on," Summer urges. "What happened when they took it out?"

"I felt empty…"

The answers come easier and easier. Something has loosened her tongue. The words fall out as easily as water from a leaky cauldron. Is it strange that she doesn't question her compliance with this witch's interrogation of her? What does it matter if a long dead child was born crying or not? It isn't as though her daughter still draws breath, yet…

"I remember hearing laughter. Not my baby's. Someone else's."
Wah-ha-ha-ha! She's perfect! Our super soldier is here!
Congratulations, sir!
Whaaah! Aaah!
"Then, my baby cried."

"Good. Now, what happened next?"

"I died."

The answer leaves her mouth without a second thought. There are two kinds of truths. There are the learned truths—the relative truths. The ones known on an experiential level and discovered through observation: Decision-making is performed in the frontal cortex of the brain; if a body does not eat, it will die; a charged battery is the only kind worth using; and if a witch does not cast, she will fade into nothing. Then there are the absolute truths: the ones known on a subdermal level. These

Laws of Physics we couldn't change even if we employed the most advanced magics. These indisputable facts of existence fall into this bracket of truth: gravity, life, reproduction, death...

Yes, death is an absolute, even to a necromancer. Having the ability to undo death doesn't make life any less finite. Unravel a tapestry and the dregs left behind will resemble nothing like what was once so painstakingly sewn together, but unravel death, and its touch leaves a stain on what is reborn from the tatters.

That's how she felt after she gave her first death rattle: like something stained.

"So the Technomancer died. And who rose to take her place? The Songstress of Lorelei? A witch of death? A deathwalker? Oh wait, no, I know. The Queen of the Damned came in her place? Tell me. I must know. Who came back in your place after your first death? What did you name yourself?"

What did she name herself? But she didn't name herself. That was other people who gave her a name, gave her a title, gave her a label. Sought so hard to shove her in a box that they put the nails in their own coffin.

"I didn't name myself."

"Sure you did. You were the one who had to figure out who you were after you lost yourself. The very nature of our magic demands such command over the self."

But I didn't... Did I?

To Jessabelle, she gave the name Amelia. Her middle name was unobtrusive, nondescript, and best of all, unknown to the vast majority of the population. And considering her near-death experience, she wasn't about to chance having her name spread throughout the land when said land tried to kill her off.

Jessabelle was the one who saved her. Jessabelle was the one who taught her how to harness her power. Jessabelle was the one who kept her from taking her own life. Well, hers and the infant who now depended on her.

Mmmm...

It would be months before she told Jessabelle what her real name was. Months beyond months as she tried to fit together the shambled jigsaw puzzle that was her new existence, and she struggled and fought and denied everything that had happened to her. It wasn't even really she who finally figured out her new identity.

Ma...

What was that identity though? How does someone go from being one of the elite soldiers of the League to a lowly witch with little-to-no control over her own abilities? She didn't know who she was. She didn't know what she was. It required a very small, very honest voice to help identify who she now was.

Mama...

Fae said her first word at six months old. A song and a poem, an unending ballad and a whole trilogy all hidden between the two most innocent syllables she has ever heard spoken together. It had been world-shattering in the best possible way. The child named her, and it was the name that would forever change her life.

"I was 'Mama.'"

"Who?" asks Summer. "Who were you?"

"'Mama.' I was 'Mama.' That was my new identity."

An emerald glow manifests from within her core, and all of her memories are returned to her, including her name. Wren Nocturne remembers who she is, the witch's magic overcoming the fairy's.

"The Lady Nocturne became a mother." A new voice enters the conversation. It's harder, rougher, meaner. "That's hardly anything to be proud of. You soft women. You've never been suitable for war."

The new ghost banishes Summer's incorporeal form. The redhead is snuffed from Wren's psyche like lead dust blown from the edge of a page. She distinctly feels sorry to see the other witch go, for in her place is a far more distasteful apparition.

"Rameses."

"Long time no see, Nocturne."

"I suppose I owe your visit to your residue still lurking in Lacuna."

"Naturally."

"Right," she growls. Never mind that her athame is hardly responsive these days thanks to a certain fairy. "What do you want?"

"From you, nothing. For you, everything."

"I don't follow."

"Of course, you don't. Girl children are so terribly unintelligent."

"This coming from the man who thought it would be a good idea to assault a known witch. That's the kind of decision-making skill that gets you locked in an athame for the rest of known existence."

"You were a guest in my home."

"Not your home, your hotel, and why should that make anyone more amiable to being accosted by a bigoted old fart like you!"

"Regardless of any hard blood spilt between us, I'll have you know I come with advice."

"Advice? I wouldn't take your advice even if I hadn't killed you."

"Surely, you understand how death is the most marvelous equalizer. It makes one gain perspective on the choices made in life. Almost makes me regret some of the decisions I made."

"I find that unlikely."

"Of course you wouldn't understand. Death has only ever been a bosom buddy for you."

"Not sure I would classify Death and I as 'buddies,' but do you mind just getting to the point?"

"I realize it might be hard to accept the idea of my being an innocent bystander, but I will have you know that my visitation of your rooms that night years ago was less a personal decision and more an orchestration."

"I had no idea you carried an inclination for the symphony."

"Oh, I don't, Nocturne. I don't, but I can certainly certify that a certain tune was played into my ear the evening after you made a right fool of Farqaad. That old dunce should rightly have failed his technomancer trials, yet they passed him anyway for some ungodly reason. Anyway, this is the kind of tune that makes it very difficult to fight off any previously felt urges. Enchanted music has quite the sway on a person, as you well know."

"Wow, just like bra straps make it oh so difficult for prepubescent boys to keep their hands to themselves."

"I find it quite hypocritical that a Songstress who uses her own voice as a conduit for her magic would dismiss my story. Shouldn't you know better than anyone how powerful music-based magic can be?"

"Oh, I am well aware, Rameses, but if you expect me to believe that a witch was pulling your strings that night, you're crazier than Yggfret."

"I understand your skepticism, but someone wasn't just pulling my strings, they were conducting an entire scherzo."

"Well, then, it would have had to be a witch who survived the siege on the Vatidome. Oh, wait, there were none." Her voice is rising in pitch, and she isn't quite sure she has any control over it, not that she cares. "And there's more because this wouldn't be just any witch, mind you, but a witch with abilities to mirror mine who snuck into the Shard just to cast a spell on you so that you would come into my rooms and attempt to rape me. Right, yeah. I can believe that any day of the week except Wodinsday which just so happens to be today."

Wren flips the bird at the former Primarch and moves to leave, not that she knows where she's going in this topsy turvy world of make-believe. Anywhere would be better than in the presence of a mad ghost.

She storms her way to the nearest door, tugs it open, and steps through. The moment she walks over the frame, unfortunately, she finds herself right back in the dining room in front of an amused Rameses.

"Not a witch, Nocturne. A machine."

"Machine? Machines can't channel magic. Such a thing defies the basic laws of Deus."

"It is not as you say. I tell you this mechanism had the power to make me act on a thought I had but once."

"So you admit that you wanted me carnally, but you just didn't have the guts to try for my body without a bit of magical incentive.

Got it. So you're still a lusty swine, just one without an actual backbone. Glad we cleared that up."

"Damnit, woman, will you listen to what I am saying! Someone manipulated me to my death, and I think it would behoove you to figure out who, because it may very well lead you to some pertinent information you were previously missing regarding a certain doctor."

"Faust... You think Faust was pulling your strings that night."

"Not just my strings, dove. Yours as well."

A pulse of force rams into her chest. It barrels into her sternum, twists, and like water carving through sand, it drips through her pores, bones, and organs to come out the other side. Wren stumbles, gasping for air. It sucks down her nose to sit thick in her lungs, heavy and viscous, before she has to heave it back out. By the time her exhale is gone, another pulse hits her in the same place to the same effect.

This one knocks her off her feet, and she falls through the floor.

When she lands, a third pulse rockets through her whole body. Only this one doesn't seep all the way through her. It stays, rocking in her core. She feels it squirming around like a parasite, kicking her edges and stroking her insides. It coils in on itself, then expands out of her skin, and the pain that comes with it sets her on fire.

"Retractor!"

She's screaming. She is screaming but no sound comes from her mouth. There are too many tubes stuffed down her throat.

"Retractor."

Cold steel stretches an incision in her abdomen open. She can feel them, the hands moving around her insides and even deeper the tiny light wriggling for survival. *Stop it!*

Arms and legs are bound to the table. She can't fight. She can't see either. Not reality anyway. The seaside portrait flickers and blackens as the VR headset affixed to her head stutters. There's a whirring sound as the machine she is strapped to strains to restart the simulation she has been trapped in for however long.

"Scalpel!"

The blade cuts into the last layer of tissue protecting her little light and her jaw locks. The seizure rips through her spine in a dizzying array of sensation. Hot, cold, heavy, weightless, nothing, everything.

"We're losing them both!"

"No we're not!"

Despite the violent shakes of her body, those foreign hands digging inside of her grab hold of what they are looking for. Her little light shudders as gloved fingers wind around its center.

No!

Her light is ripped from her body. Blood and pain and a vast void. A cry fills the room.

"Our super soldier is here. At long last!"

"Congratulations, sir."

The voices, so filled with joy and accomplishment. She has never wanted to kill something as badly as she wants to kill the source of that joy.

But she can't...

She's too busy dying.

"Take the babe. I want a full chart taken. Bloodwork, head circumference, length, weight, gestation estimations, everything. We need to know that our hope is healthy."

No, that's her light. But she can do nothing to get it back. Death has already stolen her breath away.

.

.

.

"Sir, what about the mother?"

"What about her?"

"She is still alive."

"Not for much longer. Remove any of our suppression tech and dispose of the body. We have no further need for it."

Her light leaves her, and so too does her life.

Going...

· · ·

Going..

. .

Almost gone.

.

Wires are pulled from her legs. Points of numbness disappear like needles being removed after an acupuncture session. Only these needles, strangely enough, seemed to have been sapping her strength from her corpse. These tiny synthetic leeches kept her at the brink of death even before her body was cut open.

Her foot twitches.

Something niggles at the edge of her psyche. Something light and new. It's frightened and cold. It wants, it wants, it wants its home back.

A stranger's hands once again grope at her limbs, only this time instead of restricting her, they remove the manacles binding her in place.

A growl rumbles in her ear. She's heard this sound before, but she can't place it. A phantom touch trickles up her skin like a cat winding through its owner's ankles.

No, not a cat...

Her eyes open, her fingertips curl, and at her will, the sharpest tool on the table flies into the left eye socket of her would-be mortician. The screaming hurts her head. Her hands tear blindly at the wires still attached to her body. Sockets in her thighs, monitors on her chest and belly, there's a neurological stem buried two inches into her skull, and when she pulled the breathing tube out, she didn't realize a feeding tube was primed to come out with it.

She coughs and sputters.

Her hair is matted under the VR visor. Her fingernails are jagged, broken in two and three with uneven edges and sharp points. Bits of her hair come out with the visors straps, tangled and grown around the wires as though she's been wearing the damn thing for months.

The next hurdle, getting off the table, results in her overheated skin meeting cold linoleum. If she could but lie here for just a moment, surely this would be heaven, but she can't. The want, the niggling, aching panic drives her on. That and the blood still pouring from her core.

Another growl echoes in her head.

An army crawl has never been so tricky, considering her abs have been ripped apart. Most people don't realize this, but when a surgeon worth their salt performs a C-section, they actually make a point to not cut against the line of the abdominal wall so that the muscles can heal properly. Her core has been ripped open. She's heard of a botched abortion, she's even heard of cesareans that went wrong for one reason or another, but the one performed on her was intended to end her life. She was never supposed to survive that procedure, yet here she is. The cauterizer does its job. The bleeding diminishes enough that she's no longer leaving a trail of it.

Something cries in her head. Need. Desperate need, the likes of which she has only ever felt in the weeks she lost her mother to a sea monster. Her little light. Brighter than ever before and so terribly afraid. That fear pulls her to her feet, out of this poor excuse for a room that should have been her declaration of death site and across the hallway.

Her sight, damaged from prolonged exposure to a virtual reality cyberscape, is blurred and near useless. She moves by sense alone. It's a wonder she doesn't kill herself a second time.

The pissants who try to stop her become nothing more than stains on the wall. She senses their malice, and as though by magic, their presence disappears a moment later. She hasn't the slightest idea how. There is no pain. Only need which fuels her to the door where her little light cries for her.

"Give me my light."

There are three men in the room. They are dressed in medical blacks. Masks cover their faces, reminiscent of the plague doctors of old, only not all of them wear the visage of the crow on their face. One in particular wears the mask of a crane, the beak long enough to reach his belt.

It is this one who screams, "Guards!"

But his calls fall on deaf ears, or rather, they fall on dead ears. "Give me my light!" she screams again.

Her light is there on the table, cold and alone, screaming as unfeeling hands poke and prod at the small beacon. The crane draws a gun.

Thoughts are too slow. Her actions work on their own. This strength, this terrible, horrible strength, works its way through her unbidden and turns the weapon against its owner. The bodies drop as she makes her way farther into the room.

"Stop right there." He brandishes a scalpel at her light.

"Give them to me!"

"Don't come any closer. I'll do it. I swear."

"Give me my light!"

The growl comes again, a flash of fur and emerald light. A beast the size of a horse bolts past her, attacking the crane. The scalpel falls to the floor as the crane goes down, but so too does her light.

She drops to the floor. Her knees hit hard.

"No!"

But her little light never hits the floor.

As if by her will, her light hovers mere inches from impact. Wren's eyes, wide and bloodshot, clear of the tears that were welling there as her light floats into her arms. She curls her light, frozen and in pain, into her body, wrapping her meager garments around the precious thing that was ripped from her body.

Already the calm seeps into her psyche, replacing the previous bonds of fear and panic with a feeling of safety and comfort.

"I've got you. I've got you."

She rocks on her knees and feet. The swaying comforts her light or herself; she has no idea. There is no space between them. She is the light and the light is her. She would have died without this light. She will kill for this light.

"That baby is not yours."

The crane is back on his feet. He cradles his arm in hand. Blood seeps through his clothing, down his pant leg, and onto the floor. At some point in the tussle with the great growling beast, he lost his mask.

Her vision, cloudy still and unfocused, cannot make out any aspect of the man's features. And when the fire starts, emerald flames ignite across his features, and then there is more screaming, more pain, more everything. Only for this, she cares not. Her light is safe in her arms.

The growling turns to soft mews as the flames surround them. She should be panicking. She should be trying to escape. She should be running, screaming, anything in the wake of this fire, but there is only calm. She has nothing to fear from this fire.

And as the blanket of void surrounds them, she surrenders to displacement. She has her light. Everything is going to be just fine.

"Look carefully, *min dronning*. You know who you saw." Summer's voice doesn't belong in this memory.

Wren blinks.

The memory has frozen, a still frame in the deepest recesses of her mind. She looks around. She is in a hospital room, a neonatal unit of some sort. A bassinet lies upturned. There is a weighing station. The flames are frozen like icicles rising from the floor. And amid all of that is—

There's a sickening kind of beauty behind blowing up human+ synapses. The hexen used to do it all of the time at the peak of the revolution. If you destroy the brain and brainstem, you are likely to get rid of any data collected by said human+'s neural interface. This keeps magical secrets from being discovered postmortem after an adept or technomancer's death.

An Excerpt from *Technolyze Me*
C. R. Ashworth, 1845 A.P.

24

THE SUN (PART 1)

F AUST... IT WAS FAUST, EVEN BACK THEN.
"Do you think the doctor will be pleased?"

How many times has she woken up to the sound of voices talking about her? How many times has she woken up on a cold slab of a table only to have someone shove a needle in her arm or a sharp something-or-other through her skin? It might have been many years ago as the calendar dictates, but to her... it was only three years ago.

"I think the doctor will certainly have something to say about the sample. These test results are hardly the most reliable when used on witches. Let alone recently dead witches."

"You'd think he'd be happier having a technomancer to experiment on. I can't believe that beast managed to bag one."

"Well, did you see the cam footage? The poor sod was swimming in circles. Talking to himself like a crazy person. He kept saying he couldn't remember who he was supposed to be here with. Couldn't even remember that the Songstress of Lorelei kidnapped him. The witch really did a number on him. How else could a Miyazaki prince get messed up that badly?"

Kaito? Kaito forgot me...

"I heard Faust has him in a magic bubble of some kind. Warping all of his memories so he stays content while the doc gets all the data from him he can get."

Gloved hands paw at her legs. "Well, I'm gonna take another sample from the witch just to be sure. Make sure the repression system is still active. There's only one way to be absolutely sure."

He's so focused on collecting his so-called samples, he doesn't realize that his unwilling patient was long ago released from her VR bonds by an oh-so friendly ghost.

The top button of her jeans pops open.

Oh, hell no!

Green eyes fly open. Emerald sparks in their depths, and the triskele at her brow ignites. Her molester goes flying across the room into the virtual reality generator. While the machine whines at the mistreatment, the so-called doctor wails as the electricity fries him alive.

Wren yanks herself up off the table and runs for the door. It opens to a corridor very similar to those of the hospice center she found Anna in. This must be another floor of the facility. Whether they are above or below ground though, she has no idea.

"Stop her!"

A nameless henchman tries to trap her in the room. She rams her shoulder into the metal door, and with a bit of magical might, traps him against the wall in a cocoon of steel. His last cry echoes damply through the hallway before her ghostly push crushes him into the concrete.

"Kaito!"

A cacophony of noise answers her cry. Alarms blaring, the cries of caged beasts, people yelling. None of them are Kaito. None of them are her technomancer. The adepts race for her, but in her fury, she barely acknowledges the weapons they brandish at her. Too harried. Too mad.

Fae is so small in her arms.

...Too heartbroken. Their lives are hardly a blip on her radar. They know not the consequence for hurting a Death Witch. Her necrotic touch teaches them otherwise as she races through this maze of pain. No longer are the hallways perfect and pristine. The doors and patient rooms are no longer picturesque

This is all too familiar a setting.

Hospital equipment, anguish-filled cages, pain, strife, and worst of all, despair. This is the same kind of place she once died in, the same kind of place she was reborn in, the same kind of place her curse calls for blood in.

There are creatures in the cells. Beasts, fae, hexen, human, and all manner of creature in-between. Someone has been conducting their twisted science experiments on the weak and un-championed. It's too bad they didn't make their locks telekinetic-safe. She opens each one as she passes. Barely glances at the occupant within long enough to determine that it isn't Kaito who she has spring from entrapment.

"Kai!! Answer me!"

She reaches out with her empathy and the ghosts of the facility rise to her calls.

There is only one definition for "misery" and it is in the misty specters of the tortured and tormented, horrific and vaguely magnificent in the force of their ardor.

A low growl skates over her senses.

"Silje?"

Another answering meow behind the door to her left.

She blasts the hinges off. Behind it, five doctors, each wearing black leather masks shaped in various bird-like visages, turn to her in shock. The first one makes the mistake of brandishing a scalpel her way. The instrument embeds itself into his forehead before he can even take a single step toward her.

"Guards!" shouts the shortest one, a familiar man wearing a familiar crane's mask.

Faust. Name the devil and he shall appear.

Wren's fingertips curl in mid-air, and before the man can even reach for his pistol, he is flung backward into a table adorned with various medical paraphernalia.

The remaining three duck out a side door. Wren, too focused on the sight before her, can't be bothered to go after them despite the tickling voice at the back of her neck which urges her forward.

What are you doing? After them...

The voice comes and goes like a vision more felt than heard, but no.

There are more important things to deal with.

Her familiar hangs suspended in a sack above a locked chest. At the center of the room, Kaito hangs suspended in a vat of glowing potion. Magical radiation spills from its depths. Without another thought, Wren sends Faust face-first into the glass of the tank. Said tank rattles heavily at the impact, but the glass doesn't so much as crack despite the force behind her magical throw.

"What have you done to him?"

"I can explain."

Kaito's body bobs in the vat.

"Turn it off." Wren's command echoes with the power. Only the deathly ones settle unaffected. Everything else quakes.

"It isn't a machine. I can't just unplug it."

"Then you won't mind if I break it in two."

The tray of medical equipment levitates dangerously off the ground. Sharp instruments point at the glass.

"No, you'll kill him!"

No, she won't. She can't. The array of tools fly forward, embedding themselves into the glass, still unshattered but now weakened by her constellation of murderous intent. Through the wounds, the magical mixture drips out like venom from a snake's mouth. Tiny droplets grow into streamlets to pool on the floor.

"Silje!"

The cat growls from inside the bag as the witch rips the mechanical wards from the outside. They fizzle out of commission to end up as nothing but crumbled metal on the floor, and out springs her familiar.

"Silje! What are you doing down here? I left you at the fairy's."

A flash of annoyance rings across her synapse.

"Okay, yes, I get it. You didn't want to be left behind, but if you had stayed put, you wouldn't have ended up in a cat sack, now would you?"

The cat, out of the bag, triples in size and barrels into the tank. The displacer beast's meaty shoulder thuds against the side of the tank. On the first impact, nothing gives, but on the second, the side panel buckles before rebounding. The third and fourth impact have much the same effect. It is on the fifth that the entire structure gives. The glass folds, the steel frame bends and breaks, and once the screws escape their holes, everything comes toppling to pieces.

"Kai!"

Wren rushes to catch her lover in a gentle cocoon of magic before his body hits the cement floor. She kneels in the mess of glass and rebar, cradling his body in her arms. He is covered in the veiny evidence of magic sickness. The trails of toxin-darkened blood stand out in sharp contrast against his too-pale skin. The normally brilliant purple glimmer of his augmentations flickers a dull grayish violet.

And as soon as she rests his head in her lap, the convulsions begin.

Magic poisoning. She's only ever read about it in books. Kaito's body, under the stress of filtering out as much magic as it possibly can, is rejecting his own augmentations, the very accoutrements that make him what he is.

"No, Kaito!"

"What did you do to him?"

"It's a hallucination bath. It-it isn't supposed to be dangerous."

"Isn't supposed to be dangerous?! You've submerged an augmented individual in a vat of magic. It could have killed him."

"I took every necessary precaution."

"As if you actually cared! He is your boss's enemy. Anything can be dangerous when overused."

"I didn't mean—"

"I don't care what you meant! Wake him up! Now!"

"I can't do that."

"Why?"

"Because he's too far gone by now. To wake him would be to kill him."

"Wake him up, or it will be you who dies from magic poisoning, and I promise you, you won't fall asleep at any point during the process."

Volatile spirals of emerald glitter in Wren's eyes. Faust jolts at the sight. He knows. Most things that glow such a violent green are either poisonous or very, very venomous. Wren is neither, really, but Death has always been considered a plague upon earth despite it being far more natural a thing than birth.

"I'll n-need your h-help."

Wren narrows her eyes. "Aren't you a doctor?! Don't you know how to save someone's life?"

"Knowing how to do something does not make a person able to execute it, especially when the circumstances are so... blistering."

He lifts his hand before his face to reveal the ugly red of a fresh laceration and the still resting scalpel embedded in his palm. It must have happened when she threw him against the floor. Damn doctors should know better than to wave surgical tools at witches. They have too much history with torture devices to give much opportunity for something even resembling one to be used.

"Fine! Instruct me."

"We need to start by extracting the oxygen tube. It's doing more harm than good at this point. Get the exo- off his face. I'll tell you what to do from there."

She didn't need a third party to tell her that. Kaito's shakes are startling at this point. She starts by removing the exo-skeleton mask surrounding his nose, chin, and cheeks. It comes off like a jellyfish, tendrils of viscous material clinging to his face like spiderwebs. It only makes it worse. His teeth clamp, clamp, clamp on the black tubing. The tube is probably the only thing keeping him from flat-out biting his own tongue off.

"Now the tube."

"He's going to hurt himself if I remove the tubing."

"If we don't remove it, the bubbling of air into his lungs will kill him anyway."

"Fine, what next?"

"Lay him flat. He needs to be completely horizontal."

She follows the instruction, careful not to let her lover's skull hit the cement, but Kaito's seizures only intensify as she releases him from her hold. It's as if her touch was holding back a flood of shock, and now in its absence, the stress and strain of his ordeal unleashes its full force.

"No, don't! He needs a magical filter. Your touch is like an absorbent for him. It's the only thing keeping him alive at this point."

Silje, ever attentive, shrinks down in size and curls up on Kaito's pelvis. The netherbeast glows, radiating a soft purring sound while the tendrils of magic attached to her fur sink into Kaito's body.

The cat's influx of energy, or rather, the void-like suction of the netherbeast's power drains the magic from Kaito's body like sucking poison from a wound.

Telekinetically, she carefully extracts the oxygen tube from his throat, praying to every god, goddess, and unholy artifact that she doesn't end his life by doing so. A long moment stretches between the hiss of the valve releasing and the last artificial breath escaping his lungs. He breathes, barely.

She waits, anxious for him to open his eyes and greet her, but his silver eyes never open.

"What's happening? Why isn't he waking up?"

She turns back to Faust for answers and curses. The doctor is gone. Run away like the coward he is. Why is she surprised?

She looks to Silje then back to Kaito's face.

"Please, Kai, wake up. I can't lose you. Not now."

But he doesn't answer. The blank space of his aura penetrates her empathy. It's like a space previously occupied by him has been left vacant in her own head. A cavern left empty and cold.

It's a feeling she has only experienced once before. And it was the last broken straw that drove her insane twelve years ago.

Gone... That space in her being where Fae's little psyche pulsed every hour of every day since the day she was born. It's just gone. Vanished into nothing, not even a burnt-out ember left in its place.

"Where is my baby!"

"Dead, Nocturne. Your child is dead. And it is no one's fault but your own."

The memory goes as quickly as it came.

"Kaito, please."

No answer.

"I admit it, okay. It was all my fault. Olga, Jessabelle, Fae... The bombing, the virus, the defection. I'll take all the blame. Just please wake up."

Still no answer.

Wren's tears fall, and hidden deep in their depths is the truth she has been running from since she was sixteen years old.

"Kai... I can't lose you the way I lost our daughter."

Faust runs.

He's not fool enough to wait and hope that the technomancer's death will trigger the witch's downfall. It happened once that way when the songstress's grief drove her to madness. There are some people in the world who believe it was that madness that led to her demise. That so-called suicide by fire the tabloids reported.

But Faust knows better.

Faust knows that the witch's greatest weakness is also her greatest strength, and he is not fool enough to stick around to find out what the result will be this time around.

"Mayday. Mayday."

The signal on his comm is muddy at best. He can only hope his message makes it through. There'll be hell to pay if it doesn't.

What he is about to do is so far out of the plans that it might very well make him more of a liability than an asset, but if he doesn't, there won't be any chance of him having a place at the table when everything is said and done.

"I am abandoning Project 26. All subjects will be terminated. I repeat. All subjects will be terminated."

Damned technomancers and their shitty comm systems. He'll be giving Thames an earful for giving him a defective unit the next time he sees him.

In the meantime, he reaches into his coat pocket, pulls out the trigger box, and depresses the kill switch. The timer starts to drop: T minus 5 minutes before total meltdown occurs.

It's warm inside the cabin. He hasn't felt this warm in a long, long time, wrapped up in a handknit shawl on the rocking chair. The smell of hot cocoa wafts into the living area from the stovetop. A fire crackles happily in the corner. Wren's cat snuggles content in her lap while she reads the new book he's brought her, and little Fae is fast asleep on his chest. All tuckered out from the day's festivities, the child snoozes on as the sun sets on the shortest day of the year.

It was a day of gifts. A day of feasts. A day of quiet peace. Now at the end of the day while the light dies outside his witch's cabin in the woods, he rests, closing his mind to the horrors of the outside world and allowing himself to simply exist.

When he was small, Kaito used to have night terrors. It was the winter following his father's failure to return home, and the long, dark nights made death feel more real, closer, and scarier than ever before.

"Brought on by the death of his father..." That's what his doctor used to say. "He'll grow out of it, my empress. I promise you. In the meantime, just let him cry it out."

But Mirai was never one for allowing her children to cry themselves to sleep.

On those rough nights when he would wake screaming with the visions of witches cackling in his head, his mother used to rise from her bed and carry his too-heavy body outside onto the grounds. It was there, in the midst of the temple's slumbering gardens, where his mother used to rock him to sleep between the snow drifts. She would wrap him up in blankets and shawls and rock and rock and rock until a young Kaito drifted off to sleep. And despite the snowflakes kissing his nose, he always felt so, so much warmer.

He's reminded of that time now. Warm and cozy, surrounded by love. Only he is the one doing the holding this wintery eve. The witch curls into his side, her head resting against his bicep as she looks up from her book to glance around at all the newly opened toys given to her little one for the Solstice.

How ironic it is that he sits in the presence of one of those very witches he used to have nightmares about, but, he guesses, warmth doesn't come from what a person is but who they are.

"Daa-dah." The child coos sleepily into Kaito's collarbone. He knows Fae isn't really calling him "Dada." It's just baby babbles. The child's favorite descriptor for him is "tekno man," but a man can dream.

Wren looks up from her book. She smiles that devastating smile that always seems to warm him to a boiling point before returning to her words on the page. The baby shifts against him. A small babble and then a coo followed by the smallest hush of "mama" draws Wren's attention once more.

"I should get that one to bed."

"Perhaps it would be best if we all retired for the evening."

"Perhaps it would be, *mon rivage.*"

Wren helps him to standing, Kaito balances the sleeping toddler on his hip, and hand-in-hand, they make their way to the bedroom while the snow continues to fall outside. He sets Fae down on the bed. The small child curls into Wren as the witch lies down on the far side, and Kaito settles himself on the side of the bed he typically claims whenever he stays the night. Wren's green eyes glow in the darkness, sleepy but happy. The blanket slides down her shoulder. Kaito reaches to pull the fabric back up.

"You're never going to leave us, right?"

Wren's question startles him but not in the way he expects. It's like ice has been poured down his back. Déjà vu is the hexen term for it, this inkling of doubt he feels in the back of his head.

He's lived this moment before. He regrets with every fiber of his being what he said in response. He remembers it as clearly as he remembers the feel of Fae's little tuft of hair under his hands. He wanted to tell her that couldn't make that promise yet, but one day when it was safe and he knew she would come to no harm, he would take her and Fae back with him to Murasaki, keep them safe and sound in Shinka where none would be able to hurt them. He wanted to say that he would stay there with her in that cabin until the end of their days because what did it matter that he had responsibilities at home? What did it matter that he was a technomancer and she a witch? What did it matter that there were those who would damn them in a heartbeat if they ever discovered his secret liaisons to her hiding place in Lorelei forest?

He wanted to say all of it. Those are the sensible things to say, but—

"Of course I won't. You are my home."

No, that's not right. The answer comes without his consent. It falls from the roof of his mouth unbidden. This is not what he said. He remembers. He said nothing. He's sure of it. He knows because after the time for an answer had come and gone, Wren's face had wilted into sorrow, and she closed her eyes to sleep.

This Wren has a very different response. She leans over, kisses him on the cheek, then lays back, eyes closed. This Wren falls asleep with a smile on her face.

This is wrong!

A voice that sounds vaguely like AYA shouts at him, but the sense of peace with his current reality fights against the impulse to reclaim his senses.

You know this is wrong.

But does he care? This is the life he could have had. No... This is the life he *can* have. He's here, isn't he? If only it would never end. If only this day could last forever and ever and ever... and... ever... and...

Kaito coughs/hacks his way to sitting.

"Kai, you're alright!"

Wren is there. Her hands are on his shoulders, Silje is in his lap, and his head—oh, gods below—his head is throbbing something fierce. His whole body throbs with pain.

"What happened?"

"They immersed you in a vat of potion. Illusion magic in liquid form."

"But my shields—"

"Were dismantled by Faust's hackers. I told you not to log onto the network here."

No wonder the hallucination had felt so real.

"It was a risk that had to be taken."

"It's a risk that nearly killed you."

A sigh escapes his lungs. They could argue about it all day, going round and round and round until they're both blue in the face. Was it a foolish thing to do? Yes. Was it absolutely necessary? Yes.

"Can you walk?"

He shakes his head. "I can barely even feel my legs."

"Deactivation syndrome. How long until your system resets?"

No way to tell. The last time he was deactivated by an external entity, his system was nearly kaput. At least right now he can tell his systems are functional, if badly stunted.

"I need you to reboot my augmentations."

Wren flinches. "How am I supposed to do that without an impetus? I can't log into your augmentations the way you once did mine. I need a computer."

Yes, even years ago when Wren was a technomancer, she would have been hard-pressed to do so. Her augmentations simply weren't designed for such things. Kaito nods to the far wall.

"See that over there? That's one of the new system start-up panels. We have them in Murasaki." He pulls one of the cables in his wrist until about a foot of wire is exposed and hands the end to Wren. "Plug me in and I can do the rest."

Wren takes the cable in hand and draws it to the aforementioned panel. Naturally, the metal door that protects its contents is locked. Her magic practically crumples the door into a wadded ball as she tries to get into the damn thing. The panel is a pretty straight forward construct. If you've ever messed with a control panel, you might recognize the structure of the device. Various switches, input and output slots, and of course the control levers make up the main network, but the coup de gras of the entire invention is the surge osmosis pylon that circles the entirety of the paneling. It's this effervescent column of power that she'll need to connect him to.

"Along the pylon, there should be a slot for reboot initiation. That's where you want to plant the cable."

"Why do I feel like I'm plugging you in to charge?"

"Essentially, you are."

He feels the moment his cable meets the ignition. It's uncomfortable and strange. He hasn't had to do this in years, and he certainly hasn't had to do so on someone else's panel. Were he less proper, he would describe the sensation as icky. He expects they have it here for the doctors coming and going constantly. They are pretty standard implementations in operating rooms, and he can assume with the amount of "patients" they have around here that this one is used well and often.

At least it seems to be working, if the tingling in his toes is any indication.

"You good?" asks Wren.

"Fucking marvelous." He sighs, allowing his head to fall back. He isn't being sarcastic either. It truly does feel glorious to be back online. A few more minutes of this and he'll be back to his usual self.

"Lady Nocturne, is that you? What happened to your robo man? He looks like one of your poppets."

Kaito's eyes snap open. It's Lyra and Leon. The fae flutters in the doorway, pink and pretty, looking absolutely absurd in a get-up that would have been covert were it not for how bright and flamboyant her hair and wings were. Behind her Leon has a pistol drawn and aimed for any who might get in his way. Kaito can sympathize.

"What are you two doing here?" asks Wren.

"To suffice, the human succumbed to his own human nature and lost his patience. So decide to follow you, we did."

His witch does not take kindly to this. Not in the least. Wren stomps their direction, an entire storm of energy brewing around her.

"If you were just going to follow us, then what was the point of sending us down here? You've just broken your own bargain. Return me my name—now."

"Your name is yours again, my songstress. No doubt of that, you've got. I needed you to come down here so I could follow you. The locations of my nameless, of course, are ever known to me. We'd never have found this place otherwise."

"So my name is my own again?"

Wren signs her signature across the bottom of the album cover. When the last letter falls from the pen, a purple flash shimmers across the lettering. Without warning, the lights go out, and as suddenly as Wren begins to speak, her voice vanishes.

Right, and therein lies the reason they were in the mess in the first place.

"Your name is now mine, my lady, which means your magic is at my beck and call."

If that wasn't a nightmare... Kaito will not be repeating that any time soon. Watching Wren unable to access her magic, save for at the will of another... There are few things worse than having your abilities claimed by another. Wren had been livid. Kaito even more so.

Kaito had been just about ready to end the fairy's life right then and there had it not been for Wren's hand on his arm keeping him from invoking his own ownership of the fairy's name.

"Sure, see for yourself," laughs the fairy, tossing Wren her athame.

On instinct, Wren's magic reaches out and snatches the instrument from the air. The witch is quick to draw the dagger from its sheath. Almost immediately, Lacuna glints with emerald power, once again responsive to its witch whereas before the blade could not recognize its master.

"So it would seem. I'll have to be more careful with my signature in the future."

Suddenly, an alarm screams to life above their heads.

"What's happening?" asks Wren.

"I don't know."

Kaito revs his sights back to life and immediately folds in pain. Sharp and spontaneous, a flash of agony splits his head open and his tech deactivates.

"Kai!"

Wren's touch, as much as he can't get enough of it, worsens the pain. It must be the remnant of the magical bath he was just soaking in for gods-know how long. He pushes her away. Her touch amplifies his discomfort.

"I'm fine. Just give me a minute. I need to recalibrate my system."

"Mind you never, that," inserts Lyra. "We gotta go."

Leon shoves the fairy aside. The man storms his way toward Wren, and Kaito's sights instinctively activate. The man, noticing the glow of his tech, softens his approach, addressing Wren with the respect she deserves.

"I'm not leaving until I find Thale. Do you know where he is?"

The witch blinks at the gravitas with which the former pirate addresses her.

"Yes, but Kaito—"

"Never mind your damned technomancer. My husband's life is at stake."

Wren looks about ready to punch Leon, but Kaito stalls her with a gentle hand on her shoulder. "I'll be fine, Wren. Go. Whatever that alarm is for, it can't be good."

"You can barely walk. I'm not leaving you here alone."

"You have to. I'll catch up once I stop Faust."

"That's my job. Not yours."

A mechanical voice sounds over the intercom: "Facility shut down in T-minus 2 minutes. All occupants remaining inside will be henceforth terminated."

That rat bastard. He's going to kill everyone in the entire facility. The alarms sound impossibly louder in Kaito's ears.

"You are my job. Now go."

A flash of rejection runs across her face, but he doesn't have the wherewithal to regulate her emotions for her, so he pats the back of her hand.

"Go!" he shouts. It takes far too much of his strength to push her into Lyra and Leon. The fairy, taking his cue, grabs the witch around the shoulders, and drags her out of the room. "Find Thale and get out of here."

She pauses to look at him, tears in her eyes. "Hey," she says, "don't forget me again."

"Never," and it is a promise as deep as his soul. He will carve her name into his skin if he has to, but he will never forget her again.

Wren smiles.

She disappears around the corner, and as if with her, so too goes his strength. His system is still shot through. He grits his teeth and tries to reboot his inner workings again. This time when his sights turn on, they stay on. The pain is still there, angry behind his eyes, but he ignores it. He's survived worse. Far worse. This is nothing.

And if he wants to survive long enough to get back to his witch, he'll have to bear it. After all, rebooting one's own system is *only* a level below performing open heart surgery on oneself. His vital eyes unfocus, and he sinks into his own motherboard.

His internal server, normally as easy to maneuver in as calm lake water, is turbulent. In his youth, before he could qualify for the technomancer trials, his instructors took him into the mountains, not for any kind of rock-climbing adventure, but for waterfall diving. Sometimes people die whitewater rafting;

people die all the time waterfall diving. It is a sport reserved for adepts and technomancers. His ability to undergo the waterfall dive successfully without sustaining severe injury was the last test of readiness before his training in Murasaki would be deemed complete.

His first attempt ended badly.

He lost control of his watercraft and spiraled face-first down the waterfall's torrential length. The river washed him downstream for several kilometers before his brother finally fished him back out. At least he'd been wearing the appropriate equipment.

His second attempt the following spring had been much more successful, but that's neither here nor there.

It is in the memory of the first failure where he finds the most likeness to his current circumstance, only instead of being pulled down a stream of whitewater, he is pulled into his core via the digital coding that makes up his existence. Whole segments are missing, pieces of memory shredded and floating apart like driftwood and, most disturbing, the easy access with which he should be able to manipulate the faults in coding is gone. Hacked up to nothing by the hacker that destroyed his mainframe.

If he is going to get rid of this virus, he's going to need to do it piece by piece by piece. A procedure that would normally be undertaken in a safe controlled environment where he could do it at his leisure over the course of several days, but he doesn't have the time for that now.

He goes instead to a specific location in his mainframe and churns out the necessary coding.

"Tomi, do you read me? I need your help."

After all, who better to undo the damage caused by a hacker than another hacker?

Did you know that a solar flare could corrupt a person's software? You would expect extreme heat to corrode hardware. That's obvious. But software! I mean sure, it seems improbable; why would heat have any effect on what we perceive to be just a bunch of 1s and 0s? We forget that all of those numbers and units that comprise the coding is actual matter, even if it's matter you can't really touch, but yes, solar flares can scramble software as readily as it might melt an exoskeleton.

At the height of the war, the hexen began to play with fire. Not because they wanted to burn the world to pieces but because they wanted a means to fight back against the one way technomancers knew to kill their witches. In the process, though, they figured out how to disrupt communication systems and code transmissions. And a whole new branch of magic came to be.

An excerpt from *From Hexen to Human+:*
The Rise of Technomancy
Written by W. H. Holmes

25

THE SUN (PART 2)

THROUGHOUT THE COMPOUND, THE NANO-wasps boot up. The small robots attack any and all in their path indiscriminately. Not even the workers, the doctors, nurses, and guards who worked so hard to make this lab what it is are safe.

Wren races down the hallway, Lyra and Leon tight to her side. It is utter chaos throughout the compound. The trapped fae creatures all scramble to find their own means of getting to safety, and in the process, they have no problems barreling over one another to the detriment of the smaller fairies, pixies, and gnomes struggling to escape.

Things don't become truly dire until Wren sees the first of the nanos round the corner.

"Look out!"

Lyra shrieks as a small swarm flies for her head. Leon fires his shotgun, primitive but effective against these tiny murderers, and a slathering of the bots falls dead or damaged to the ground. The remaining bugs sizzle and fall once Wren telekinetically swipes them into the wall.

"Damn it!"

"Do you even know where you're going?" Leon's voice is filled with agitation which really doesn't help Wren's own annoyance.

Where is that place? She knows she hasn't passed it by; she would have felt that dawning of negative energy again if she had. She's still worried about Kaito. Oh, that stubborn man! But she can't worry about him. He says he can take care of himself, so he can take care of himself. Not like she can help him anyway. That her touch was making his situation worse is hard to take, but the truth of the matter is, handling his tech was giving her more than a headache as well, considering she had just been hooked up to who-knows-how many wires and cast into a hellscape of a simulation. She would have been able to help him reboot his system about as much as he would have been able to help her regain her name from the damned fairy—which is to say a minor/somewhat vital amount which once done accounted for the full extent of their helpfulness.

No, she's already helped Kaito enough by plugging him in. Not much more she can do for him. Thale on the other hand...

She closes her eyes and lets the dead speak. Their voices are everywhere in the infernal place. Easy to hear but hard to place. There are so many of them. Lost souls trapped in their own personal purgatory, trapped by their hatred for the one who killed them. She owes Faust for more than the sorry souls who summoned her back from the waters of death.

Green eyes snap open. *There!*

"This way," she calls to her companions and woe to the one who falls behind. Right, right, left, center, another right. There it is! The tapestry she found. The one she felt the immense amount of anguish from. The same unicorn tapestry that she couldn't help but sneer at for its placement in a hospital. At the time, she'd assumed it was merely the fabric exuding such malignant emotions—objects do retain auras, you know, but what if she was wrong? Perhaps she should have ripped it off its hangings earlier. Then she would have been able to solve this mess a hell of a lot faster.

She rips the tapestry from its place. A wall as plain and lifeless as the rest of this hospice center greets her.

"Oh, how marvelous! A wall. So glad we are ripping down the décor on our way out of here."

As much as she doesn't care for the man's sarcasm, Wren walks up to the wall, hands before her, disbelief in her eyes. "This can't be right."

"Where is my husband?! You said you knew where he was!"

"I swear it came from here."

"What did?"

"The feeling," she answers, short and sharp. If he would just leave her alone for ten seconds, she would be able to figure it out. He doesn't. Leon keeps on without any regard for the witch standing before him.

"'The feeling' she says. This is what you bet my husband's life on?! Some half-crazed witch!"

"Now, Leon, I highly doubt that Miss Nocturne here is on the rocker."

Now the fairy is getting in on the argument. Wren's head throbs.

"It's 'off her rocker,' Lyra. Not 'on the rocker.'"

"Oh, posh pish. Listen, I know her witchliness is the most reliable source of magic I could get my hands on, and for that I am not sorry in the slightest."

She can't concentrate with their racket.

"You think I care about—"

"Shut up!" Wren shouts. "Both of you."

She almost adds that she is trying to think but doesn't bother. She isn't thinking, not really. This is deeper than thinking, deeper even than feeling.

It's anger and hatred, pain and anguish, abject horror and physical helplessness. It's people in cages, living self-aware beings in chains. It's the sheer volume of despair that drips up from behind the solid wall blocking her path. But what if a solid wall is not actually so solid?

Wren drops to her knees and focuses on calling upon her witchsight.

Look within to see without...

She's never seen void water captured between touchable matter, yet here it is, hidden even from her, a witch capable of seeing into the very heart of the void.

"Lyra, I need you to dust this wall."

"What?"

"This is not a wall. It's a dam. Someone has been manipulating the void waters in this place. The flow has been cut off. I need you to weaken it so I can tear it down."

"Okay!"

The fairy spreads her wings and takes flight. Glitter falls in torrents from the móg-fae's fluttering wings, and the more she dusts, the easier it becomes for Wren to see the cracks in the dam.

"This is a waste of time. You're going to get us all killed."

"Well, shouldn't you consider yourself grateful then?"

"What?"

"If I get you all killed, then you and your merman will be able to float together eternally through the seas of the dead."

She hears him huff, probably to give a retort, but Lyra's voice chimes down sweetly from the rafters. "I found something! Wren, I think I found what's powering the dam!"

"What is it?"

"A mechanism of some sort."

"What mechanism?"

"I don't know. Here—look!"

The fairy pulls open a loose hatch on the ceiling and a great hunk of metal lowers into the hall. Wren's immediate reaction is to slam her hands over her ears. She didn't realize that a worm had been niggling its way deeper and deeper into her ear until the full brunt of it was pried from the wall.

"Turn it off! Turn it off!"

It's making her head split open.

Lyra pulls a switch on the mechanism, and the noise in Wren's head amplifies, dropping her to her knees. Leon looks on in confusion.

Above, the fairy presses every button and lever she can find on the device until finally relief floods Wren's system as the deafening noise comes to an end.

"Holy pixies! Are you alright?" asks Lyra.

Wren breathes hard through her teeth and nods. When she opens her eyes, her vision is blurred around the edges, but at least there aren't weird colors flying everywhere anymore. The void waters trapped behind the dam rage at her, asking her, no, demanding she release their anger into the world.

"Both of you step back."

Wren holds her hand up to the wall and narrows her focus to the weak points between the bric-a-brac. Funneling magic into the cracks, she pushes and pushes and pushes until bit by bit the barrier keeping the waters at bay crumbles to nothing.

Wren holds her breath as she pulls her magic back into herself.

"So what happened? Was something supposed to happen?"

"Shh, Leon. Sometimes these things take ti-eeeeme!"

A pulse of magical force so strong it knocks Wren off her feet and onto her backside barrels out from its holding pin. Lights break and alarm systems fizzle out and die. Even some of the nanos that were pursuing them farther down the hallway die on impact.

"All of that was trapped in here."

She isn't sure who says it, but someone curses. She doesn't care who. She's too busy riding the wave of magic pulsing in and over her body. Wren thrashes on the floor, her indicia lights up, brighter than the sun on her forehead, and the wild script across her arms flashes in erratic rhythms. She's never experienced such a flood of magic. She is overwhelmed by it, conquered by it, wants to be washed away with it. She is a sole point in the universe and a sea of stars all at once.

"Wren! Goddamnit, pull yourself together!"

She opens her eyes to Leon shaking her. She shoves him off and stands. There is magic everywhere. She can feel it ricocheting through the entire island. Wren can't even fathom how much collateral damage might have just occurred citywide from the veritable explosion of magic she just unleashed on the city.

Gears clang behind the walls. She can hear it as plainly as any songbird's chorus. The works grind out a rhythm of clinks and clanks or "clank clinks" as Lyra would say, and a passage opens up.

"Where does this go?"

"Down."

Wren can't take the steps fast enough. She is soaring with energy. This is it. This is where they are, all of those suffering under the doctor's malpractice. They have to be down here. She doesn't care if the human+ or the fairy are behind her. There are more important things to worry about.

"We keep going down like this, we'll never get back out in time."

"We'll just have to hope there's a way out where we're going."

The stairs end, the hallway opens, and Wren pelts her way through a thick sheet of plastic hung from the ceiling. Another sheet blocks her, then another, and another, and another until finally she comes out the other side and stops.

Lines of tanks, each one colored to match the captive creature within, and at the base of each sits a vital signs monitor. There are mermaids and lycans, vampyres and trolls, goblins and elves frozen in time, and witches... There are witches trapped down here. More witches than she could have ever expected. And among them...

"Jessabelle?"

There is something profound about reaching into your innermost wirings. It's cathartic in the same way finding oneself can be as equally exhilarating as it is devastating. The inexplicable vulnerability being known at any point in your life only to learn that you need to rediscover yourself all over again and again and again, the feeling only made worse because you thought, once upon a time, that you knew yourself. But that whole visage was shattered the moment you looked deeper and found yourself wanting.

That's what it felt like when Kaito lost the one he knew better than he knew himself. She knew him better than anyone could have ever known him, and when he lost that, he lost everything.

"Daddy, why do I have to wear different robes than you?"

Well, not everything. There had been one precious gem saved the day he lost himself. One precious gem saved the day he failed to save the other. The only person who ever knew him.

He was known then. He had always been known, really. He just didn't realize it until far too late.

"Wren! Fae! Jessabelle! Anybody!"

The voice that screams through the forest is hoarse, panic-stricken, and alien to his ear. The words are his. The names fall from his throat at his own command, but he doesn't recognize his voice. Is he even sure it is his own voice?

"Wren! Chikushō! Answer me!"

But the only answer that comes is yawning silence. No answering call of his name, no shout of excitement, nothing. Just too-quiet forest.

Wren's clearing has been destroyed by anti-magic. Even he, technomancer status aside, can feel the uncomfortable burn of the radiation seeping into his pores. Is it even possible anyone could have survived this?

He searches. Under downed tree and broken shingle, under the ruins of a play yard now destroyed by man-made chaos. Somehow, Wren's witch's cottage is left intact.

"Wren! Fae!"

The door comes open with ease. His terror driving him to panic, he knocks over a chair as he races around the small space. The hearth, always lit by this time in the evening, is ashen cold, naught but broken pieces of char and wood. Wren's athame, normally kept safely on the mantle, is missing, taken either by the witch herself going to battle or by another thief.

"Wren! Wren!"

A hushed moan greets him. So small and quiet, were it not for his enhanced hearing he would have missed it all together. He rushes toward the sound. Through the hallway and into the bedroom. The wardrobe has fallen over, one of the doors hanging off its hinges. The few items of clothing he's left here over the past months have spilled out onto the floor. Wren's clothes however are huddled and shaking in the back of the fallen wardrobe.

A toddler lies whimpering and scared under a fallen piece of ceiling.

"Fae..."

The child cries even harder at the call of her name.

"K-k-k- ...Baba?"

The toddler slurs through the first letter of his name before settling on baby talk she should have outgrown long ago. At least, that's what he tells himself she says. Any other option would make him break down himself.

Kaito hunches down, pulling dresses and scarves aside to get a better look at the babe. There's blood dripping from a cut at the top of the little girl's temple. When he feels the area, his hand comes back wet. Her hair is slick with it, and the shivering of the clothes is a testament to the violent tremors wracking the child's form.

"Come here, Fae. I've got you."

She's cold to the touch, yet her forehead burns with fever. Kaito grabs one of his own discarded robes from the floor and wraps her up tight. The bulk of the cloth does nothing to mask the shaking of such a small frame. Far more fragile than anything else Kaito has ever handled.

"W-where's m-mama?"

The girl's teeth are chattering. Kaito is acutely aware of just how dangerous it is that the two-year-old's eyes do not react to the light he shines in them.

"I don't know, sweetheart. I don't know."

He does know. Wren is not here, yet her ward is. It can only mean one thing for his witch. She is in League custody which means he has less than no time to get to her side before the worst happens. But the child in his arms will not survive her wounds without immediate medical care.

He tucks the toddler into his chest and makes his choice.

Wren would never forgive him if Fae died.

More importantly, he would never forgive himself if he let his own daughter die.

Kaito's memories slide back into place. The hard drive he left with Tomi now fully uploads into his system. The memories rush into his neurons with a vengeance not even his lover could match.

It takes his breath away. So much more was lost than he even suspected. Whole days spent with Wren and her ward in Lorelei forest. Times before and between when he presented so many ideas to the council only to be shot down like he'd never spoken. And somewhere hiding in that space is the answer to the question: who hacked his servers to trick Wren into meeting someplace unsafe?

There's a knock on the door. Far too soft to be anything but suspicious.

"Aniki? Are you here?"

He is but he won't be for much longer. His bags are packed and his light cycle is waiting for him in the garage. He can't waste any more time. Not even on his brother.

"Didi?"

"Nii-san," he addresses his brother in a crisp and straightforward way. The only bow he offers the young emperor is a slight tilt of his head. "Forgive me, but I am on my way out."

"Kaito, please. I know what you are thinking, but this is the only way to ensure a peaceful future for all of us."

"If by 'peaceful' you mean unchallenged, you're correct. The elimination of whole groups of people does indeed tend to result in lasting peace, if only because the opposition is too weak to ever rise up again."

He sidesteps his brother around the doorway.

"Kaito!" Hikaru shouts.

He stalls.

"You can't save them."

"I have to try."

"No, Kai, there is no time. Gewalt has chosen not to wait. The rest of the council agreed. You'll be too late."

Kaito turns. "You mean you agreed?"

"Yes, I did agree with the decision, but Kaito, you must consider—"

"But it was decided. The detonation is scheduled for the 10th day in the Month of Dirt. Even if she rallied now, it would take them at least eighteen hours to prepare."

"Yes, but—"

"All the more reason for me not to waste any more time."

"Kai, there's nothing you can do."

"There is always something that can be done."

"Don't you understand! You've been offline for an entire day."

He stops, frozen as though his limbs have just stopped working. "What?"

"It's too late, Kaito! The bombs have already been detonated."

Why is this memory cropping up? There is nothing new in this information. His brother was the one who told him that the bombs had gone off over Lorelei. His brother was the one who informed him that his systems had been damaged from some unseen attack. His brother had been there to tell him he had done too little too late. His brother was the one...

Hikaru is the one who finds him. Of course Hikaru is the one who finds him. Who else would know his habits so well? Who else could predict his moves with such precision? Fae is still feverish, sleeping fitfully under the heated blanket Kaito has thrown over her. Most alarming is how the cranial-repair helmet he strapped onto her head is taking so long to repair the damage done by the anti-magic bombs and the resulting head trauma.

Hikaru, however, cares nothing for the small child. His concern is with the mad witch currently comatose on the floor. He looks at Wren the way one looks at a rabid beast.

"There is more going on here than we know, Hikaru. The last time I saw her—"

"The last time you saw her? When did you see her, exactly?"

"Two weeks ago."

"You've maintained a relationship with her all this time!"

"That's beside the point."

"If the council knew about this, you'd be—"

"You are on the council, brother, and don't lie to me now by saying you did not know. Have you become so blind?"

"I—" Hikaru stumbles over his words. He's never heard his brother stumble over his words before. *"I hoped it was not true."*

Kaito fumes. *"Wren has been in total control since leaving the League."*

"You think she has been in control. You can't know that for sure."

"I know."

"You know nothing, brother. Your judgment is clouded by affections that are naught but illusions at this point. The child can come with us, but that thing behind you isn't capable of love anymore."

"I don't believe that, and I will not."

"Then you leave me no choice."

He knows what happened next. The scar on his chest still aches sometimes at the memory.

The river that is Kaito's mainframe system smooths. The whitewater turbulence dulls and gives way to the gentle currents Kaito is used to navigating.

Wren's body goes cold.

"Jessebelle..."

This is the anguish she was feeling from the other side of that hidden door.

In the tank before her, her old lover hangs suspended in time. Drifting in a vat of some unknown substance, Jessebelle doesn't look to have aged a day despite the years since Wren last saw her. The woman she long thought dead, killed in the anti-magic siege of Lorelei with everyone else she knew and loved, is before her: barely alive with countless wires protruding from her skin as a specimen for experimentation.

Who would do this to another person?

Her skin, normally a lovely auburn, is blue-tinged and dead-looking. The veins stand in sharp contrast to the pale barely-living flesh, but she is alive nonetheless.

Across the top of the tank scroll the witch's vitals—a looping repetition of numbers and digits. There was a time in her prior existence when Wren would have understood those scrolling stats easily. She would have been able to interpret the data without any problem, without any emotional involvement, without any understanding of the person held within. The Wren of today can do no such thing.

The numbers flash across the monitor, and she can't make heads or tails of them. They're just numbers, meaningless representations of something that should not be quantified: a life. A soul. An existence.

There is a chair pushed under the desk five feet from her and a computer sitting on top. Without even a thought, the whole set-up lifts off the ground and flies into the glass of the tank. The fluid within spills, a waterfall of preservatives, splashing against Wren's skin in cold, icy droplets as she rushes forward to catch the falling witch before she can hit the floor.

Wren catches Jessebelle's limp body and lowers her to the ground, disconnecting wires and monitors as quickly as she can. Jessebelle was the kind of witch who could barely even listen to the radio without getting a headache. What could being hooked up to all this equipment have done to her? The other witch is heavy and lifeless in her arms.

"Jessebelle, I'm so sorry."

The generators of the surrounding machines and tanks whine as Wren removes the last of the nodes. It's as though Jessebelle's magical reserves have been powering the whole facility. One by one, each of the remaining tanks and cages shut down. The creatures within, hexen, fae, and netherbeast alike make their way to freedom amid a growing swarm of nanos.

"I didn't know. I didn't know." Her face is wet with tears.

"Miss Nocturne, are you alright?"

It's Lyra. In her shocked state, Wren forgot she wasn't alone. The fae looks at her in concern from where she kneels next to Wren.

"I'm fine. Jessebelle..."

"We can fix her. I'm sure. Once we get back to my workshop, I can work on her."

"You don't understand! This is my fault!"

"Nocturne! We have to go."

Leon's voice rings in her ear. The man has already claimed his prize. In the ex-pirate's arms is probably the most beautiful man Wren has ever seen. Well, not man but merman.

"Is that?"

"Thale. Yes, he's alive, but if you don't pull yourself together and get us out of here, I don't know how much longer that will be! He needs the ocean, or he'll die."

Right. Mermaid, sea water... it's kind of a necessary thing for them.

Lyra holds her hands open as though offering to take the unconscious witch off Wren's hands. "No," answers the songstress. "Jessabelle is my responsibility. I'll hold off the swarm for as long as I can."

"But Lady Nocturne—"

"Just go. Help the rest of these fae out of here." With a shove of magical might, the fairy is pushed up the stairs without further discussion.

"You know," Leon's voice is gentle compared to what she has come to expect from the man, "you're kind of alright for someone who grew up rich."

"Yeah, thanks for the half-compliment. Head for the surface. This may get messy."

Leon, Thale still cradled in his arms, follows after Lyra and the other released prisoners. Wren, however, stays put. She knows what's coming and unless she can come up with a better answer than she did 14 years ago, everyone in this facility is going to die.

26

THE SUN (PART 3)

WHEN KAITO SURFACES FROM WITHIN HIS interface, it's like breaking through the sound barrier on an aircraft—a shot of immense discomfort followed by a calm sense of weightlessness. Maybe a better way to think of it is to compare it to the freefall before opening the parachute. An instant jerk before a quick and easy float down to the ground.

He turns his sights on. The data panels on the edges of his vision recalibrate. Measurements flow before his vision: electric currents, activation panels, heat-sensory data, even the simple lengths and widths of nearby items. There's an imperfection in the floor to his right and a light fixture above his head is burning way too hot for optimal operation. All it would take is a small flick of water in the wrong place and that bulb will explode into a jumble of pieces.

"Everything back in order?" Tomi's voice echoes into his cochlear comms. They are operational now. He's been having to run everything from his auxiliary units, something he hasn't had to do since he was around ten years old. He can't imagine how Renki and Akari manage. He's lost the damned thing more times than he can count.

"Blissfully so."

Tomi laughs. "Well don't go too ham on your systems yet. My monitors say you're functioning at about 90% capacity."

"It is reading the damage to my blade ensembles." Has it really only been a few hours since that poor abomination of magic and tech attacked Wren and him in the tunnels? "Those will require physical maintenance before they are fully functional again."

"Do you need to find a mechanic? Not sure I have any friends in the Tai Tai, but I can check."

"No. I think I have someone who can make decent work of it."

An outburst of noise from the door, followed by the banging open of said door.

"Get him!"

The two thugs come at Kaito before he can fully finish rebooting his system. The first one wrangles him into a chokehold while the second punches him in the abdomen.

The second thug doesn't get a chance to aim a second punch. Kaito flings a leg up and kicks him square in the chin.

"What's wrong with you?! Get the damned tranquilizers," shouts the one holding him. Kaito reaches up and back. His sword cables extend, grabbing the fool by the back of his neck, and when he folds his body forward, the man goes flying straight into a cabinet of medical supplies.

The second man, seeing that Kaito is now free to move, gropes at his belt, no doubt looking for an ill-placed laser or pistol. Kaito doesn't let him find it. He cartwheels forward and punches him across the jawline. As he attempts to retaliate, the technomancer swings his other fist, planting it straight into his gut.

The thug crumples, bile spilling out his mouth at the forced evacuation of his stomach through the path of least resistance. Kaito grabs him around the collar and lifts him off his feet.

"Where's the doctor? Where's Faust?"

"Faust, that bloody coward, he made off with the records and—Ahhhh!"

The man's screams cut off, and as quickly as his agony begins it ends, going lifeless in Kaito's hold. In shock at the man's sudden expiration, he drops him with a wet thud onto the ground.

What happened? The other thug—the one he threw into the wall—is also still as can be, showing not even the smallest of life signs, but he didn't throw him hard enough to kill him, just to subdue him.

He scans the bodies and is horrified to find that their brains have been turned to mush. Internal detonation of a small bomb or perhaps a small robotic insect.

Kaito hurries to the nearest monitor and hooks himself directly into the mainframe.

Faust has set the facility for total lockdown, and apparently with total lockdown comes the destruction of any and all assets, including those who maintain said facility. He finds details for a three step "abandon ship" sequence. Step One: Lock all doors and exits. Unnecessary systems such as life support will be cut for the purpose of maintaining an absolute 0 movement in or out of the facility. Step Two releases the nanobots to deal with active patients, personnel, or even visitors caught within the walls. Step Three: In case the nanos failed to take care of everyone, the next stage would be the burning of the facility. All hardware, software, and physical evidence of operations within shall be deemed fodder for the furnace.

Right now, the lockdown is initiating Step Two. He thinks he can shut it all down or at least buy them time to get out if he can just reshuffle the coding. He needs to get the doors unlocked and stall out the final phase, maybe even stop the nanos from finishing off everyone else still living in this hell hole. It's an easy enough code to counter, but only if Kaito can gain access to the mainframe.

"Tomi, I need you to get me into the system."

"But you just finished repairing your software center. Don't you think it's a bit premature to try and do anything more than, oh, I don't know, function?"

"Faust has damned every creature in the facility to death to protect his own hide. I'm not about to let him erase his sins so easily."

"Fine. Give me five minutes. In the meantime, I recommend getting yourself somewhere that isn't where you are presently."

"Why ever for?"

"Because there is a swarm of ro-bees flying straight for your location."

And sure enough, a buzzing sound penetrates the silence. With a flick of his sword cables, the doors to the lab slam shut to buy him some time.

Flashes of Club Harborage echo through his head. He has seen this enemy in action, and had hoped he would never come across such abuse of robotics again. He had made sure to include the instance of the robots' usage in his end-of-mission report to Hikaru. His brother made a movement to the council about the occurrence, citing such atrocities as inhumane and excessive. The meeting ended in a vote to ban the technology as too volatile for proper management and too tempting to abuse; even the Primarch could not deny that the potential for the bugs to be turned against them was too high a risk for further production. Yet here they are yet again—used as a termination method for an illegal research facility in the Tai Tai.

Kaito scoffs. The first mechanical insects *tink, tink, tink* against the closed doors.

Human nature is as predictable in this case as can be. Humans will always favor methods of cruelty over methods of peace.

"I don't know, man. How do you expect to hack a computer while dealing with all this shit?"

"Just get me in, Tomi. I'll take care of the rest."

"I promise to take great care of Renki after your funeral."

"That won't be necessary."

Kaito draws his swords. His tanto and katana gleam lavender in the low light of the room, and his sights shine brighter than they have since he and Wren woke up on the shoreline.

He snaps the water suit's hood over his head and fixes the mask over his mouth right as the wasps scream into the room. He swings and spins into the cloud of mites, keeping a close guard on his ears and nose lest they try to wriggle their way through his suit and mask.

It isn't long before he begins to wonder just how much longer he can sustain this kind of defense against thousands of tiny attackers.

In the quiet of the facility's belly, Wren cradles her ex-lover to her chest. Jessabelle's head has been shaved, so the songstress strokes her fingertips over the top of her scalp in a slow, circular pattern.

"I'm so sorry about all this. If I had just been there..." Well, she doesn't know, does she? After all, she wasn't there. She wasn't there to stop the bombs. She wasn't there to protect Fae. She wasn't there to keep Silje from being used like a battery. She wasn't there to keep Jessabelle from falling prisoner to the technomancers.

Wren swallows her grief. There's so much more to lose if she doesn't.

The nanobots haven't penetrated this deep into the facility yet, but she can feel their effects all throughout the compound. Panic, pain, and abject terror color her psyche in streaks of graying-yellows and puke-tone greens. Fear is a unique texture: it tastes like a knotted bowel but feels like your spine is being crushed from both ends and is the color of bloody piss. It's everywhere and spreading rapidly.

Fourteen years ago, she tried and failed to stop a swarm just like this. She does not have the option today.

Loo-lee... Loh-lee... Loo-lee-loh...
Look long enough into the eye of a fire,
you'll soon discover the heart within.
Look long enough into the heart of any thunder,
you'll find calm and peace forsworn.

Scherzo

Wren's voice, once more hers and only hers, rings out into the darkness of the room. The shards of glass on the floor reflect the glow of her indicia and wild script. They even start to dance as her song opens into a second verse.

Loo-lee... Loh-lee... Loo-lee-loh...
There is no such thing as immortality,
only dreams of the eternal.
No man, no beast, no god, nor deity
lingers here forevermore.

Time... Time is the slayer once more.
Loo-lee... Loh-lee... Loo-lee-loh...
Dearly beloved, we gathered today
With ashes for ashes and earth for earth
The bride walks a path most wandered at dusk.
When she reaches the end, her groom will ascend
while she is left nothing but dust.

Time seems to stall at the witch's behest. The nanos throughout the building flutter, frozen in space. The words make no sense (The rhyme scheme is off, there's no consistency between the length of her phrases, and there is no chorus to speak of), but neither does trying to stop a massive assault of robots.

It's 3 in the morning and I wish you were here.
You're sleeping beside me so peaceful and warm,
yet I can't seem to sleep through this made-up storm.
It's 3:10AM and I see you so clear.
Your breath flutters near, like a butterfly, sweet,
yet still, I fear you'll soon disappear.

She is not herself. Not anymore. She is the Wren from the past. The Wren who broke down walls and screamed her way into a doctor's room to find her little light. She is the Wren who was rescued by a strange witch. That witch brought her into her home and made her almost whole again.

Now her light is gone, snuffed out years ago with the travesty that should have killed Jessabelle as well, yet here she is. The witch who should have been dead is alive in her arms. But then again, Wren is supposed to be dead herself, so what makes their situations here so different?

Oh right... Wren had actually been dead.

Kaito's systems strain to keep rhythm with his movements. Every swing of his sword is a fight against a rusty hinge. His muscles work to their exertion point, and sweat beads at his brow. Even his lungs, biomechanically optimized, labor against the limitations of his physical body. With another side slash of both blades, a handful of the nanos fall to the floor, tiny electrical bursts color their demise, but they are instantly replaced by two to three times as many.

He can't keep this up.

"Tomi? An update would be nice."

"Hacking takes time."

"I don't have that kind of time."

A dozen nanos land on his left armguard. He releases his hold on Amatsu. The tanto rises up on its cables, circling around Kaito's form to fend off another assault. As the blade dances around him, Kaito closes his fist. Electricity dances up his arm, short circuiting the nanos working their way up his arm to his face. They fall dead to the floor.

As Amatsu returns, Tsukuyomi leaves his hand. The katana, as though possessing her own thoughts and autonomy, flies to defend her master with sweeping spirals and whirling slashes. The katana's blade is longer than the tanto's, meaning her reach extends farther. She is stunning, truly, as she clears the space, giving Kaito more breathing room.

The man breathes heavily.

"Kaito, I can't get these nanos to deactivate," shouts Tomi over the comm.

"Just get the doors open. I'll do the rest."

"Working on it."

Kaito fights on. A nano lands on his face and is swiftly brushed aside before it can climb up his nose. A whispering tendril of emerald magic curls into the room, the magic forcing its way in through the split in the door. At first, he cannot hear the song over the buzzing of the nanos or the swishing of his blades as they cut through the air. His breath hammers against the edges of his lungs, but as the magic engulfs the room, the sound becomes apparent. No, it becomes all-consuming.

The song crescendos higher and higher in volume, winding in and out of the swarm of nanos. It wrangles them in, a lasso to an untethered ox made of hundreds of thousands. The nanos struggle against the magic.

Kaito's battle fervor is allowed to dull, the pressure taken off now that only dozens of nanos swarm him rather than hundreds.

The magic spirals, turns in on itself, and then implodes, a blinding emerald explosion that does no harm to him but blows every single nano off its course, and the buzzing, the incessant, volatile buzzing announcing his impending death, comes to an abrupt quiet. The finality of it is as brisk as the final pump of a conductor's baton at the end of a symphony.

Kaito's boot crunches over the lifeless bodies of the small robots.

They're dead. Wren's magic killed them.

But he doesn't have the time to celebrate. The destruction of one obstacle paves the way for him to take care of a second.

"I got the door!" Tomi announces as said door slides open.

"Thank you, Tomi. I'll talk to you later."

He disconnects and strides forward. Faust must be found, and when Kaito finds him, the "good" doctor will answer for the atrocities he has committed.

Double, double toil and trouble:

Fire burn, and cauldron bubble.

By the pricking of my thumbs,

Something wicked this way comes.

Taken from the old world play *Macbeth*,
By William Shakespeare, 1623 A.D.

27

THE TWO OF SWORDS (REVERSED)

15th Day in the Month of Falling - 6:01PM - Wakeville

"RENKI," ZENZA'S WHISPER IS HARSH IN HIS rear, "are you sure we can trust this guy? We have no idea where he might be leading us."

"He says he knows who is behind those murders. If he can help us clear your aunt's name, it will be better for everyone." *Especially Kaito-sama,* he finishes in his own head.

"Yeah, but are you sure? Like I get that I have trust issues, but how do you even know him?"

"A man picked my pocket and stole my pistol. I gave chase without realizing he was a lycan. I would be dead right now if it wasn't for him."

"He said his name was Gideon."

"Yeah."

"How was a normal able to help you defeat a lycan? Is he a witch?"

"I don't know. I don't think he's augmented, but there are plenty of adepts who exclusively use external tech. Not all of us rely on augmentations or implants."

"It just doesn't make sense."

"Zenza, you don't have to be augmented to be able to fight or defend yourself. There are plenty of people who defend their homes every day from animals, robbers, and even murderers with regular, run-of-the-mill shotguns."

"Still. I don't like it."

"He's one kid, Zenza. If he really were to try anything, don't you think the two of us could handle him?"

"Yeah, I guess."

This seems to pacify the girl. Truth be told, Renki is starting to feel more than a little on edge as well. They've been following Gideon for several hours now, and with winter right around the corner, sundown is coming earlier and earlier. Already, he can see Koi in the sky, a waning gibbous with Dei sparkling just beside.

"Hey, Gideon, where did you say we were going, exactly?"

The boy turns his head. "I didn't."

"Right..." growls Zenza. Renki shoots the girl an ugly look.

"Do you mind sharing?" Renki asks.

"There is a cave not far from the village. The creature we are looking for lives there."

"But aren't there dragons and stuff around here? This is part of their protected reserve."

"The dragons aren't the problem," answers Gideon. "They keep to themselves and never involve themselves in human affairs. It's the centaurs and satyrs you have to look out for. They hate humans, and any fae that hates humans is sure to try something or other with a band of idiot kids walking through the forest."

"So why are we going through here?" asks Zenza.

"Did you ever stop to wonder if your culprit is actually a fae, not a hexen?"

"Fairies can't do that to a body. He was basically taxidermized while still alive."

"Different fae folk can do different things. Some will steal the teeth out of your mouth. Some will taint the honey of the local bees. Some will blow you a kiss and leave you a mushroom to hurry up and eat, if only for the opportunity to claim you as their own. You technomancers really take for granted all of the mystical things lingering in this world beside vampyres, lycans, and witches. If you'd open your eyes wider, maybe you would understand things better than you ever had before."

"My eyes are open," says Renki. That anger, once again, pushes against his voice. He doesn't like feeling angry.

If you're angry and you know it, blow it out.

The song dances unbidden across his memory. He can't, for the life of him, remember where he's heard it before. An image flashes across his data feeds of someone holding their index finger in front of his mouth and pretending to blow out a candle.

If you're angry and you know it, blow it out.

The woman's face is obstructed. He knows it's a woman even though she feels more like an extension of himself than a separate person. The voice is too feminine.

If you're angry and you know it, and you need to calm down, if you're angry and you know it, blow it out.

A big gust of wind across his memory's face. At the time, he didn't know how to blow out a candle, but he pursed his little lips and made an effort to pass air through them. The woman's praise makes him feel like he is the best in the whole wide world.

As quickly as the memory comes, it goes, and with it, so does his anger.

"What kind of fae are we talking about?"

"Ever heard of a doppelganger?"

"Doppelganger? Yeah, they usually inhabit big cities or heavily populated areas. But Miyazaki-sensei has said time and time again that they are virtually harmless. Even when they want to cause trouble, they only ever pull pranks. They don't kill people."

"Doppelgangers don't, but mimics will."

"What the hell is a mimic?" asks Zenza.

"Think of it as a doppelganger that has been tainted by witchcraft. They get sucked in by the unnatural magic and it nests inside them. Makes them crazy. My dad used to tell me all sorts of stories about mimics. Different cultures call them different things. Buho, Skinwalkers, Face-stealers, etc. They are the dangerous ones."

"So you know where one of these creatures is?" asks Renki.

"I've been tasked by my master to track it down. It killed one of our best clowns the other day."

"Wait, you live with a traveling circus?"

"You could call us that. We prefer 'entertainment troupe.' We go from town to town bringing joy and merriment to any and all who meet us."

"I hate clowns." Zenza crosses her arms and pouts. Renki can't help but wonder if there is anything in the world that Zenza actually likes other than her uncle and her father's old rifle.

"Too bad. They are some of the best people you will ever meet. Funny and great with children but horribly sad when not in costume. It's hard living off of the laughs of others rather than your own goals and dreams. Believe it or not, vampyres do really well in the profession. They feed of the laughter as a replacement for blood."

"Being a clown is a profession now..." Zenza grumbles.

Renki elbows her and looks up into the trees. There aren't many animals about, no squirrels and not a single bird, which is strange. On top of that, it's eerily quiet. He stops walking. "Hey, how much farther did you say this cave was?"

"Not far," says Gideon, turning back to look at him. He seems surprised that the other boy has stopped. Zenza too seems to shuffle back and forth in discomfort. "Why?"

"It's too quiet."

"I'm going to message my uncle," declares the princess. She pulls out her comm unit and types in a message. However, when she presses the send button, instead of the sweet, high-pitched chime that indicates at message being successfully delivered, there is a *duh-dump* sound. "What the—! My message didn't go through."

"We are kind of in the middle of the woods."

Zenza turns to him, a look on her face that speaks volumes for her feelings on his level of intelligence. "I don't own second-rate technology like you. My messages always go through."

Renki doesn't bother to explain that there is a good chance his comm unit is a more up-to-date version of her own. The Miyazaki family, as frugal as they are reputed to be, does not spare the expense when it comes to the technology their very livelihoods depend on. Renki may not have as advanced of a comm as Kaito, but it's up there.

Zenza tries several more times to send her message to her uncle. None of her attempts are successful. *Duh-dump, duh-dump, duh-dump, duh-dump.*

It crosses Renki's mind to message Akari at least of his whereabouts. He probably should have done so earlier, but he'd been angry.

He types out: [Following a Lead. Check back in 5.]

He hits the send button expecting the message to fly through the cyberscape as easy as a bullet through water, but instead, he gets a very similar *duh-dump*.

"What?" he hisses. His finger slams over the send button again and again and again. *Duh-dump, duh-dump, duh-dump.* Nothing is going through.

"I imagine you'll find it rather difficult to get a message through."

"What do you mean?"

"This is a dead zone. Didn't you realize?"

Renki blinks. "What do you mean this is a dead zone? My tech is working fine."

"Of course it is. We've only been in the dead zone for about ten minutes. You won't experience tech failure until at least fifteen."

"Why did you lead us into a dead zone?" asks Zenza, an accusatory tone to her voice.

"You don't honestly think fae enjoy hanging out on the grid, do you? It interferes with their systems the same way it can disrupt witch magic. Magical beings don't do well under the constant pressure of an invisible cyber network."

Renki frowns. "We have to head back. Neither one of us is connected to the network."

"Oh, you'll be fine. It's just for a few minutes more."

"You don't understand. I—"

Renki bites his tongue. Kaito always stressed that it was never anybody's business what his augmentations did for his system, but this... He's never been in a dead zone.

Adepts die in dead zones because they aren't prepared for the consequences that result from their tech shutting down.

They are taught often in school that witches and the like have trouble accessing their powers in major metropolitan areas because of the saturation of metal, steel, and the pollution of industry. The ley lines are interrupted by the networks made by all of the internet connections flitting about the place. If you want your best odds against a witch, you face them in a city. If you want to get yourself killed, you go hunting in a dead zone.

The negating effect goes both ways.

It isn't like losing cellular service or having a bad connection. Dead zones are the antithesis of technology: places of the world so saturated with magic that tech cannot function.

Renki grits his teeth. "Twenty minutes more, then we head back. I cannot stay in a dead zone longer than thirty or forty-five minutes."

"The cave isn't far at all. Fifteen more minutes max. Then, I promise I'll have you both well within network structures."

Zenza nods, an excited grin on her face. "It's a deal. Now, let's get this bastard and go back already."

Gideon is true to his word. Just a few more paces and they find themselves at the aforementioned cave.

"Welcome to The Maw."

The reasoning behind the name doesn't escape Renki. The cave entrance is a giant orifice in the side of the mountain. The purplish dirt for which Murasaki's mountain ranges get their namesake doesn't reach this entrance. The purple geothite in the ground which comprises the rest of the mountain turns to a rusty red around its edges. The ground at the base is a particularly bloody shade of red. He doubts it's actually blood. He'd be willing to bet that a scan of the soil would come back with some heavy iron deposits.

"The Maw?" Renki repeats.

"That's what the locals call it."

And just from looking at it, Renki understands from whence it gets its name. It is from the cavernous opening decorated with fang-like stalagmites and stalactites. The rocks hang down like blades from the top of the cave entrance. Sinister bottom "teeth" protrude up from the earth. It looks like a giant prepared to chop down on any who might decide to enter.

"They say that no one who's ever gone in has made it back out."

"Bullshit!" shouts Zenza.

Gideon shrugs. "I don't know if the stories are true, but I have heard them quite a bit in the time we've been here."

"Any idea what keeps people from returning?"

The younger boy shrugs again. "No clue, except maybe the mimic. The locals say it is full of demons just waiting to latch on to the nearest host. I've never put much stock in demons, myself, but there are plenty of people who believe in that sort of thing."

"Just like they believe in angels."

"Personally, I think there are just too many fae, too many netherbeasts, and not enough education for people to understand that not everything that happens in the world has to be linked to the unexplainable."

"Well, what are we waiting for?" declares Zenza. "Let's go take care of whatever it is that is causing a ruckus." The girl then strides forward, head high, rifle at the ready, uncaring about what may be in the darkness waiting for them. The mechanical hand, scurrying about after her on the ground, gives off a flash of light, as though in warning, but the adept disregards it. She is far too confident in her abilities. No wonder Wren left him in charge when she left them on their own to go solve a zombie apocalypse.

Turning on his night vision, he goes in after her.

Upon entering the cave, Renki doesn't see anything particularly interesting about their surroundings. Not at first, anyway. As fearsome as the outside of the cave might be, the inside looks like any other cavern he's ever been in.

"Doesn't seem all that creepy on the inside."

"Just wait," says Gideon, now at his shoulder. He follows him, much quieter than he should expect for a tenacious child. There's an edge to the younger boy's voice, but Renki can't decide if it's fear he's hearing or something else.

"Hurry up, you two," calls Zenza, already halfway down the incline into the tunnels. "I don't know about you, but I don't want to be here forever."

"Zenza, wait."

Renki hurries after the girl, lest she stumble on something and kill herself. It takes about five minutes to descend into the cave's depths. He doesn't really notice it getting darker, not with his night vision on, but there is a ledge that they have to climb down, and once he is back on the solid ground of the cavern, they find themselves enfolded in complete darkness.

"Ah! How did it get so dark all of a sudden? Shouldn't there still be light from the entryway?"

Zenza lands in a heap on the ground. Without night vision to help her see, she must have been seeing complete blackness.

Bheee!

Her little mechanical hand makes an annoyed sound at her before its index finger opens up and a small but powerful flashlight turns on. The beam alights on a dark blur. The blur is gone from the light faster than Renki's augmented eyes can track.

"What the hell was that?!" shouts Zenza.

"Over there!" Gideon's beam flickers over the opposite corner of the cave. The black shape is there once again. Renki draws his pistol, but Zenza is faster. She aims Agni and a deafening boom echoes throughout the cavern. Rocks come loose, bats leave their roosts, and pieces of the ceiling tumble down onto their heads.

"Zenza, don't! Agni will bring the whole cave down."

"I have no other weapon."

"Then get out of the way," snarls Gideon, drawing a pair of blades from his belt. Before he can launch his assault, the shape tackles him to the ground.

Renki cannot describe the chaos that unfolds over the next five minutes. The glimpses he catches of the creature are beyond imagination. There are gunshots, clangs of metal, and the gripping cry of a creature's dying breath, a cry loud enough to incite a cave-in.

"Look out!" Zenza tackles Renki to the ground as a rock crashes to the floor beside him.

"Move it! We have to go deeper into the cave!" shouts Gideon.

"But we have to get out!"

"There's no time!"

He grabs Renki's arm and all but drags him into the cave's depths. He hears Zenza following close behind, using Agni to blast away the rubble tumbling their way.

By the time the earth has stilled and the cave no longer rains down on their heads, the three are not so deep underground that Renki's night vision struggles to find the small bits of light that will feed his scopes, but those are beginning to fail him. Even the conversation happening beside him comes in tattered snippets.

"Now what?" Zenza says, sounding horribly annoyed.

"I know another way out," says Gideon.

"How? I thought you'd said you've never been here before."

Renki's vision is getting blurry. He can't breathe. The damage caused to his lungs when he was a child, damage which is normally circumvented by his augmentations, is aggravating his ability to breathe. His pulse echoes in his ears. He reaches for his regulator. The device lights up when he touches it but then instantly dims as though the battery were dying.

"Oxygen levels dropping," it reads, but it dies as he tries to get his systems back online.

"You don't honestly think I would come down here without a map, do you?"

"Renki, are you alright?"

He can't draw enough air into his lungs to answer.

"Renki—" A loud thump interrupts Zenza's words, like the butt of a blade being rammed against a skull.

I'm sorry, Uncle...

Zenza's voice echoes in his head.

What a pair of suckers.

Gideon's voice echoes in his head now, even as his sense of the world around him diminishes.

The static of a walkie cuts through the pain in his chest. "Gideon to Zero."

"Go for Zero."

"Mission successful. Get me a pick up. I've even got a spare to go with the payload."

"I've got your coordinates. Xena and I are on our way for extraction."

The walkie disconnects.

"You... You planned this."

Gideon shines a light in Renki's face. The boy winces.

"It's nothing personal... Well, no that's a lie. It's totally personal. You're going to be the bait that catches us a witch."

Is he talking about Lady Nocturne? Why would Wren Nocturne care what happens to me?

As Renki's system fails, Gideon looks down on him, a smile twisting his lips.

"Magic and logic were never meant to be at odds with one another."

From Merlin to Queen Mab after a scientist caused
the deaths of several fairies
An unrecorded exchange - 1100 A.D.

28

TRIUMPH

WREN AND KAITO COLLIDE IN THE HALLWAY, a literal collision in which both technomancer and witch end up hitting their asses on the linoleum. The only reason Jessabelle doesn't hit the floor as well is because Wren has the control to keep her hovering in midair with her ghostly touch. Score 1 for telekinesis.

"Kai, did you get the doors open?"

"Tomi did, yes. The patients and various prisoners should be escaping right now as we speak."

"Good."

"You did it," he says, reaching for her hands. Kaito's palms turn her face this way and that as he examines her for injuries. "The last time you nearly killed yourself trying."

Wren frowns in confusion. "Did what? When did I nearly kill myself?"

"Fourteen years ago, in Club Harborage. You tried to avert the massacre, but it was too much for you to handle."

Wren blinks, the memory coming back in spurts. "I remember now."

"How did you manage it this time? Your song squished them to bits."

Wren shrugs. "I don't know. I just wanted it. I wanted it so badly, I willed it into existence. The flood of void water might have helped."

"Is that what that was? It felt like a bomb went off."

"Yeah, it was... It was something alright."

Wren shifts Jessabelle in her arms. Kaito looks down at the unconscious witch. She cuts him off before the question can even finish forming in his mind. "I don't know how, but yes, it's Jessabelle. I found her in a tank being sucked dry of her magic."

"They've been using her as a conduit."

"I don't know, but we're getting her out of here. Will you take her?"

Kaito takes the injured witch out of Wren's arms, hoisting her over his shoulder. "Come on. We need to find Faust."

"I don't care about Faust. Jessabelle needs a doctor. Ah—" Wren winces as a deep pang of pain resonates from her arm.

Blood for blood.

The souls of the vengeful remind her of her pact.

"Okay, we'll find him and take care of him quickly. I don't want to be here any longer than necessary. We may have gotten the doors unlocked, but there's no telling if another failsafe is going to blow this whole place sky high." Or worse. When she escaped into Silje's vortex, the whole place went up in flames with the massive expulsion of magic she had unleashed. Unleashing a dam of void water, there's no telling what the repercussion will be to the prison that kept it stalled for so long.

With a short nod, Kaito takes Wren by the hand, and they both take off running down the hallway.

"Any idea where he is?" she asks.

"My tracker last saw him in the control room at the front of the facility."

The front of the facility, where the bot had greeted her and then promptly directed her to the long-standing patient room where she was pretending to be a good Samaritan. The patient in question was a victim of magical radiation who had been stuck in a coma for years—Snow White without a true love to come and wake her up.

"Wait—His daughter. He's probably in his daughter's room."

"His daughter?"

Wren nods. "She and her mother were attacked by a witch more than fifteen years ago. She's been in a coma ever since. Faust won't leave without evacuating her, too."

"Show me."

Wren veers left in the direction of Anna's room.

"Where's Silje?" asks Kaito.

As though on cue, a large explosion echoes from down the hallway. A door bangs open, and Silje's growling form rolls across the floor, followed by the same amphibious monster that attacked Kaito in the tunnels.

"Silje!"

The monster rolls and wrestles with the great cat. Silje's claws, sharp as daggers and glinting silver in the low light, find purchase in the monster's flesh, ripping it apart. Green, gelatinous blood spills onto the tiles. Silje somersaults off the creature and sprints toward them.

"Let's go!"

Wren takes off running, her familiar right on her heels, and not far behind them, Kaito brings up the rear. Behind him, she can hear the monster crashing after them.

"Wren, we need a plan here."

"Um, I'm partial to 'Grab the girl and run like hell.'"

After all, isn't that what the fairy and the pirate did with the mermaid? Seriously, that could be the punchline of a joke.

"That's not a plan!"

The witch ducks as a gurney flies over her head. "Well, then, you come up with something better!" she shouts back.

The snarling behind them crescendos. The sound becomes more aggravated, angrier, and just all around more worrisome. Wren pools magic into her fingertips, the familiar feel of her own magic once again at her beck and call. She turns and throws the force at the creature with all the vengeance of an angry ghost.

The emerald magic hits its target and the monster collides with the wall, buying them more time. They round the corner, taking another right to swing up the stairs. Wren takes them two at a time, Kaito keeping stride with her. Behind them, there's a crash. Silje turns on her hind paws and springs at the monster.

"Silje!" Wren shouts as the netherbeast and the monster go tumbling down the steps.

Wren stops for a second on the landing. Which way? Does she go back for Silje or does she keep pushing forward. They are back on the surface level, even with the street. All they would have to do is walk out the front doors to get out of the facility, but escape isn't enough. She pushes power into her familiar's energy signature and makes her decision. They have to end this once and for all, so Wren turns left toward the comatose patient's room.

"Wren, are you sure about this?"

"Positive."

And they are at the door. Kaito draws his katana as Wren kicks it open.

Inside, they find Faust.

"You!" he shouts, pointing at Wren. "This is all your fault!"

"I beg to differ," she announces, flinging a ball of power at his head. The good doctor presses a button on his lab coat and an anti-magic field springs up around him. Wren's magic dissolves against the barrier. There is a moment where everybody takes a breath, and then an explosion rocks the entire facility.

"Leave us alone! Your kind are the ones who did this to my daughter. Your kind should be the ones to fix her."

"You can't fix Wuxing Syndrome," says Kaito. "Once it takes hold, it is irreversible. You know that. You're a doctor."

"I have spent my life trying to find a cure for Wuxing. If only I could figure out a way to harvest the cells in a witch that synthesize the destructive qualities of magic that hurt normal humans so badly! I was so close. I thought I would break through."

"Your breakthrough would have come at the cost of dozens of magical folk: fae, hexen, witches, merfolk alike were the victims of your work."

"I could cure Wuxing Syndrome. I could give everyone who has ever suffered from magical poisoning their lives back. They wouldn't need to run anymore. They wouldn't need to find help from witches. They wouldn't need to butcher themselves with augmentations. They could just live a clean, magic-free life. That's all any of us normals have ever deserved."

Wren's memories flash through her mind. The experiments that were performed on her had been horrific, chosen for her due to her status as a technomancer and the attractiveness of affecting the unborn babe that was in her womb. They had been after her baby. They had wanted to see how they could change her infant during gestation using her body as a filter. She would say it was a miracle she survived all of the torments she was submitted to, but miracles have little to do with magic.

"You think that justifies the means? You have been torturing people. Ending lives. There is blood on your hands. Blood that I highly doubt your daughter would have ever wanted. Is that what you want? For your daughter to wake up knowing that hundreds of peoples' deaths made her life possible?"

Wren can barely handle the fact that six people had to die for her to return. Those innocents should not have died for her, yet here she is due to no choice of her own. Maybe she can accomplish something worthwhile in this second chance. At least that way, she would know people gave their lives for a paragon rather than a boogeyman parents warn their children about.

"It doesn't matter what you say or even what she might think. She is my daughter, and I am going to do everything I can to bring her back."

"You can't bring back the dead, Doctor."

"She's not dead."

"But she's not alive either," inserts Kaito.

Wren looks over at the technomancer. Kaito's sights are bright with saibaki, his power reclaimed and his tech back at full force.

"I can see her energy signature. It is that of a living dead. Deader than a vampyre but too full of life to be a ghost."

"You're lying."

"I am not. There is no future for her beyond the current state she is in. Even if you could bring her back from her slumber, she will never be the person—no, the child she was before she went into her magic-induced coma. To bring her back to the waking world, even if she would not be unchanged, would be cruelty that I think even you are incapable of."

"Shut up! You don't know what you're talking about. You—you—"

"You took my life from me!" Wren's voice booms through the room. Magic quivers at the edges of the space as though in anticipation of her command. "You, with your experiments and your selfish mission to help a lost cause, destroyed everything that I was. You made me what I am today. You woke the magic in my blood. You're the reason—"

He's the reason Fae is dead. The reason Fae never got a chance to grow up.

Wren's magic lashes out at the doctor. The barrier breaks, and Faust stumbles over his own feet. Magic swirls around Wren's fingertips, blackened nails sharpened beyond normal and ready to plummet into the man's spinal cord and yank it out.

"Please, don't. I—"

Her right hand lifts, but just as she is about to bring it down—

Slam!

"Silje!"

The door to the room flies open. Silje rolls into the patient room, the beast right behind her, having thrown the netherbeast aside. Wren rushes to her familiar's side as Kaito lunges to deflect the creature before it can turn Anna's bed over. Faust jumps up to protect the medical equipment keeping his daughter alive.

"Cease! Desist! I command you!"

As Kaito's sword locks with the creature's maw, Wren gets a good look at it for the first time. Amphibious by design, the creature is part shark, part salamander, with tentacles spouting out from his trunk instead of arms or legs. She would call it a chimera, but the creature isn't stitched together the way Summer's experiments were, from the various spare parts of netherbeasts she'd killed. This is a whole beast, born and bred to be a freak of nature designed in mottled shades of blue and green.

"Stop this instant!"

The monster doesn't listen to the doctor. However, the man's cries draw the creature's attention. Its eyes, all twelve of them, glow a hostile blue, the kind of blue found on poisonous lizards and toxic flowers. It disengages from Kaito and lunges for the doctor. Wren dives away before she becomes collateral damage. Her back meets the machinery keeping Anna alive.

"No! I created you. You belong to me!"

The words sound familiar to Wren, a distant echo of a time when a little light had been pried from her body and the thief laid claim to what was hers. The babe he called for then was no more his to claim than this creature. It goes for Faust's throat. The doctor dodges his death by a hairline.

Kaito, attempting to intervene in the man's demise or at least to prevent the room from being completely destroyed, drives his tanto into the creature's back, severing spinal tissue and vertebrae.

The beast howls with a mouth not meant to do so. Its blood falls in torrents onto Faust, and like acid, it seeps through his clothes. He screams, seeing the effect of the blood on his clothing and begins feverishly to try and rip off the tainted garments. It's no use. The fluid eats through the skin of his fingers, gnaws at the sinew of his knuckles, and melts away the muscles of his hands and wrists at an alarming speed.

It doesn't take long for the blood, still pouring, to consume his clothes, making contact with flesh, and well, you can imagine the rest.

A wretched smell fills the room as the doctor is virtually melted alive by the blood of the beast he created. It's so bad that Kaito pulls his sleeve over his nose and backs away, making sure the beast's blood doesn't get on him as well.

Wren's arm throbs, drawing her attention. The wound at the center of her forearm is bleeding, pulsing with anger seemingly in tandem with Faust's death throes until finally, with a glimmer of green light, the slash closes. No more blood. No more pain. There isn't even a scar left in its place.

Only one left.

The blood continues to seep into the floor beyond Faust's miserable end. A hole opens up, sizable enough that the creature's corpse falls through into the lower depths of the facility. Wren can only hope it stops eating away at the building before coming in contact with the water below. Though, surely the flooded train rails will dilute the acid enough to prevent much damage to the nearby infrastructure.

"That's it? It's over." Kaito seems to be in disbelief at how the whole situation has unfolded.

"It would seem so."

How fitting that the doctor who brought about so much pain would leave this world with a whimper. Is it fitting? Or is it disappointing? Regardless, this is the unfolding of the event. It is what it is.

A part of Wren is disappointed, but that's vengeance for you. People expect revenge to make the hurt go away as though making another person suffer in turn makes up for the fact that you've lost something more important than gold.

A small child, a spirit barely older than Fae was before she died, looks at Wren from the corner of the room. It is standing in the exact same place it was before. Only this time, hope shines from those unliving irises.

Wren's hand slips from the top of the respiratory machine, and with a flick of her fingers, she turns the machine off.

It takes a moment. The quiet sound of artificial breathing ceases. The body on the bed stops moving. The heart monitor flatlines. Wren turns the sound of that off as well. No need to disturb this passing with the taint of mechanical buzzing.

From the corner of the room, the child ghost of the living smiles.

29
THE WORLD

AFTER THE GHOST DISAPPEARS INTO A TRUE afterlife, Wren and Kaito flee, flicker, fly from the facility. Down the hallway, through the sliding doors, and outside onto the streets of Calypso City where a whole host of Faust's victims have gathered to catch their breath. She sees Leon and Thale immediately. The merman is awake, scaly, humanoid hands gripping either side of the former pirate's face as they kiss.

Lyra flits back and forth between several injured fae creatures. There are a few other high fairies; their wings have been damaged, their magic dulled from their experiences, but they are alive, and as Lyra washes them with her own glittery magic, theirs too will heal and return to full strength. A petticoat of pixies flutter close to the ground, gathering as much strength from the soil as they can. They need to be relocated to a forest as soon as possible. There's only so much organic energy they'll be able to scrape up in a city as wan as Calypso City. There are more creatures of course: a few trolls, other sea creatures, even a yeti seemingly from the Wastes.

Faust has spent a long time collecting his menagerie, collecting prisoners from lands near and far.

The doors slam shut behind Wren, Kaito, and Silje, and just as her boots hit the pavement, the explosion rocks everyone collected in front of the building.

"Wren, are you okay?"

She nods, sizing Kaito up to see if he too is alright. His tech, fully restored as it would seem, is alight and on high alert. Amatsu and Tsukuyomi are nearly vibrating in their sheaths. Even his weapons can sense that something has passed. They are on edge. They are at the ready even though there is no longer any foe to fight. Faust, who killed so many, died a pathetic death at the hands of his own creation.

Sirens echo through the streets. It is late enough at night that not even the vampyres would prowl the sidewalks, yet here is a small collection of ambulances, patrol cars, and security drones. The local force must have been alerted to the fire.

There are hexen, too. A few lycans, a handful of shapeshifters, and a vampyre. The vampyre is currently being offered blood from one of the shifters that was also kept in the facility. It's not the vampyre's typical choice for a meal, but it will be enough to keep the poor thing from dropping dead until he can get a proper meal of human blood and energy. The lycans will have to rejoin their packs, if they even have any. She has no way of knowing what kind of lycans they are. They could be Koi or Dei lycans. The Koi lycans will most likely be loners, cursed to wander alone in the night waiting for the next time Koi is full before they can shift again and heal their wounds. The Dei lycans, however, weakened as they are, will need to rejoin their pack mates before they too can shift and heal from their ordeal.

That being said, that means they could be local citizens or be in need of a ship to New Chernobyl, where most of the wolf packs are. The only witch, however, is tucked away safe in her lover's arms.

"Is she breathing, sir?"

Wren dons a glamour—not a terribly extensive one, just enough magic to change the shape of her nose, her eye color, and the shade and texture of her hair—as one of the paramedics rushes up to Kaito.

"Yes," answers Kaito. "She needs a doctor, quickly."

"She a lycan, vamp, human, what?" asks the medic, a youngish man with a touch of elfish blood in him. She can see it in his pointed ears.

"She is a witch," answers Wren.

The paramedic looks at Wren in shock. "That can't be right. She has virtually no magical aura."

"She is a witch," Wren repeats. She is a witch who should rightly be long dead, much like Summer, much like her. This present she has been brought back to life in proves yet again how little of the truth she truly knows.

"Then we need a specialty unit. Stacy!" he shouts to another paramedic. "We need to get this one to the hospital. Stat!"

"What's the matter?" asks the other medic, a bouncy-haired blonde, as she runs over with a stretcher under arm.

"I got a WSM. We need to get her stabilized and get her to Oakley."

"What's a WSM?" asks Kaito.

"Witch Sans Magic. I've never seen one, personally, but it's an emergency. We need to get her out of here. Set her down here, carefully, and try not to jostle her. We don't want any more magic leaking out of her than already has."

Jessabelle sleeps on as Kaito places her on a gurney, her magic drained from her. She needs medical attention, and she just might get it at the local hospital. The medics load her up into an ambulance.

"Can I go with her?" asks Wren, running after the pair as they load Jessabelle into the back end of the vehicle.

"Family only, ma'am. You can meet us at the hospital if you want to stay up-to-date on her prognosis."

Then, the doors are shut, and the ambulance takes off in the direction of the hospital. Wren can only stand and watch as it disappears around the corner, her former lover inside, fighting for her life.

The weight of the last thirty-six hours comes down on her heavier than hell's largest boulder.

"Wren, talk to me." Kaito's hand hovers above her shoulder, scared to touch her as the tumult of emotions wash over her. Grief, rage, and bitterness, all wrapped up in one, rocket around inside of her. She just killed a child, well, a woman who in essence was a child, and the person she was supposed to kill died as the result of a total accidental spilling of blood. She didn't kill Faust. Kaito didn't kill Faust. The doctor, for all intents and purposes, killed himself.

"She was barely older than Fae when a stray spell landed her in a coma."

"What?"

"The coma patient. She's been frozen in time since she was a little girl. Her spirit was that of a four or five-year-old. It's the only eternal youth that exists. The ghost of a child. Just like Fae."

"Wren."

"I wonder if I'll ever find her ghost or if she is resting peacefully in the fields of Elysium."

"Wren, you don't have to worry about those things. Fae is—"

"I never told you the truth about her. Granted, I'm pretty sure you figured it out the very first time you met her. I told you she was an orphan I found on the side of the road. I didn't want you to know who she really was. She was my daughter—"

"Wren, stop."

"—She was our daughter. She was born while I was MIA. Faust cut her from my body and tried to keep her for himself. I-I couldn't let him take her. I didn't let him take her, and it was in that moment that I became the Songstress of Lorelei. It wasn't for revenge; it wasn't to quench my blood thirst. It was to protect the only light I had left."

Kaito doesn't speak. He doesn't question. He simply pulls her into his chest and holds her in his arms as the tears begin to fall.

"Jessebelle found us. She kept us both alive when I was too weak to do so. She helped me learn how to control my magic. She took care of Fae while I went to war. She—" Wren chokes on her grief. "I always thought she had been killed by the same siege that killed Fae."

Kaito holds her tighter.

"Wren," his voice is soft in her ear. "There is something I have been trying to tell you ever since Shinka."

"What? Did you know Jessabelle was alive?"

"No, not Jessabelle. I didn't know Jessabelle was still alive. Fae though," Wren looks up at Kaito's face. Fear, uncertainty, and, perhaps, a little relief. "You're correct. I did see through your lie that day. I knew Fae was ours."

Wren cries harder. *Goddess above and below!* She is just the worst. How can he even look at her, knowing that she is the reason his only child is dead?

"After the bombs were dropped on Lorelei, I went to your cottage. My plan was to find you and Fae and bring you both back to Shinka with me. I wanted to hide you away until the world decided to leave you alone. I didn't know that you had already been captured by the League, so naturally, I couldn't find you. I did, however, find Fae."

"You found her body."

"No, Wren. I found *him*." He stresses the last word.

For a moment, Wren doesn't understand. What does he mean? He would have found a body, surely, but that's not what he means, so... And "him?" Fae was a little girl.

"Our child is alive, Wren. I found Fae and I brought our little one to Murasaki. You've met the adept Fae has grown into. You've met *him*."

Him? Him.

A boy with too-wide and too-watery eyes looks at her from a nearby tree. It's the same adept who found her at the asylum. He looks at her with too much curiosity and intrigue. He tells her about his long-dead mother. He tells her that he was raised by his father. He looks at her with eyes that are too determined and naive at the same time, and she sees a bit of herself in him.

It clicks. Fae isn't Fae anymore. The child she always struggled to see as a daughter is in fact—

Location Unknown - 16th Day in the Month of Falling - 4:11 AM

It's dark. Renki's head aches something fierce. No, not aches. It pounds.

Didn't realize he would be bringing two in.

Great, now, we'll never hear the end of it.

Voices echo in his head. So many voices, but he recognizes one of them. This one is the closest and the most panicked.

What's going on? Where am I? What's happening?!

"Zenza?"

"Ah! Renki, is that you? I can't see anything."

"It's me. Do you know where we are?"

"Why are your eyes glowing? Renki, what's happening? That's not your tech, is it? I thought you were disconnected. I thought they killed you!"

"I am not dead." He awkwardly shuffles around so he can look at her. Through the cotton in his brain he figures out the question buzzing around in there. "What do you mean: my eyes are glowing?"

"They are, they're glowing. Just like… Just like hers…"

"Whose?"

"Her. My aunt. Wren Nocturne. You know, the Songstress of Lorelei? Why do you have eyes just like hers, anyway? It makes no sense. It's not like you're related."

"Eyes like who?"

"*Her*. Wren Nocturne. The Songstress of Lorelei. It's not like you're even related to her or anything. Are you really a witch? Is that why your eyes are like that? My uncle once told me all witches have the same weird glowy eyes. I always thought he was just full of it."

For a whole minute, Renki feels like he's been slapped. Zenza doesn't notice or care; she simply keeps going, ranting about her uncle said this and her uncle said that.

"Tousan always said I had my mother's eyes," he whispers to himself.

"What'd you say?"

"Nothing."

"You said something."

Renki doesn't respond, too engrossed in his own thoughts. It can't be, can it? He couldn't possibly have Wren's eyes because Wren Nocturne can't possibly be his mother. It would be... well, it just couldn't be.

"My father always told me that I have my mother's eyes, but... she's been dead for years."

"So, my aunt has been dead for years. What's that supposed to prove?"

"He should have told me."

"Told you what?"

Told me who I was... The sharp pain returns, and he feels like his head is about to split open.

"Renki, Renki. Hey, Renki, stay with me here. We need to figure out where we are. We have to get out of here!"

He wants to focus on Zenza's words, but the voices are back. Dozens, no hundreds of voices echoing in his head. He can't focus on any of them, yet they are all vying for the forefront of his attention.

"Stop it!"

"Stop what? I'm not doing anything."

"The voices. Stop the voices."

"What voices? Renki, no one is talking."

Renki's screams are the only response he is capable of giving.

FIN.

The song will continue in *Berceuse*.

GLOSSARY OF CHARACTERS BY FACTION

Deriva:

- Tlanextli Moctezumo – Vulcan of Deriva – Father of Atzi and Xipilli Moctezumo with his first wife, Elisabeta De Claré and Wren Nocturne with his second wife, Freya Nocturne.
- Elisabeta De Claré – Vulcana of Deriva – Mother of Atzi and Xipilli Moctezumo.
- Freya Nocturne – Second Wife of Tlanextli Moctezumo – Firefly and Mother of Wren Nocturne.
- Atzi Moctezumo – Princess of Deriva – Eldest daughter of Tlanextli and wife of Chike Nagi. Mother of Zenza Nagi.
- Xipilli Moctezumo – Current Vulcan of Deriva – 247th Trials Graduate – Wren's older half-brother.
- Wren Nocturne – The youngest child of Tlanextli Moctezumo – 247th Trials Graduate – Known Alias: The Songstress of Lorelei.
- Zenza Nagi – Princess of Deriva – Wren and Xipilli's niece via their elder sister.
- Irene – A Landless technomancer who graduated with Wren and Xipilli. Declared loyalty to Deriva.

Murasaki no Yama:

- Mirai Miyazaki – Empress of Murasaki no Yama – Mother of Hikaru and Kaito Miyazaki - Died in the Technomancer Civil Wars.
- Fumiko Miyazaki – Grandmaster of Shinka Temple's Adept Training Program – Twin sister of Mirai and aunt to Hikaru and Kaito.
- Hikaru Miyazaki – Current Emperor of Murasaki no Yama – Elder brother of Kaito.
- Kaito Miyazaki – Crown Prince of Murasaki no Yama – 247th Trials Graduate – Younger son of Mirai Miyazaki.
- Akari – Miyazaki trainee under Kaito's tutelage.
- Renki – Miyazaki trainee under Kaito's tutelage.
- Orson Thorgard - A Murasaki technomancer. Attended Empress Mirai's funeral and is the next highest ranking technomancer in Murasaki. He is appointed mentorship of Renki and Akari after Kaito's defection.

Ebele:

- Chike Nagi – Crown Prince of Ebele – 247th Trials Graduate – Husband of Atzi Moctezumo and Father to Zenza Nagi.
- Chiamaka Nagi – Princess of Ebele – Younger sister to Chike Nagi.

Sekhmeti:

- Rameses Sahra – Pharaoh of Sekhmeti – Father of Jamar Sahra.
- Jamar Sahra – Crown Prince of Sekhmeti – 247th Trials Graduate.

Seraphim:

- Donarick J. Thames – Son of the former pontiflex. Present Primarch of the League.
- Montwyatte – Archibald's right-hand man.

Aighneas:
- Morrigan "The Morrigan" Gewalt – President of Aighneas Killed by Summer Helsdottir.
- Arturo Lionheart – 247th Trials Graduate – Student of The Morrigan.

The Tai Tai:
- Lylilria "Lyra" Mchelogdea - A Móg or High Fae who tricks Wren into giving up her name.
- Thale - A merman, kidnapped by unknown entities.
- Leon De Mare - A former pirate and Thale's lover.
- The Creature - A genetic construct of Faust's. The Creature has been lurking below Calypso City's streets, kidnapping fae to places unknown.

Miscellaneous Human+:
- Tomi - Kaito's friend and confidant. An A-class hacker and techno-savvy operator outside of League sanctions.
- Selene Fitzroy - 247th Trials Graduate - League country allegiance unknown.
- Gideon - A young boy Renki meets in the streets of Wakeville.

Miscellaneous Hexen:
- Yggfret Bloodfang – The Goblin King.
- Summer Helsdottir – Witch - Married Donarick Thames during the Technomancer Civil War. She was a powerful summoner, capable of calling giant beasts from the abyss. Now deceased.
- Jessabelle – Witch - Rescued Wren after her time spent in the facility. A healing witch.
- Unnamed Ice Witch - Attacks Wren in the diner with her first couple of hours in Calypso City.

The Facility:
- Dr. Johannes Faust – Head Doctor.

- Atalia Vaishi – Asylum inmate who led a group of patients to summon Wren back from the dead.
- Anna Elizabeth Faust - The comatose daughter of Dr. Faust.

Notable Weapons of Deus:

- Mångata – Wren's Ætherkalis
- Lacuna – Wren's Soul-Eating Athame
- Tsukuyomi – Kaito's Katana
- Amatsu – Kaito's Tanto
- Agni – Chike's Blast Rifle – Currently in use by Zenza
- Serket - Jamar's triple bladed katar.

Notable Heavenly Bodies:

- Koi - Deus' larger moon. Exists on a six-month cycle as far as waxing and waning goes.
- Dei - Deus' smaller moon. Due to its volcanic activity, it is almost always full.
- Ør - Deus's sun, a white dwarf.

BOOK CLUB QUESTIONS

1. How is the relationship between Wren and Kaito different in this book compared to *Sonata* and *Prelude*?

2. When did you figure out Renki was Kaito and Wren's child? What gave you the hint?

3. How do you think Renki's newfound powers are going to manifest in the next book?

4. How are the fae within the Nocturne Symphony different from the various folklores we know in the real world? How are they similar?

5. Now that we are beginning to get more into the different creatures of the world of Deus, which are you more likely to be: a human, a fae, a hexen, or a human+?

6. What would you do if you forgot who you were? How would you recover your identity?

7. How do you think the League's campaign against Wren is going to be altered thanks to the temporary erasure of her

person from their records? Do you think it will affect the hunt at all?

8.   If you were to be forgotten, who would be the last person to forget you? Why that person?

More books from 4 Horsemen Publications

Fantasy, SciFi, & Paranormal Romance

Amanda Fasciano

Waking Up Dead
Dead Vessel
The Dead Show
Dead Revelations
Dead Carnage

Beau Lake

The Beast Beside Me
The Beast Within Me
Taming the Beast: Novella
The Beast After Me
Charming the Beast
The Beast Like Me

Chelsea Burton Dunn

By Moonlight
Moon Bound
White Moon
New Moon Rising
Bloodthirsty

D. Lambert

Rydan
Celebrant
Northlander
Esparan
King
Traitor
His Last Name

J.M. Paquette

Klauden's Ring
Solyn's Body
Hannah's Heart
The Inbetween
Call Me Forth
Invite Me In
Keep Me Close
Heart of Stone

Kait Disney-Leugers

Antique Magic
Blood Magic
Heart Magic

Kyle Sorrell

Munderworld
Potarium

Lyra R. Saenz

Prelude
Sonata
Scherzo
Ragtime Swing
Midnight Cumbia
Sea Song de la Corsaire
Falsetto in the Woods: Novella
The Devil's Trill

PAIGE LAVOIE

I'm in Love with Mothman
I'm Engaged to Mothman
Dear Galaxy

ROBERT J. LEWIS

Shadow Guardian and the
Three Bears
Shadow Guardian and the
Big Bad Wolf
Shadow Guardian and the Boys
That Went Woof

T.S. SIMONS

Project Hemisphere
The Space Between
Infinity
Circle of Protection
Sessrúmnir
The 45th Parallel
Orenda

VALERIE WILLIS

Cedric: The Demonic Knight
Romasanta: Father of Werewolves
The Oracle: Keeper of the
Gaea's Gate
Artemis: Eye of Gaea
King Incubus: A New Reign
Queen Succubus: Holder
of the Crown
Val's House of Musings: A Mixed
Genre Short Story Collection

V.C. WILLIS

The Prince's Priest
The Priest's Assassin
The Assassin's Saint
The Champion's Lord

DISCOVER MORE AT
4HorsemenPublications.com